KAYNDO

Book 1: Ring of Death
By: Terri Luckey

Copyright © 2014. Terri Luckey. All rights reserved.

Diverse Pixel (**www.diversepixel.com**)

Kayndo 'Ring of Death'

By Terri Luckey
© 2014 Terri Luckey

ISBN-13: 978-0692327531
ISBN-10: 0692327533

This is a work of fiction. Names, characters, places and incidents are either the product of the author's imagination or, if real, are used fictitiously.

Cover by Diverse Pixel (http://www.diversepixel.com)

© 2014 All rights reserved. No part of this book may be reproduced, transmitted or stored in an information retrieval system in any form or by any means, graphic, electronic or mechanical, including photocopying, taping and recording, with prior permission from the publisher.

For more information about the book contact:
www.terriluckey.com

What others have to say about KAYNDO, Ring of Death:

"Kayndo: Ring of Death was one of my favorite reads of the year! Entirely engaging! Be prepared to keep the book by your side until you've finished!"
Precarious Yates- author of the 'Revelation Special Ops Series'

***

"Terri Luckey is a master at crafting fictional cultures. Her depth of detail and intense plots will impact you long after you close the book. Days later, I miss spending time with her characters."
Nadine Brandes- author of 'A Time to Die'

Dedicated to John, my late father, a former paratrooper who told us to believe in ourselves and jump for our dreams. Even if we fell, the journey's still worth it. This book is my jump.

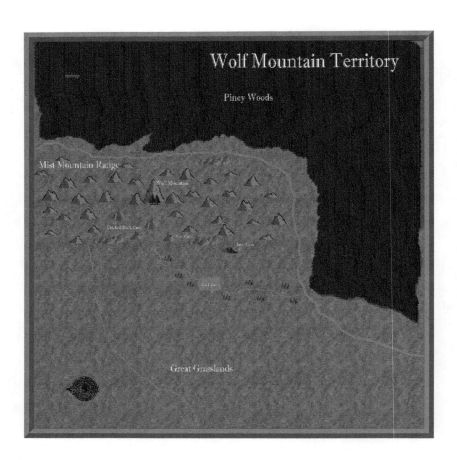

TABLE OF CONTENTS

TABLE OF CONTENTS…………………………………………...……… 7
PROLOGUE………………………………………………………..……… 9
1: THE TEST…………………………...……………...…………..……...13
2: CALUPI………………………………………………………....………21
3: PACK LAW………………………………………………………..…… 33
4: BEYOND DEATH……………………………………………...……… 41
5: THE CHOOSING…………………………………………...…..……… 49
6: HONOR OR HARDSHIP……………………………………..……… 58
7: NO REGRETS……………………………………………………..……65
8: A NEW PUPPY……………………………………………………..……72
9: DECEPTION……………………………………………………..……… 82
10: GAMES………………………………………………………..……… 91
11: A VISITOR………………………………………………………..…… 98
12: TRIALS………………………………………………………..……… 104
13: HELP OR HURT……………………………………………………112
14: BARING TEETH……………………………………………..……… 120
15: THE ANCIENTS………………………………………………..…… 130
16: KUN'S REWARDS…………………………………………..……… 137
17: COURAGE……………………………………………………..……… 150
18: STRANGE LAND……………………………………………..………160
19: CHILLY RECEPTION……………………………………..……… 166
20: DEFIANCE……………………………………………………..……… 175
21: OUR HEARTS BLEED……………………………………..……… 188
22: WISDOM……………………………………………………..……… 198
23: HUNTING BUFFALO……………………………………..………206
24: UP IN SMOKE……………………………………………..……… 214
25: THE SCENT OF TROUBLE………...……………………..…… 221
26: WOLF POWER……………………………………………..……… 225
27: LEETO'S WRATH……………………………………………..…… 230
28: MIXED MESSAGES……………………………………………..……240

29: DARK TIMES..246
30: DECISIONS..255
31: EVIL'S LAIR...266
32: THE CHALLENGE..276
33: THE PACK...283
34: THE JUDGEMENT..291
35: THE RING OF DEATH..302
36: THE KAYNDO...309
EPILOGUE...319
GLOSSARY...322
ACKNOWLEDGMENTS... 325

-Prologue-

Wolf Mountain Pack History: Story of first alpha of Wolf Mountain Pack, Herrick, meeting JoKayndo.

The putrid fumes from a world on fire choked Herrick, but he forced the cough back.

He ran his tongue—as dry as a wad of leather—over the grooves in his split lips. The sting and the sharp tang of blood a reminder of his thirst. His foot began to slip, so he dug his boot in further behind the outcropping of shale he used for cover. The grade of the rocky slope kept his perch precarious above the winding mountain road. He cupped his hand over his eyes to peer through the smoke—as futile as seeing through strong coffee to the bottom of the cup.

He barely made out the closest charred black husks. They looked like gnarled poles—all that was left of the former thick forest. Where were the sounds of men on the move—steps, groans, or weapon creaks? Silence came from his front, and only a few rustles betrayed the twenty soldiers remaining of his platoon hidden behind him.

Over a week had passed since their last bloody encounter. Since then, they heard nothing of their foe. Even the wave of humanity fleeing the ravages of war had slowed to a trickle, then stopped.

Gravel crunching warned him of someone coming up the road.

Herrick lifted his gun to his shoulder, the familiar weight a comfort as he slid back the safety. Clicks came from behind him as his soldiers did the same. Out of the dark smoke a man emerged. His uniform hung ragged and torn, but the tell-tale green saved him. Another deserter? Herrick lowered his weapon.

To determine any rank was impossible since his sleeve was missing. He didn't recognize him, but they all looked similar with premature grey shocks of hair and faces worn with creases. Herrick's own blond hair and traces of youth were stolen by the war long ago.

Herrick left his outcropping, and with his feet sideways, descended the slope to the road without falling. Three of his men did the same, while the others stayed hidden with their weapons trained on them. At their approach, the man's face drew back in a huge grin, and he skipped closer. Skipped? Was he crazy? And when was the last time Herrick saw a smile?

"Did you see it?" he shouted.

The noise was a risk. One whack from the butt of Herrick's gun should quiet him. But what he had to say might be important.

"What?" Herrick whispered.

"A giant wolf." His voice still rang too loud. "He told me the war was ending, that peace is coming."

Herrick groaned but only inwardly. Crazy for sure. Wolves didn't speak and this war didn't end. "Where's your unit?"

The man blinked several times. His voice was barely audible. "I think they're all dead, sir."

How could he not know? Maybe his separation was by accident. Herrick gave him the benefit of doubt. "You better come with us, son."

The man took several steps back. "No. There's nothin' left worth dying for. Just ash."

So he was a deserter. A whisper came from one of Herrick's soldiers. "Air thief."

Herrick agreed. He'd never desert his few soldiers left or admit all the others' deaths meant nothing. "The enemy's out there, somewhere."

The deserter's voice rose. "The wolf said peace is coming."

"He qualifies for extinction," came another whisper.

His orders did say to shoot deserters, but Herrick was tired of spilling blood. Besides, they were low on ammo—his gun held only one bullet. The deserter would need restrained and gagged for his sake and theirs.

"It's okay." Herrick moved toward him, palms out.

The deserter jumped back and ran down the road to be swallowed again by smoke. "Peace is coming! The war's over!"

Herrick wouldn't chase him. The man's shouts grew distant.

"One is none." A soldier gave a heavy exhale.

Herrick lifted his hand for quiet, then climbed back up behind the outcropping. An enemy bullet would find the dead man still shouting, and anyone unfortunate enough to be near him.

The silence returned. Since the war began, he had longed for quiet, but now that his prayer had been answered, it seemed unnatural and filled him with foreboding. Their foe spread bullets around on the slightest provocation. Where did they lie in wait?

After taking the risk to break radio silence, his impatience grew. His parched throat scraped down a swallow. Safe drinking water grew harder to find. Every canteen empty since their last drink yesterday.

The assignment was simple. Stay hidden in the mountains and impede the enemy's superior numbers with fast strikes. Without supplies, how could he continue the mission? Their last drops weren't delivered, and the terrain held too many places a radio signal didn't get through.

A soft footfall announced another presence coming from the opposite direction. Herrick's gun jabbed back into his shoulder. The cloying soot stung his eyes as it rained around him. A man in green clothing stepped out of the smoke with a black cloth wrapped around his nose. His hair and skin bore a willful cover of mud—but his deep blue eyes were unmistakable.

"Just me, lieutenant." Jared pulled the cloth down, the corners of his mouth turning up.

Another smile? Maybe he had good news. Herrick removed his finger from the trigger and reengaged the safety. "See anyone?"

"No, sir."

"And you made it to the top?"

"Yes, sir." Jared's whisper sounded resolute. "Only static."

Command should be in bunkers, far below the sweeping destruction—so why didn't they answer? He turned his attention back to his sergeant. "Water?"

Jared handed his canteen to him. Liquid sloshed against the sides. "Comes out of a cave. Tastes of minerals, but good."

"Pass the canteen around. I'll drink last."

Jared nodded and held the canteen out to the closest, Rochelle. She lifted it, took a swallow, and passed it back. Pride in his troops filled Herrick as none guzzled greedily. They'd shown loyalty to him and each other again, and again.

"I found a deer hiding in the cave." Jared ran a hand through his hair. "Must have been in shock. It didn't run, just waited. I killed it silently, with my knife, strung it up, and came back for you."

The canteen returned to Herrick. He poured cool water into his parched mouth. The taste was strong, full of minerals, but sweet. He swallowed, then pulled his own covering back over his nose. The smoke choked him just a little less. "Well met, Sergeant. Take point."

"Yes, sir."

That night, Herrick allowed a fire. It shouldn't alert their enemies since smoke hung everywhere. Some dead branches provided the fuel from a copse of trees that had somehow been missed in the inferno that burned their world. They had eaten their fill, and now sat huddled around the flames just inside the cave—all that still lived. Flickers of light danced against the rough stone and dirt walls. The water's gurgle from the stream flowing through the cave below made a pleasant refrain.

His parents, most of his friends probably lay dead beneath the cities' rubble. Hard to believe their destruction. Those towers of stone and glass had blotted out the stars. Now, people sheltered again in caves, and the stars were hidden by smoke.

Concentrate on the moment. He drew a breath and registered the roasted meat aroma mingling with the cave's soil and mineral scent. His stomach ceased its growl for the first time in days; he'd slaked his thirst, and the cave sheltered them from the ash rain. Things were looking up.

Then, Herrick heard it—soft shuffles against the stone. He sprang to his feet, stared toward the entrance, and strained to see. Shadows played against the wall.

Out of the darkness a white wolf glided toward them. Several smaller grey ones followed to form a ring around Herrick and his men.

His spirits sank. Not enough bullets.

1
The Test

"Base your decision to add a story to the history on how a Calupi lived, not died." ~Kwutee to Chayla

Story of the 5th Kayndo, from Wolf Mountain Pack history, written by Chayla:

Tearing fabric broke the quiet. *Oh, cackles.* Dayvee's heart pounded. How could he have been so careless?

Buckskin from his sleeve and a blonde strand of hair dangled from thorns on the Hawthorne thicket, announcing his hiding place. A sinking feeling flooded Dayvee—as if he were drowning and unable to propel himself to the surface for air. The most important trial in his sixteen years of life, and he may have just blown it—his future, too.

The small gap he peered through in the weave of reddish-brown branches revealed the mountain lion. It twisted around to bring amber eyes to bear on the brush that hid Dayvee. Would the mud on his face keep the lion from spotting him? The lion's short rounded ears twitched. Oh, no.

Stories of lions hearing deer a mile away came to Dayvee's mind. He dared not let his breath escape. A hush had fallen in the gloom beneath the trees, and the entire forest seemed to wait with bated breath, too.

Dayvee was Calupi—well almost. Yet, here he hid like a scared turtle, only the thicket wasn't near as safe as a shell. What other option was there? His uncle's words resounded in his head. *"Sometime prudence is necessary for a successful hunt."* Dayvee's fear sharpened his senses. He could pick out the lion's nose as it wrinkled its broad face. Thankfully, a cat's sense of smell wasn't as keen as a wolf's.

The light feather tied to his weapons pouch swayed toward him with a slight gust of wind. Good, his scent carried away from the lion. The predator took a step closer. Dayvee curled his fingers over his chakram. The rawhide grip of the weapon against his sweaty palm gave him some comfort, but even if he managed to kill the lion—he'd fail the test. *Please Kun, don't let the lion discover me.*

A sudden crash ripped through the air, a deer bursting from cover between them. With leaps and bounds, the doe streaked through the trees. The mountain lion catapulted after it, stretching out for greater speed. Dayvee's breath rushed out as he ran in pursuit, but the animals' four legs soon outdistanced his two. The forest revealed only trees and brush. He'd lost the lion.

Fingers of despair choked his heart. Two and a half days he'd watched this mountain lion laze while he only risked short naps, ate dry rations, and worried. The disgusted look their leader, Leeto, would level at him if he failed the test haunted him—and that wouldn't be the only consequence.

No, Dayvee couldn't think about it. He wouldn't let it happen. Pine and cedar trees reigned predominant, greening these woods even in winter, but enough oaks and other trees bare of foliage let the sun dapple through the branches. The rays hit his shoulder. He glanced up to confirm it. Maybe two hours before the sun marked the center of the sky, and he was at least thirty minutes from camp. Not much time left to complete the test.

Unwilling to accept defeat, Dayvee scrutinized the forest as he trudged on. A low hanging pine bough had lost its covering of snow. Something must have knocked into it. He found the print among the brown needles underneath, and his despair turned to hope. As big as his hand, the indentation showed four toes and a tri-lobed pad with no nail marks. Cats retract their nails when walking. It must be his lion.

His scan almost missed the impression under the white oak's shadow—three upside down teardrops—the deer's track. He followed the prints as swiftly as he could without betraying himself. Not over thirty paces ahead the lion's long swishing tail appeared, then the tan body that gracefully stalked through the trees, muscles rippling. *Yes.* His heart skipped as excitement charged into him.

When the lion slowed and dropped to a crouch, Dayvee imitated it. Thankfully, the few inches of snow on the ground didn't crunch. The small doe nibbled on some bark ahead. She couldn't weigh seventy pounds.

Don't fail lion. It inched through the scrub to a walnut tree less than ten paces from the doe. Her ears flicked toward the hidden danger, and she froze. The lion broke cover.

The deer accomplished one jump before the lion vaulted on top of her to wrap giant paws around her chest. The lion's teeth clamped down on the back of her neck. She staggered, then fell to the ground. The sharp odor of blood tinged the air. The doe's eyes glazed as her life blood poured out and turned the pristine white blanket of snow redder than Elayni's lips.

Dayvee might never know the taste of Elayni's lips or gaze on these familiar woods of his mountain home again. He must prove himself worthy. He must become Calupi.

The sharp teeth clicked on bone as the lion tore flesh from the doe's belly, so recently bounding with life. Respect for the lion's prowess rose in him as the white patch around the mountain lion's mouth turned bright red. Dayvee shuddered. The lion could slaughter him just as easily. He scanned the trunk of the hickory tree he hid behind—did his six-foot frame protrude?

The predator devoured its fill. Then scraped snow, leaves, and mud over the carcass to conceal the meat. It would leave now and return later to gorge again. Dayvee needed that deer. Go, lion.

The mountain lion retreated ten paces to where the sun's rays blanketed the ground and snow only partially covered the leaves and moss beneath. The lion stretched out and licked the blood from its paws. Apparently satisfied with their cleanliness, the cat worked on its stomach.

Just Dayvee's luck. The cat seemed content to stay. He shifted on his feet. His tingling toes signaled they'd soon be numb. The sun warmed his neck. He peered at the sky. Couldn't be much over an hour left, if that. In his scramble for a solution, he latched onto the only idea that dawned. It might work, even if it was risky.

He retreated to a small clearing out of the lion's sight to gather two long sticks, leaves, dry brush, twigs—anything flammable. Heavy rocks went into his pockets. When he grabbed another, he felt the smooth texture—too smooth, too round, too perfect. Must be something of the ancients. Kwutee's warnings bombarded him. "Avoid the ancient's things or your soul will be contaminated and separate you from Kun." Dayvee snatched his hand back and left the rock. He'd touched it, but not for long. Maybe his soul would be okay.

Using his knife, he cut away some fringes from his shirt. He still had plenty to wick away water when it became wet. Retrieving his fire kit, he lathered the birch tree fungus soaked in oil on the fringes and tied them around the top of two sticks—the only part of this venture Dayvee felt certain about. Those diligent hours learning the materials and skills to craft good torches after he learned their worth at age eight weren't wasted.

Now to light them, but the lion was sure to hear that. Dayvee shrugged. If the noise bothered the lion, wonderful. It might leave. Striking his quartz rock striker and pyrite hand stone together, Dayvee threw a spark on the torch. The flame erupted. He lit the second. Heart racing, he finished his preparations and drew a deep breath to calm himself. He had to do this.

Openly, he moved back toward the mountain lion with a torch in each hand. "Get out of here! Go!"

The predator sprang to its feet and faced him. Mouth wide, it released a bloodcurdling scream. Then spat and hissed.

Dayvee's hands shook. All his senses cried out to flee. He struggled to keep his legs moving toward the mountain lion.

The beast snarled. A ripple moving through the predator's taut body exposed the menace. Its muscles flexed, and then bunched, ready to unleash and spring.

I'm going to die. Dayvee's knees weakened and his legs trembled. His mouth went dry. Terror hammered his galloping heart into his chest. He snapped his arm forward—the torch flew through the air and landed in front of the lion. The beast jumped to one side. Dayvee pitched the other. The fiery stick plopped onto the lion's back but tumbled off.

"Go!" Dayvee screamed. Loading his hands with the rough rocks, he flung them. They pummeled the lion.

The beast shook its head, backed a few steps, then displayed its teeth and hissed again.

Dayvee desperately hurled more stones. One crashed into the lion's face. The predator turned, moved a couple steps in retreat, then stopped. Dayvee strained and heaved his last rock using every bit of his strength. A dull thud filled the air as the stone hit the animal's flank. The lion fled.

Dayvee stood rooted to the spot for a second surveying the woods. Did he dare believe he'd driven the mountain lion away? "Yes!" Dayvee's body still shook, but euphoria surged through him.

He dashed to extinguish the torches, unearthed the bloody carcass, and heaved on the legs to maneuver what was left of the doe onto his back. A messy job. The legs finally hung over his shoulders. He staggered to his feet—a step back helped him keep his balance. An ache settled between his shoulders from the weight, but all that running with a loaded rucksack in training prepared him. Blood soaked through the buffalo hide of his coat and his soft buckskin shirt to ooze against his skin. He lumbered away in the opposite direction from the lion.

Would the predator now stalk Dayvee? He hurried his pace. Sunlight played over his face. Almost where it had marked the sky when he started three days ago. Even so, he couldn't risk a mountain lion following him—and finding the others. A few sharp turns to double back over his trail assured him nothing pursued him.

He slated for camp. There, the creek. He turned to follow its bank. Before he reached the clearing, the trees thinned, and the smell of wood smoke permeated the air. Anticipation and dread poured into him at the same time. The pulsing emotions stretched his body tight like a drum and begged him for release.

"Dayvee's back." Brando's voice rang out. No surprise his friend spotted him first. Brando, like Leeto, missed little.

The group gathered to greet him where the trees stopped. The Calupi alpha leader stood in front. His face chiseled like stone under his short, sun-yellow hair with a white-streaked cowlick that jutted out above his forehead. His dark-blue eyes fixed on Dayvee as he approached. Everyone told Dayvee he looked just like his father, except his own eyes were bright green like the stalk of an onion.

Leeto's wolf companion, Luko, moved to the leader's side. The alpha wolf's ash-grey body weighed over two hundred pounds and sported a zigzag scar on his muzzle.

Behind Leeto, Dayvee's uncle Codee waited. He and Leeto shared similar frames, tall and solid with muscles that strained against their clothes, but Codee's long oak-brown hair hung down his back in a single braid. His grey-blue eyes glinted as they met Dayvee's, and his mouth parted in a broad smile. Dayvee dropped his gaze to Wilee, who stood at his uncle's side. His torn and ragged ear made him an easy wolf to recognize. The five trainees that bunched in a group behind the leaders studied Dayvee, too.

He slogged into camp and dumped the warm carcass on the snow, then checked the sturdy branch planted in the ground nearby. The shadow from the trees had almost reached it but not quite. Relief poured into him. He made it.

Leeto must have noticed his gaze. A derisive snort came from him. "Another few minutes and you'd have failed." If Dayvee could forget about the family tie, it might not hurt as bad when the criticism came.

Both Leeto and Codee bent over to examine the deer. Were the leaders impressed?

The two wolf companions nosed the carcass. His worth needed proven to them, too. Dayvee stopped his foot tapping the ground as the men and wolves decided his fate. Why were they taking so long? Did he pass?

"Wilee says the deer smells like a mountain lion." Codee clapped Dayvee on the back. "That took courage. Well met. What do you say, Leeto?"

A sense of accomplishment swelled in Dayvee's chest. Now if only Leeto was pleased.

"I'll wait until we hear the story to decide whether it was courageous or foolhardy." Leeto eyed the deer carcass. "Is that all you have?"

As if Leeto's expectations would ever be satisfied with Dayvee just getting one like the test required from everyone else. He'd probably want three from him. Why had he thought if he pulled off a mountain lion Leeto'd be impressed enough the amount wouldn't matter? Would he fail Dayvee?

Righteous anger filled Brando's voice. "No one else brought more than one."

Leeto crossed his arms. "No one else used all three days."

So definitely not impressed.

"Or was brave enough to take on a mountain lion." Elayni jumped in.

Dayvee's heart overflowed with gratitude for his friend's loyalty, but it wasn't a good idea to confront the alpha. They could get in trouble. He pulled a pheasant from his rucksack. "No, but this is. I took it from a fox. The other two and a half days, I spent waiting for the mountain lion to hunt." Would it be enough to satisfy Leeto? Dayvee ran a hand through his hair, and smoothed his cowlick. His foot tapped again. He stopped it.

"Pack up everyone," Leeto ordered.

Dayvee bit back his groan. Leeto rewarded Dayvee's anxiety with another patience lesson. He'd need to wait to learn his fate.

2
Calupi

"Our reputation—Calupi make terrific friends and terrifying enemies." ~ Chayla.

Two sentinel pines appeared first since they towered at least one hundred feet, piercing the blue horizon of the sky.

Dark-green boughs, covered with a light frosting of snow, and the russet, scaly bark stood prominent in the light of late afternoon. The trail's grade leveled off on the snowy plateau dotted with trees. Dayvee inhaled a deep breath of the pine-laden air. His boots skidded on the slick, marbled ice of the frozen stream as he trailed the leaders across with the other trainees.

The rock escarpment of the mountainous cliff loomed ahead as people and wolves materialized from nowhere. Their home's entrance lay hidden beyond the trees.

Wolves bounded up to Luko and Wilee, then surrounded the trainees. A cold nose on his hand startled Dayvee and left a moist impression when his mother's wolf companion, Skylay, greeted him.

Milay approached next. Dark circles surrounded her soft brown eyes and her face appeared pinched. She hugged Leeto, then wrapped her arms around Dayvee. Why would his mother act affectionate? It's not like she loved him. Brando's advice filled his mind. *"They can't hurt you so badly if you don't care."* Dayvee stepped back from her.

Her chin quivered. Guilt assuaged him. A corner of Leeto's mouth turned down, enough to signal his displeasure. Dayvee lifted his chin. Why should he expect anything other than criticism and indifference from his parents? He'd already endured sixteen years of it. His conscience pricked him with Kwutee's teachings. *"Treat others how you wish to be treated."* Dayvee took a deep breath and forced his anger aside. He shouldn't have rebuffed her.

"Sorry," he mumbled.

Milay's eyes lifted to Leeto. "Did they do okay stealing meat from a predator?"

"Yes, they all passed," Leeto replied. "We should hear some interesting stories tonight."

The worry Dayvee'd hauled around like a huge boulder lightened. Only two more barriers to topple to prove himself as Calupi—the strength test and choosing.

Several other Calupi clasped Dayvee's arm as they swarmed forward to greet the trainees. He returned their warm smiles and arm clasps with enthusiasm as they congratulated him and the others on passing the test.

A tall, gangly kid with features too large for his body hung back while the others met with them. A stranger? Must be his new brother, Bunjee. Why would Leeto and Milay volunteer to adopt a twelve-year-old from bear clan when they couldn't love the son they already had?

"You made it." Leeto moved over to clap Bunjee's shoulder. "Welcome."

The boy beamed Leeto a full smile. "Thanks."

Milay folded her arm around Bunjee. "I just started showing him around."

Apparently Milay would give Bunjee the affection Dayvee had spurned. His foot tapped the ground, but he stopped it.

"Has he seen the pool room yet?" A corner of Leeto's mouth twitched.

"No." Milay's long, tawny braid swung as she shook her head. "He barely got here."

"You should join us then." Leeto strode toward the entrance. "He might enjoy seeing the trainees' next test."

Bunjee stayed at Milay's side as she followed. Wouldn't they make Bunjee go to the rear, today? Leeto held up his hand and spread his fingers. Good. They didn't have to keep single file. Dayvee dropped back to walk next to Elayni, and Brando moved up beside him.

Elayni's eyebrows rose. It made her light blue eyes appear even larger—the shade of a mountain stream and easy to get lost in. "Are you okay?" she whispered.

Dayvee couldn't hide much from her or Brando. They knew him too well. Dayvee forced a smile.

Elayni's return smile lit her face and divulged her dimples. Dayvee stumbled and caught himself. Did she notice? Her lips twitched as if repressing a laugh. He inwardly groaned. Why did his body betray him like that?

Brando threw a punch at his arm, but Dayvee dodged to let it sail past. Another miss. "Ha, how about that reaction time?"

Elayni rolled her eyes. "Still breaking the rules and playing that game you made up?"

"Hey it works." Brando shrugged. "And it only breaks the rules if we get hit."

"We don't do it when they're watching." Dayvee glanced at the adults who faced forward.

Brando flipped his hand toward Leeto. "You'd think your parents would wait to replace you until after you failed and left." His deep blue eyes sparkled with merriment. "Maybe they figure it's a foregone conclusion."

Bunjee's reddish-blond head bobbed next to Milay. Even though Brando teased, his comment mirrored Dayvee's own doubts.

"Yeah, right." Dayvee drove his fist at Brando. His friend sprang back, and Dayvee's fist hit air. "Maybe your father should look for a new Brando."

Brando chuckled as they moved around the giant trees that hid the dark circular opening in the face of the cliff. His dark-brown, shoulder length hair barely ruffled as he shook his head. "I'm one-of-a-kind and irreplaceable."

"You're one-of-a-kind all right." Elayni brushed back the golden lock that escaped her braid. Her hair gleamed in the light, but Dayvee and his friends left the sun behind when they stepped through the cave's mouth in the cliff face.

Dayvee's vision took a second to adjust. The mounted wall lamps couldn't make up for the sun's loss. Mottled browns and tans on the stone and soil surfaces of the cave varied between cracks and textures, but all absorbed light in the vast network of caves that ran for miles through Wolf Mountain. The smell of burning wood, the water's sharp mineral fragrance, and the terra aroma filled Dayvee's nostrils. The scent of home.

The corridor they traveled twisted, widened, and narrowed as the walls and ceiling butted out in some areas or bowed back in others. They passed openings that led to other caves, and several others joined the procession, many with wolf companions at their sides. Calupi did love competitions, and the test drew them.

They entered the oval shaped cavern as large as ten family dens. Bunjee craned his neck back at the roof that hovered as high as five men on each other's shoulders. His gaze dropped to inspect the pool that spanned half the room. The textured walls claimed his focus, and his mouth fell open. The water's flow shaded them with orange and red-layered patterns against the larger background with its mottled tans and browns. Like small versions of red sunsets they formed a more exquisite wall painting than could be done by human hand.

"Buzzing," Bunjee whispered.

"What?" Leeto stared at the kid.

"It's what Ursans say when something's pretty amazing. Buzzing is a good sound to a bear. They love to eat bees, their larvae, and honey."

"I like honey, too." Dayvee let out a chortle. "But not bees."

"How did you make the pool in here?" Bunjee scratched his head, pushing some reddish-blonde tufts up.

"We didn't, Kun did. The underground stream comes in there." Leeto pointed to some brown and orange stones where strands of blue glinted as water trickled down them. "It forms the pool, then flows across the chamber and down to a lower corridor where it leaves the cave." He shrugged. "We just added this wall to keep it from flooding."

Bunjee scrutinized the four-foot wall. Shaped from rocks in a variety of textures and color, it restrained the dark blue water beyond.

"The pool meets our needs for bathing, drinking, storing food, and of course, tests." Leeto smirked. "Tests should never be too easy."

Sometimes Dayvee hated Leeto's theory. The water's inky surface of the cave pool never froze, but it would be cold.

Codee strode to the other side. Leeto tossed one end of the rope to Codee so it stretched across at the deepest depth. The trainees would get soaked.

"Renay and Chayla will go first," Leeto ordered.

Probably wouldn't be much of a contest. Renay must be thirty pounds heavier. Chayla scaled the wall slowly. The back of her auburn head only came parallel to Leeto's shoulder blades. Renay's black braid swung as she swaggered around the pool to ascend the stone barrier next to Codee. They had no choice but to stand on top of the slick rocks since the water at its deepest pressed against them. Both men handed a girl one end of the rope and retreated.

With the drop of his arm, Leeto signaled. The two girls jerked the rope with all their strength in a tug of war. Tiny Chayla drew Renay from her perch. The splash sounded as Renay landed in the pool. A wide smile spread across Chayla's face.

Leeto called each of the other trainees to compete. Finally, he called Brando, leaving Dayvee until last. Dayvee's foot tapped as Brando defeated Tayro. That only left Brando and Dayvee dry. Like last year, they would be pitted against each other.

Dayvee removed his weapons and rucksack and slid his gloves on. The coarse texture of the buffalo hide snugged his fingers and hands to protect them from rope burns.

He took a step forward, then stopped when Leeto announced, "Elayni, Renay, Chayla and Tayro, will have their chance to get even against Brando."

Leeto would have to come up with something new and harder. Four against one. Even with three girls, the challenge would be formidable. Brando's face turned red as he strained, but his feet slipped against the rocks, and they dragged him in.

"Your turn to try, Dayvee." Leeto indicated Brando's former position.

Dayvee went around and climbed the rocks. He wrapped the rope around his forearm, clutched it with his gloves, and placed one leg in front of the other.

Leeto raised his arm in the air, then signaled by dropping it. Dayvee yanked with all his strength. Pain stabbed his shoulders. Were they being torn from their sockets? Chayla's small feet inched forward in front.

Dayvee's body was almost lying down on the rocks as he towed the girls in. Then, Tayro with his round owl face—teeth gritted and feet scraping to resist—plunged in the pool and let go of the rope. Dayvee fell on his back, and then scrambled up. The watchers stamped and clapped in appreciation.

The pack's applause buoyed Dayvee as if he floated on water. He'd done it. Only one more obstacle left—the choosing.

"I wouldn't want to leave one dry. That's not fair to the others." Leeto glanced at Codee. "Shall we?"

Luko's tail wagged. The wolf shared Leeto's thoughts and emotions so Leeto must be pleased with whatever he planned.

Leeto's voice rang out. "Brando and Dayvee, you'll go against me and Codee."

Figures. Leeto wouldn't allow Dayvee to bask in his win.

Brando laughed. "Time to get the leaders wet. I hope they won't be too sore about it."

Leeto jammed his gloves on. "You two better have towels ready."

Brando joined Dayvee on the pool's far side. Codee pitched one end of the rope to them. Up front, Brando caught it. Dayvee anchored. He dug his feet in between the rocks to give himself secure footing. Leeto and Codee both curled fists around the rope across from them.

"Now," Leeto yelled.

Dayvee and Brando hauled against the rope. Dayvee's gloved fingers stung, then burned.

Leeto and Codee moved in tandem like one person. They both dipped back together and Dayvee and Brando rose. Then, Leeto and Codee reached one hand further up the rope and pulled it.

Brando's feet shifted. Dayvee clenched his teeth. His shoulder ache from the last round turned sharp and burned as he tugged. Sweat stung his eyes. Brando's back stiffened and his biceps protruded stiffly.

Leeto and Codee's faces looked relaxed. The rope's tension eased, and he and Brando careened back. A huge jerk came and Brando flew into the pool. Dayvee scrambled to halt his slide as his feet scooted forward. Then, he, too soared through the air. The shock slammed into him as cold water enveloped his body. He shot to the surface.

Brando's hair, the shade of a buckeye nut, appeared almost black when wet. He shook droplets out that sprayed Dayvee. "Hey."

They swam to the shallow side where the rocks didn't meet the pool edge and their belongings waited.

Elayni's golden locks framed her face as she bent to greet them. "Good try."

Dayvee and Brando clambered out. When Dayvee gained his feet, he reached for his towel. Something leaped at him. Elayni's scream pierced the air.

Dayvee jumped and almost landed back in the pool. A toad hopped away. Embarrassment flooded him. He should have known.

Brando held his stomach as he bent over laughing. Leeto's eyebrows arched.

When the gazes of the adults left them, Dayvee slugged Brando. It actually hit Brando's shoulder since he wasn't paying attention, but Dayvee hadn't put much force in it. "Thanks. Great friend you are, making me look like an idiot."

Elayni's hands rested on her hips. "Brando, you need to grow up and stop these pranks."

"It was funny,—"Brando straightened"—and I didn't make you look like an idiot. You did."

Leeto, Milay and Codee strode over to them. Codee's chin lifted in a quick bob to signal his approval. "Nice effort. You put up a good fight."

"Thanks," Dayvee said, but Codee's praise and time were easier gained than Leeto's. What would he say?

Brando chuckled. "Dayvee needed to wash the mud off his face and the blood from his clothes."

Codee smiled. "He could have done that afterwards."

Brando's hearty laugh rang out again. "Yes, but then you oldsters wouldn't be so pleased with yourselves."

Codee's eyes twinkled. Brando had that effect on almost everyone. He kept them laughing. "If you want a rematch—"Codee chortled once"—now that Dayvee's clean, it can be arranged."

Only a corner of Leeto's mouth turned up. Usually, that passed as a smile with him.

Brando shook his head. "No, we'll let you keep your illusions for now. Dayvee can beat you another day."

Dayvee almost cracked a smile. Sometimes his friend's confidence bordered on delusional.

Leeto tilted his head toward Bunjee. "Dayvee, show him around." He moved away with Codee and Milay. Three wolf companions padded silently behind them.

Poor kid. Leeto was already dumping him off. Since Leeto hadn't said anything about how Dayvee did, it must not have been good enough.

Dayvee lobbed another punch at Brando, who blocked it. "I'll hear it worse if Leeto thinks I didn't give my best effort."

"Did you?" Brando asked.

"Of course, and so did you."

Brando's smile broadened. "Did I?"

Elayni rolled her eyes. "Surely even you wouldn't hide how strong you are during a test."

"That wasn't the test. Dayvee won it, even if Leeto didn't want to admit it. We're supposed to compete against each other." Brando clicked his tongue. "That, my naïve friends, was Leeto's attempt to learn how we'd do against them."

Had Brando really rolled over? Dayvee's tone sharpened. "Still, why wouldn't you show him?"

"Maybe I think we should wait to reveal that until one of us meets him in the ring."

Most people underestimated Brando. They thought him lucky when he won his wagers, but Dayvee never bet against him. Behind Brando's laughter lurked a brilliant mind.

"I saw your straining muscles." Dayvee ducked under Brando's return punch. "You worked."

Brando's blue eyes lit up. "Think what you want."

Maybe he really hadn't. But how could Brando do that to him? Heat rose to Dayvee's face. "If you didn't try, Leeto will think we're weaker, and you just gave him something to fault."

"You'd hear it regardless. Just quit believing it."

A deep breath helped calm Dayvee. What if Brando was right? No, he couldn't be. If Dayvee was judged good enough to be a high status Calupi, Leeto'd be proud of him. Dayvee might even gain his love.

Dayvee clasped Brando's forearm, then Elayni's. "I'll meet up with you later."

The pack felt everyone should care for the future. Dayvee had his duty to do. It didn't matter whether today might be his last. He went to where the gangly Bunjee waited. "Come on. I'll show you around."

The kid jumped up. "I hope you don't mind sharing your family with me."

Dayvee pulled back the hide across the opening to the corridor and motioned for Bunjee to go through. "If you're talking about Leeto and Milay, I don't mind sharing them." Dayvee let the hide fall after joining Bunjee. "My friends, Brando and Elayni, are more of a family to me." Dayvee walked down the corridor, and Bunjee fell in at his side. "We've trained, eaten, and slept in the same clump for years."

Bunjee's big brown eyes blinked a couple times. "Don't your parents mind?"

"Have you ever heard what they say about Calupi?"

Bunjee cocked his head. "My father said Calupi are like their wolves, they love and hate with equal ferocity."

"Yes." Dayvee crouched to move past a low spot in the ceiling. "And mostly that's true. We're taught not to hate, but Calupi are passionate, except Leeto and Milay. Neither reveal their feelings." He couldn't bring himself to tell Bunjee they had none for Dayvee.

"Why?"

"Leeto believes that emotional displays make a person appear weak." He touched the hide that draped over an opening. "This is the communal den. We'll go in later. Just about everyone eats and sleeps in there with their sub-packs."

Bunjee's nose wrinkled. Maybe he didn't understand.

"Sub-packs are smaller groups with close friends or relatives. And you'll like evenings in the communal den listening to stories, singing, and dancing."

"In bear clan, kids stay with their mother and her companion. When the bears hibernate, Ursans socialize and teach the kids."

That would be different. "This is Codee's den." Dayvee cast his hand toward the entrance. "You don't need to remember every family den yet, but this crooked column that looks like a bent leg is where you turn for Leeto and Milay's. But they're not there much."

"Are they always gone?"

"No, but if there's trouble anywhere, Leeto or Codee go, and Milay travels to other packs to negotiate. If they're here, they stay busy so don't count on them." Were Bunjee's eyes tearing? Sympathy tugged at Dayvee's heart. "Everyone else will help you. I will too, if I can, but tomorrow's my choosing."

Even if Dayvee was chosen, he'd see little of Bunjee this year. New Calupi trained separately.

"If you're not chosen, don't you have to leave? What will you do? Are you scared?"

Did Bunjee think Dayvee wouldn't make it? "Yes, I'd have to go, and I don't know what I'd do." He wouldn't admit to being terrified. A Calupi's life was the only one he wanted. They squeezed around the formation that looked like a man's beard.

"Remember the beard." Dayvee touched the point on the rock. "It marks this den where you'll train."

"Our teachers said I was too sociable to be a bear's companion. They said a wolf might choose me, but I don't have much hope."

Compassion gushed through Dayvee. "You'll do fine."

"I always thought a brother might be good to have."

"Me too. Maybe my parents will focus on your mistakes instead of mine." Dayvee chuckled. "Can you make sure to mess up often?"

Bunjee grinned. "I'll try."

"Thanks." Dayvee smiled and turned down a different corridor. He stopped to press a finger against the rough striation on the walls. "See how the ridged lines make this wall look like a waterfall? If you memorize what's different in each area, you'll have a map. Right beyond it is the ceremony room. The lamps aren't lit, but you'll see it tomorrow. Across from it is the tunnel to Kwutee's den. He's our keeper if you're sick."

Bunjee stopped to gawk. "I've never seen caves like this. They're amazing."

Dayvee agreed. Kun displayed his art all over their home. Seeing it through Bunjee's eyes made him appreciate it more. He said another silent prayer, *Please, Kun, let me be chosen.*

An elderly Calupi faced the wall at the end of the corridor. His thin-white hair and bowed legs gave away his identity. Dayvee stopped. "That's Miko. He can't walk very far now so it's his duty to fill the lamps. Miko became alpha leader after my grandfather was killed by a bear."

"My grandfather died, too." Bunjee sighed. "I miss him."

"I never knew mine. Leeto was seventeen—just a year older than me—so he didn't have enough status to lead. The pack calls that the year of challenges since Leeto and Codee fought someone nearly every week. When Leeto gained enough status, he challenged for the right to be alpha, but Miko stepped down and handed leadership over to him."

"Would your father have won?"

"Leeto doesn't lose fights, but Miko told the pack that even though Leeto'd be our youngest Calupi alpha ever, he'd do a great job—better than him. Codee said Miko could have formed a new pack and taken several Calupi with him. He chose not to split us, but supported Leeto, instead. Codee and Leeto both respect him."

Dayvee moved again toward Miko. His grizzled face turned from a lamp to greet them. "Hello Dayvee. Who's this?"

"Bunjee, my new brother."

Miko smiled. "Welcome to our cave."

"Thanks," Bunjee said.

"Did you hear Rayvo went missing yesterday?" Miko asked.

"No," Dayvee replied. "What happened?"

"He decided to explore the Nowhere tunnels, and his torch went out. Like you. What were you, eight?"

"Yes." Dayvee shuddered as he recalled the paralyzing fear when darkness closed in and his agonizing crawl through the cave's blackest corridors on the longest day of his life. Leeto and Milay never noticed him gone. Brando and Elayni alerted the pack when he didn't show up that evening.

"Did it take the wolves long to find him?" Dayvee asked.

"No. He only went a mile—unlike you." Miko chuckled. "He said he couldn't see them, but felt their noses stuck in his face. He grabbed on, and they led him out."

"That's good." Dayvee still didn't like the dark.

Bunjee's eyes opened even wider. "I could get turned around in here easy."

"As long as you stick to the used tunnels with lamps, you'll be fine. Someone will come along to ask. But if the light stops, go back." Miko turned to the lamp. "I've got to get these last few filled. I'll see you later."

Dayvee's stomach growled. Time to go to the communal den to eat and—no avoiding it—face his father.

3

Pack Law

"The pack will grow weak and die if our will to keep the law isn't strong." ~ Kwutee

As Dayvee entered the communal den with Bunjee at his heels, the voices like a babbling brook hushed. Everyone turned to look.

Bunjee fell silent. The egg-shaped room had an entrance at each end. Pitted stone walls curved around like in most of the cave's chambers. A rock shelf protruded in one section. Brando and Elayni gave Dayvee a wave from beneath it.

Several lamps and a fire in the center cast light in the room. Some of the sub-packs clustered around the fire's flames. A rough table made of lashed branches held food nearby. Bedrolls and pillows lay scattered. Bunjee goggled as he craned his head up.

Bears only spent winter in caves so Dayvee asked, "Do Ursans have ceiling platforms?"

Bunjee shook his head no. His forehead furrowed.

"They're in all the dens we spend much time in," Dayvee explained. "Those poles support the ceiling and help prevent cave-ins." He pointed up. "The treated hides are sewn together, and hung between the poles to catch the cave's drips." He waved at the closest clay pot in the corner. "The water runs into those, and we stay dry."

Dayvee led his new brother to the food. "The night before the choosing, trainees' parents make their favorite dishes."

Milay didn't know Dayvee's current favorites, but she prepared the dishes he preferred as a young child. He still loved the nut crisps, but why did she bother? Just following tradition?

Would Dayvee's stomach ever stop its churning? Like a tiny puppy running inside. Maybe after the choosing tomorrow, he could relax. Should he try to eat? To keep from hurting Milay, Dayvee selected a little from her dishes—the roasted pigeon with seasoned grains in mushroom sauce, the watercress, and the nut crisps made from crushed nut and grain batter, fried, and topped with honey or berries. The crisps' crunchy sweetness usually had him cramming in as many as he could.

His hands full with his bowl and a cup of tea, Dayvee tilted his head toward the sub-pack closest to the fire. "That's the leaders' sub-pack. The alpha's are Leeto and Milay, and the beta's are Codee, Jolay, Kwutee, and Clunee. And each sub-pack has a beta leader. Kids stay with their parent's sub-pack if they aren't on rotation and with a relative or friend if they are. They're welcome everywhere. Sometimes older kids just stay together." Dayvee chuckled. "Like us but we started a lot younger."

Bunjee trailed Dayvee to the other side of the room where Elayni and Brando sat under the shelf of rock that resembled a chipped piece of driftwood. The adults avoided the area, not wanting to duck. After they claimed it, the other kids wanted to use their spot, but Brando considered anyone except his 'family' trespassers.

Dayvee knelt down so he didn't hit his head. "Brando, are you going to welcome my brother, or should we go somewhere else?"

Brando let Dayvee and Elayni make the decisions about everything with a few exceptions—Brando's list, and who was 'family.' Not very much to ask for.

"If you want him here, that's fine—he's family of family." Brando took a swallow of tea, and placed the empty cup down. "But I don't want Leeto."

"Alphas go where they want, but I don't think Leeto's interested." Dayvee motioned to Bunjee. "Sit anywhere that's comfortable. You can sleep with us, too, if you'd like." Then, he plopped on a pillow in his normal place and touched the pebbly wall with his hand. Not wet. The shelf usually kept it dry. He rested his back against it.

Bunjee sat a few steps away and huddled where the wall recessed back a little. His eyes darted over the pack while he ate.

"Remember to duck when you stand, or you'll bang your head," Dayvee warned him.

Bunjee nodded, still not speaking.

"Do you want me to light this?" Brando retrieved their lamp from the nook beside him.

"Yes." Dayvee might not want to admit his weakness, but the shadows already made his skin crawl and his breath seemed harder to gain. The lamps and fire, struggling to dispel the pitch black of the cave, didn't illuminate very far under the shelf.

Brando took his fire kit out and struck his stones together to throw a spark on the lamp's wick. The light flared, chasing the shadows back.

His relief let Dayvee's breath and muscles relax. "To take the leader's lamp with them sitting there has to be your best prank yet, but Miko sure was angry."

A mischievous crooked smile lit Brando's face. "He came around. My charm's hard to resist."

Brando caught the pillow Elayni threw at him. "Charm? The only reason he let you keep it is you offered to help him until you earned it."

Wilee came over to sprawl near Dayvee, then Luko joined him. The wolves often sought out the kids or clumped together in the evenings. The wolves' presence comforted Dayvee, but he'd need to be careful about what he said. Luko and Leeto's thoughts were shared.

"So now that our tests are done, who do you think did the best?" Elayni asked.

Such an overachiever. Dayvee picked at the food. "You."

"You won more tests. Strength, hunting, and speed. Brando won fighting and wrestling. And he has the most blades. Negotiations and trading are the only ones I might have won.

"It isn't based on tests, alone." They'd know soon which trainees impressed them enough to be chosen, and what rank they gained. Dayvee put his bowl of food down. "So did your parent's make it back?"

"Not yet, but sometime tonight." Elayni tumbled her words together. "They'll be so proud of me—I mean if I make it."

"You don't have to act." Brando chuckled. "We know you'll make it."

Elayni swallowed her last bite. "You're too talented to fail, too—but they might make you wait to mature." She took out a dyed bone bead from a pouch beside her and slid it on a sinew strand. "You shouldn't have pulled that prank today."

"Dayvee needed a laugh to lighten up. We're not facing death." Brando's fist flew toward Dayvee. He twisted but not fast enough. It brushed the back of his arm.

Luko growled at Brando. A scuffling sounded as Bunjee scooted further away. Frightened? Dayvee spoke reassuringly, "Luko won't hurt us." He touched Luko's head. "He just reminded Brando that if he wants to fight me, to take it to the ring."

"It's been a long time since I got a punch through, but why does he remind me of the law so much more than you?" Brando asked.

Dayvee chuckled. "Do you need it more?"

Brando flung Elayni's pillow at him. "No. I'm going to fix a basket tomorrow, Luko."

Luko growled again. Dayvee snorted. "He wants to know if you like nips."

Elayni and Brando laughed. Dayvee filled Bunjee in, "Brando tied a basket with a snake inside to Clay and asked her to find me. Wolves don't like snakes."

"Clay raised Dayvee so she tolerated a lot, but I pushed it." Brando grinned. He drew his knife from his weapons pouch, picked up his latest wood carving, and shaved a slice off. "She only nipped me once when I poked her in the eye. A little pinch to my finger was all that was."

Dayvee's heart wrenched. If only Clay could be there tomorrow.

"When a companion growls, it's just a warning." Elayni's long graceful fingers flashed as she strung the beads for a necklace. "Either their chosen's angry, or they want us to think about whether we're following our Pack Law."

It might calm Dayvee's nerves to do something. Like Brando, he really didn't like sitting still for long. He pulled his shoe snow from his rucksack. He had damaged it when he walked over a rocky area that didn't hold enough snow. The rounded ash frame was okay, but the center lashing was torn and frayed. He undid that section.

"Here, Dayvee." Elayni handed him a long strip of rawhide.

"Thanks." Dayvee wound an end around the center of the frame.

"Ursans don't have a pack law. What is it?" Bunjee asked.

"To defend the Vita and protect the pack." Dayvee wove the strip hexagonally. "Ursans don't need it since they don't live together. What do you think would happen if the wolves attacked us?"

"You'd die."

"Yes." Dayvee looped the strip again around the frame. "But if companions attacked Calupi, we'd use our weapons. Everyone would die, and there'd be no pack. So we follow the law. They don't sink their teeth in us, and we don't sink our weapons. And Calupi fights between each other are controlled in the ring."

"Do they know I'm part of their pack?" Bunjee asked.

"Yes." Dayvee answered. "But if you weren't, you'd have to be trying to harm the Vita or the pack to be attacked. Not even wild wolves want to harm humans. They retreat from us." Dayvee touched the soft fur on Luko's head. "He wants to come over and reassure you."

"All right." Bunjee's eyes widened as the wolf moved to him.

"Put out your hand and let him smell you."

Bunjee stuck his hand out, and Luko nosed it.

"Are you frightened now?" Dayvee asked.

Bunjee shook his head. "No."

"Good, he likes you." Luko returned to plop by Dayvee, and nudged the pillow between them. "I did forget to return it, thanks Luko." He held out the pillow. "Here, Elayni."

She took it and leaned forward to slide it behind her against the wall. "I can only tell the obvious stuff, Dayvee. It sure seems like you talk to the wolves."

Bunjee's eyes goggled. "Can you?"

"No." Dayvee knotted the rawhide lashing together and cut the remainder off with his knife. "Calupi are like all clanspeople. We can only mind-speak to our own companion after we're chosen. The keeper's the only one who can speak to all the pack's wolves."

"A Kayndo can speak to every animal." Brando's crooked smile flashed.

Dayvee choked back a chortle. "We haven't had an animal master in over a hundred years. I'm not that old. I just read their body language. Everyone does it some. Codee knew someone better than me."

"Who?" Elayni caught the strip he tossed over.

"I don't know, he didn't say." Dayvee stowed his repaired snowshoe back in his rucksack. "I'm not as good at figuring out people so I study their companions." He slung a fist at Brando who pulled his shoulder in enough for it to miss. "And I did need a laugh, but not tomorrow."

Brando put his carving and knife down. "I'm not a turkey." He flapped his arms. "I know better than to gobble when I don't need to stand out."

"Then promise no acting up during the ceremony." Elayni wrinkled her pert nose.

"All right, you have my word. *Satisfied*, mother Elayni?"

"Yes." Calupi valued their word.

"But afterward, if they don't choose me, I'm giving the pack something to remember me by." Brando sheathed his knife, his mouth turned serious. "If I don't make it, would you walk away with me?"

He must really be concerned to drop the smile and nothing-bothers-me act. Elayni studied her feet and shook her head. "It'd hurt my parents if I did that."

"Dayvee?" Brando asked.

He'd like to lift Brando's spirits, but he couldn't lie. "I don't know. That would convince Leeto and Milay, I was worthless."

Brando's voice turned glum as he rocked slightly. "My father wouldn't either. That killed my mother."

"Jonesee had his companion and the pack." Dayvee spoke gently. "He couldn't leave."

"I could for you or Elayni, but you are my family and my pack," Brando declared. "I won't abandon you."

"We'll make it." Elayni grabbed his hand, then reached over Wilee to clutch Dayvee's. Her fingers sent warmth traveling up his arm. Sweat moistened his palms. Would she notice?

"We'll know soon." Dayvee pulled his hand back and turned to Brando. "Will Jonesee be here?"

"He volunteered to cover again." Brando's lips clamped tight in a stiff smile. "I didn't expect him." Jonesee had delivered another deep cut to Brando's heart.

"Sit with me, tomorrow." Elayni stared at Brando.

"No, I'll be all right alone. We won't be seated long anyway." Brando drew his knife and the shavings flew as he attacked the wood carving, again.

Luko's head rose and alerted Dayvee. He followed the wolf's gaze to Milay's approach. "Bunjee, come with me," she called. "Leeto's going to introduce you."

Bunjee rose, and smacked into the overhang. He gave Dayvee a sheepish grin as he rubbed his head. Milay took Bunjee's arm and led him to Leeto standing in front of the fire.

Leeto put a hand on Bunjee's shoulder. Dayvee stopped his anxious foot tapping. Leeto didn't like him to exhibit weakness. The room hushed when Leeto cleared his throat. "I'd like to introduce my new son, Bunjee, and ask you to make him welcome. We're very pleased to have him join our family."

Leeto's words hit Dayvee like a fist in his gut. Maybe Leeto couldn't wait to replace him. At the tilt of Leeto's head, Milay and Bunjee sat.

"Rodnee come up," Leeto commanded.

The lanky Calupi startled. He stood and went to Leeto.

"Two sub-packs were short members so they decided to merge," Leeto announced. "I asked their Calupi to choose one leader, and they've selected Rodnee." Leeto clapped Rodnee's back. "Do you accept the burden of leading them?"

Rodnee squared his shoulders. "Yes."

"Congratulations, I know you won't let me down." Leeto flicked his hand. Rodnee returned to his seat as Leeto studied the pack again. "Now for the trainees. Most of you saw the strength test and how they did…"

Miko called out, "Were you worried after Dayvee pulled in four that the pup might defeat his father?"

Leeto's gaze picked out Dayvee under the shelf. "What have I always told you about being worthy of Wolf Mountain pack?" Leeto asked.

Dayvee swallowed hard. "That no sacrifice I make will be too much."

"Yes. Before I touched the rope, I knew we'd win. You need to work much harder to be good enough to worry me."

Was every gaze in the room locked on Dayvee? Now, he wanted to disappear in the shadows, so he slid further down from their lamp. Dayvee had really strived in training and given his all on the test. Why did he always fail to convince Leeto? The weight of Leeto's expectations for Dayvee to become alpha pressed heavily down upon him.

The pack's gazes returned to Leeto. The crushing criticism was proof Dayvee hadn't worked hard enough. A lump choked his throat and tears threatened, but he widened his eyes to stop them. He threw his head back and banged it against the stone wall. It hurt, but he deserved the pain.

Dayvee flung himself a second time, but before he reached the wall, both wolves sprang up. Their lips curled back to show their teeth.

4

Beyond Death

"Our memories don't fade with the last breath. Sharing stories parts the curtain of death." ~Chayla

Luko and Wilee's teeth latched on to Dayvee's pant leg. Brando and Elayni each seized an arm and helped the wolves haul him away from the wall.

Elayni mouthed, "You are good."

What would Dayvee do without them? His fate seemed clear. Leeto just told them all. "Not good enough."

Brando turned hooded eyes on Leeto. Dayvee gave him a small jab with his elbow. If Brando kept glaring, Leeto might challenge him.

Leeto's gaze fixed on them. Did he notice? "Each trainee will come up now to share the story of their predator test. Dayvee, go first."

Dayvee drew a big breath to calm himself. Was he just a trainee while Bunjee was the son Leeto was pleased to have? Dayvee went forward and related to the pack how he'd faced the mountain lion. Then, he returned to their spot.

"Elayni, you're next," Leeto called.

She put aside her bead necklace and went to Leeto. Dayvee shook his bedroll to get a few of Brando's wood shavings off and crawled in. Brando smiled. "This is early even for you. Aren't you going to hear the other stories?"

"I'll listen from here. I didn't get much rest waiting on that mountain lion."

"Then sleep." Brando chuckled. "You're grumpy without it. If your brother comes back, I'll help him get situated."

"Thanks." Dayvee never heard the end of Elayni's story.

...

The fog of slumber cleared, and Dayvee snapped open his eyes. Today was the day. His chest was like a hide stretched too tight. Excitement might rip it in two. Then, Leeto's words came crashing back. *"Not good enough."* The lump rose again, but he fought for composure.

He wiped his gritty eyes, and rose. Brando and Elayni had already left. A few people in the communal room still slept, including Bunjee. In his pile of fur, he resembled a hibernating bear. Dayvee blew out the lamp.

Bunjee's eye cracked open. "Brando said the lamp's almost out of oil, and I can use your spot while you're gone."

"That's great," Dayvee returned the lamp to the nook. "He must like you."

"Why do they call him tiger?"

"Who said it?" Dayvee's voice came out sharper than he meant.

Bunjee's hand ran through his mussed hair. "Leeto told Codee the tiger was making a mistake glaring at him."

There wasn't anything he could do about Leeto using that term. Dayvee sighed. "When we were younger, kids called Brando that since tigers are alone. They tried to make him an omega."

"What's an omega?"

"The lowest status wolf the rest pick on. They ganged up on him when I was hunting with Codee. Five against one. I thought no one called him tiger anymore, but apparently I was wrong."

"I won't call him tiger." Bunjee stretched his arms.

"Good. If you start moving, you can have breakfast before we wash for the ceremony."

The kid jumped to his feet. Was his stomach bottomless? Dayvee's still churned. After Bunjee devoured two bowls of gruel, and they scrubbed themselves clean, Dayvee led Bunjee out of the pool room.

"We store our things in our family den, and Leeto holds his meetings there." A sharp pain stabbed Dayvee's temple. Not very smart to beat his head against the wall last night. A sudden urge to leave swept through him. Why wait and go through this?

No... Leeto would think he ran from his duty. He'd never respect Dayvee. Besides, he wanted to be Calupi. To relinquish his dream, he needed to know for certain he failed. He and Bunjee found their den as empty as a nest after the birds flew south.

"Nice painting." Bunjee pointed.

The mural painted on the rock wall depicted wolves stalking an elk. The only other things relieving the starkness were a fireplace, some shelves, a few trunks underneath, and a low table with a small carving of a wolf. Calupi didn't need much, but Bunjee could be used to more. There were two other rooms, each entrance covered with a hide.

Dayvee ambled over to one, pulled the hide aside, and went in. "This was my den—yours now." Smaller than the main room, the one lit lamp showed this half of it—and the two trunks on the floor. Dayvee didn't bother lighting the other lamps. He wasn't staying.

"You can have my sleeping pallet on the other side." Dayvee chuckled. "But you'll need to get better at ducking your head if you sleep there. The ceiling's low."

"Thanks, but are you sure?"

"Of course, I haven't slept here since I was eight, but the pallet's big enough for you. I just finished making a larger one."

"Why didn't you sleep here?"

Should he tell Bunjee? If he didn't, the kid might be hurt. "I decided to go where I was wanted."

Bunjee's eyes teared. Dayvee rushed to undo what he caused. "Leeto and Milay usually sleep in the communal room, anyway. Codee will help you if he's not busy, but don't tell him anything you don't want to get back to Leeto. Did Brando say you can bring others to our spot?"

"He said I can invite friends, but I'm not sure how to make them. Ursans aren't real sociable."

"You're going to be Calupi, and they are. Start by asking Rayvo. He's your age. See Miko about earning some more oil and light the lamp. Rayvo will like that after being lost in the Nowhere tunnels."

"Thanks."

Dayvee nodded and ran his hand along the rough bark of his trunk—nothing special, just made from branches cut to the right length and lashed together. "Tomorrow, what's left in here you can have. We're only supposed to take what will fit in our rucksacks."

Bunjee's brow furrowed. "I'll keep your things for you."

"No, I want you to use them if you can." Dayvee opened his trunk's lid. A new ceremony outfit lay on top. He lifted it out and rubbed his fingers along the soft texture, breathing in the scent of freshly treated deer hide.

Bunjee gasped. "Buzzing, that's a lot of beads."

The array of beads on the fringes dazzled. An embroidered mountain, wolf paw, and circle decorated the shirt. Paw prints emblazoned the knees and teeth were painted on the side seams of the pants. His companion's face might embellish the shirt's circle—if Dayvee received one. Why did Milay invest the time in the elaborate outfit when she cared so little? Maybe she wanted the alpha's son dressed to reflect their status.

"I have new clothes, too." Bunjee drew a shirt out of his trunk with one hand and pants with the other. The same symbols minus the circle adorned Bunjee's outfit—all painted—with not as many beads but ideal for his first ceremony outfit. Milay must have made it after her and Leeto met with Bunjee in the fall.

"What do they mean?" Bunjee's nose crinkled.

"The teeth show we belong to a predator clan, the wolf prints are for Wolf Clan, and the mountains are the symbol for our pack, Wolf Mountain." Footsteps crossed the other room. "We're back here!"

Milay came in dressed in her ceremony clothes. Wet hair lay smooth to her neck, but she twisted the strands below in her hands to form two braids.

Dayvee jiggled his hand holding the outfit. "Thanks, it's perfect."

"Yes, thank you." Bunjee stroked his shirt.

"You're welcome." She finished braiding her hair and pursed her lips into a strange half smile. "Give me your rucksack."

Dayvee took it off and handed it to her. Was that a tear on her cheek or water from her hair?

"Now, hurry and get dressed." She left the room. After dressing, Dayvee tried to smooth his cowlick that stuck out above his forehead, but deemed it a rabbit in the hole—a lost effort. "Let's go."

They entered the main den where Leeto and Milay waited.

"They're a little large." Milay eyed them. "But you'll fill them out shortly."

"Dayvee, you're still missing something." Leeto held out both his hands, each had a small bundle wrapped in hide with a thin cord twisted around it.

Dayvee snatched them, plopped on a pillow, and placed them on his lap. He rushed to untie the cord on one and pulled back the hide to reveal a long narrow pouch. When he picked it up, the new leather and fringes that ran along each side felt stiff in his hand. He noted the weight and opened the flap to draw out the Calupi knife. It slid into his palm. The opalescent blade gleamed in the light. His heart missed a beat. A familiar wolf's face was carved into the hilt. "Clay," he whispered as he found the etched name on the back.

Memories engulfed him—Clay's soft eyes, her body curled against his, the soft tongue that licked his tears and cuts, and the sound of her paws padding behind him to keep him safe. Dayvee choked back his tears. "This is real!"

Milay nodded. Tears *were* in her eyes. Probably missing Clay.

He hefted the knife, checked the balance, and tested the sharpness by cutting hair from his forearm. The blade sliced them as easily as fingers travel through water.

He opened the second package. Another leather pouch, only shaped in a half circle. Decorative brown fringes dangled down the sides. He opened the flap to reveal the grip of a chakram, and drew it out. Around the sides and bottom of the circlet twelve sharp blades bristled. Rawhide strips wrapped around the circle to grip it firmly without harm. Padded wood lined the pouch to make it safe to carry.

Dayvee scratched his head. First, Leeto told Dayvee he didn't work hard enough and then handed him a valuable gift? Some Calupi took years to acquire the wealth for 'real' weapons. His parents already gifted him with good weapons after he proved his ability to use them. An apprentice crafted them instead of a master, and the material originated from a deer. He never expected these—not good—superb.

"What are they?" Bunjee asked. "And why do you call them real?"

"This is the Calupi tooth." Dayvee passed the knife to Bunjee, hilt first to inspect. "And the nails." He rotated the chakram to present Bunjee with a rawhide grip. "With them, we can fight as fiercely as wolves."

Leeto shifted his weight. "Real ones are crafted from the teeth and bones of a deceased wolf companion. Our histories tell us Calupi buried our companions at first, but the wolves didn't approve. They asked the clan to use their bones, teeth, and hide to protect the pack."

"Clay," Bunjee read aloud. "Didn't Brando say she raised you?"

Dayvee called Clay mother from the time he learned to say the word until Codee told him Milay didn't like it. Clay always showed him unconditional love.

"Yes, and she died protecting me." He still couldn't bear the memory and pushed it aside. *A wolf companion fights for its pack beyond death.* The old saying took on new meaning as Dayvee held the weapons. A part of Clay would still be with him and keep him safe.

"Thank you doesn't begin to express how grateful I am to have these." Dayvee reverently placed the tooth and nails back in the pouches and stood.

Leeto crossed his arms. "Just use them well."

"I will." Dayvee turned to Milay. "But how can you part with them?" Didn't she blame him for Clay's death?

"She loved you and wanted to keep you from harm."

"I loved her too." Dayvee wiped away a tear with the back of his hand. "But what if I don't make it?" His voice quivered.

Leeto lifted his chin. Dayvee pulled his shoulders back, raised his chin, and straightened his face. Leeto nodded once. "They're yours, to wield however."

Milay reached her hand up and smoothed his cowlick. "Whether you're Calupi or not—make us, Clay, and the pack proud."

"If I have to leave…" A lump rose in Dayvee's throat. "Will you forgive me if I'm not good enough?"

Leeto's brow furrowed. "What have I told you about your doubts?"

"They're the same as fear. I have to face them and defeat them."

"If you had worked harder, you'd be certain of today's outcome."

"When? I needed to sleep."

Leeto's face turned stern. "I'd suggest sacrificing some rest to improve enough so you don't fear failing."

No matter how hard Dayvee tried to stay awake, sleep generally found him. "I won several tests against the other trainees."

Leeto's eyes locked on him. "How many adults did you best?"

"None."

"An alpha's son can't be weak. Youth aren't going to be your only challengers if you lead." Leeto flicked a finger at the pouches. "Now put your weapons on."

Dayvee removed the old pouches and attached the new to his belt. "Bunjee, I want you to have my other set. They aren't real, but they're good weapons and kept me from harm." He swapped out the red fringe on his old pouch with one of the brown on his new. "You have to earn red fringes by risking your safety to protect pack mates or to defend the Vita."

Leeto had given Dayvee and Brando a red fringe when they carried Elayni home with a broken leg and fought off the coyotes that came after them. They were the only trainees who had one. Most of the adult's weapons' pouches displayed several red fringes, and all forty on Leeto's and Codee's pouches were red.

Dayvee drew out his old chakram and removed the other blades. "Everyone begins with two blades. You'll gain more after you improve your accuracy." He handed the pouches to Bunjee. "You're right handed. Most prefer the nails on the right side of their belt and grab them first, but you can decide."

His brother's eyes lit up. "Thanks, Dayvee."

"Just use them well." Why did his parents give him a sibling, now, when Dayvee couldn't help him? Dayvee squeezed Bunjee's shoulder. "I'm sorry I won't be able to teach you to wield them. Ask Miko for pointers. He helped Brando and me." He handed the blades to Leeto. "I'm sure Bunjee will need these, soon."

Milay's voice caught as she held out his rucksack. "I added a few things."

"Thanks." Dayvee grabbed it.

"Remember, they won't just judge you, but us by your actions." Leeto lifted his head. "Stand proud—head up."

Like Leeto would ever let him forget it. Dayvee drew himself up and took a deep breath. *Be strong.*

Leeto pulled back the hide, and they took the corridor to the cave's mouth. Dayvee placed his rucksack down by five others already there. No one knew who might be forced to leave abruptly. As they turned toward the ceremony room, Dayvee's legs shook. *Don't fail me now. My destiny waits.*

5

The Choosing

"A creature that can easily take your life, but instead shares it. That is the choosing." ~Chayla

Dayvee traveled the corridors with Bunjee trailing his parents and their pack, all headed the same way. Spasms kept his stomach tumbling.

Tobee, the pack's only unchosen adult, hobbled around to corral the children under age eight. His youthful features were a contrast to his grandfather-like shuffle. Even with Tobee's deformities—small crooked legs, bowed back, and twisted hands—he got them to cooperate.

The first choosing Dayvee was old enough to attend was one trainee short—Tobee. His parents thought he'd fail and be forced to leave, so they urged him not to take the tests. He contributed to the pack by growing things others couldn't, helping with the children, and cooking. Regardless, he held the low status of a child and couldn't garner respect. Tobee wasn't Calupi.

Dayvee followed his parents past the pool to enter the large ceremony room with its sand-colored walls that stretched over a hundred feet long. The entire face of one wall sloped back from below and displayed alcoves and niches that formed groups of natural seats. Their ancestors had only needed to carve a few steps to have a ceremony room where everyone could be seated and watch activities below.

Bunjee looked up at the stalactites that hung down in rows of jagged teeth from the ceiling and whistled. The lamp light sparkled against the colorful array like glittering icicles with shades of white, rose, tan, and yellow from the minerals in the cave.

"It's a stunning room, isn't it?" Dayvee asked.

"Buzzing."

Elayni already sat by her parents. Brando was a little further down—people all around him, yet alone. An island in a sea of faces. Dayvee followed his parents up a few steps to an oval shaped niche, near a rock chimney and close to the ring. Leeto's preferred spot.

"Can I go sit with Brando so he's not alone?" Dayvee asked.

Leeto sighed. "What did I tell you last year?"

"I had to sit by you during the ceremony, but after that, when you mingled with the adults, I wasn't to bother you."

"And before you attended your first ceremony how did I say you should act?"

"Sit down, be still, and get quiet."

"Your memory doesn't seem to be the problem, but leaders don't expect to keep repeating themselves. If something changes, we tell you. Now I'm ordering it. Get still and quiet."

Why did Leeto bother with his charade? He already told everyone how he felt about his son—*"not good enough"*—but Dayvee couldn't defy the alpha's order if he wanted a place in the pack. And Brando wouldn't join him or Elayni with their parents. Dayvee situated himself near Leeto and Milay but left a gap between them. His parents' companions sprawled out in front of them. Dayvee leaned back against the cave wall, and the rough pitted texture bit through his shirt. Bunjee plopped next to him.

Their position gave Dayvee a good view of the ceremony ring consisting of rocks placed in a large circle around the thick sand cushion on the floor. It took a few minutes for everyone to file in, find places, and greet neighbors. Leeto shot Dayvee a glare, then glanced at Dayvee's foot. It was tapping again. He stopped it. The savory odor of roasting meat wafted through the room from the feast preparations.

Dayvee's uncle, Codee, and his life-mate, Jolay, joined them and filled the space between Dayvee and his parents. Good, that might make it harder for Leeto to scrutinize Dayvee.

Codee clasped Leeto's and then Milay's forearm. He turned to Dayvee. "Ready?"

Should Dayvee shrug? No, Leeto ordered him to be still, too.

Jolay's smile lit up her heart-shaped creamy face. Jolay had life mated Codee in the fall, but with the couple leaving on Rashee to twine their souls, and Dayvee busy with his tests, he'd barely said two words to her.

"I was so nervous at my choosing. Are you okay?" she asked.

Dayvee glanced at his father. Leeto turned to Jolay. "I've ordered Dayvee not to talk or move."

As he entered the ring, Kwutee's small stature didn't diminish his authority. His white robe matched his short, curly gray-white hair. A small limp and the staff he used for support betrayed his age and frailty. Wrinkles from nature and time etched his dark face. Keeno, his wolf companion, strode proudly at his side, head high, his muzzle and face silver. Kwutee halted in the center of the ring—his black marble eyes glittering as he turned a penetrating gaze on those gathered.

Kwutee's presence radiated power. He held the rank of beta and the knowledge of Kun and the Vita. As the oldest keeper, other packs often consulted Kwutee for his wisdom and healing. His gaze sent a prickle of apprehension through Dayvee, but he must not be alone. All those assembled hushed. So quiet, Dayvee heard water dripping from somewhere in the caves.

"As Keeper of the Vita for Wolf Mountain Pack, I've asked you here for an important occasion. I'd remind you of the first choosing, and how we became Calupi."

Brando shifted in his seat. Thankfully, he'd promised not to act up. If a snake appeared now, and people jumped or screamed, Leeto would be livid.

"After the ancients nearly destroyed his creation with waste and wars, it saddened Kun. He sent the first Kayndo, JoKayndo, to teach us the Vita—rules to live in harmony with Kun and each other. Some animals volunteered to guide us—our first companions. Kun gifted them with intelligence, longer lives, and the ability to communicate with us. The animals selected people in that first choosing who formed the first clans. Some of our ancestors were chosen by wolves. They called themselves Calupi and formed the packs that make Wolf Clan. Herrick founded Wolf Mountain Pack.

Everyone but Dayvee chanted. "As our ancestors followed the Vita, so do we."

"Today it's time for another choosing, those who believe they are worthy may come down." Kwutee extended his arm with his palm open and motioned them toward him.

Dayvee turned his gaze on Leeto again. "You may move now, but keep silent until I release you."

Dayvee rose and proceeded to the ring with the other hopefuls. Usually the large room chilled him, but now he wiped at sweat that trailed down his forehead and stung his eyes. His legs wobbled as if he'd run all day. Easier for him to walk toward the mountain lion.

He ran a hand through his hair to smooth his cowlick and glanced back. Leeto gave him a stern look and signaled with a snap of his head. Milay gave him a weak half-smile.

To project a confidence he didn't feel, Dayvee drew himself up taller and lifted his chin again. He'd probably put a crick in his neck soon, then Leeto might be happy. *Come on legs.* He lined up with the six other Calupi hopefuls. The two older Calupi, Nero and Rudee, were here for second companions and stood a few feet apart from them.

Kwutee peered at the youth first. "You've worked hard preparing for this, and helped with the wild wolves, but companions are more intelligent. The bond is so strong, it will be hard to separate your thoughts." Kwutee raised his staff to point at the entrance. "Calupi don't break vows, and these require sacrifice. You shouldn't swear them lightly. If anyone wishes to leave now, they may."

Kwutee paused. No-one moved. "If you're chosen, do you vow to put the Vita, your pack, and your companion's needs before yours? To treat your companion as an equal partner and to follow our pack law until your death or your companion's?"

Each of the trainees answered in turn with shaky voices. "Yes."

Brando answered, and then Dayvee's turn came. He met Leeto's eyes. *Come on. What are you waiting for?* Kwutee shifted impatiently. Dayvee clenched his jaw and his face warmed. Finally Leeto nodded.

"Yes." Dayvee snapped. The echo returned. He hadn't meant to shout. Dayvee glared at Leeto. His father's mouth turned up in that little smile of his. Codee's face wore a broad grin. Then, Dayvee understood. Leeto had meant for that to happen. By craning to see his father, Dayvee's head was up, and his anger made his voice come out strong. But by waiting so long, Leeto made Dayvee appear an idiot—too dumbstruck to answer. Dayvee wanted everyone to believe he should be judged worthy, but on his own merit.

Kwutee's voice rolled around them. "The wolves will examine you. They may decide you're immature, and you can try next year. If they believe your temperament isn't compatible with theirs, you can try another clan. They may sense you fear or don't like animals. If so you'll have to leave this pack and travel to some town or city to take up a new life. Are you prepared to do this?"

Dayvee stopped his foot from tapping. What choice was there? To accept this test or leave without taking it. Dayvee loved his home but not enough to stay without respect or status—like Tobee.

Dayvee needed water. His mouth felt as parched as if he ran several miles on a hot summer day. He squawked, "Yes, I am."

Kwutee turned to Nero and Rudee, the older Calupi. "Are you sure you're ready to take a new companion and let them take the place in your soul once held by another?"

Both replied, "Yes."

Some never wanted another companion after they lost one. Dayvee gulped as Brando's mother popped into his mind.

If the older Calupi failed the test or weren't ready for a new companion yet, they'd still be Calupi. Not forced to leave although they might choose to. Not so easy for the rest of them.

Kwutee projected his voice. "Now, the wolves will decide…cide…cide." The echo filled the cavern. "Take your places." Kwutee swung his staff.

They spread out like they'd rehearsed. Nero and Rudee stood closest to the opening in the ring, across from each other. The rest situated themselves according to their birthdates with the oldest youth next to the two Calupi. Dayvee was the youngest—Brando was one month older, and Elayni three, so he assumed his place at the far end facing the opening, leaving several wolf-lengths between Brando, him, and the perimeter of stones. Plenty of space for the wolves to move around him.

Kwutee tapped his staff on the ground. "The older companions will look you over first. If you're judged worthy, the pups will come in and choose." The companions left the alcoves and leapt down to enter the ring. Wolf Mountain Pack boasted thirty-five companions. Everyone tried to attend the choosing, so there must be thirty here today. They approached Nero first, sniffing and circling him before continuing on to the next trainee.

The wolves finished Elayni and approached Dayvee to ring him. It didn't matter that the wolves loved the Calupi children like their own pups, or that Dayvee's father was alpha. They'd do what they considered best for the pack. His future was for the wolves to decide.

Was he imagining it, or were they taking longer on him? Some crowded so close they rubbed against him. The soft touch of noses pressed against him, and their hot breath seeped through his clothes and left moist impressions on his skin. *Oh no.* Usually if they took longer it meant the trainee failed. Desolation washed over him as if he'd fallen down one of the bottomless shafts in the caves, and the sensation of being too hot changed to one of freezing. The wolves turned and loped over to Brando.

They circled Brando once and moved on. *Whew.* He and his friends must have passed their inspection. The wolves continued until they finished with Nero. They should go back to Kwutee, now.

Wait a minute. They were headed back toward Dayvee. Leeto warned him he wasn't good enough. All the wolves crowded around him. His legs turned wobbly, but he needed to stay on his feet. If the wolves thought he feared or hated them, they'd charge him and give him a good nip if he didn't leave the cave and Wolf Mountain territory. The wolves weren't bristling, they crouched. What was going on? He'd never seen this before. All the wolves plopped over on their sides.

Keeno's head lifted off the ground, and a quiet voice whispered in Dayvee's mind. *Don't worry, we find you worthy, pup.*

This couldn't be happening. Dayvee tried to project his thoughts back. *Are you talking to me? I don't understand.* Confusion and relief flooded him. Did the wolf say they found him worthy?

Yes, it's Keeno, and you should get used to wolf voices in your mind. That's what it's like to have a companion.

But you're Kwutee's companion. And why are you lying down?

We're showing you respect. All the wolves rolled over and showed him their bellies—a huge submissive gesture.

But why? I don't deserve it. I should show deference to you. There was no room to lay with the wolves surrounding him, so Dayvee sat, lowered his head, and bared his neck.

All the wolves bounded to their feet as Keeno's whisper filled his mind. *We believe in you. You'll deserve our respect soon.* Dayvee checked Luko's body language. He stood tall, head up, with an ear slightly tipped. That stance would normally reveal his pride in a wolf—but his ear and muzzle pointed at Dayvee.

The wolves parted as Kwutee made his way through them, limping quickly to Dayvee. "Get up."

Dayvee jumped to his feet and tried to brush the sand off his ceremony clothes. He smoothed his cowlick. What would Kwutee say? He must be talking to Keeno from the distant look on his face. Were they discussing Dayvee? He couldn't hear Keeno in his head anymore.

He longed to ask Kwutee why the wolves had acted so strange, but he mustn't make Kwutee more upset. Dayvee checked the wolves' body language. Their head and tails were up, and they almost pranced as they left the ring. Were they…pleased?

Kwutee turned toward the crowd. "I'm sorry but the wolves wanted my attention. They've judged all of these Calupi worthy! Welcome new Calupi of Wolf Mountain Pack!"

The crowd clapped loud and long.

Shooting stars went off inside Dayvee's head. He was judged worthy! The desire to throw back his head and let out a howl rose, but he stifled it. *Thank you, Kun.*

Kwutee beckoned. "Come forward for your marks."

Dayvee took the last place in line. Kwutee pointed to his own hand. "This tattoo tells the world your companion's a predator—a wolf—who is your right hand as you are theirs." With a bowl of soapy water, he washed each of their hands between the knuckles and wrist. He dipped a needle in an ink pot and drew the wolf teeth mark. Two fangs pointing down separated by a line, then underneath, and inside, two fangs pointing up divided by a line.

He pointed to his other hand. "This tattoo shows you're a member of Wolf Mountain Pack, and just like you need your left hand, you need your pack." He drew their pack mark. A large triangle with a point and another line on both sides—the symbol for mountain range.

Not one trainee flinched. When Dayvee's turn finally came, he clenched his teeth, determined not to reveal the pain either. Maybe he'd make Leeto proud. The sharp prick of the needle penetrated his skin and scratched him as Kwutee etched the marks. Dayvee smiled when Kwutee finished. Not near as bad as his worry built it to be.

When Dayvee received his only other tattoo as a baby, Codee told him he cried hard enough Kun surely heard. The open circle around his heart was drawn as soon as he was cleaned after his birth and dedicated to Kun. The reminder for all clanspeople their heart is a gift from Kun and should be open to Him.

He examined his new tattoos. Calupi. His chest puffed as the thrill surged through him. "We will turn each pup loose in order of status to choose which of you will become their companion. Since the highest status pup is the prince's companion, I'll ask all the senior Calupi to come forward now so he may choose who will have the honor of training him." Kwutee flung a hand toward the back of the ring. "The rest of you can wait there."

Dayvee was glad to go to the back. Calupi didn't consider training a pup for another person an honor but a hardship. Only one other time had Leeto allowed it, and that was when a Calupi broke his leg.

Rudee, one of the older Calupi came with the trainees, but Nero stayed up in front. This was his tenth year as Calupi, so he qualified as senior. Couldn't be over ten other Calupi who joined Nero and that included Leeto and Codee.

"Release the prince's pup," Kwutee ordered.

The stunning pup drew Dayvee's attention as it entered the ring. The pup had ash grey tones on his head and back blending into creamy sand yellow along his ribs, flanks, chest, and upper legs, into snow white patches on his muzzle, cheeks, and lower legs. Only nine months old, he seemed big—had to weigh at least a hundred and twenty pounds. The largest of the adult wolf companions, like Luko and Wilee, topped two hundred pounds when they finished growing.

The pup approached the seniors. He passed Leeto, Codee, then each one in the line that ended with Nero, and circled around them. Without wavering the pup came clear to the back and sat down facing Dayvee. What?

Kwutee raised his hand. "The pup has chosen Dayvee and the other wolves are agreed. Dayvee should be given the honor of training the future king's pup."

A black hole of despair reached out to swallow Dayvee. Train the prince's pup? Wouldn't he get his *own* companion?

6

Honor or Hardship

"Don't jump off cliffs hoping there's a ledge to stop your fall."~ Leeto.

Gasps and the hum of murmurs filled the cavern. Dayvee's throat turned raw and his stomach clenched as if he'd eaten winter berries by mistake.

Kwutee held up his hand and it quieted. He gently said to Dayvee, "It's quite a responsibility for someone so young to be given and it will be hard for you to give the pup up. Will you accept this honor?"

Leeto and Codee turned to face Kwutee. Leeto's fists clenched and his back was as unyielding as stone. "We agreed to only let a senior train the pup so why are you asking him to do this?"

"I'm not asking, they are." Kwutee's face pinched in a frown. "It was never our right to decide. The wolves chose Dayvee."

"It is my right to be concerned." Leeto crossed his arms. "You shouldn't do it, Dayvee."

Since when did Leeto show concern for Dayvee? And if he refused, would another wolf choose him? He might end up with none. "Would I get another companion, too?"

"No." Kwutee shook his head. "You're so young, you'll have your hands full."

Codee shook his head. "Leeto is right, Dayvee. A senior Calupi with a companion would have a hard time losing the bond. For you, it will be as difficult as when Clay died."

Could he go through that devastation again? Dayvee glanced at Brando and Elayni, both faces held worry lines.

A stab of pain shot through Dayvee's temple. Putting a hand to his forehead Dayvee rubbed it then smoothed his hair where he'd roughed it up. To meet a wolf's eyes was a sign of aggression, but those soft golden eyes pulled at him and he couldn't resist. The pup lowered his head. It considered him worthy.

Dayvee squared his shoulders. "Kwutee, do you believe I could do as good of a job as another if I trained him?"

"I'm absolutely convinced of it." Kwutee's black eyes pierced him. "It's not your father's, your uncle's, or your friends' decision, it's yours."

Leeto raised a brow and a corner of his lip twitched down to show his displeasure. "I don't understand why you're encouraging this."

Kwutee signaled with a touch of his lips and a drawing back of his hand. They'd talk more later.

Leeto uncrossed his arms and gave Kwutee a curt nod. "All right, but if there's a fox in our midst, you'll find me a vicious opponent."

Did Leeto really think Kwutee was conniving against Dayvee? Kwutee was usually among the few Leeto trusted, and he was as powerful as the alphas. Leeto spoke for the Calupi, but Kwutee spoke for Kun and all the pack's wolves. Could it be that Leeto really did love Dayvee and was showing concern for him? He better get off the delusion trail. It only led to disappointment.

"What do *you* want to do, Dayvee?" Kwutee's tone demanded an answer.

The pup's tail was up, his head sat high. His stance showed pride in his decision. The belief in Dayvee's abilities warmed him. Wasn't hunting the rabbit in front of him better than waiting for a deer he might never get? Rabbit meat didn't last long, but it beat none. "I'll accept."

Leeto and Codee frowned, but they filed out of the ring with the other senior Calupi.

Kwutee gestured with his staff to the pup. "When training a companion for another we use a partial bond so it isn't as difficult to separate. You won't share his every thought. To speak to him you'll need to concentrate and focus on him. And you'll have to be fairly close to one another. You won't feel his pain or hunger so you'll need to watch carefully to learn his needs."

"What do I do?" Dayvee asked.

Kwutee's wrinkles parted as he smiled. "It helps establish the bond to place a hand on him. He'll do the rest."

Dayvee extended his hand. The pup sniffed it and then Dayvee gently laid it across the wolf's head, the soft fur enveloped his palm. The pup didn't back away.

Kwutee put his finger on his own temple. "Now mind speak to him."

Was every eye on Dayvee? Did the pup feel his fingers trembling? He thought, *Hello.* What name would the pup select? It probably wouldn't be close to Dayvee's since he'd be the prince's companion.

Nothing happened. Hadn't he been told to focus? He shut out everything—Kwutee, Leeto the watching pack—and left only one thing in his mind. Speaking to the pup. *Hello.*

The soft response filled his mind. *Hi. You can call me Jaycee.* Dayvee sucked in his breath. The knot in his stomach unclenched. His struggles to get to this moment faded. Joy rose in him like a creek dammed by a beaver and it threatened to overflow the bank. His eyes stung and he widened them in an attempt to keep the tears back.

"I can tell by your expression he's established the bond." Kwutee turned to the pack. "Dayvee's partially bonded, and although he's training the prince's pup, he's considered Calupi with all the rights and privileges." He tilted his head toward the exit. "You can leave now and go to the training rooms until the games to get acquainted."

Dayvee left the ring to scattered applause. The pack seemed as confused as Dayvee—at least he didn't need to leave his home. He'd enjoy every minute with Jaycee without regret, and when they separated, Dayvee'd at least have the memories.

He went to the cave entrance and grabbed his rucksack and threw it over his shoulder. Then, he headed toward the training dens. The pup padded beside him with his tongue out. Jaycee could go to the pool to drink but water was kept available in the dens, too. *Are you thirsty?*

I can drink.

Dayvee turned and entered the puppy den. Some raggedy pillows, hides, and bones the pups had nearly destroyed lay scattered around. A large cask of water sat in the corner.

Several clay bowls, with padded leather on the outside lay nearby. Jaycee nuzzled his. Dayvee filled it with fresh water. Jaycee drank his fill.

Afterwards, Dayvee and Jaycee strode to the dens set aside for new Calupi where they'd live until they finished training. Dayvee reached out to pull aside the hide that covered the entrance but stopped when he heard his name. Jaycee bumped Dayvee's leg as he halted.

"If you ask me, Dayvee got what he deserved, the privilege of training the prince's pup." From inside the room, Nero's voice dripped with sarcasm.

Dayvee's breath caught. Who was Nero talking to?

"Everyone could tell he was judged unworthy when the wolves took so long on him." The hushed voice was Rudee's. "Kwutee must have asked the companions to let him train the prince's pup."

Dayvee's heart leapt to his throat. They didn't believe him worthy.

"No one else wanted the job." Nero harrumphed. "Did Kwutee think that if he called it an honor, we'd believe it? The alpha's son and keeper's pet couldn't fail and no matter how he acted, Leeto had to be in on it."

Kwutee and Leeto would never do that. How could they even think it?

Dayvee strained to hear Rudee's soft voice. "Leeto already treated him as if he'd be the next alpha when there are more experienced Calupi to replace his father."

"Leeto won't be alpha much longer. He's too weak to make an unworthy son leave." Nero's voice sharpened. "Dayvee's dung stinks. He'll refuse to follow an order or fail in his duty and I'll prove he's unworthy. Then, we'll be rid of him."

Dayvee's stomach knotted. Jaycee pressed against his leg. *Someone comes.*

A footfall fell behind him. Dayvee jumped and almost dropped the bowl. Just Elayni with her new companion. Relief swept over him. She put her finger to her mouth to signal quiet and crooked her finger for him to follow. Dayvee and Jaycee trailed her and her companion into the deserted room he just left.

"Did you hear?" Dayvee couldn't keep the anger from his voice.

She filled her companion's bowl with water. "Not much. I wasn't the one listening at the door." She grinned. "You're lucky I'm the one who found you."

"It wasn't intentional. I heard them as I started in—Elayni, they acted like I was a stranger."

"Don't overreact."

"I'm not. They said my dung stinks."

Her eyes widened. "So they're renouncing you as a pack member."

Dayvee clenched his jaw and nodded once.

Elayni chewed her bottom lip. "I heard some others claim you weren't really Calupi if you were only training a companion."

Dayvee wiped the sweat away from his forehead. Jaycee pressed against Dayvee's leg as if to reassure him. He tried to keep the desperation from his voice. "What will I do, now?"

Elayni gave his arm a squeeze. "Nothing. They're just howling. The companions don't lie and they say you're worthy."

The heat rose on Dayvee's skin where Elayni's fingers circled his arm. He took a deep breath. Focus.

"Maybe Nero's still angry at Leeto." She dropped her hand.

The memory surfaced of that first challenge Leeto let Dayvee see. After Leeto caught Nero's guard post empty twice, he broke Nero's nose and front tooth in the ring.

"But that was years ago." Jaycee went over to Elayni's companion. They nosed one another.

"Calupi have long memories." The old saying she spouted did hold some truth.

"But I'm not Leeto and Rudee blasted me too."

"Ignore it. Maybe they want to be the next alpha and feel threatened by you."

Dayvee's nerves were wound as tight as a sapling bent to make a rabbit snare. "I can't just brush it off. Nero's senior and he can fail me even if I do everything right." He let out a heavy breath. "I went through all this for nothing."

"It's not that bad. We train with each other so he'll have to find an excuse. Don't give him one. I'll watch your back and I know Brando will too."

Dayvee grabbed onto the hope. Maybe it wouldn't be as bad as he feared. "Thanks Elayni."

"You're welcome. But don't trust anyone else." She tilted her face and gave him a hard look. "You should tell your father what they said."

"He'd just criticize me for not being able to handle the problem, if he believed me." Dayvee refilled Jayvee's bowl. "Congratulations on being chosen, your companion's beautiful."

"She says she'd be honored to meet you. Her name is Evee."

"Hi Evee." Dayvee reached out his hand and Evee came over and smelled it "This is Jaycee." Jaycee approached Elayni.

She touched Jaycee's head. "Is it difficult to speak to him with just a partial bond?"

"I have to focus really hard and not let anything distract me. I'm not that good at it. What's the full bond like?"

Elayni's nose wrinkled. Having someone else in my mind is overwhelming, but she's wonderful about it and keeps sending me encouragement. And the physical thing is strange. When she's thirsty, my throat feels parched. Elayni picked up Evee's bowl. "We better go. The other trainees should be there now."

Dayvee didn't want to go back, but they needed to. He grabbed Jaycee's bowl and strode out. Elayni and their wolf companions followed. At the training room entrance, he pulled the hide aside and went in. The trainees all stood there now with their new companions. They stared at them and the room fell too quiet. Had they still been berating Dayvee?

"There you are." Under Nero's thin, light-tan hair his face appeared too long, especially for the small features like his narrowed brown eyes. "Didn't you understand you were supposed to come here?" Nero's sneer exposed his broken front tooth. His new companion bristled—a female. Companions chose the Calupi they believed merited them, regardless of sex—the sex of pups in a litter rarely matched ready trainees.

Jaycee's hackles rose at Dayvee's side, a low growl emerged. Nero's companion lowered her head and body.

Rudee's face wore a frown and his companion had stiffened. When Jaycee's muzzle swiveled toward Rudee's companion, his posture loosened. Jaycee showed them. Dayvee'd *really* like to growl at Nero, too.

7

No Regrets

"Kun doesn't promise you an easy climb, but he'll be with you, guiding and aiding you, to the summit." ~ Kwutee

If Dayvee didn't show respect to the senior Calupi, it would give him justification in his attempt to get rid of him. He jiggled the bowl in his hand and softened his voice. "We needed to retrieve our companions' bowls. They were thirsty."

"You didn't have to take so long." Nero puffed up like a defensive opossum. "I'm trying to explain a few things."

Dayvee and Elayni joined the other trainees to stand in front of Nero. Brando flashed Dayvee a smile.

"Everyone repeat your companion's names again for Dayvee and Elayni. Mine's Nesi."

They went around the group with each trainee naming their companion. Jet black hair and a square face caught Dayvee's attention. Fifteen-year-old Geno wasn't part of their regular group. He touched a hand to a wolf's head. "My companion's name is Graydee."

Nero smirked at Dayvee. "Since you're training the prince's pup, we had one extra. The companions felt Geno, even though he's younger, is worthy to be chosen."

Dayvee bit off a retort. He hadn't spent time with the younger boy, but he didn't look special—short, and muscular with those dark brooding eyes. The companions must like something about him. He was chosen to have a companion, not train one.

He drew in a cleansing breath. Stop traveling the self-pity trail. Jaycee wasn't just any companion, but the best. He shouldn't blame Geno.

"Welcome to our group." Dayvee reached out to clasp his forearm. "If there's anything I can to do to help, just ask."

"Thanks." Geno returned the arm clasp. His thick eyebrows crinkled as his smile filled his face.

Nero crossed his arms. "Since I've been a Calupi for ten years, I'm the most senior here, and that makes me the training leader." He shifted his weight. "You'll be learning to work with your companions to perform Calupi duties. If you fail, you won't be here long."

His beady eyes burned into Dayvee. A tingling ran through the back of Dayvee's neck. A sudden compulsion to flee or hide came over him. He dismissed it. Stop overreacting.

"Sub-packs usually hold no more than six Calupi with companions. Since there are nine of us, we'll break into two groups." Nero pointed to Rudee. "I'll lead one, and Rudee the other." He shook his finger at the trainees. "I can't ensure your safety unless you follow my orders, so I won't tolerate defiance." He flipped his finger toward Dayvee. "I want you in my group to make sure the prince's pup is treated right."

Sure you do. Dayvee forced himself to walk over and stand next to Nero.

Nero wore a sour face as if he'd bitten into an apple with a worm. "From now on when I tell you something, you answer, yes, sir."

Dayvee snapped. "Yes, sir."

Nero's nose wrinkled, but he turned his gaze on the others to inspect them like a trader looking over wares. "Anyone else want to join my group?"

After a second, Elayni and Brando stepped forward. "We'll join you, sir," Elayni said.

"Aren't you close friends with Dayvee?" Nero asked.

Elayni shook her head. Her errant lock fell in her face, and she pushed it back. "We know each other. We're close in age, but I don't think of Dayvee as a close friend."

Dayvee's heart plummeted. She had told him she'd watch his back, but must have reconsidered. His gut ached as if he'd just been punched hard. Making her parents proud and gaining status meant a lot to Elayni, but she wasn't the only one. To show support for Dayvee against a training leader wouldn't be in any trainees' best interest. Would Dayvee find himself friendless, now?

No, Jaycee sent. *You'll still have me.*

Brando's mouth dropped partially open, but he closed it. "I'm proud to be Dayvee's best friend."

Dayvee's heart warmed as he smiled at Brando. He could count on him and Jaycee, too.

"Elayni, you can be in our group." Nero turned to Brando. "Why do you think they call you tiger?"

Bruno's ruff rose, but Brando just lifted an eyebrow as if to say, *Is that the best you got?* "I don't know." The corner of his lip twitched. "Maybe because no one wolf can take on a tiger and win."

Dayvee sure admired Brando's confidence. Would Nero be as impressed?

"You already learned a pack can win against a tiger. Don't forget it. You'll be in Rudee's group so you can make some new friends. Choose them wisely, and you could join the pack."

Nero had struck low, but he was right. Even together Brando and Dayvee were outnumbered by far.

Brando replied in his sarcastic tone, "Yes…sir." He moved back by Rudee as Elayni lined up on Nero's other side away from Dayvee. She had her bottom lip in her mouth again.

No one else volunteered to be with Nero. None of their former teachers had treated them like the kingdom's soldiers, the kagards.

"We have three," Nero said. "I'll take Tayro and Renay, so that's five. Rudee, you get the rest."

Tayro blinked his hazel eyes several times. His thin frame ambled after Renay to join them. When Tayro's gaze met Dayvee, he lifted his chin, and his haughty look returned, as he turned his round-owlish face away.

When they were ten-years-old, Tayro made Elayni cry, and Dayvee threw Tayro down to pound his head against the floor. Brando pulled Dayvee off, thankfully. Luko judged Dayvee's apology sincere, but Tayro never forgave him. Dayvee made sure to keep control with every opponent he faced in the ring, now.

Nero laid a hand on his companion's head. "Don't look a companion directly in the eyes, and don't invade their space unless they come to you. They're not a pet, but a partner."

Dayvee released a heavy breath. Was Nero going to tell them things they knew since they were five? Did he like the sound of his own voice? Dayvee didn't try to stop his tapping foot.

Nero scowled. "Wolves are resting and sleeping at least six to eight hours a day; pups and older companions often need more. We've assigned each of you a den. Get settled, and we'll meet back here before the introductions."

Dayvee took a few steps toward the rooms. Nero's voice rang out again, so he stopped and turned back.

"New Calupi trainees have the lowest status, except for children who have none. But even among the lowest, there are differences. Your names are written on the hide entrance of the dens. The front partition is for the highest ranked companion. The last is still Calupi. That's better than anyone else, and status does change, doesn't it?"

"Yes, sir," everyone replied together.

"You can go, but don't forget to come back for your pallets." Nero waved a hand toward them stacked against the wall.

Dayvee might as well collect his now. He shoved Jaycee's bowl down in his rucksack, then grabbed his pallet's rectangular frame of branches with its rope mesh woven between. Then clutched his mattress with his other hand and dragged both, careful not to let the dried grass spill out. He hadn't sewn the bottom of the two hides, but tucked the flap so he could change the stuffing as needed.

Dayvee was written in chalk on the first partition entrance. Unease about overstepping his place made him pause. It didn't feel right to take the room ahead of the older Calupi, but Jaycee had been judged as the best pup.

Tayro and his companion, Topay, pulled his pallet into the next den. As Kwutee's apprentice, his status would be beta when he became keeper. Elayni and Evee entered the next room. She must be happy.

Nero stomped into the fourth partition with his companion, Nesi. Probably hard for Nero to be placed fourth. With the prince's pup and the future keeper in this class, the senior didn't receive the highest status pup like normal. Even Elayni surpassed him. Following Nero, petite Chayla stopped at the next partition. She glanced back toward Dayvee. Her almond eyes sparkled with delight. She bounced in with her companion, Cato.

No surprise Chayla had ranked higher. Even at sixteen, everyone liked her stories since she asked people what they felt and thought to tell them better. Kwutee and Clunee encouraged her to write them down. With Clunee's failing vision, they'd need a new writer of the pack's history soon, and it would surely be Chayla.

Just beyond Rudee, Dayvee barely made out Bruno. The biggest wolf after Jaycee, he was easy to spot with Brando. It was as far as Dayvee could see.

Nero and Rudee must have been writing the names when Dayvee overheard them—another reason for them to be angry at him.

Dayvee would trade the first room for his own companion. He shook his head. No regrets. If he did a great job, maybe he'd receive a high-status companion like Elayni at the next choosing. He hauled the pallet into their new home with Jaycee on his heels. The small den only held two lit wall lamps, and a full water bag hanging by the door. No shelves with food, pillows, wall paintings, or hearth. He shrugged. They wouldn't be here much, and they'd eat in the training communal area.

He placed the frame down and put the mattress over it. He made it plenty long enough for Jaycee, too. He took his bedroll of two hides from his rucksack and spread it over the top. *Jaycee.*

No answer. Even without a room full of people, this wasn't so easy to keep his mind focused.

Dayvee tried again. *I hope you like the pallet. Are you tired now?*

I can rest. Jaycee circled to inspect the pallet, then flopped down on the bottom and stretched out on his side.

The pallet took his weight without collapsing, and the grass didn't fly out. Dayvee let out his breath. Maybe he had done it right, and they wouldn't end up on the floor. The sewing had been difficult for him.

He shivered. The cave stayed damp and held some chill year round. Not so cold a released breath came out with a puff of steam, but even on the warmest summer day, he wanted a long-sleeve shirt on inside. He eyed Jaycee's warm coat with envy.

Elayni's betrayal returned to his mind, and a lump choked his throat. A black fog of despair threatened to engulf him. Why was so much working against him? Like he was in a flooding river swimming toward shore against the swift current, but the incredible force of the water was determined to drag him under. Focus on something else.

He should check if he left anything behind and learn what Milay packed in his rucksack. He hauled out his bowl and Jaycee's, his cup, spoon, coat, and clothing and laid them on the pallet in front of Jaycee. One of his two everyday outfits was replaced with a new one. Strange, Milay acting like she cared. Jaycee peered at him through slitted eyes.

Jaycee, are you sure you want me to train you instead of a more experienced Calupi?

I chose you. Are you having second thoughts?

No. Dayvee pulled out his food pouches, two empty for gathering, three full with his rations of jerky, dried vegetables, and various grains. Milay replaced the jerky he ate during his test. *I am worried I won't be good enough. You could have Leeto and he's alpha.*

The wolf raised his head a little. *I want you.*

Dayvee's snowshoes, the preserved and tanned stomach bag for water, the wolf rucksack, a short rope, and two small leather bags joined the pile on his blankets. *Are you sure?*

Yes.

Dayvee opened the two small sacks—one held his fire kit with his stones and oil soaked fluff, the other his sewing kit with needle, sinew, a few feathers, beads and leather strips. Milay had added the strips. *I'll try not to let you down.*

That's all any companion can ask. I pledge the same.

He removed the folded waterproof ground hide. On the bottom of the rucksack lay the pot for cooking. He had all he needed and more.

Jaycee cocked his head toward the door. *You have company coming.*

"Can we come in?" Elayni called softly.

Invite them in. Jaycee lunged off the pallet.

"Yes."

Elayni pulled aside the hide and walked in with her companion at her heels. Evee's ears and tail hung down as she minced in cautiously, normal behavior for a wolf entering another's den.

"I'm kind of busy." Dayvee began to repack his rucksack. "And do you think you should be seen with me?"

"Will you at least let me explain?" Elayni whispered.

8

New Puppy

"Kings need to put their kingdom over their own desires." ~King Layton to Prince Tibalt.

Tib raced through the dimly lit castle halls. His shoes clattered as they hit the stone floors, warning the servants who scurried to get out of his way.

Some shot him rude glances, but that was the most reproach he'd receive—one advantage to being a prince. Most people were too afraid to say much to him. Not his father, and he wouldn't be happy Tib was late.

He should have risen earlier, but what fifteen-year-old wanted to sit still for four hours? Most mornings for the past year, Tib sat at his father's side while he received petitions to learn a king's duties. Maybe Father would excuse him today? Not likely. At noon, he could escape and go to his other lessons. Not exactly fun, but better than endless rounds of petitioners asking for more land, more of Taluma's resources, more kagards, and reduced lease payments. Blah, blah, blah.

Tib arrived at the audience hall just a few minutes late. After a pause to smooth his mussed sandy-brown hair, wipe the grit from his eyes, and catch his breath, he entered the large hall. A painting of Father hung on one wall and hid the plain stone blocks. On the opposite wall a tapestry depicted Kun smiling at people. Above the throne a large map showed their continent and the kingdom of Taluma with all the cities and towns marked. Morning light dappled the room from the small windows above his head.

Father sat on the large ornamental throne with red fabric, carvings, and scrolled decorations around the edges. Tib made his way to the plain chair beside his father's throne and plopped his slender frame into it. Seemo, Father's eagle companion, shook his head from his perch. Twin red spots colored Father's cheeks. A match to the red hues revealed in the morning light in his father's otherwise brown hair. Neatly combed in contrast to Tib's own. Father's eyes narrowed as he met Tib's.

Still, Tib asked, "Can I be excused today?" *And every day?*

Father's green eyes flashed. "No Tibalt. A special visitor will arrive sometime this morning, and you won't want to miss it." The curt tone left no doubt the futility of argument.

Tib sighed and shifted to get comfortable in his chair. *Can't blame me for trying.*

The attendant made the introduction for the first petitioner of the day. "Owen, mayor of Portia to petition the king."

Tib fidgeted. As the mayor of such a prominent coastal city, he received the first appointment. Surely *he* wasn't the special visitor. He came in escorted on each side by a pericard—often called the 'king's fists.' The mayor stopped at ten paces in front of Tib's father. A rope and more of the pericards barred any attempt to get nearer. The mayor bowed. "Your Majesty."

Father's gaze fell on the mayor. "A pleasure as always. Do you have a petition?"

"Yes, Your Majesty. Our city has grown, and we need land to meet the growth. We need permission to cut the forest back so we can lease the land for more homes and crops."

Tib had studied the maps of Taluma. Portia was ringed by ocean, marshes, and forests. Another mayor who thought his city should be exempt from the clan's restrictions. How did his Father keep from sighing or yawning when he heard the same thing over and over?

"Reed, have you studied the mayor's request?" Father asked his Botanee advisor, the clan charged with protecting plants and trees.

Reed stood. "We have Your Majesty. The city cannot expand. It has grown to the marsh and forest edge. Several species in the marsh will be impacted if the city grows further. And the forests took two centuries to regrow after the ancients wiped them out. The city of Portia should encourage some citizens to move."

The mayor's body stiffened. "The forest and marsh have grown. And where would the population move?"

Tib's father seemed preoccupied. "Seemo informs me the city has doubled its size since he's been flying over it. Your city's out of room. Portia's main food source is fish. Even if I were to grant your petition, how can you support your growth without going over your share of the fish quotas for the area?"

"By farming, Your Majesty."

"To support your population from farming would require many fields. In time, you'd decimate the entire forest there."

"We also have fine craftsmen who trade goods for supplies, Your Majesty."

"Farming and tradesmen don't require a port location, only fishermen do. The population is sparse in many other areas and will support more farms and tradesmen. You should encourage your farmers and tradesmen to move and limit your city to fishermen."

"What if there're still too many, Your Majesty?" The mayor frowned.

"There are smaller northern port cities needing fishermen."

"They won't want to go, sire." The mayor threw his hands in the air.

"Hold a lottery if you need to. Some have to leave, and Portia can't allow new residents."

"If the farmers move, how do we feed the rest of us?" The mayor left off the honorific, which gained him a nudge and a hard stare from the pericard.

"You can trade fish for food, but you can't cut down a forest to maintain growth which an area can't sustain. Both people and animals need to keep the balance."

"My citizens won't like it. I won't be mayor for long, Your Majesty." He sighed.

"If you're replaced the limits will remain." Tib's father frowned. "Your city's in this mess because it focused on today and didn't worry about tomorrow."

The mayor stared at his feet. "Yes, Your Majesty."

"Kagards and Botanees will accompany you to make sure the population is limited to a sustainable level for your area." The king dismissed the mayor with a hand gesture. "You may wait in the entrance hall while your escort is assembled."

"Yes, my king."

The mayor turned and took two steps out of the hall, but the pericard on his left snapped a finger and pointed toward the king. The mayor started, turned on his heel, and delivered a hasty bow to the throne. Then, as if overly cautious, he backed away from the king until through the door.

Would the pericards clout the mayor? It wouldn't be the first time they'd been over zealous in reminding citizens the pericards did not pledge their loyalty to an unworthy king. Tib would probably never know since his father didn't condone it.

Tib had heard that the pericard's captain, Blake, had even administered a few lumps to fools after they were escorted out. Father finished writing his order and handed it to Blake. Tib couldn't help but stare.

Normally the captain wasn't easily distinguished from any other pericard. Blake's explanation was that an enemy didn't need to know who commanded, and his own men knew who they answered to. They all wore padded leather outfits and helmets died black with flat pieces of bone sewn in over areas they wanted protected. But now, Blake sported a black, swollen eye, just open a slit.

Was Blake in a fight or did a lucky blow get through in sparring practice? A few stray pieces of his dark brown hair escaped his helmet. Unusual for him to allow any disarray. The captain's one eye must have felt Tib's stare and his flint-grey eye met Tib's—his face as expressionless as a rock.

Blake rose and strode to the rope. The courier dressed in the brown leather uniform of the kagards met him there. If a kagard moved beyond that rope without permission, the pericards dealt them as quick a death as anyone else.

"Reed, do you have some Botanees to accompany them?" Tib's father's gaze turned to his advisor. Reed's name suited the thin, willowy man.

"Of course, Your Majesty, I'll see to it immediately." Reed left and returned a few minutes later. The attendant made his next announcement. "Drako, a Calupi from Wolf Mountain Pack has arrived with a companion seeking audience."

Drako had to be a man's name. Men's names in the clans ended with an E or O and women's with an A or I. They pronounced all the vowels in their names hard.

"Show him in immediately." Father waved.

This would be a first. Tib had met other clan members but not any Calupi.

Grumbles came from the foyer. Must not be happy about the line being passed. As the man came in, Tib took in the high cheek bones, strong forehead, and prominent chin. His forehead had a decorated band wrapped around it holding his black hair back. The muscular body pressed against the ornamental clan clothing, with all the drawings, embroidery, and beads. Liquid brown eyes met his.

Tib dropped his gaze to the large silver-grey wolf on the man's right. The pericard that escorted him on that side kept a few feet between the wolf and himself. Tib didn't blame him. They stopped at the rope. The Calupi bowed, and the wolf nodded his head.

Then, the wolf's amber eyes locked onto Tib. Was the wolf thinking what a good snack Tib might be? He wanted to bolt for the door. His muscles tensed, and his mouth dried. The beast's mouth parted into a strange smile that showed his sharp teeth. Tib's gulp came unbidden. He needed to stop. There was nothing to be afraid of—the pericards would protect him. When the wolf turned his head away, Tib slumped in his chair.

Father raised his eyebrows at Tib, then concentrated on the Calupi. This must be the special visitor. "And whom do I have the honor of meeting?"

"I'm called Drako and my companion is Juno. We're messengers from Wolf Mountain Pack, Your Majesty."

"We appreciate your long journey on our behalf. May I meet your companion?"

Drako glanced at the wolf and turned his gaze back. "Juno says he'd be happy to meet the king who keeps the Vita, Your Majesty."

Tib's father left his throne, went to the wolf, and ducked his head. "I'm pleased to meet you, Juno."

Tib squirmed in his seat. How embarrassing. Why would Father bow to an animal? He scrutinized the pericards, trying to determine what they made of this spectacle. Their faces were unreadable.

The wolf sniffed Tib's father and licked his hand. Father touched the wolf's head and returned to the throne. Tib let out a heavy breath. At least the wolf didn't hurt Father. But what was he thinking?

Drako smiled. "Your Majesty, a pup has been selected for the prince. He was judged by the companions as the best of all the Wolf Clan litters. He'll make a wonderful companion to his royal highness."

Tib's mouth dropped open, but he quickly shut it. A wolf? *Oh no.* Couldn't they have asked him first?

"I'm certain he will." Father turned his head to include Tib. "What do you think?"

He needed a companion to be king, but a wolf? Not Tib's idea of a good match. Maybe something like a rabbit? Tib attempted to swallow his rising panic. He stole another look at the wolf again and couldn't imagine living with it. Not the blasted eagle either.

His first memory was being attracted to one of Seemo's shiny feathers. After Tib pulled it, the bird bit him so hard his hand bled. When he cried to his parents, they scolded him. Tib gritted his teeth. Father spent almost every minute with that bird and relegated his son to tutors.

The wolf's eyes focused on Tib again. He worked not to reveal his fear but his hands shook. If the wolf felt that Tib wasn't worthy, it would be a huge disappointment to his father.

Why would Tib want to be king? A life like Father's—full of duty—didn't appeal to him. And now they expected him to live with a wolf. Why not just tell Father to forget it? Surely he'd get over his disappointment sometime.

Tib shivered. Would they ask him to meet the wolf? Father continued to stare at him.

"Um yeah, it's great." Maybe no one else noticed the tremor in his voice.

"May I be granted a short private audience, Your Majesty?" Drako asked.

After a quick glance at Seemo, Father's attention returned to the Calupi. "Yes, of course."

Odd. Father rarely met with anyone but Tib and his mother without his pericard retinue. Blake frowned, but he didn't say anything. His good eye stared at the Calupi. A warning or just to read his intentions? And what did the Calupi need to see Tib's father alone for? Had the wolf already judged Tib unworthy?

Father turned to Blake. "I'll meet with Drako and his companion in the meeting chamber. I'll resume audiences on my return."

At least the diversion might let Tib escape. Probably three more hours until noon, and he didn't intend to spend them here. Father stood and motioned to the pericards to allow Drako and Juno to pass. Tib craned around in his chair to watch as the Calupi and wolf followed his father to a meeting room at the rear of the large audience hall.

Tib's father pointed at the door. "Take up positions outside."

The pericards brought their right fist over their heart, then back down to their side. Their salute acknowledged his father as the heart of their kingdom, Taluma. His father's return salute recognized the pericards as the fists that protected the heart. No one expected Tib to salute, yet—not that he wanted to.

Father motioned. Drako and the wolf entered, trailed by Seemo. Father went in and shut the door behind them.

Tib jumped out of his chair and strode toward the entrance.

Blake cut him off. "Prince Tibalt. I don't think your father would want you to leave."

"Has Father ordered me guarded?"

Blake's forehead wrinkled. "No, he hasn't."

If he spoke with any hesitation, Blake would pounce. Tib made sure his voice was haughty. "Then, I don't think it's your concern." Blake stepped back, and Tib broke into a run. There were things he needed to do. Two more turns down the castle's halls and he was in the library, which backed up to the meeting room behind the throne. He'd learn what the Calupi had to say.

A servant was dusting the books as he ran in. "Leave, now. I don't want to be disturbed while I study." She flounced out.

The room contents appeared simple with the central table over a Kwin rug which warmed the stone floor, two lamps, and some scattered chairs, but Father felt the room held riches beyond any other in the castle. The few shelves that spanned one wall held the maps and the books with the histories—Taluma's, Harthome's, several other cities', and a few of the clans'. There were probably more books here than anywhere else in Taluma. Paper wasn't as plentiful everywhere.

Tib carefully removed the two books that hid the crack in the stone wall and pressed his ear to it.

"This is my fault." Father's voice was faint but clear. "I should have made sure he spent time with all Taluma's inhabitants."

What was he talking about? A sense of foreboding filled Tib.

"He won't be chosen unless he can conquer his fear," Drako said.

Tib's secret was out. What a disappointment he must be to Father. "You've probably seen people afraid of animals before. Do you have any advice?"

"He has to confront the fear to lose it." Drako spoke with surety. "In his case, spend time with wolves."

Tib mouthed the words in a silent plea to his father. *Don't make me.*

"He has to learn to rule, too," Father said. "That's why he's not doing the training."

"There are wolf packs closer," Drako replied. "He could go for a month and take the other tests. Then, he could complete the choosing when his companion comes."

Several heavy sniffs sounded. "Sire," Drako sounded puzzled. "Juno's informed me someone's listening to us." His voice dropped to a barely-heard whisper. "He hears breathing on the other side of this wall."

Tib's heart raced. He jerked away to run from the room.

"He thinks the scent is the Prince's." Drako's voice rang out.

Caught.

"Tibalt, hold," Father shouted. "I want you to hear this. Are you there?"

Tib pressed his ear back to the crack. "Yes."

"Drako, is it true that packs are good at teaching their youth respect?" Tib's father asked.

"Yes, Sire."

"Good. As you can see, Tibalt needs to learn some for others' privacy."

Those wolves would probably kill him. How would Tib dying teach him respect? "Don't send me."

"Make the arrangements for Tib to spend a month. But if he needs longer to learn, so be it," Father said. "I trust you'll continue to be discreet?"

"Of course," Drako replied.

Father's voice rose. "Tibalt, you'll only have defense lessons this afternoon. I'll ensure Blake makes them difficult."

"Yes, Father."

"Drako, I hear Calupi are excellent fighters. Maybe you'd like to participate in Tibalt's sparring lesson?"

"That's the second offer today, but I don't fight children. Challenges are serious to us. If you step in the ring with a Calupi, blood spills. Just ask your captain."

All the pericards held Blake's abilities in awe. The Calupi must be good.

Father chuckled. "I wondered about the black eye. Tibalt, go to the throne room. If you're not there when I return, you'll have several longer defense lessons."

Tib fled and raced back through the corridors. After his haughty attitude earlier, Blake would have him sparring until nightfall, and he had no desire to do it tomorrow, too.

9

Deception

"A successful hunt requires cunning, perseverance, and patience." ~ Codee

Elayni chewed her bottom lip. Was she worried? That loose strand had worked out of her braid again. Dayvee's heart careened. Mustn't let her presence do that to him.

"Your whispers are explaining plenty." A lump rose in Dayvee's throat, but he forced the words past. "You're afraid others might learn you're here, aren't you?"

"Yes."

He stuffed the rest of his piled belongings on the pallet back in his rucksack, none too gently, but left the small sack with his sewing supplies out. "At least I have one loyal friend."

"And look what happened to Brando since I wasn't able to warn him in time." Her eyes snapped, a contradiction to her quiet tones.

Dayvee took a feather and some dried sinew out of the sack. "Even if you did warn him, Brando wouldn't betray me."

"Stick your head out of the den," Elayni whispered. "If Nero thought we were friends, he'd have separated us. Then who'd watch your back?"

His heart skipped a beat. "You mean you planned it?" With Elayni, Brando and Jaycee for him, what did it matter if Nero and Rudee weren't? Dayvee's despair gave way to hope like the sun peeking out after a terrible storm.

"Of course. I told him the truth, just worded carefully. I said we're not *close* friends. We're not, we're *best* friends."

Dayvee's mind reeled. She hadn't betrayed him. He wanted her in his arms, at least to hug her if not kiss her.

A corner of Elayni's lip twitched in a half smile revealing one of her dimples. "You can't act friendly either, or Nero will put me in the other group."

"Calupi don't lie. And remember what happened when we deceived Leeto?"

"He made us pick berries for a month. And no, I don't love berry picking, but this is necessary. We won't lie, just word things carefully."

Dayvee finished tying the feather under his new knife pouch. "Leeto will still consider it deceitful."

Jaycee nudged Dayvee's arm. *Mother wolves practice deception to keep predators from finding their dens. You're not hurting anyone, and it's only a precaution. If nothing happens, pretend to make up later.*

Dayvee put the sack back in his rucksack. *Won't Nero's companion know?*

Yes, if she pays attention. But I doubt she'd care. It isn't uncommon for humans to hide their feelings.

Dayvee ran a hand through his hair. *Then, Nero will know.*

Perhaps a man loves a woman, but she's already mated. The mate might be jealous so the other man hides it. Do you think it would be better for the pack if we told? Jaycee's head tilted toward Dayvee.

No. But I don't understand. I thought in a full-bond it was impossible to keep things from one another.

With a full-bond it's impossible to keep emotions from one another. And Calupi can't seem to divide their thoughts. When they think to try, they've already shared.

Maybe Dayvee should be glad he didn't have a full-bond. Wouldn't it be uncomfortable if his companion knew his every thought? He smiled at himself. Who was he trying to convince?

A few Calupi block their mind from their companion for a period of time. Not many know how. Jaycee's tail thumped once. *Wolves don't block their Calupi, but they can and do separate their thoughts and pick those they wish to share.*

Somehow that didn't seem fair. But maybe they could deceive Nero.

If we're asked to judge truthfulness, we will, but Elayni told the truth. Jaycee glanced at him then looked away. *My advice is to keep pack members that can help you close.*

"I'm sorry I doubted you, Elayni."

"I'm not a hyena. I don't tear out my friend's throats." Elayni rolled her eyes.

Dayvee loved those big blue eyes, even if they were rolling. "My heart knew that, but the rejection hurt too much to listen. Can you forgive me?" He used Brando's exaggerated sad face and stuck out his bottom lip.

She crossed her arms. "Yes, but don't do it again."

"I won't. You're right. We do need to be deceptive, for now."

"When we're around the others, I'm going to treat you coldly. You do the same. Like acting a part in a story."

"I understand."

"I'll start." Her eyes glinted. "Sometimes you don't know how to treat a person!" Her shout echoed through the cave. "I came here to help you, and you're acting so rude to me. I can't be friendly with you." She flung the hide aside and stomped from the room.

Her exit left him breathing ragged. Elayni's long legs were hard to ignore when she stomped. The room felt much emptier.

Jaycee stood. *More company coming.*

"I'm coming in." Nero's voice grated as he charged into the den uninvited. Didn't Nero know better? Jaycee's low growl sounded as Nesi slunk in behind him. "What was that all about? Elayni sure was angry."

"I reconsidered a friendship, sir," Dayvee replied cautiously.

Nero's eyes narrowed. "Sometimes you need to work with Calupi who aren't your friends. Don't let it be a problem."

"I'll work with her, sir…" Dayvee met his gaze. "…but I don't like it when someone from my pack wants to hurt me."

Nero's chest puffed. "Let's get one thing settled. The prince's pup has high status. You're just training him so you have none, and what I say goes. Understand?"

Nesi's head snapped up, and she growled softly. One look from Jaycee and she lowered her head and quieted.

Dayvee stopped his foot tapping. "Yes, sir. I realize with any other training group you'd have the first room, and it must be difficult for a senior Calupi like yourself."

Nero tossed his head. "It doesn't *bother* me. Like I said before, things change. We're going to meet back in the training communal room. It's neutral ground, and the wolves won't fight to defend their dens."

"Yes, sir."

Nero and Nesi left his room. *Are you hungry or thirsty?* Dayvee asked Jaycee.

I can wait for the feast.

...

When Dayvee entered the training communal area with Jaycee, he found the other new Calupi already there with their companions. One of the children called from the other side of the door, "If you're ready, the games are about to start."

Nero cast his gaze on Dayvee. "Since you're training the prince's pup, and he has the highest status, you have to lead us there."

Dayvee and Jaycee walked past the hide to the corridor beyond. The others fell into line. He might not read people as well as Brando, but he could see Nero's disdain.

His worrying was interrupted by Tayro's voice behind him. "Are you disappointed to be a pretend Calupi?"

Was Tayro speaking to him? Must be. Dayvee's nails bit into the palm of his hand as he glanced over his shoulder. "I'm not a pretend anything. You heard Kwutee. I'm Calupi with all the rights and privileges, and it's an honor to train Jaycee."

"I'm sorry." Tayro smirked. "I didn't realize you believed it."

Dayvee pushed his fists into his legs to keep them at his side. He turned his head and fixed his gaze straight ahead to keep from showing Tayro his new tattoo up close by punching that self-satisfied smirk from Tayro's face. Dayvee couldn't fight Tayro without a challenge, and the day of the choosing was no time to issue one.

Nero, Rudee, and Tayro could be counted among those who wanted Dayvee to fail. He couldn't let them win. But how many others were there? Dayvee forced himself to take even, deep breaths until he could unclench his fists and focus on the task at hand. *Kun, help me get through this.*

As Dayvee entered the ceremony hall again, even with all his problems—his pride surged. He did it. The entire pack stood lined up from Leeto down to the children—where Dayvee and his friends waited last year.

Before he made it to them, Leeto spoke in his booming voice. "Wolf Mountain Pack, I present to you the future!"

Everyone clapped as Dayvee and Jaycee approached Leeto and Luko. Jaycee's tail tucked as he slinked toward Luko and licked his muzzle, completely different from when Jaycee was around the other pups, and they deferred to him.

Leeto clasped Dayvee's forearm with one hand and put his other on Dayvee's shoulder. "Well met, Dayvee, I'm proud to welcome you as Calupi."

The thrill flooded Dayvee as he returned the arm clasp. Leeto was proud? Did Kwutee's talk with him change his mind? Did it really matter? Dayvee was just happy to have it.

"What name did your companion choose?" Leeto asked.

"This is Jaycee."

"Hello Jaycee." Jaycee nudged Leeto's hand. Milay reached out and hugged Dayvee. "He is a handsome wolf."

Dayvee let his gaze travel over Jaycee again. "Yes, he is." Was she proud, too?

After she greeted Jaycee, he moved to Kwutee. The keeper gave him a beaming smile. Then, he went to his Uncle Codee and on down the line with the entire pack. Most congratulated him. Maybe Leeto's enthusiastic greeting swayed them.

After they came to the last, Leeto called out, "We'll begin the games."

Dayvee clapped and stomped his feet with everyone else while the wolves howled. They loved games. Dayvee sat closest to the ring, the spot reserved for the new Calupi to honor them on this special day.

"Nails first." Leeto waved to some Calupi carrying targets made of hides stretched tightly over a frame. The hide wouldn't damage blades. They entered the ring to set them up with their support props. The first target displayed two lines painted five hands apart, and they placed it ten feet from the throwing line. The lines on each target narrowed until, the last, at the far end of the ring, revealed only a space of a few fingers between its lines.

Leeto called, "Eight and nine-year-olds come down now."

Three children holding wooden, practice chakrams with two spikes, entered the ring first. At age eight, training and competing began, but you weren't allowed to use good weapons with blades until you earned three sets of spikes.

The first boy came to the line and held his chakram underneath, with his thumb on one side and his fingers in the hole. Not the normal grip. He flung it with a straight arm. Dayvee heard the thud. It hit the target but not between the lines.

The second boy held the weapon between his thumb and index finger on the rawhide strip edge like most Calupi did. He curled his arm and flung the weapon out by flipping his wrist. It landed between the lines on the first target, but he missed the second.

A little girl came next. She spun her chakram around her index finger in the center hole, and then flicked her finger to let it fly. A whoosh sounded as it sailed past two targets but didn't come close to hitting them. The weapon did fly in the right direction, even if she missed. It impressed Dayvee, especially for an eight-year-old. To manage the spin and release to control the flight using that method proved difficult. Only a few in the pack had mastered it.

Leeto handed the second boy two more spikes for his nails. His face lit up, and he danced around happily, holding up a prize spike in each hand while the pack clapped and stomped their feet for him. The memory surfaced of Dayvee's pride at eight when he received his second spike set.

When it was their turn, Dayvee and Brando made it to the fifth target. Elayni surprised them when she made it to the sixth and beat them. Dayvee did better than Brando and Elayni when his knife sunk in the sixth target in the tooth competition. In the races, he finished fourth for his best finish yet, and Brando placed fifth. In wrestling, Brando beat him as usual. Dayvee couldn't knock Brando from his feet. Brando bested several adults, too. It came down to Leeto against Codee, and Leeto won.

Leeto stood. "The sub-pack competition will be next!"

This was the first year Dayvee could compete. He lined up with all the other sub-packs in the center and tagged several Calupi in other sub-packs trying to get through to the other side. If they could get more members through, their sub-pack would win.

When their sub-pack's turn came, Nero decided their strategy. "The training sub-pack's larger, so we have the best chance. Dayvee, Brando, Tayro, Geno, and their companions will run first and be the decoys. Try to keep as many as possible chasing you and away from the rest of us while we run behind you to get through."

Dayvee shook his head. Why did Nero put Dayvee and Brando as decoys when they finished better than the others in the race? They should be running for the line. The slower ones like Nero, Rudee, and Renay, should be distracting. Dayvee and Jaycee raced forward. Renay came behind them. As Dayvee approached the line, Calupi ran forward to tag him. Companions tried to swamp Jaycee.

Dayvee dodged and ran to the side to draw them away. "Come get me if you can."

They followed, but more came from his front. He cut back the other direction and went wide to bring them further away. "Is that the best you can do?"

Some of them cut across. He turned, and fled back. Calupi swarmed him from all directions. They tagged him.

A shout sounded. "Renay's through the line." *About time. Run, Renay.*

They chased her down and tagged her before she made the ring's other side. Jaycee still hadn't been caught. Dayvee laughed. The wolf streaked like a blur in front of several others pursuing him. Luko raced from the front to cut him off. Jaycee launched himself in the air over him. Would he make it? Luko jumped up to nose his leg. Jaycee was tagged.

Dayvee concentrated hard at Jaycee. *Well met.*

It was fun, Jaycee sent. *My father said I gave them a good chase.*

Luko should be proud of Jaycee, Dayvee was. Elayni and her companion Evee followed Brando and Bruno. Elayni and Evee made it to the line, the only ones from their sub-pack.

As he and Jaycee trotted back toward the group, Dayvee flashed Elayni a smile and moved to congratulate her and Evee, then stopped himself. He couldn't act friendly. Elayni's cheeks were flushed from her run, and she was breathing hard. Tayro intercepted her and slapped her back, then draped his arm around her shoulders. Heat rose to Dayvee's neck. *Leave her alone.* She smiled at Tayro, but moved away, letting Tayro's arm drop.

Nero and Nesi stalked toward Dayvee and Jaycee. Nesi held her head up and her legs were stiff. Jaycee didn't put up with that. His ruff rose, and his head came up higher. Nesi lowered her head a little in deference.

Nero's lips pursed. "Why couldn't you help Renay through?"

Would Nero blame him for his own poor choices? Dayvee raised his head and drew back his shoulders. "I did."

Nero spluttered. "It was a mistake to think you might be of some use."

Jaycee's growl split the air. Bruno's joined it as he and Brando moved to Dayvee's side. Brando tilted his head toward the rocks outlining the ring. His crooked smile lit his face, and he bumped Dayvee's shoulder. The message clear. He had Dayvee's back if he wanted to challenge Nero to a fight.

10

Games

"Hunting isn't a game for predators but a risky act of desperation. If they succeed, they live another day." ~Codee

Brando rose on the balls of his feet as the energy coursed through him. Would Dayvee challenge Nero?

Leeto probably wouldn't want him to challenge a senior, but Nero deserved it. And Brando would support him. Leeto trained his gaze on Dayvee and crossed his arms.

Dayvee met Leeto's gaze, released a heavy breath, then lowered his head to Nero. "It's not my fault she got chased down, sir." He stomped away with Jaycee.

A small frown flitted across Leeto's face. Why was Leeto upset at Dayvee this time? He hadn't lost his temper. If Leeto was what having a father around was like, Brando was lucky his wasn't. He and Bruno followed Dayvee.

Leeto's voice reverberated. "Blind Calupi will be our last game. Those with companions may compete. Calupi can come to the ring while their companions help from above."

The crowd stomped in appreciation for the favorite.

Dayvee's posture relaxed. "Are you going to compete?" Brando asked.

"No. I'm not that good at speaking to Jaycee yet. I'll watch and cheer for you."

Brando scrambled to the ring with all the other trainees. Some people set up poles and scattered logs of firewood in the ring as obstacles. Codee handed out the mink hoods.

Brando slipped the dark cover over his head and face. It really did make him blind. No light came through.

"Go," Leeto yelled.

Brando ran.

Dodge to your left, Bruno sent.

Brando dodged.

Now to your right.

Brando dashed to the right.

Jump.

Brando jumped, but tripped over some wood. He regained his feet and raced forward.

Stop.

Not fast enough. Someone slammed into Brando, and he crashed to the ground. A Calupi fell over him and landed on top with a cry of, "Cackles!" Another collided with them and an "umph" sounded as a new weight pressed down to flatten him.

Brando tried to regain his feet but got tangled up with the others. Laughter rang out from the watchers, and he cracked up, too. He crawled out from under the pile up but slammed his head into a pole. "Ouch." He grabbed the pole and brought himself to his feet.

"Miko won." Leeto announced.

Brando removed his hood to cheer and applaud for Miko with everyone else. The older Calupi's fastest gait was a broken trot, not a run. But he came in first, proving his rapport with his companion—two thinking as one

The games were finished, so Calupi carried an entire haunch of buffalo, turkeys stuffed with seasoned grains, fish wrapped in leaves, several ducks, and pheasants from the cooking pit over to the tables.

Brando's stomach grumbled as they added the spoils from the pack's garden and gathering—bowls of flower and plant bulbs, squash, carrots, onions, and potatoes. Somehow, they managed to crowd a rice dish, a hearty stew, a sweet dish of stewed fruit and nuts, flat bread made of grains pounded to flour, honey cakes, and Milay's nut crisps onto the laden tables.

Leeto grinned. "The scent of all this food is torture for this hungry Calupi. Kwutee, lead us in a prayer to thank Kun for this bounty."

After Kwutee said the prayer, Leeto added, "Let's eat," and headed to the tables. As usual, status determined who went first, but no-one could doubt having plenty. The aromas made Brando salivate.

When his turn came, he filled Bruno's bowl with the things he wanted—duck, fish, stew, and a steamed wild rice dish with meat, garlic and eggs. Then, Brando heaped his own bowl to overflowing. Somehow he found room for a few honey cakes, and liberally spooned maple and berry syrup over them. The best feast, ever.

His sense of accomplishment swelled. This day marked the end to their childhood. Just the transitional training year to complete, then they'd be assigned a sub-pack and den, be able to choose a life mate, join the rotation, and if he gained enough status, he might finally get respect.

After he ate until he could hold no more, Brando and Bruno joined the others around the fire. Razi, a fermented drink highly regarded among Calupi that they claimed made them sing like a wolf, was passed. For the first time, the Razi came to the trainees. Brando swallowed a drink of the honey colored liquid. The bitter taste surprised him, and it burned as it slid down his throat. He coughed and passed it to Dayvee, who took a drink, sputtered, and then choked.

"What does anyone see in this?" Dayvee asked.

Brando shrugged. When they passed it to him again, Brando forced himself to gulp down another drink, but the taste didn't improve. He declined more. The adults who guzzled too much often lost control, and he needed to stay alert. Even the little he imbibed made him light headed and kept a grin on his face.

A drum beat pulsed through the room. The trill of a flute jumped in. Kwutee began singing a song praising Kun. Everyone joined in and wrapped their voices around his, with the wolves accompanying them. A yip, yip turned to a howl as they drew out the notes and harmonized. Oooohhh, ooohhh, ewwww, ewwww, yip, yip, they sang. They finished the song, then Leeto started another about the joys of being Calupi. Brando's voice melded with all the others.

He clapped, stomped, and sang. Calupi went to the front side of the fire to dance. Some of the new trainees joined the dancing, so Brando went, too. He moved his feet in time with the beat and formed the actions to depict their lives. When the songs spoke of journeys, he stepped as if he trotted. As the words described battles, he leapt, pounced, and made a throwing and slashing movement. When they sang of Kun, he raised his hands above his head and stomped in approval.

Brando danced until his legs ached, and his lungs burned. He stopped and wiped the sweat from his brow. Bruno lay watching with several other wolves, nearby. The wolves didn't dance, but they sang. Brando moved away from the dancers.

Calupi who weren't dancing relaxed around the fire. Brando was tired of dancing, but where should he sit? Dayvee sat on the left side of the flames, Elayni on the right. The split tore at Brando. He'd created their family years ago when Dayvee parroted Leeto's words, "Family comes before friends." Brando asked Dayvee if he wanted to be in a better family—one of choice, not birth. Dayvee had quickly agreed, and Elayni begged to join.

Bruno bounded up to him. *Am I your family now?*

Absolutely.

A chirp sounded. Aha. Brando walked over to the corner where it sounded. Another squeak. Brando bent down. A cricket. He grabbed it up and put it in his pouch. Going to be even harder now to make his family happy if they split, but he couldn't fail.

It wasn't only Jonesee's fault that his mother died. When she wouldn't get out of bed after her companion died, Brando didn't cheer her. He complained about her not getting up with him and condemned her actions. She eventually rose. Some bits of torn clothing and a few bones the searchers found at the bottom of the cliff were evidence of that. Some claimed it must have been an accident. To kill oneself was against the Vita. But Brando knew she willingly left those who brought her misery.

And who could blame his father for working all the time and not wanting to come home? Why would Jonesee want to see the son that added to his mother's sadness? Brando wouldn't make the same mistake again. He made an extra effort to keep Elayni and Dayvee laughing and happy. They were all he had left.

Could he keep both as family? Probably not. He'd be forced to choose. But how could he? Elayni had held him after his mother died and rocked with him. She was only seven when she declared herself as his new mother. And Dayvee fought five challenges without waiting for Brando to heal, even though Leeto made him do them back-to-back. Brando situated himself in the closest spot, not near either of his friends. It wasn't the first time he'd been alone.

Bruno sat by him. *You forgot me. You're not alone, and I'm not leaving you.*

Mist came to Brando's eyes. *Thanks. And I'm sorry for forgetting.*

He took out a block of wood and whittled, plastering a smile on his face. No matter how badly he hurt, he didn't expose his neck. "Tiger," came a whisper.

He lifted his head. Who? Hard telling, but it was far from the first time. Supposedly, children didn't have status. In reality, they shared their parents. As the alpha's son, Dayvee had been at the top. Elayni was just behind him, a beta's daughter. Brando had been at the bottom of the bottom. He was the abandoned cub of Jonesee, considered the pack's tiger since he worked alone and came home seldom.

When Dayvee befriended Brando, they were too little to know about status. After they became older, Dayvee's belief in the tiger's cub never wavered. And Elayni had always followed Dayvee's lead—until today.

I believe in you too, Bruno sent.

You and Dayvee are the only ones.

The only difference now from when he was young was they dropped the "cub" and whispered "tiger" instead. But not too softly.

They should know better, now, Bruno sent. *You're Calupi. You belong.*

Since Dayvee and Elayni fell out, would she turn to him? Guilt pricked him for even wanting her, too. He should get over it. Dayvee loved her. Besides, look who she chose to sit next to—Tayro, the next keeper of the Vita. Tayro would be beta, someday, and Elayni needed status for her parent's approval. Brando snorted. He won several tests, beat every trainee in the ring and several adults, but, still, they placed him seventh out of nine. Seventh?

The song ended, and Nero stood. "Thank you everyone for the welcome, but it's getting late, so I'm ready to rest. New Calupi should seek their bedrolls, soon, as we'll have an early morning. Your companions will decide for themselves whether to stay or go."

Are you ready to leave? Brando asked.

Yes. The firelight reflected off Bruno's eyes as the wolf rose to his feet. They walked away from the fire.

"Brando." Dayvee and Jaycee intercepted them. "Let's take the back way." Dayvee touched an elbow.

The signal Dayvee wanted to talk. Brando flipped a hand in the air. "Lead on."

In the corridor, Dayvee chose the longer route that passed several family dens before getting to the training area. He must hope to avoid people since most would sleep at the gathering.

Dayvee and Jaycee turned into the pool room. A good place not to be overheard. The water's gurgle muted voices, and at night the room usually stayed deserted. Brando and Bruno followed them in. Only a few lamps lifted the shadows on the rock wall and pool beyond.

Dayvee turned to him. "I need to explain about Elayni."

Elayni was wrong to deny their friendship, but would Dayvee want him to drop her from the family? A sigh escaped.

Dayvee smiled. "She's just pretending not to be my friend so Nero doesn't separate us. We overheard Nero and Rudee claiming that since I'm training Jaycee, I'm not worthy."

Relief poured into Brando. His family wouldn't be broken. Brando let his laughter escape. "I must be finally rubbing off on her. Elayni pranked us good."

"Yes, she did." Dayvee's frown revealed how much Elayni hurt him. She should have signaled.

"Nero's a hyena," Brando said. "Whenever he looks at Leeto, he has hate in his eyes. He's using you to get to him."

Dayvee's foot tapped the floor. "I don't think Leeto will mind how he treats me."

"Nero must not know that." Brando exhaled heavily. "I wish Elayni had shared, so I could be with you."

"Nero might have suspected if you both changed loyalties."

Brando shrugged. "How do you want me to act now?"

"Don't. Be friendly with us both."

Brando had to chuckle. "I think I can handle that, but I'm not going to be friendly with Nero. He's getting added to my list." Those who harmed his family received his special attention. Just another way to ensure his family stayed happy. He hoped Nero enjoyed frogs.

"I can fight my own battles."

Bruno nosed Brando's leg. *Someone comes.*

Dayvee only had a partial bond. Brando better warn him. "Somebody's coming."

A head tilt toward the entrance was Dayvee's quiet response. They hurried out. Brando didn't see anyone, but he heard soft singing.

When they reached the training corridor, Dayvee yawned and pulled aside the hide to his room. "Good night."

"Night." Brando, Dayvee, and Elayni had slept apart very few nights in years. Even with Bruno, he'd miss them. And now he'd be stuck in the other group. Brando groaned softly. How would he keep his family happy if he wasn't with them?

After Jaycee followed Dayvee in, Brando moved further down and entered his own room with Bruno. It *was* nice to have an assigned den. Almost like he belonged. He stretched out on the pallet. Invisible weights pulled his eyelids closed.

"Rise and shine trainees!" Nero called. Wait, morning already? "Time to go to work. We meet in the communal room in fifteen minutes, dressed and with your rucksacks."

11

A Visitor

To find your prey, you must leave the den. ~ Companion saying.

Excitement hung in the air. Rumors swarmed from one end of the castle to the other, all about the man who washed up on their shore. Tib arrived early to the audience hall to hear morning petitions.

As he entered, Father angled his head. "Good morning, Tibalt. Aren't you going to ask to be excused today?"

He smiled. "I thought I'd wait a little before asking."

"Until after you see the visitor from the Eastern continent?" The corner of Father's mouth twitched. Seemo ruffled his feathers. "At least you're on time, but don't plan on leaving until noon."

Could it be true? They had no contact with the other continent for centuries. Prior to today, Tib doubted the Eastern continent even existed. Part of Tib's required studies, Taluma's history, claimed at one time Terra held several continents. But after all the wars only two continents and a few islands in the oceans remained. No one really knew for sure.

People streamed in. Not just Father's advisors, but his scribe, some relatives, a few of Tib's tutors, some Botanees and Gollees, and the mayor of Harthome were among those Tib recognized taking seats at the back of the large room. "It's crowded today."

The attendant announced the first audience—no stranger. "The Calupi messenger, Drako and his companion, Juno, from Wolf Mountain Pack with a message for the king."

Drako strode in with the wolf at his side and stopped in front of the rope, to bow before Tib's father. Tib eyed Juno. Juno still looked ferocious. Tib sank back into his chair.

"Drako." Tib's father smiled. "What news do you bring?"

"Sire, the prince's wolf companion has a name now, Jaycee. He's training with a young Calupi. They'll complete the training next year and journey here for the choosing."

Tib sucked in his breath. That soon?

Father leaned closer. "Good. And were you able to make the other arrangements?"

"Yes, Your Majesty. White River Pack—only a day's travel—has agreed to the prince coming there. He'll spend time with young Calupi his age, training with new companions." Drako's eyes locked on Tib. "The prince will learn much from them, Sire."

Maybe Father would change his mind. Did he really expect Tib to spend time with a pack and deal with more wolves?

Father bent his head toward Seemo, then turned back to Drako. "Good." Father's eyes fell on Tib. "I think it's wonderful you'll get to learn about your companion and be ready for him when he arrives, don't you?"

Father must be speaking for the benefit of those listening. He knew Tib's feelings, but he didn't want them spoken. Tib couldn't even muster a show of enthusiasm.

"Y-yes." When he ended up eaten by wolves, everyone would know what a terrible idea it was.

Father's attention returned to Drako. "I invite you and your companion to stay and have lunch with us."

Drako glanced at Juno. "We accept, Your Majesty."

Father gestured to a pericard. Drako bowed and backed away. Juno flipped around and followed as the pericard led them to a seat.

A stir came from the outside foyer as some grumbling rose about the line's interruption. Two pericards came in holding the arms of a man who stood between them. They propelled him forward.

Tib scooted to the front of his chair. The man's face held sharp angles—a pointed chin and pronounced nose under curly hair. His beard was scraggly and seemed black, but it was hard to tell under the dirt. His shirt, although torn and stained, held a square neckline and sleeves that reached only his forearm. That wasn't a Harthome fashion or any other Taluma city that Tib knew of. Did he make clothes to match his story?

The pericards stopped him at the rope. "Bow before the king."

The man bowed and straightened. His obsidian eyes darted between Tib's father, the pericards, and the advisors.

Tib's father waved a hand. "You may tell me how you come to stand before me."

The stranger lifted his chin, and an arrogant smirk donned his face. "My name is Varian. I sailed from my continent to yours, so we could reacquaint ourselves with our neighbors."

Tib strained to decipher his strange way of speaking. Varian had pronounced vowels soft that should have been hard. The consonants came out slurred as if his tongue couldn't form them right; and his emphasis was all wrong. Not an accent Tib had ever heard. He *must* be from the Eastern continent.

"My boat ran into your reefs and began to sink, so I swam ashore." Varian frowned deeply. "I expected a warm welcome, but your kagards accosted me. We don't treat guests so rudely."

Gasps and murmurs filtered through the room. "Guests are invited," the pericard on his left snapped. "Even intruders should know to address the king as Your Majesty or Sire and show proper respect."

If Father was shocked, he didn't show it. "You're cutting down trees to make boats again?"

According to Tib's history lessons, boat travel stopped during the wars. Varian nodded once. "Yes, you'll have more visitors from my continent, Your Majesty."

Tib's father shifted on his throne. "You must have many trees if your Botanees are letting you cut them down for boats."

Tib leaned forward to hear Varian's response. Father would never give permission to fell enough trees to build large boats.

"Are you talking about the Vita?" Varian asked. "I've read a little about it, but we haven't practiced it in a hundred years. We don't believe in Kun."

They didn't? Tib nearly fell off his seat. Soft grumbling came from those listening.

The pericard on his left side knocked Varian's feet out from under him, and he fell to the floor, landing in a heap on his side. The pericard raised his fist. "I told you to show respect, and you belittle what we hold sacred!"

Tib's father motioned to the pericard. "Enough."

The pericards pulled Varian back to his feet none too gently. Varian straightened to stand proudly as if he were king, and addressed Tib's father as if he spoke to a child. "Those stories about JoKayndo and Kun were invented by misguided ancestors—the animal and plant lovers." Varian snorted. "You don't still believe in Kun, do you, Your Majesty?"

Tib shut his open mouth. Was this Varian stupid? He looked at Blake. What would he do? Blake's eyes narrowed at Varian. Both pericards raised their fists.

Father motioned to the pericards to desist. "If his story is true, he doesn't know much about our beliefs. Show him some compassion." His gaze turned back to Varian. "I don't believe. I *know* Kun is truth, and we proudly keep the Vita as JoKayndo taught us. I pity your continent if you've lost it. Doesn't your king have a companion?"

"No, Your Majesty. Animals don't tell us how to live anymore. And since then we've made great strides. We retrieved some of the ancient writings that weren't dust and gained some of their knowledge. They didn't have one Kun, but many made up by people to advance their own causes."

Tib sucked in his breath. A place with no companions might be a good thing.

"Didn't Kun send an animal master?" Father asked.

"Someone claiming to be a Kayndo tried to stop our great grandparents, Sire. But they were tired of the Vita." Varian smiled. "After they learned about the ancient's weapons, they duplicated some and killed the so-called Kayndo and those with him. Now, we tell the animals what to do."

The histories told of the ancient's weapons killing thousands of people. A chill of unease ran through Tib. Could anyone have a chance against them?

A scraping on stone sounded. Juno scrambled to his feet, his ears lay flat against his head, and his lips curled back to reveal his teeth.

"This is blasphemy," shouted Drako. "Kill him before he spreads this poison."

"Remember"—Tib's father sounded strained—"he's a stranger. Allow him *some* leeway."

Juno sat, and Tib tore his gaze from the terrifying animal. Varian was safe—for now. Seeing Juno angry didn't make Tib any happier about having a wolf companion. What would happen if his wolf companion got mad at him?

"More of my people will come here, Your Majesty. Will your guards kill everyone who doesn't agree with you?" Varian asked. "They'll use the ancient's weapons against anyone who tries to keep them from living their lives as they choose."

Tib's father leaned a little forward. "We have no proof that any of your wild claims are true. For all we know you could be crazy. We'll discuss it more later." A fist with his thumb out let the pericards know he wanted the man guarded. Since the thumb wasn't inside his fist, Varian wouldn't be taken to the dungeons, yet. "Allow him to eat and clean up." Tib's father locked eyes with Varian. "I can't permit you free roam until I know you're sane."

A flip of Father's hand dismissed Varian. One of his pericards ordered, "Bow." As soon as he finished, they escorted Varian away.

Tib wanted to talk to Varian alone. But if he tried to see him now, his father would be notified quicker than a squirrel could run up a tree.

A few more petitioners were seen before Tib's father stood and addressed the attendant, "Inform any waiting petitioners I have important business to attend to. I'll resume audiences in the morning." He glanced at Drako. "Will you join me, the queen, and a few of my advisors for that lunch?"

Juno jumped to his feet as Drako rose. "Of course, Your Majesty."

"Blake and Reed, you may come." He turned to Tib. "Get your lunch and go to your afternoon lessons." Tib would have to wait to learn the visitor's fate.

The pericards rushed to surround his father as the invited few followed him out. Tib left in the opposite direction, striding toward the kitchen for lunch. As he passed people in the halls, their whispered conversations got cut short too late for Tib not to overhear. The castle buzzed with the news of the visitor.

Varian's words thrilled Tib. An ancient city ruin lay on Harthome's outskirts and had always interested him. To act on that interest was against the law in Taluma. Could Tib convince Varian to let him accompany him back to his continent? Maybe they could build another boat to sail there and not come back. It would solve so many of Tib's problems.

He wouldn't have to be king, stay with a pack, or live with a wolf. And he had his own doubts about Kun. He used to pray constantly, asking Kun to make Father care about him like he did Seemo. His prayers weren't answered.

Varian was probably right. Kun wasn't real.

12

Trials

"If you suffer for following the Vita, you are blessed. Kun will reward you." ~ Kwutee.

Nero's shout for the trainees to rise resounded. Dayvee groaned. Today was the first day of training with Nero, and he couldn't give him a reason to find fault.

Dayvee jumped off his pallet, got dressed, and grabbed his rucksack. He and Jaycee joined the other trainees rushing into the communal area. Nero glanced at them and gestured at the rough table near the hearth. A cask of water and pots filled with meat and gruel sat upon it. "Good morning trainees, see to your needs."

After filling his companion's bowl with meat, Dayvee placed it in front of Jaycee. The other trainees did the same. As the companions tore into their food, Dayvee took his own bowl of gruel to sit beside the others around the hearth.

Growling followed by a sudden yelp pierced the air. Jaycee had his ruff raised and teeth showing toward Nero's companion, Nesi. She slinked a few steps from her food with her tail between her legs. Jaycee advanced toward her, stiff legged. Nesi crouched lower. Jaycee pressed his muzzle toward her, and she licked it.

It wasn't the first time puppies and adult wolves asserted their dominance with food, so Dayvee returned his attention to his own bowl.

Nero stalked over to Dayvee. "Tomorrow, you'll rise sooner, fix breakfast for everyone, and feed Jaycee early since he's the most dominant!"

Dayvee clenched his teeth. "What's the difference? You're not going to change their minds if they decide on Nesi as the omega. If it's not food, it will be something else."

Exactly. He's wrong, Jaycee sent.

"I don't remember asking your opinion. Just follow the order."

"Yes sir." Dayvee focused to send his thought back to Jaycee. *I don't think he cares if he's wrong.*

Nero strode to the center of the room. "I'll now explain something about sub-packs and the duties you'll be learning. We have eight Calupi sub-packs in Wolf Mountain."

Rudee moved to Nero's side. Dayvee finished his last bite and stood facing them with the other trainees. The companions joined their Calupi.

"Four sub-packs are assigned to the rotation and switch duties every two months. They guard our territory, monitor wild wolf packs, hunt and gather, and check leases." Nero must love his own voice to keep telling them stuff they knew. "The other four sub-packs hold the teachers, traders, leaders, and ours—the Calupi in training. Their duties are more fixed. The leadership sub-pack includes the alphas and the betas—Leeto and Milay, their seconds, the keeper, and history writer."

Brando and Bruno had circled behind Nero and Rudee. Brando's taller height made it easy to see him as he screwed his face and mouthed silent words. Dayvee suppressed his laugh.

"You'll learn each duty this year." Nero licked his lips. "We'll start with hunting."

Elayni made a quick finger-slash in front of her throat to signal Brando to stop. She escaped Rudee or Nero's attention, but Brando wagged his tongue and crossed his eyes. Dayvee couldn't hold back his grin. The other trainees smiled, too. Elayni's hand on her hip left no doubt to her opinion of his jests.

Nero shifted his weight. "You'll spend most of your time away from the cave and separated from the pack so you learn to work with your companion and sub-pack."

Dayvee stifled a yawn. *This is what we needed to get up early for?* Brando clamped his thumb and finger together. His signal for a prank. This was *not* the time for him to start his campaign against Nero. Brando didn't need to get in trouble, and they didn't need more problems. Dayvee shook his head, no.

Nero noticed Dayvee's head shake and his lips tightened. "Hunting is a valuable tool in teaching you to work as a team. We're a large pack, and we don't want to deplete the resources for the wild wolves, so we'll keep well inside our quotas."

Brando's face set, and Bruno's ear cocked beside him—a wolf laugh. Jaycee tilted his head. He apparently thought Brando's antics humorous, too.

"It probably isn't necessary for us to hunt," Nero said. "We could trade for our needs, but the companions wouldn't be happy."

Brando held up a cricket in his fingers. "No," Dayvee mouthed and sidled behind the others to get around Nero and over to Brando.

Nero droned on. "The best place to locate herds is the grasslands. We'll be traveling light and fast. Pack coats, blankets, snow shoes, and rations if you haven't already. We leave soon, so finish your preparations and meet me and Rudee outside."

Dayvee made it to Brando. He grabbed for his hand but missed. Brando threw the cricket so it landed on Nero's head. Nero startled, threw his hand up and brushed it off. Everyone laughed. Nero pivoted around, beet red. He stared at Dayvee and Brando.

Dayvee sucked in his breath. Brando was sure to be in trouble now.

"I hadn't realized I'd be dealing with an immature child instead of a Calupi taking his training seriously." Nero spoke the words quietly. Deadly.

Nesi stiffened just enough to let them know that Nero was angry. Bruno's ruff rose to stand erect, and Jaycee's lips curled back. Nesi softened her stance.

"You'll learn, and you won't be laughing when I finish with you." Nero rose up on his toes. "This isn't the time for pranks, Dayvee."

Dayvee's jaw dropped open. Everyone knew Brando was the pack's prankster.

Nero's gaze turned to Brando. "You should find a different friend." The training leader stomped from the cave.

"I'm sorry." Brando's face fell. "I'll tell him I did it."

Brando targeted Nero for Dayvee's sake, and he couldn't be mad at that dejected face. "Don't bother. He'll just find another excuse to fault me."

Are Brando's teeth sharp? Jaycee asked, wanting to know if Brando would be good in a fight.

Dayvee focused to deliver his thought. *Very.*

Nero wanted you angry with each other.

Dayvee washed his bowls and stowed them in his rucksack. He had enough provisions, so he walked outside with Jaycee.

Within a few minutes everyone gathered around Nero. "Some of you may think wolves hunt in a pack all the time, but normally they go alone or in pairs unless they're chasing a herd. Calupi split up, too, so we can cover more ground. We'll spread out and make our way to the grasslands, hunting and gathering as we go. Regroup at Cracked Rock late this afternoon." Nero moved off alone.

Dayvee walked away from the cave, Jaycee padding beside him. Thankfully, they were rid of Nero for a while. He soon forgot the morning's crisp chill as he and Jaycee set a quick pace. The sun rose over the top of the eastern mountain and lit the horizon with shades of pink, red, and orange. Finally, the yellow globe lifted in the sky.

Frost covered the ground. A beautiful white blanket—so pristine. It seemed wrong to dirty its crust, and the ground crunched in complaint as Dayvee left footprints on its surface. The noise would make it hard to sneak up on any game. He tried to tread softly but found it impossible.

With every breath, he and Jaycee exhaled a steam cloud that marked the frigid morning air in front of them. The pine scent hung thick among the trees as Dayvee trod the path along the winding stream. Partially coated in ice, the water still ran free in the middle so animals would drink there. Maybe they'd scare up game along the trail over the rough banks. He glanced back at his home before descending to the valley. What a difference a day made. Yesterday, he thought he might lose his home. Today, he was Calupi.

The two pine trees that acted as sentinels blocked his view of the cave entrance. Brush and trees covered three other entrances in different locations—a precaution the companions insisted upon although it had been over a hundred years since the pack answered the animal master's call to overthrow false King Marcello and went to war. The fighting never even penetrated their mountain home.

Most animals made a wide berth around their cave, aside from a few bats in the Nowhere tunnels and mice that tried to invade the storage rooms. Although it was never left unguarded, with all those human and wolf scents, animals would have to be crazy to attempt to enter Wolf Mountain. The wolves' precautions made more sense after Dayvee found dead pups, the result of a bear digging up a wild wolves' den.

Jaycee trotted ahead with his nose to the ground and flushed a rabbit. Jaycee chased it from behind, but his body blocked Dayvee from throwing his weapon unless the prey reversed direction. The rabbit made it to his hole and escaped the wolf's pursuit.

Jaycee. The wolf looked back at Dayvee. *If you leave me some room, I can help without fear of hitting you.*

I'll try next time.

Dayvee found a few frozen berries the birds missed on some brambles. They were shriveled and puckered, but they'd still hold flavor. The morning's gruel might taste better with them. *Jaycee, if I gather these, we won't be completely empty handed.*

Yuck. Jaycee nosed around while Dayvee picked the berries. A strong whirring of wings broke the silence. Kok! Kok! Kok! A pheasant broke from the bushes, launching into the air. Dayvee pulled his nails, but the bird rose above the trees, out of sight.

Dayvee slammed his nails back in his pouch. This was going to be harder than he thought. Without the full-bond, he and Jaycee weren't that aware of each other. He was going to need to stay close and really watch Jaycee's body language. *Jaycee, can you wait till I'm close to flush birds?*

The wolf stopped poking. *I'll try.*

Jaycee's trot was quick and sure footed, and Dayvee struggled to keep up. He found himself sliding on the loose rock and slipping on the frozen ground. After a few close calls, he eased his pace. To his relief, Jaycee also slowed. Dayvee spotted some cattails along the stream, and with the help of a digging stick, gathered some of the roots.

He scrambled down the steep grade of the mountain path to the valley below. The snow deepened to his ankles, but his boots kept his feet dry. He didn't need his snow shoes, yet. Jaycee traversed the valley and started the climb up the next mountain. Dayvee followed. The meeting place lay just on the other side. The snow accumulation lightened to only a dusting.

Dayvee needed to find something besides a few berries and cattail roots, so Nero didn't have more reasons to fault him. Pine cones littered the ground. He gathered some to add to his pouch. When heated by the fire, the cones would open to reveal the nuts inside. Everyone always enjoyed the crunchy treats.

When they clambered higher up the steep mountain face, the stream went underground and disappeared. The water probably carved another cavern similar to their home, and they'd have another cave to add to the several in their territory. The steam would surface again at some point and converge like all the rest into the river that flowed from the mountain range they called home.

The trees grew scarcer as the elevation rose. Jaycee dropped into a hunting crouch. He must smell something. Dayvee emulated the wolf. He tread quietly and used the few scrawny trees for cover. Above the last of the cedars, a small group of elk grazed. Dayvee dropped to the ground and crawled closer.

Nine cows and three calves. The calves had to be going into their first winter. They didn't have any antlers yet and couldn't weigh a hundred and fifty pounds. The meat would be tender. Jaycee glanced at him. Dayvee tilted his head toward the closest adolescent. Any nearer, the elk would be sure to detect their presence. Luckily, the wind blew toward them. Dayvee opened his pouches. The hilt of his knife slid into his palm. His other fingers wrapped around the rawhide grip of his chakram.

With nails in his right hand and tooth in his left, he jumped up as Jaycee sprang. Dayvee threw his nails. The weapon hit its mark, cutting the elk's front leg above the hock. The herd bounded away, and the young calf trying to follow on three legs, couldn't keep up. Jaycee beat him to the injured elk and clamped his teeth around the tendon of the calf's other front leg to keep it from fleeing. The elk bleated, barely able to stand.

Dayvee raced in, grabbed the calf's head, and cut its throat with his knife. "We honor you, noble elk, for the sacrifice of your life, so we may receive nourishment from your body. May your spirit be at peace and with Kun."

He turned to Jaycee. *Jaycee, we did it. Our first kill together.*

Dayvee's chest puffed with pride. He skinned the calf. Cracked Rock wasn't too far. They'd probably reach it in two more hours of hiking. There'd be a fire there to smoke the meat. He cut the meat into more manageable pieces, and wrapped the bigger chunks in his waterproof hide.

Jaycee nosed him. *I'll help you carry.*

Thanks. Dayvee took out the wolf rucksack and attached the harness with its side pouches around Jaycee's chest and under his middle. To make more room, he tied his snowshoes and pouches to his belt. After filling both rucksacks with the chunks of meat, he rolled the elk's hide and secured it above with his bedroll. Only a few scraps left for the scavengers. The rucksack's weight settled against his shoulder blades. Maybe eighty pounds. Jaycee probably carried forty.

The butchering was messy but done in a little less than an hour. He and Jaycee moved across the mountain's crest and proceeded down the other side. In other areas of Taluma, the traders and messengers claimed that the mountains were much higher and had to be detoured around or traveled over through rough passes. In some places they even needed ropes to traverse them. Their mountains had trails to follow, and the tops were rather flat.

As they drew close, Dayvee smelled the smoke, and the landmark came into view—a big flat rock table with several cracks running through its face. An ideal camping place their pack had used for years. A small cave was located behind the rock—a good shelter for a small group like theirs. A stream ran nearby for fresh water, and although frozen now, the ice could be broken through or melted for water.

Brando and Bruno approached Dayvee. His arms held several branches. He must have been gathering wood. "Your rucksack seems full. Did Kun bless your hunt?"

Dayvee slipped his rucksack off his back and showed him the hide. Bruno nosed it.

"An elk. Well met," Brando said.

"Thanks." Dayvee put his rucksack back on, and they moved toward the camp. "Did Kun bless you?"

Brando nodded. "We nabbed three pheasants and some nuts the squirrels missed."

"Good for you and Bruno. Jaycee flushed a pheasant, but I was too late." Dayvee hit a slick spot and skidded. He scanned the ground before glancing again at Brando. "Is everyone here?"

"All, but Elayni." They reached the shadowy mouth of cracked rock's cave.

"Look everyone, Dayvee and Jaycee're here." Brando called as they ducked through.

The heavy scent of soil, wood smoke, and smoked meat filled Dayvee's nostrils. Jaycee lifted his nose high, sniffing, and trotted ahead to scout the cave. It hadn't changed any since Dayvee had been in it with Codee—one room with two recessed areas. The first not much more than a hole used to store meat; the other had a few rough shelves. The brown walls appeared to be more soil than stone. Nothing like Wolf Mountain. The fire burned in a small pit. Racks perched over it, and strips of meat smoked on them. The trainees sat around the fire.

"Kun blessed Dayvee and Jaycee with an elk," Brando said.

"Good hunting, Dayvee." Geno smiled.

Chayla nodded her agreement. Jaycee came back and brushed Dayvee's leg. *Someone comes. A dragging sound penetrated the cave.*

13

Help or Hurt

Chase away the stranger who dares to trespass, or they'll kill your children while you sleep. ~Companion saying.

Tib hurried through the castle halls. He should be at his weapons lesson, but he'd heard his father was interviewing Varian again. His curiosity needed quenched like a plant needed water. He had to find out more about Varian and his continent.

Two pericards stood sentry at a door of one of the castle's rooms. They met Tib's gaze. "Is my father interviewing Varian in there?"

"Yes, but he's left instructions not to allow others in, Prince Tibalt."

Tib's eyes met the pericards. "But you can go in. Tell him I'm out here, and I want to watch."

"Wait here." After a minute, the pericard came back. "The king will allow you entrance."

Tib strode in. The stone block walls of the castle stood unadorned. The small room held only chairs and the room's occupants. Father, Blake, Drako, his wolf companion Juno, Varian, and the pericards all gave Tib their perusal. Varian sat between two pericards facing Tib's father with several feet between them.

"Why are you here, Tibalt, instead of your lessons?" Father demanded.

Tib detoured around Varian and his pericards to stand in front of his father. Unusual that Seemo wasn't there to give Tib a sharp eye and ruffle his feathers. "If I'm to be king, I need to learn how best to conduct an interview."

Father gave him one curt nod. "You may stay, but you'll make up any lessons you miss."

Tib released his held breath. "Of course." The pericard sentry brought Tib a chair, so he could sit beside his father. Tib sank into it. "Thanks."

His father waved his hand at the pericard. "Take back up your post and see we're not disturbed."

The pericard put his fist over his heart. Tib rolled his eyes. The salute was ironic. He'd eavesdropped on the pericards often enough to know they believed the king had too soft of a heart, and they had to have iron fists to protect him. The pericard left the room.

Varian appeared cleaner, but his hair and beard still lay long and straggly. The pericards probably wouldn't permit him anything sharp to cut his hair. They leveled stern expressions at Varian as they stood over him. A new red lump stuck out of Varian's forehead, like a shell on a turtle. Not surprising after his earlier disdain. Father must've noticed and wouldn't be pleased.

"Hello, Prince Tibalt. What lessons are you studying?" Varian asked.

Tib's eyebrows shot up. Why would Varian ask him a question familiarly?

The pericard on Varian's right stiffened. "You shall address the prince as Your Royal Highness."

Varian scowled at the pericard. "Your Royal Highness."

Tib glanced at his father to see if he should answer. Father gave him a small head bob.

"I'm taking lessons in defense, reading, math, writing, communication, negotiations, politics, geography, and the teachings of the Vita."

"I'm also a prince, Your Royal Highness." Varian lifted his chin. "On my continent, I'm known as Prince Varian, and I took lessons in all those, except the last."

Tib scratched his head. How old was he? Late twenties, early thirties? And he spoke of lessons.

"My studies also included archeology and languages, including the ancients. It's a good thing I did learn them since yours isn't the common language in our land."

"What is archeology?" Tib leaned forward. He wanted to know. Hopefully, his father wouldn't mind.

Varian smiled. "Archeology is the study of the ancient people's way of life and their artifacts, how they work, and whether they can be duplicated to help us, Your Royal Highness."

Tib returned the smile. He'd like to take those lessons.

Drako's head jerked as if he'd been slapped. "He's broken our laws and the Vita by using the ancient's things. His soul must be contaminated." Juno stiffened beside him.

"That's not true." Varian's eyes crinkled. He cleared his throat as if he were trying not to laugh. "There's nothing wrong with me or anyone else on my continent. Your views are considered myths there."

Tib might as well ask. "What else is normal on your continent?"

"War." A corner of Varian's mouth turned down. "War can be normal when one of the kings decides he needs to have more land and people to pay taxes to him, Your Royal Highness."

Why did he sound so bitter? Did he have to flee his continent, like some of the rumors claimed?

"How many kings are on the Eastern continent?" Father took over asking the questions.

"There are four now." Varian shifted in his seat. "When I was a boy, there were eight, Your Majesty."

Tib's jaw dropped open. His father was the only king on the Western continent. With that many kings, no wonder there were wars.

Father's forehead furrowed. "Are there more from your continent coming here?"

Varian looked down at his feet. "Yes, Sire."

More coming. Yes. His father couldn't guard everyone. Tib would be able to learn more and maybe convince them to take him back.

Juno growled and bared his teeth. Drako's disdain showed in his voice. "Juno says he lies."

Tib's hopes crashed. About what part?

Father's eyes pierced Varian. "Companions always know."

"I heard stories." Varian blinked a couple times. "I never gave them credence, Sire."

"You should have." Father's voice hardened. "My pericards want me to lock you in a cell or worse, but I'll give you one chance to tell the truth."

"All right. I don't think anyone is coming now, but I think they'll come later, and you won't be prepared for them, Your Majesty."

Tib tried to mask his disappointment. Later wouldn't help him now.

Father raised an eyebrow. "To make war on us?"

"Some make war wherever they go, Sire."

"Would you help them defeat us?"

Varian's mouth firmed into a straight line. "No, I'd help you, Your Majesty."

The stranger would help them. But why?

"Drako?" Father asked.

Drako glanced at Juno, then up. "He believes he's speaking the truth, my king."

Father rubbed his chin. "If I allow you to stay, how can you aid us?"

Varian's face broke into an arrogant smile. "I can prepare you. If you want to speak to them, you'll need to learn our common language. I can teach that to you, and how to make and use our weapons, Sire."

If Tib did manage to escape to the Eastern continent, he'd need to know Varian's language.

"Why would you help us?" Father demanded.

"Those who will come are my father's enemies, Your Majesty."

Juno growled again. Drako shook his head. "He's lying again. I can teach him to answer truthfully." Juno snapped at the air.

Varian slid his chair away from Juno. His Adam's apple bobbed up and down. Tib didn't blame him for being scared. The wolf was terrifying. But Varian didn't seem frightened by the pericards or Father.

Varian held up his hands. "All right. They aren't my father's enemies, they're mine, Your Majesty. My father is dead." His shoulders sagged, and he took a deep breath. "King Nolan of Lucendo is a tyrant who invaded our kingdom and wants to rule all of Terra." He spoke with surety. "When he's defeated our kings, he'll send his soldiers here."

Wait. Tib didn't want soldiers to come to Taluma.

Father's forehead creased. "Don't you think your kings can stop him?"

Varian shook his head as another smirk donned his face.

Tib's father commanded. "Tell me the entire story so I understand why you believe otherwise."

"I began building the boat some time ago just to learn if I could. I never finished it, But after Nolan declared war on us, my father sent me in it to the other kings to try and get them to stand with him."

Tib scooted back in his chair. No wonder Varian's boat sunk.

Varian gritted his teeth and took a deep breath. "They didn't want to antagonize King Nolan. I warned them without an alliance, Nolan would defeat us each. While at the third kingdom pleading for help, I learned the last of our defenses had fallen, and my father was dead."

Tib frowned. How awful.

Varian slumped in his chair. "None wanted me to stay since they were all afraid of Nolan." Every time he said that king's name, Varian's eyes flashed. "I promised my father I wouldn't return if we lost the war. Nolan would kill me. So I set sail hoping my boat would make the Western continent. And it almost did."

Tib sighed. So much for an escape with Varian to his continent. They wouldn't welcome him back.

Father glanced at Blake, then turned his attention back to Varian. "Does anyone else know you're here?"

Varian's fingers drummed against his leg. "No one, and I have no interest in aiding King Nolan." He met Tib's father's eyes. "I didn't realize you still lived like animals, Sire. I wanted to ask your help to regain my kingdom and attack Nolan before he came here, but you're like an ant to him." Varian stomped his foot. "You'd be stepped on."

Tib stared at Varian. His father might be soft, but he wasn't stupid. If Varian kept it up, he'd be in a cell for sure. Then, Tib wouldn't be able to talk to him.

Father's back stiffened. "Drako?"

Drako angled his head toward Juno. "He believes what he speaks is truth."

Father narrowed his eyes. "If we allow you to remain, you'll have to honor the Vita, not speak of your continent to our people, nor blasphemy Kun."

If Varian wasn't able to speak about his continent, how would Tib learn anything?

"I don't know the Vita, so how can I honor it?"

"We could teach you," Father answered. "After we do, you'd need to give an oath to honor the Vita and pledge your loyalty to me. And if it wasn't sincere, my companion would know." He shook his head once. "You won't be free until you've sworn those oaths."

Father snapped his finger at the pericards. "Take him to his room. Continue to guard it. Blake, Drako, and the prince may remain. The rest of you can wait in the hall." The room emptied out.

Tib wouldn't have to wait to learn Varian's fate. He'd been included.

"Speak freely. What do you think?" Father asked.

"Lock him in a cell." Drako spoke passionately. "Juno sensed hate in him when he spoke of their King Nolan. He's a threat, a willing pawn of the deceiver, and contaminated by the ancients' things."

Blake's mouth was set in a straight line. "His arrogance and contempt toward our king and kingdom tells me he's already plotting against both." One corner of his mouth twitched up. "But we can still use him. Learn about their weapons, their language, and how to defeat them. Use him, and then kill him, Sire."

"I have no intention of using their weapons." Father crossed his arms. "It's against the Vita."

"He said we'd have no chance without their weapons." Tib spoke out. "We have to use them."

Father smiled. "With Kun on our side, we need not fear."

Tib was at a loss for words. Father had probably never seen the ancients' things like he had. They were far better than anything they made, but he didn't dare tell him he broke the law.

"What if we don't use their weapons, Sire, but learn about them in order to defeat them?" Blake asked.

"That's fine. Find out what to expect, but don't let Varian convince you they're unbeatable. I'm sure they have flaws, but I don't have time for lessons."

"I'm willing to learn about his language and weapons." If only Father would let him, he could find out more about the Eastern continent and the ancients.

"You may be the one to deal with them in the future, so it might be wise. But I don't know that I want him near you when he doesn't share our beliefs."

"I can be careful. I want to help."

"If you had a companion to advise you, I wouldn't be worried." Father rubbed his head. "I'll think about it."

"If you have no further need of us, we'll take our leave, Your Majesty." Drako stood. "I have a few more messages to deliver in Harthome."

"We're done. Thank you, and I look forward to the prince's companion joining us."

Tib gulped. He wasn't.

Drako's gaze fell on Tib. "Yes, Sire, if he's chosen."

"Of course. We'll plan on those arrangements we discussed earlier." Father flicked his hand. "Safe travels to you and Juno."

"Thank you, Sire." The Calupi bowed, and he and Juno left the room. Tib wasn't sorry to see them go.

"I can assign a few guards, Sire, to learn Varian's language and weapons knowledge," Blake offered.

"Good. Varian will need lessons on Kun and the Vita, too. I'd like to gain him as an ally, so go easier on etiquette lessons. I don't want to see any more lumps."

"As you wish, Your Majesty. Do you want me to assign pericards or kagards to take his lessons?"

"Aren't we stretched thin on pericards?"

"Yes, sire, but I can assign extra shifts again, or I have some in training. But they've barely started and haven't completed any tests yet."

"One of these days you might have to lower the standards so more pass the tests."

"We have plenty of kagards we can use to fill in. If I lower the standard, there will be no difference, sire."

"All right, pick two kagards from the ones training as long as they're loyal." Father rose, went to the window, and opened the shutter.

Seemo flew down to perch on the sill, and with a flutter of his feathers, closed his wings. Father's finger stroked the eagles' head. "He says he talked to the geese and most avoid the Eastern continent. If a flock flies over, they slaughter them without any regard."

"It's true then," Blake said. "They don't keep the Vita."

"Yes." Father turned to face him. "So the peace Kun has granted us may be shattered all too soon. Pray for Taluma. We may need it."

"I always do, Your Majesty." Blake saluted. Father returned the salute, then flicked his hand in dismissal. Blake pivoted and left.

"Don't you have lessons to finish?" Father asked.

"Yes, father." Tib hurried out. If his father let him take Varian's lessons, he'd enjoy going to them.

14

Baring Teeth

Mark your foe with teeth and nails til your last breath. And you will be remembered past your death. ~ Wolf companion song verse.

Dayvee rushed out of the cave with everyone else to learn who approached.

Evee held her head high as she trotted in front of Elayni, who pulled a travois loaded with a large mountain lion. Dayvee sucked in his breath and stopped himself from running to her. She seemed okay, but that lion must weigh a hundred pounds. The companions gathered around it growling.

Brando's gaze darted between Elayni and the mountain lion. "What happened?"

"We were flushing birds and came over the mountain to find tracks—a wolf, a human, a blood trail, and a mountain lion's—on top. We couldn't let it attack someone unaware, so Evee and I followed. The cat never looked back as we drew close." Elayni shrugged. "My nails sank deep in her neck, and she bled out."

Dayvee's heart thudded in his chest. "My thanks, Elayni. We followed the creek, so it must have been us she stalked." His earlier elation at their successful hunt disappeared.

Elayni crossed her arms. "I'd have helped anyone, but you should use more caution." Her tone dripped with smugness. "Next time I might not be there."

Even though Elayni acted, her reproach still stung—but not as much as the one Dayvee gave himself.

Well met, Elayni." Nero's chin lifted. "A mountain lion can be tough to handle, but you did great." He turned to Dayvee. "How did you act carelessly?"

"I should have backtracked across my trail to make sure nothing followed."

"Yes, before you slated for camp. You not only risked something catching you and your companion unaware, you endangered the entire camp." Nero smirked. "Pack Law says we protect the pack. You jeopardized pack members, so you've earned a white fringe."

Dayvee had never known anyone but Leeto or Codee to give one of those out, and he had never heard of a trainee receiving one. "You can do that?"

Nero's eyes flashed. "Do you admit your actions put other pack members at risk?"

Dayvee couldn't lie. "Yes."

"Then, I can do it." He handed him a white rawhide fringe. "Now put in on."

Dayvee's heart sunk to his toes. Shame and embarrassment spiked in him. He tied the white fringe under the red one he already sported on his weapon's pouch. White were wide on purpose so plenty still showed. It was supposed to remind him to protect the pack and earn red. If he had two red, he could swap them and lose the white, but he had to earn another before he could do that.

Most adult Calupi had plenty of red fringes, so if they received a white, they'd exchange two red and get rid of it. It would still shame them to receive one. Only two adult pack members in all Dayvee's years had lost enough red that they had to wear a white until they gained enough red to cover their shame. Both were given omega treatment and assigned the chores no one else wanted so they'd learn to make their pack's safety a bigger priority.

One was Nero. Any white showing would give most Calupi an invitation to make Dayvee an omega, too. Maybe Nero did want to get even with Leeto and use Dayvee to do it. It was stupid. Leeto wouldn't care.

Kwutee said any teaching was to be done with love, but too many enjoyed giving the lesson. The certainty Nero would be one, sent a chill racing through Dayvee.

Jaycee nuzzled Dayvee. *I'm sorry.* The wolf hung his head and tail. *I should have warned you. I got a whiff of a strange scent, but I didn't know it trailed us. I'll recognize it now.*

Don't blame yourself. You must smell lots of strange odors. Dayvee kicked the ground. *It's my fault. I know to double back. I'm glad Elayni prevented our ambush.*

She's a good friend.

Yes, she is.

Nero gestured at the cat. "If you haven't yet, take care of your day's bounty. But don't draw danger to camp." Nero scowled at Dayvee. "Do your butchering outside on carved rock, and clean up afterwards." He gestured toward the cave. "We set up racks to smoke meat and stretch hides. There's a stew pot on the fire so add a little meat and any roots or vegetables you found. Put any other food you collected in the appropriate baskets." Nero turned and ducked back into the cave's mouth.

Brando put his hand on Elayni's travois. "I'll help you pull your load."

Dayvee's large chunks of elk needed to be sliced thin to be smoked, so he went to the large rock table. Geno and Renee were already there cleaning their bounty.

Jaycee, let me take off your rucksack.

He undid it as Brando pulled the travois over. Elayni drew her tooth and made a slit in the cat's hide. "Go do yours, Brando."

Brando sank down beside Dayvee to clean his pheasants.

Jaycee's head and tail still drooped as he stood nearby. Bruno and Evee went over to him. Evee nudged Bruno, then licked Jaycee's muzzle. She streaked away. Both Bruno and Jaycee chased her—their legs a blur as they raced.

"Can I help you skin the lion?" Dayvee asked Elayni.

She shook her head. A golden lock had worked free from her braid again to fall into her face. She flipped it back. "No thanks. It needs done right."

It might be an act for Geno and Renee, but the implication still seared him. Dayvee tore into the elk's meat with a vengeance.

Elayni slid her tooth down from the top of the cat's head around its body and to the top of the head again. Then, she worked her knife underneath the skin to cut the sinews and muscles that kept it attached.

Brando finished with his pheasants and winked at Elayni. "Would you like the carver's touch since it's such an art to hack up a carcass?"

She gave him a smile, scooted down, and made room. "Yes. Thanks."

Geno and Renee finished and wondered back to the cave, leaving Dayvee alone with Brando and Elayni. Her blue eyes met his gaze. "Elayni, I appreciate what you did, but I don't want you putting yourself in danger for me."

"You'd do the same. I just said that stuff for the others' benefit." Her nose wrinkled. "Anyone can have a predator trail them, and Nero shouldn't have given you a white fringe."

There was nothing Dayvee could do about the fringe, but he didn't want Elayni taking on more mountain lions alone. "I wish we could hunt together." His voice came out strangled. Why did her presence steal any calmness?

Brando slid the hide out from under the lion. "Yeah, me, too. Once we leave the others, we could meet up."

"Nero's sending us out on the grasslands. Be pretty hard to hide there." Dayvee finished with his meat, so he chunked his cattail roots to put in the stew for tomorrow. "I'm done. Are you sure I can't help you?"

Elayni glanced up from butchering. She blinked as if unsure how to answer. "No, we'll be done shortly."

"All right, I'll go hang this meat on the racks, but I'll be back to help with clean-up."

Elayni shook her head. "Don't come back, Dayvee. We can do it. Otherwise it might seem like we're getting along."

Jaycee, Bruno, and Evee's tongues lolled as they loped into camp. Jaycee drank from the creek, then trotted up to Dayvee as he entered the cave.

Dayvee put his pine cones, nuts, and berries in the baskets. They almost overflowed. Calupi always knew where to find food even in winter. They might need to eat travel rations if they were in a hurry, injured, or snowed-in, but, otherwise, they'd rather hunt and gather. He hung his meat on the racks with all the rest to smoke. Tayro finished relating the story of his and Topay's trek today.

A frown darkened Nero's face when Dayvee sat. "Did you clean up?"

"Brando and Elayni are doing it. She didn't want my help."

"Go gather more firewood, then."

Dayvee and Jaycee searched the nearby wooded area. He collected dead limbs and sticks and even found a small dead tree to drag to the cave. Jaycee grabbed the branches on the other end of the tree in his teeth and pulled it the other direction.

Scamp. Dayvee chased the wolf.

Jaycee's ear cocked in a wolf laugh when Dayvee gave up. He never even came close. *You needed some fun.*

That wolf and Brando must think alike. After Dayvee brought several bundles back, he broke the limbs into smaller chunks and stacked them close to the fire. Brando and Elayni had joined everyone in the cave. Dayvee fed Jaycee and helped himself to stew. He sat on the other side of Brando from Elayni. Jaycee flopped by Bruno and Evee.

Nero threw another chunk on the fire. "I remember a mountain lion that surprised us at your age. We were on the grasslands coming back from hunting caribou and pulling travois' piled high with meat. As young trainees, we wanted to prove ourselves. Hugo brought up the rear, carrying probably twice as much as normal."

Dayvee leaned forward to listen to the new story. Everyone else did the same.

"A mountain lion dropped from a tree onto his travois and grabbed a caribou haunch. We heard Hugo yelling at the cat and went running to help. He pulled his nails and threw them, but they did no real harm and only angered the lion. It let go of the meat and sprang at Hugo, raking his face with claws and shredding his skin to leave it hanging." Nero shook his head. "I'll never forget it."

Dayvee's heart skipped a beat. What if it had been Elayni?

Nero paused and scanned their faces. "The rest of us left our loads and ran to help. Our companions attacked the lion, but our fear of hitting them or Hugo prevented us from loosing our nails. We could only yell. The lion stopped mauling Hugo, picked up the haunch of meat, and fled. If Hugo had hunted alone, he'd probably be dead. He wears the scars from his encounter with the mountain lion to this day."

Dayvee nodded with the others. Hugo wasn't from Wolf Mountain, but they'd seen his terrible facial scars at the pack meetings.

"Today reminded me that young trainees make mistakes." Nero glanced at Dayvee. "Some more than others." His brow furrowed. "So, I'm going to split you into groups of two or three. I'll take Tayro and Renay with me and Dayvee and Elayni will go together tomorrow."

Elayni put her hands on her hips. "Sir, there are some people I'd rather not pair with."

Nero's eyes rested on Dayvee. "What about you?"

"I'd rather work alone than go with certain Calupi." Like Nero. Dayvee looked down at his feet. He took a quick peek. Jaycee tilted his ear to show his laugh.

Nero scowled. "Going alone didn't work well today, and you don't always have a choice. You'll go together tomorrow."

"Yes sir." Dayvee kept his eyes trained on the ground so Nero didn't read his elation.

"Tonight will be the last night we're all together. Rudee will take his sub-pack to Pair Cave, tomorrow. Since Pair Cave is smaller and doesn't have a cairn, they'll use the racks and store meat here. If we find a large herd, we'll come together to hunt it."

Dayvee sighed to himself. He wouldn't get to see much of Brando, even though Pair Cave wasn't more than ten minutes away. Any hope Dayvee could get away from Nero by spending time with Rudee's group, died. The cave had an entrance you had to kneel to get through, before it opened up into a small chamber that was perfect for two. It would be crowded for four.

"Everyone will be on the grasslands early, so you should find your bedrolls soon," Nero said. "We won't post guards. The companions will warn us if anything approaches."

Leeto wouldn't approve of that, and Nero must know it. But there wasn't anything Dayvee could do about it.

Nero motioned Elayni to follow with a hand flip. "Come with me. I need to talk to you."

"Yes, sir." Elayni, Evee, Nero, and Nesi quickly faded from view, as they moved away from the fire and out of the cave into the dark night.

#

Brando glanced over to see Dayvee's head fall on his chest and his eyes lower. Dayvee jerked his chin up and stood. Then, he pulled his bedroll from his rucksack and headed to the rear of the cave. Jaycee followed him. Bruno bounded to his feet as Brando rose. They walked to the back, too. The light from the fire didn't reach far enough to see Dayvee and Jaycee very clearly.

"Great spot," Brando said.

"I knew you'd like it."

"What about you?" Brando whispered.

Dayvee wheezed. "I'll be okay."

Brando took off his rucksack and found the flask by feel, then the bowl. He carefully poured some oil in. With a strike of his fire stones, he lit the wick attached to the piece of bark. Light sprang up, and he threw the piece of wood into the bowl.

The light revealed the rough cave walls and Dayvee's pinched face. His expression softened and his breathing leveled out. "You told Bunjee you were out of lamp oil."

Brando set his make-shift lamp on top of an area of the wall that jutted out. "It was true."

"You filched more?" Dayvee's eyes widened.

The look of awe sent Brando's pride surging. He had made Dayvee happy and convinced him again that he could do the impossible. Miko called the oil a fire hazard, kept it in his own den, and guarded it fiercely.

"It's probably not enough until we get back. It's all I could get." Brando might be in huge trouble when Miko learned, but he'd make it up to him.

Dayvee's wide smile spoke his gratitude. "Thanks."

"Aren't families supposed to take care of one another?"

"Yes. But if Miko ever suspects why, tell him it's me." Dayvee spread out his bedroll.

Miko already wrongly assumed that Brando feared the dark. It didn't matter. Leeto wouldn't care about fixing Brando.

Brando shook out his bedroll near Dayvee's and whispered, "I don't know how you take Nero."

"I don't have much choice." Dayvee's foot tapped. "I can't quit, and if I defy him, he'll kick me out."

"He's trying to throw you out anyway, and he's getting others to help him."

"How's he doing that?"

"Tayro told Renay that Nero thinks you're incompetent. They're to watch and inform Nero if you mess up training Jaycee. And they're not supposed to endanger themselves to help you."

Dayvee sighed. "Great, but I already knew Tayro wasn't a friend, and there's still nothing I can do."

Jaycee grabbed an end of Dayvee's bedroll and took off with it. Dayvee did a flying leap and caught the other end. Brando bowled over laughing.

Dayvee shook his head. "Jaycee and you are an awful lot alike."

Then, Bruno took Brando's bedroll in his teeth. Brando clutched the other end, and they both tugged. "Hey, you two. I'm in charge of pranks."

Bruno's wolf laugh filled his mind. *We don't agree.*

Dayvee chuckled as he sat on his bedroll. "I think you like having a companion."

"Bruno's great." Brando jumped on his own bedroll. He hushed his voice. "Let's give Nero some reasons to worry. I have a great idea."

Dayvee ran a hand through his hair and smoothed his cowlick. "What?"

Brando threw Dayvee a smile. "There's a big black snake I found in a hole in a stump." He waved his hand toward the entrance. "Let's put it in Nero's bed tonight."

Dayvee laughed. "We can't. That will give Nero another excuse."

"Nero won't catch us, and even if he suspects, he won't be able to prove anything."

"I know you could pull it off, but he'd blame me, and I couldn't lie. He'd ask Nesi to judge the truth. So for me it would be foolish."

What if Dayvee did challenge Nero? They'd have to go back to the pack for the challenge. The details of what was going on would come out, and Leeto might assign them a different training leader. But Nero probably wouldn't accept the challenge.

"Not foolish, funny. A black snake is harmless. Are you sure you don't want to?" Brando tilted his head, and raised his eyebrows. Bruno and Jaycee both slanted their heads. They thought it would be funny.

Dayvee removed his boots, and got inside his bedroll. "I'm sure I don't want us kicked out."

Elayni and Evee returned. Elayni spread her bedroll away from them. Brando missed her. Their trio seemed incomplete. Elayni looked over, and smiled at Brando. It sent Brando's pulse racing. She gave Dayvee a scowl. Heat rose to Brando's face, and he inwardly groaned as guilt assailed him. The small hope she'd turn to him had resurrected Brando's old crush, but it felt wrong. Dayvee was still crazy about her. How could he want to hurt him?

Elayni's act was too good and left Brando confused. She really didn't seem to care for Dayvee anymore. Tayro went over to Elayni. She greeted him warmly. It didn't take her long to find another to fill the gap, and it wasn't Brando. Dayvee's heavy breathing told Brando he slept. He turned over and shut his eyes, too.

Brando woke and rose. He ducked out of the cave, and the stars greeted him. They were as numerous in the sky as fireflies on a warm summer night. After retrieving the black snake, the eastern sky turned a dark gray instead of black, and the stars faded. He went back in the cave and crawled into his bedroll. He heard Dayvee get up, but he let sleep reclaim him.

Yelling broke the predawn peace. Brando snapped open his eyes to see Tayro launch out of his bedroll and shake it. The snake dropped out and slowly slithered away.

Laughter came spilling from Dayvee at the front of the cave. The fright on Tayro's face put Brando in stitches—tears even came to his eyes. Awakened by the noise, the other trainees joined their mirth, and Bruno's resounded in his mind.

Maybe since Dayvee laughed first, Tayro turned on him. "Did you do this? Is this some prank of yours?"

"No, it isn't." Dayvee snorted. "You know snakes like a warm place to curl up."

"I think you lie." Tayro's eyes narrowed at Dayvee.

Brando could take the responsibility. But he wanted Dayvee to challenge Tayro.

Will he slink? Bruno's thought rang in his mind.

I hope not, Brando sent back.

Bruno's ear cocked in a wolf laugh. *Jaycee won't advise it.*

"Ask your companion if I lie." Dayvee gestured to Topay. Both Topay and Jaycee had stiffened. Jaycee's lips drew back to reveal his teeth. Dayvee's head rose, and he clenched his fists. "Maybe you'd like to challenge me, or how about I challenge you for calling me a liar?" The invitation hung in the air.

15

The Ancients

Choose a mate wisely since you will share her kills, and she will share your den. ~Wolf companion saying

Dayvee clenched his teeth, and his fingernails dug into his palms. He was tired of receiving accusations and blame.

If Tayro accepted his challenge, would Nero call it a training fight and let them do it today? He'd probably make them wait to return to the pack. No matter where they fought, Dayvee might not win. But, he'd find out if Tayro didn't tuck tail.

Give him your growl, Jaycee sent behind the wolf's own.

Dayvee let a growl surge forth.

Nero jumped up and hurried over to them. "There's no reason for challenges. Nesi said Dayvee spoke the truth, Tayro. He didn't put the snake in your bedroll." Nero's gaze locked on Dayvee. "You both have other things to do than argue with each other. See to them."

Tayro pivoted and strode away. Topay trailed him. Dayvee controlled the urge to crack a wide smile. It felt good to defend himself for a change. He searched for Brando, who winked at him and smiled. Brando struck again.

"See to your companion's breakfast and your own." Nero ordered the trainees. "I want you to cover ground today and try to locate a herd."

Nero served himself a bowl of gruel Dayvee had prepared. Dayvee halfway expected praise for getting up early to prepare breakfast.

"This breakfast tastes awful. You certainly can't cook." Nero harrumphed. "You'll learn. It shouldn't take much for you to improve on this tomorrow."

Dayvee's jaw tightened. The gruel tasted fine. He choked back the angry retort that came to his lips and drew in a deep breath. Jaycee's ruff rose beside him. Unlike Tayro, Dayvee needed to ignore the senior Calupi.

Nero glanced at Elayni. "You two head north-east. At midday, turn around and return. If you find a herd, send a companion to let us know. Don't hunt them alone or spook them."

After filling his water bottle and collecting his rucksack, Dayvee and Jaycee stopped to tell Brando and Bruno goodbye.

"Hurry up, Dayvee." Elayni's tone dripped acid. "A herd isn't going to wait for us, and I don't want anyone slowing me."

"I'm not the one who might have trouble keeping up." Dayvee strode briskly out of camp with Jaycee. Elayni and Evee scurried to catch them.

The path they followed was well-worn and only held a gradual grade to the grasslands below. It had enough room to stride two abreast. Once they left the sight and hearing of the camp, Dayvee slowed, and Elayni came alongside him. Evee and Jaycee glided ahead to investigate the trail.

With only an inch of snow and the trees and brush scattered, Dayvee found it easy going except for the rocks that littered the area and hindered their footing. His breath showed an absence of steam—unusual this early in the day.

Elayni stubbed her foot on one of the rocks. She hopped a few steps. "Cackles."

"Are you okay?" Dayvee steadied her with a hand.

"Yes. I'm fine." She took a normal step. "Does the stuff I say in camp upset you?"

Dayvee couldn't let her know how much. The alternative might mean her taking on another mountain lion without him. "I'm really glad that it convinced Nero to let us hunt together."

Her face screwed up. "Okay, if you're sure?"

"Yes."

"That little talk with Nero last night was just him telling me to watch you and not to help you if you run into trouble."

Dayvee scanned the rocky terrain ahead. "Brando said Tayro told Renee the same thing."

A corner of Elayni's mouth twitched. "That's why Brando put the snake in Tayro's bedroll."

Dayvee stumbled over a stone and then righted himself. "He thinks I should give them reason to worry."

"I'm glad Brando's on our side, but if he starts causing mayhem, and they suspect you, it will bring more trouble."

Dayvee examined the ground, stepped over a fallen tree limb, and then glanced back at Elayni. "Rabbit in a hole. It's hopeless. Nero will have the same talk with everyone and keep pointing out my shortcomings."

"Just do your best, and he won't find anything to fault."

Surely she didn't believe that. "If that was true, I wouldn't have a white fringe. I'm going to make mistakes, and even if I could be perfect, Nero can make up faults." Dayvee groaned.

The ground leveled as they trekked out onto the grasslands. The brown grass of winter was still tall. It brushed against Dayvee's waist, and the powdered snow came up to his ankles. In areas where the snow drifted, Dayvee sank to mid-calf.

Elayni slid on a slick spot, and Dayvee grabbed her before she fell. "Thanks."

He preferred it when Elayni needed his help instead of him needing hers. Dayvee let his hand reluctantly fall away. He searched the ground for any sign of game tracks, then glanced at Jaycee and Evee ahead. Jaycee marked some of the grass.

Elayni's forehead wrinkled. "Isn't it time you tell your father?"

"No, I want to handle it." For Leeto to take Dayvee's side over Nero's seemed as likely as Tayro wanting to be friends.

"Okay, do you want to formally challenge Nero?" Elayni asked.

Dayvee ran a hand through his hair. Not something to do lightly. But if he challenged Nero, would he accept? It seemed unlikely. "I don't think the alphas and betas would believe I have enough status to challenge Nero. Jaycee's isn't mine."

Elayni rolled her eyes. "That only matters when you're challenging for status. Any Calupi can challenge another if they wrong them."

"But they have to believe I'm wronged. What will I say? I challenged him for giving me a white fringe or assigning me chores? They'd laugh at that."

"What about not risking ourselves if you do something stupid?"

"He'd just cite pack law. Protect the pack over one individual." Dayvee shrugged. "Besides he'd never accept. It's hopeless."

"Cheer up. I'll keep watching your back. We're working together like we wanted, and it's a beautiful day." She gave him her amazing smile that dimpled her cheeks and put a sparkle in her eyes.

She shouldn't be able to melt his cares with one look, but that smile begged for his in return. Why not enjoy this time with Elayni alone?

The sun's rays blanketed them and warmed Dayvee, but not enough to shed his coat.

The ground turned slushy in areas as several patches of snow melted. It was too early for spring, but weather like this could fool one into thinking it anyway. Jaycee and Evee returned to walk with them for a few minutes. They got bored at Dayvee and Elayni's pace and trotted ahead.

The day wore on as they traversed the grasslands, scrutinizing the ground for any sign of a herd. Some hills appeared. The view from the top might allow them to see further. Jaycee and Evee loped up to them and blocked their path. The wolves alert ears signaled danger.

Dayvee pulled himself up short, and grabbed Elayni's arm to stop her. Please get it right the first try—this time. *What's wrong?* he asked Jaycee.

Jaycee pointed his muzzle at the hills and back at Dayvee. *If you continue on this path, you'll be in the ancient ruins.*

Elayni's eyes widened. "I didn't realize we were so close." Evee must have informed her, too. "I'm glad this is the only one in our territory."

Dayvee ran his hand through his hair. "We'll have to cut around." Most of the ruins had been swallowed by the ground, but a few of the ancients' rubbish piles from their larger cities still marred Taluma. The piles could slide and crush those foolish enough to tread them.

Relief flooded Dayvee. The wolves had kept them from harm. *Thanks.*

You're welcome, Jaycee sent back.

Kwutee warned them often about the soul sickness caused by touching the ancients' things. Their narrow escape sent chills racing through Dayvee.

Dayvee trekked a wide berth around the hills and studied them in case he ever came across another. Even covered by snow, the hills weren't uniform, but jagged and, in many areas grass still didn't grow. How had he missed that?

The ruins behind them, Dayvee turned to Elayni. "Should we break for lunch?"

"Yes."

They fed their companions, then themselves. The warm weather sent Dayvee's spirits high. How about some fun? He picked up some of the melting snow, formed it into a ball, and flung it at Elayni.

She dodged, but the snowball hit her arm. "Hey." Elayni retaliated and threw one that landed on Dayvee's neck.

The cold soggy mess fell apart on impact and slid into his coat, sending a shiver through him. Jaycee and Evee joined the action. They ran around and jumped on them as they battled each other in the snow fight. Evee tripped Dayvee, and he fell to the ground. Elayni stood over him with a huge mass of packed snow poised over her head.

"Do you give up?" She raised her eyebrows.

Dayvee swept her ankles with his leg, and she fell, almost landing on top of him. He caught her and spun her around on her back.

He kneeled over the top of her with his weapon of snow in hand. "No, do you?"

She laughed. "Possibly."

Dayvee stood and extended his hand to help her. Her hand fit inside his like it belonged there. The skin smooth like cream. He pulled her to her feet and into his arms, where he caught her. The light blue pools that were Elayni's eyes trapped his gaze. *She's so beautiful.* Her scent fresh, like the breeze with a promise of flower's waiting. The hope of spring after a long winter.

Her long eyelashes fluttered. Those lips were so inviting, he couldn't resist. Dayvee leaned in and kissed her. The taste—as sweet as the first strawberry. Time slowed and, there was only Elayni. A jolt of pure joy traveled through him like a lightning bolt. She trembled. Did her lips move? He howled inside.

Jaycee slapped his paw into Dayvee's leg. *There's a deer moving in the grass not far from us.*

Cackles. Dayvee pulled back. He dropped his arms from around her shoulders to put his wrists together and spread his hands and fingers partially—the signal for deer.

Elayni gave him a nod and dropped her gaze. Pink splashed her cheeks. Flushed with what—excitement, embarrassment, anger at him? If only he could read people like wolves. He tried to meet her eyes, but she studied the ground and followed Evee.

Dayvee's breaths still came ragged. When he took a step, he stumbled. Had he alerted the deer?

Focus. Jaycee sent. *We don't hunt, we don't eat.*

Jaycee was right. Push it aside. Get his mind on the stalk. Together, he and Jaycee took cautious steps through the tall grass, after Evee and Elayni. The tawny coat appeared.

A doe—she grazed, pushing her nose through the melting snow that blanketed the ground to forage on the grass below. Her head bobbed up, then swiveled around.

Dayvee released his nails in tandem with Elayni. Hers hit the deer in the shoulder while his landed on the doe's forehead, stunning it. The wolves rushed in to each grab a leg and bring the deer down. Dayvee sprang forward, only a second behind them. He grabbed for the deer's muzzle, and the bleating sound it made stopped short as his hand clamped down on its damp, black nose.

Steam from the deer's breath filled his palm. Tilting the head back, he used his tooth to cut her throat and end her life quickly, so she didn't suffer. The sharp scent of blood filled the air. They said the hunter's prayer. Afterwards, he and Elayni skinned the deer and cut up the meat. They divided it between their rucksacks and the wolves for the trek to Cracked Rock.

A perfect afternoon. Why did they have to return to camp? Did Elayni like the kiss? Did she like him? His feelings for Elayni had grown stronger and were getting harder to control. She sent his blood pounding and turned his breath ragged with one look.

If anyone harmed her now—just thinking about it made Dayvee crazy. The realization hit home. Elayni had his heart snared, and the knots were strong. He didn't think the binds could be cut. But if he let Nero drive him from the pack, Elayni'd never leave. Making her parents proud by achieving high status in Wolf Mountain pack meant everything to her. The closer they got to camp, the slower his feet traveled.

When he recalled the kiss, a thrill ran through him as if he had killed a bear with one throw of his teeth. He'd like to try that again, but Calupi frowned upon kissing before a life-mating ceremony. Probably for the best the deer interrupted them. They were supposed to show restraint—not exactly easy.

Dayvee wanted to ask Elayni to life mate with him. If he got through this year, and they assigned him a permanent sub-pack, he'd ask her. Right now, he needed to slow down. His future remained uncertain, and Elayni's happiness depended on Wolf Mountain. So hard to keep control around her, but Dayvee needed to keep his distance. If only Nero'd treat him fair, he could make it.

16

Kun's Rewards

"To a wolf quitting and dying is the same word." ~ Codee

It had been three days since Dayvee kissed Elayni. Since then, he kept a few feet of space between them. He'd been careful not to penetrate that barrier and backed away if she crossed it.

Maybe Elayni regretted the kiss since she seemed so testy. When she snapped at him this morning in front of Nero, she convinced Dayvee she meant it. She stormed ahead on the trail as they put the camp behind them to search for the ever elusive herds. Evee and Jaycee loped off to investigate something.

Dayvee checked over his shoulder. He couldn't see the camp. Elayni glanced back. "You kissed me and now act like it didn't happen." She stopped walking. "Why?"

Dayvee took a breath. "I've been meaning to apologize for kissing you."

"What?" Elayni's confusion showed in her tone. "You don't like me?"

"Of course I do. But I shouldn't have kissed you before a life-mating ceremony. I'm sorry I lost control."

"I'm not sorry."

"You're not?" Elation rose in Dayvee. Elayni must care for him, too, but it didn't change anything. He scuffed his foot. "You should be. I have no status to offer you. Nero might even kick me out before we finish training."

Elayni rolled her eyes. "You're worrying too much, again. Nero can't get rid of you without a reason. And you'll be high status, I know it."

Red fringes and the companion that chose them showed a Calupi's ability to aid the pack. Dayvee couldn't gain any status until he finished training Jaycee and got rid of the white fringe. Neither seemed possible with Nero in charge. He reached out and lightly brushed a finger under her chin. Elayni's lips trembled. He wanted to pull her close, but didn't. "Would you want to leave, if he manages it?"

A long silence met his question. She finally shook her head. "You know what my parents expect of me, and yours expect from you."

"I knew you wouldn't, and I couldn't ask you to." Dayvee let a heavy breath escape. "You're going to be high status and have several offers, but we don't know what will happen to me. I can't act on feelings alone."

Red splotches lit her cheeks, and her hands clenched. Even Dayvee could read those signals. But he couldn't pretend his future at Wolf Mountain was certain. Did she expect him to deceive himself and her? He walked away in the direction they were assigned.

Her icy retort followed him. "You're right, I'll get many offers. Did you really think I'd wait for you?"

Dayvee'd be willing to wait for her. He just shrugged and kept walking, not trusting himself to speak. His voice might crack or break. He needed to be strong.

#

As soon as Elayni and Dayvee arrived at the cave with their companions on their seventh evening in camp, Nero turned his habitual scowl on Dayvee. "Dayvee, collect wood and build a fire."

Jaycee bristled. Even with just a partial bond, the wolf could sure tell Dayvee's feelings. "Yes, sir."

Everyone else sat and told stories of their day's exploits while Dayvee collected wood with Jaycee. He carried another pile back, stacked it, and found a place to sit.

Nero glanced at his pile and narrowed his eyes. "I don't think that's enough for the entire night. You can't do anything right. Go get some more."

"Yes, sir." Dayvee rose. He couldn't help the drag in his step as he headed out.

Jaycee brushed against him. *The rabbit isn't in the hole yet.*

No, although it usually seemed hopeless. But he couldn't let Nero win. Hunting with Elayni and their companions formed the only bright spots in his misery. Even though his and Elayni's relationship was more strained, now. He messed up kissing her, but that memory got him through the awful times at camp. After the next load of wood, he lit the fire with his stones.

Nero stood and swaggered closer to Dayvee. "Quit messing around. It shouldn't take you all day to make a fire."

Dayvee lowered his eyes. "Yes, sir." He couldn't quit. As the stew heated, he hung venison steaks over the fire from the deer he and Elayni hunted. They had brought in more meat than any other group.

As they ate, Nero complained. "This steak is too pink and the stew is burnt."

Dayvee expected it and didn't even look up. According to Nero, the food was always burnt or raw. Dayvee sat apart from everyone, with Jaycee, and concentrated on his own supper.

Tayro handed Nero a bulging pouch, then smirked as he put his head together with Renay's and whispered to her. Elayni situated herself next to Geno. Dayvee glanced at the fire—thick smoke billowed from it.

Nero yelled, "How many times have I told you not to put wet wood or leaves on a fire? But look…"

A pile of wet leaves smoldered on top of the fire. Dayvee picked up a long branch and fished them out. Tayro and Renay's laughter confirmed his suspicions that the responsibility for the soggy mess lay with them.

"Can I help it if others sabotage what I do?" Dayvee asked.

"More excuses for incompetence?" Nero smiled. "When will you learn to stop blaming others for your own failings?"

Why did Dayvee even bother? It just gave Nero an excuse to lecture him again and call him names—incompetent, inept, useless, and hopeless. He'd heard them all before, and so had everyone else. It was one of the few times Nero smiled.

"Dayvee really can't make a decent fire," Tayro said smugly.

Renay shook her head. "You think he'd learn."

The heat rose to Dayvee's neck. Jaycee's ruff rose.

Nero shook his head. "I'm beginning to think it's impossible to teach him."

As soon as he finished eating, Nero's eyes traveled to Elayni, Tayro, and Renay, but they stopped on Dayvee. Did Nero always need everyone's attention? "Go get water from the stream and wash the dishes. Make sure you fill all the water bags."

"Yes, sir." Once Dayvee was no longer a trainee, he'd challenge Nero. He collected the water bags and took them to a lightly frozen section of the stream. Jaycee glided at his side. After Dayvee broke the ice with a rock, he filled them and washed the dishes. Only partially finished, he stopped when Nero hollered out from the cave. "Dayvee come in and put more wood on the fire."

Dayvee went and chucked some logs on the flames, then returned to finish cleaning the dishes at the stream. Someone threw dirt on those he already had done so he needed to rewash them. He drew a deep cleansing breath to push down his anger.

Dayvee almost finished the dishes before Nero called. "Dayvee, get in here. This fire's too smoky—fix it."

Dayvee stomped inside to the fire and retrieved the new clump of foliage someone threw in. He returned to the dishes to find them dirty once again. Heat rose to his face and his ears pounded as his anger threatened to boil over. He fought a battle to stay in control of his emotions—and won his composure.

How long would Nero and his accomplices play games tonight? Jaycee nosed him in sympathy. The wolf had sorted out his own dominance issues—nicely. All the young wolves showed deference to him. Dayvee had to do the same—and deal with Nero. The wolf's body language made it clear that Jaycee thought Dayvee should stand up to Nero.

Dayvee dipped a scrap of soapy hide in the dirty bowl. He glanced at the wolf. *I can't stand up to Nero as you couldn't to Luko. I'm just training you and don't even know what my status is.*

Why do you think your status is low? Jaycee cocked his head. *It's only as low as you let Nero convince you it is.*

Dayvee poured rinse water over his rewashed dishes. *New Calupi trainees have the lowest status. Otherwise, I'd stand up to him even with the white fringe.*

Jaycee flicked an ear. *Isn't Nero a trainee?*

It's not the same. He's learning to work with his new companion, but he's still an experienced Calupi, and I'm not.

Rudee's group brought their day's bounty to put in the cache inside. When they came out, Brando and Bruno trotted over to Dayvee and Jaycee. "Hi."

Nero stuck his head out of the cave. "Brando, get back with your group and stay away from mine."

Brando looked at Dayvee. He didn't want Brando targeted. "Go." Nero turned on anyone that treated Dayvee friendly. Brando still tried whenever Rudee's group came to Cracked Rock. No one else did. Dayvee understood why, but it still hurt.

Rudee strode over. "Come on, Brando." Brando moved away, shoulders drooping. The face Rudee leveled at Dayvee appeared sympathetic, but he turned and led his group away from Cracked Rock. Rudee never commented on anything Nero did, anyway.

Dayvee finished the dishes and took them in.

Jaycee, is it going to snow tonight? The wolf always seemed to know.

Not tonight.

I'm going to sleep outside. You can rest in here where it's warmer with the other companions if you want.

I think I'd rather see the sky. Jaycee and the other wolves were Dayvee's only friends in the evenings.

Dayvee grabbed his rucksack to leave the cave to get away from Nero's incessant demands. How would he ever do this for a year? Jaycee followed him toward the entrance.

"Dayvee, you need to share Jaycee with the other companions," Nero screeched.

"Jaycee chooses to stay with me, and the other companions join him. I can't order him."

"You don't have to beg him to stay." Nero said in a derisive tone.

Having valid complaints never stopped Nero. Dayvee turned and left before he said something he regretted. As he spread out his bedroll, Jaycee grabbed the other end with his teeth and tugged. Dayvee pulled back.

Scamp. He dropped his end of the bedroll to chase him.

Jaycee retreated. Dayvee leaned over to straighten his bedroll again. Jaycee crept up behind him and jumped on his back. It knocked Dayvee down to sprawl on the bedroll. Jaycee bounced on top of him. So Jaycee wanted to play? Dayvee rolled and grabbed Jaycee around the middle to roll him away.

He smiled to himself. The pup knew him well. Whenever Dayvee gave into despair, Jaycee always developed an urge to play. Dayvee couldn't stay focused on his problems while wrestling with the wolf.

Dayvee crawled into his bedroll, reclined on his back, and focused on the stars. He searched and found the star group resembling a wolf's head. *Jaycee, look there's the wolf.*

Jaycee sat with head craned back and muzzle pointing up, as he scrutinized the sky. *We wolves believe Kun made the wolf star pattern to show us his appreciation for our loyalty and protection of the Vita.*

Dayvee clasped his hands behind his head. *I don't think humans have a star grouping.*

Keeno said the wolves' trials have been large, but so has Kun's reward. I think it's the same for Calupi.

Just how many stars could Jaycee see? A wolf's night vision was better than a human's. Dayvee tried to mark the locations of the star groupings in the sky. Many senior Calupi claimed they used the stars to keep their course true at night. Nesi joined them. Then, all the wolves of their sub-pack came and curled up around Jaycee and Dayvee studying the stars.

Dayvee could string his hide over a rope tied between two trees for a tent, but then he couldn't see the stars. He'd stay as warm snuggled in his hides, as long as it wasn't snowing. Jaycee and the other wolves slept in balls with their heads tucked under their tails. Thankfully, their winters didn't hold the bitter cold of the northern part of Taluma.

#

The eighth morning in camp, Brando woke early. Everyone else still slept. He got up, and Bruno bounded to his feet. *Let's go over to Cracked Rock, he sent to the wolf. I want to try to spend a few minutes with Dayvee and Elayni before Nero wakes.*

Good. I'll see Jaycee and Evee.

Brando approached the cave warily. As he entered, Dayvee and Jaycee stood close to the entrance. The others lay still sleeping across the fire. Dayvee snapped punches and kicks, faster and faster, as he moved through his routine. His breaths turned ragged and sweat dripped from him.

Brando crept toward Dayvee. Bruno glided over to Jaycee.

Dayvee glanced up and whispered, "No one saw. Not that they'd care. Everyone trains."

"Not like us. Most of it's our ideas. So you never stopped?"

"No. I will prove to Leeto I'm good enough, but I don't do the blocking since it takes two."

Brando bit off his response. To say something too negative about Leeto angered Dayvee. "I would have trained with you."

"Nero keeps me too busy to get away."

Brando pulled six small balls made of strips of rawhide wrapped around each other from his rucksack and his water bag. "I'll wet them."

"By firelight?"

"Just like training with the hoods. Trust your senses." Brando heard some scuffling. Jaycee had jumped on Bruno, and the two wolves wrestled. Playing.

The cool water splashed on the stones and wet his pant legs, as Brando poured water over them. "Are you going to get in the ring with Leeto?"

"No. He wants me to be alpha so he'll step down. And you'll be my second."

Step down? Not a chance. "My rank's number seven out of nine. No one's going to accept me as beta."

"Ranks change," Dayvee said. "Both you and Leeto keep telling me I need to be alpha, but I can't without you. I'm not confident or brilliant."

Brando wasn't everything Dayvee believed him to be—he should tell him, but he couldn't. "You'll be a great alpha, but I don't need to be second. I'm not giving up pranks. Low rank is fine. They don't expect anything from me."

"You're not getting off that easy. And I expect you to keep us both laughing. If we're too good to best, the worst anyone can do is grumble."

"Or leave. Get ready, I'm throwing them."

Dayvee chuckled. "You missed me." Retrieving the balls in the near dark was the most difficult part. "My turn to throw."

Brando strained to part the darkness with his hearing and his warning sense—that prickle that his body always sent when the balls came close, regardless of whether he could see them. He managed to dodge five. He felt the damp impression as the last hit his arm.

"You got one fist through," Brando admitted.

"Now block."

Brando knocked all six balls away from his body with his arms and feet. They took a few more turns.

Dayvee stopped. "Even as much as I worry, it's stupid to be concerned about Leeto wanting me to lead now. I need to get through Nero first." He handed Brando the balls. "It's getting light. I have to get the gruel ready."

Brando stayed, taking the risk Nero might catch him. Dayvee was miserable. Brando needed to help. "Your ignoring strategy isn't working. Nero's getting worse, and too many others are joining in. He's made you the omega."

Dayvee put some grain in a pot. "I know, but I have no choice. Even if I was willing to break the law, I can't fight them all."

"You can always leave."

After he poured in water, Dayvee hung the pot over the fire. "Just walk away from the pack?" His tight lips showed his disappointment—like Brando had asked him to jump off a cliff. "I can't."

"I didn't mean like a tiger. I'd go with you."

"I don't want you to throw your future away." Dayvee tossed some berries in the gruel. "You should stay away from me, too."

"Like Elayni? Her act is really good."

Dayvee sighed. "I'm not going to doubt her again."

"I love her, too." That earned Brando a sharp look. "Just be careful. She might choose her parents over you."

Dayvee's face fell as if Brando kicked him. "Or you? I know she deserves better than me." His shoulder's fell. "I'll..."

"No you won't. Elayni's capable of deciding who she wants." Brando grinned. "Is my charm so easy to resist I'd have to win by default if I was interested?" Brando would need several more than Dayvee to default before Elayni turned to him.

A corner of Dayvee's lip turned up in a tentative smile. "So you're not?"

"Elayni's great and all,"—Brando chuckled—"but she doesn't like pranks."

Dayvee's gaze moved to Bruno, and his smile faded. The wolf's ears flopped. He felt sad for Brando.

Sorry, Bruno sent.

Don't be. I know wolves don't hide their feelings. I should have known he'd check.

He was saved from more conversation about Elayni when Nero rose and stomped over. "Brando, I've told you before to stay with your group and find a different friend who's not so inept."

Nesi's head was up and her ruff rose. Bruno stiffened.

Brando let insolence color his tone. "Dayvee's not inept."

Do you want him to challenge you? Bruno asked.

He won't. My ring reputation's too good. But he might make a mistake.

Nero kicked wood from the fire and screamed. "This fire's too large as anyone who's not inept can see. We're lucky Dayvee hasn't set us all ablaze." He gestured to Brando. "Get back to Rudee's group, Tiger."

Dayvee's hands balled into fists, and he took a step toward Nero. "Don't call Brando that, ever. He's Calupi."

Nero just made his mistake, Brando sent to Bruno.

Nero retreated a step from Dayvee. "Brando, if you don't go, your useless friend will collect more wood."

Cackles. Nero wasn't stupid enough to do it again.

Bruno's head tilted. *Why does Dayvee let Nero call him names?*

Dayvee's used to criticism of himself thanks to Leeto. But target those he loves, and you risk his wrath.

Brando hated when his own actions gave Nero an excuse to punish Dayvee, but he couldn't resist one parting shot. "We won't be trainees forever."

"Are you threatening me?" Nero demanded.

"I'm just explaining that if the stars don't shine tonight, it doesn't mean they won't tomorrow."

Bruno cocked his ear. The wolf's chuckle resounded in Brando's head.

"Dayvee, I want a large pile of wood before you leave today," Nero yelled.

Brando left with Bruno.

#

Dayvee and Elayni wasted no time leaving Cracked Rock. The further they traveled from camp, the lighter Dayvee felt. Their companions ranged out to the front. Dayvee brought up the rear, and Elayni had the center, but he had to keep slowing so he didn't run into her. Heavy brush and trees abutted the narrow path they followed so, he couldn't hike at her side. After he bumped her for the second time, Elayni accelerated to a lope.

Yes, Jaycee sent. *Come catch us.*

They put distance between them and Nero as Dayvee matched his strides to Elayni's so he didn't run over her. He enjoyed the exertion even though the breeze buffeted his body in the light of the grey morning. Elayni slowed to a walk.

Dayvee mulled over his and Brando's conversation this morning. Brando was right. Ignoring Nero wasn't working. After about thirty minutes, they left the dense brush behind, when the trail opened up to the tall grass of the grasslands.

We're not picking up any herd scents. Jaycee's thoughts filled Dayvee's mind. *We're going to lope a circle and scout.*

Dayvee focused. *Okay.* He moved up alongside Elayni to talk. "I've decided I have to do something about Nero."

Her cheeks were red from the cold. "Like what?"

He sighed. "I don't know, but I know who will."

She blinked a couple times. "Your father?"

Those eyes were so mesmerizing that Dayvee avoided meeting them. "No, as soon as we get back to the pack, I'll ask Codee. I can't deal with Nero for a whole year."

She cocked her head. "That's great, but I think you should ask Leeto. Even if you and Codee are closer, won't your father be hurt if you ask for Codee's advice?"

He searched their surroundings. Nothing moved in the tall grass. "Leeto doesn't have the time for my problems, and he'd probably criticize me for having them. Codee will tell Leeto, anyway, but he'll give me good advice first."

"I *am* glad you're going to ask someone." She smiled, showing him her dimples. The first real smile she'd given *him* in days. "After we hunt a herd, we'll have to take the meat back, so you won't need to wait much longer."

They scoured the grasslands all day but didn't see any sign of herds.

We're chasing a rabbit back toward you, Jaycee sent.

The rabbit raced toward them, caught sight of them, and froze. Dayvee's nails landed in its neck, almost decapitating it. Elayni didn't need to release hers.

As Dayvee retrieved it, Jaycee and Evee came up, tongues lolling. The only thing they had to show for their day was the rabbit.

Everything's sheltering, Jaycee sent. *Sleet or snow's coming.*

That's why the grasslands seemed empty. "Should we head back?" Elayni asked.

"Yes." Cracked Rock held no joy for Dayvee, but it meant shelter in bad weather. It was nearing time to return anyway.

On the way back to camp the wind picked up and the sky turned dark. Sleet fell from the sky and crackled as it covered the ground. The strong winds carried the sleet into Dayvee's skin, stinging it like a swarm of mosquitoes. Dayvee put a cupped hand above his eyes and spied a black scar in the mountain ahead.

"Look, a cave." Elayni pointed at it. "We can get out of this sleet." She ran forward.

"Be careful, it's slick," Dayvee yelled.

She reached the cave and ducked inside. Evee disappeared in after her. Dayvee followed a little slower, not wanting to fall on the rocky ground. Jaycee jumped in front of him. *I smell an odor I don't recognize coming from the cave.*

Fear for Elayni stabbed Dayvee's heart. *Elayni and Evee are in there. We have to get them out.*

Dayvee and Jaycee plunged into the cave. The light from the entrance didn't penetrate far. A black void lay in front of him. Jaycee sniffed the air. A musky smell, unlike a cave's natural odor, assaulted Dayvee's nose. A putrid scent, like a dead animal, wafted. He needed a torch. Elayni and Evee could barely be made out ahead. Heavy breathing came from beyond them.

"Elayni, we need to get out of here." Dayvee's urgent whisper echoed on the cave walls sounding louder than he intended.

Elayni stood still. He took a few steps, reached for her arm, and brought her to his side. Together they backed.

Jaycee growled. A deeper growl answered. A blur moved towards them. "Go! I'll cover you."

"Not without you," Elayni's strained voice answered.

Huffing filled the air. In the dim light a huge mass rose and stood on two legs. It opened its mouth wide. *We woke a hibernating bear. Kun help us.* A huge roar blasted him. The bellow resounded through the cave and hurt Dayvee's ears. Warm breath assailed him. The smell of death.

Dayvee and Elayni fell back toward the entrance together as they faced the bear. Their companions retreated with them, growling, tails tucked. The bear advanced—arms outstretched, giant palms with nails extended. As it moved into the light, Dayvee stared at the giant mouth stretched open to reveal the teeth. Saliva dripped. The huge body with the shaggy brown fur lumbered closer.

Dayvee's heart lurched. "Run!"

17

Courage

"To show courage it may be necessary to throw away caution."~ *Leeto*

Dayvee pushed Elayni ahead of him and fled, the wolves flanking him. He glanced back over his shoulder.

The bear dropped to all fours and barreled after them—too fast. They couldn't hope to outrun it. His heart walloped his chest, and he barely felt the pummeling sleet as he dashed out of the cave. His slick palm grabbed the grip on the rough rawhide of his nails.

Would one nail—even two—stop a bear? It didn't when his grandfather died. The bear gained ground. Just a few more seconds until it was on them. Dayvee's desperation insisted he try. "Don't stop running, Elayni."

Dayvee drew his weapon and turned. Elayni skidded to a stop and drew hers. Jaycee and Evee joined them. Their growls resounded. The bear hit some of the sleet on the ground and his legs splayed, sliding. The beast stopped and shook its head at the sleet pounding it. It crossed one front foot over the other and lumbered slowly around. The huge grizzled head retreated back inside the cave, looking back over one shoulder to give them one more warning huff before the rump disappeared inside.

Dayvee's heart slowed as relief poured in. "Whew, it's gone, but you shouldn't have stopped."

Elayni set her mouth in that stubborn line. "Like you'd have done differently, but that was too close. Thanks."

Dayvee took off his rucksack and dug around inside. He found his hide blanket and shook it out. He and Elayni each took an end and lifted the hide over their heads as they continued walking. Their companions jumped in the middle between them.

The sleet stopped stinging. "Don't thank me, but Kun. He delivered us."

"I will thank Kun and you, too. I froze." She wrinkled her nose. "If you hadn't come, I'd have been that bear's lunch."

Dayvee's relief at their escape made him giddy. He chortled. "Brando would say the bear should thank me since you'd have caused it a stomach ache."

Elayni's laughter joined his. "Are you trying to do the impressions, now?"

"No, you're much better."

"Yours was good for Brando. He does drive me crazy, but things never seem as bad when you can laugh about them."

Dayvee returned his nails to his side. "I miss him, too. It's like one of my arms is gone, but I'm glad I still have one, at least, during the day."

"I know it's been really rough at camp for you, but if Nero discovers we're friends, we won't even have this time."

"I'm grateful, Elayni. Our days and Jaycee are the only things making the evenings bearable. But as soon as I talk to Codee, we can drop the pretense."

Thirty minutes later, the sleet changed to a slow, cold rain that showed no sign of letting up. The slick ground kept them fighting to remain on their feet.

Elayni skidded a little and regained her balance. "I don't think we better tell Nero about the bear."

"If he doesn't ask, I'm not saying a word." Dayvee sighed. "He'll just blame me for it."

"It wasn't your fault, but mine." Elayni lowered her gaze. "I ran into a strange cave without heed."

When they arrived at camp, no one was in view. They must all be sheltering in the cave. As they entered, the fire's light flickered against the walls. Rudee's group was there, too, hanging their meat over the racks to smoke it.

Nero stalked up to them. "You're late, Dayvee, and someone else had to do your chores."

Nesi's hair rose, and Jaycee stiffened. Nesi lowered her head.

Dayvee shrugged. How hard was it to light the fire? He'd already gathered the wood. "With the treacherous footing, we couldn't make good time."

Nero's eyes narrowed. "Was that your only problem?"

He should have known Nero would ask. "No, it wasn't." He took a lesson from Jaycee. Didn't have to disclose everything.

"I'm waiting." Nero's chest puffed.

Jaycee's rigid stance revealed Dayvee's feelings. But he remained silent.

Nero shifted his weight. "Elayni, what other problems did you have? Did Dayvee do something stupid again?"

Elayni put her hands on her hips and met Nero's gaze. "No, I did. I ran into a cave with a bear."

Evee's head lifted. Elayni better be careful. Nero would know she was on Dayvee's side.

"If you can believe it, Dayvee did something right." Elayni raised her eyebrows. "I froze. The bear woke and moved to attack, but Dayvee rescued me. He grabbed my arm and got me out. The bear chased us, but stopped when it slid on the ice. Apparently, bears don't like sleet."

"It was the wrong thing to do. You can't outrun a bear. Bears can run thirty miles in an hour." Nero's habitual scowl turned on Dayvee. "Who made the decision to run?"

Dayvee's smoldering anger lit. "I did. To take on a bear is foolish. I used the last option, and it worked. We weren't hurt."

"The last, not the first. I knew you were incompetent, but I didn't realize you were a coward, too."

Heat rose to Dayvee's face. Nero's constant belittling became too much. "I went in a cave, knowing something waited in there, to get Elayni out." Dayvee couldn't stop. "You wouldn't have come after me, yet you call me a coward?"

"You fled." Nero glowered. "I won't have a coward endangering us by running when we need him. If you want to stay, you'll have to prove yourself and pass a courage test." His lips peeled back in a smirk. "You don't have to take it—just flee to some town. I'll finish training Jaycee and explain to the pack you were too cowardly to be Calupi." Nero crossed his arms. "Your father may not like it, but an alpha who raised such a failure of a son isn't very fit to lead."

Dayvee put a hand up to rub his temple. Leeto made it clear Dayvee's actions reflected on his pack and father. Could Nero really convince the pack if Dayvee failed his training, Leeto bore the fault? Would Leeto lose his alpha position over Dayvee?

He dropped his hand and set his jaw. "I'm no coward. I'll take your test, and I'll pass it."

Nero gave Dayvee one of his rare smiles. A tingling pricked the back of Dayvee's neck. What had he agreed to?

Nero turned on his heel. "Follow me." Nero led him close to the fire and pointed. "Stand there and take off your rucksack, coat, and shirt."

Dayvee followed Nero's orders. Goosebumps rose on his flesh, despite the heat from the fire.

Nero took a stick from the fire and drew a tight circle with ashes around Dayvee's feet, almost touching them. "Everyone come here, Rudee's group, too."

All the trainees and Rudee soon surrounded them.

Nero's chest puffed as he crowed, "Dayvee has agreed to take a courage test to prove he's not a coward." Nero smirked. "I say he is, but we'll see. He grabbed another stick—with a flame at one end from the fire—and met Dayvee's eyes. I'll take this stick and burn a C into your back. If your feet or body moves across that line in any way, if you flee or faint, you will be marked forever as a coward, and you must leave this camp, a failure. If you can keep your feet inside the circle, the C will stand for courage, and you'll have proven yours and may stay."

"I've never heard of that." Brando's fists balled. "You have no right to do it."

"I've heard of it," Chayla said. "It's in the histories. In the war against the second Kayndo, the false king used the test as punishment for soldiers who ran from charging animals. If they proved their courage, they could stay and fight again. If not, they were imprisoned or killed for desertion."

Nero's chin jutted out, and his chest puffed. "Appropriate don't you think?"

"No, we're not at war," Brando snapped. "To use a burning stick as a weapon against a pack member, that's breaking the law."

"It's not a weapon." Nero fumed. "It won't kill him. I keep telling you to find a different friend."

Brando drew himself up. "What if I challenge you?"

"You're a trainee, you don't have enough status for me to consider. I wouldn't accept, but I'll have you bound and punished next, if you keep interfering."

"Leave it, Brando. I can do it." Dayvee stopped his foot tapping.

"You don't have to do this." Brando beseeched him. "We can go to another pack."

Dayvee searched Elayni's face. Tears filled her eyes. A corner of her lower lip was in her mouth again. Surely she knew what he wanted to ask. Would she leave? She shook her head, no. She couldn't go.

Could Dayvee ask Brando to throw his future away? Bruno would have to leave his pack. Elayni wouldn't leave—he always knew that.

He's right, Jaycee sent. *You can still spring the trap and get away.*

But not without leaving most of my pack behind. I'd have to relinquish you, too, so someone else could finish training you.

He didn't want to give up Jaycee, his pack, nor hurt Brando or Leeto. Dayvee needed to sacrifice like Leeto'd expect.

He straightened his shoulders and forced his chin up. "I'll pass his test. Do it, Nero."

Jaycee moved away, with his head and tail both low, to join several other wolves at the side of the cave. The sticks flame had died, so Nero stuck the branch back in the fire and blew on it. The end glowed red.

Nero circled around Dayvee. *Kun help me not move.*

Pain exploded into Dayvee's brain as the branch seared into his skin. He locked his knees. Couldn't move. The smell of burning meat. His own flesh. Every inch Nero carved into his back ever so slowly, agony. Nero began above his shoulder, then traveled across his back and down one side.

Water leaked from Dayvee's eyes and down his cheeks. The white hot pain consumed every inch of his mind. He gnashed his teeth and his knees felt weak. *Oh Kun, don't let me faint.*

He tried not to give Nero the satisfaction of hearing him cry out, but he couldn't keep a few moans from escaping.

About halfway down his side, Nero stopped. "The stick has cooled. I need another."

Oh no, not again. Nero returned and plunged another hot poker into his skin and continued down his side. Excruciating. Was his whole back on fire? He needed to get away. His muscles tensed, ready to run. But he couldn't move. The anguish filled him. A scream escaped.

Brando leapt toward Nero. Geno, Tayro and Rudee grabbed Brando and held him.

Dayvee needed to think of something else. *I am not in pain. My flesh isn't being burnt to a crisp.* He bit his lip, and the blood dribbled down his chin. Would the torment never end? Nero got almost to Dayvee's pant line and finally turned to bring the C across. Dayvee's strength waned. The cave's walls were spinning. His eyes locked onto Jaycee. So sad. The wolf's ears and head drooped as he paced back and forth surrounded by other companions.

"A wolf will gnaw off a paw caught in a trap." Nero rasped. "They'll self-inflict more pain to guarantee their survival and return to their pack. They're not cowards. Calupi must face and defeat fear and pain."

Dayvee prayed for endurance harder than ever before. His mind seemed to separate from his pain-racked body leaving him as an onlooker—but he felt smooshed as if others pressed against him. A wolf howled in distress. Did the howl originate from him?

He watched as Nero twisted the stick back and forth, trying to inflict more pain as he finished the last part of the C. How could he see Nero, behind him? When Nero stopped, Dayvee's conscience slammed back into his body, and the pain returned. It bent him over and stole his breath away, but his feet stayed planted.

Nero came back around to face Dayvee. "I'm not convinced you aren't a coward, but you passed the test. For now, you may remain. Let this be a warning to you and a just punishment for your actions today. I hope it teaches you not to act cowardly again."

Brando flung off the arms that held him and flew to Dayvee's side. "He passed your test. The C stands for courage." Brando's took Dayvee's arm. "You can move your feet now."

Dayvee unlocked his knees. The burns on his back still raged. His legs wobbled, and he swayed like a tiny sapling buffeted by heavy winds. Jaycee came to his other side and pressed close.

Brando reached his arm up to his back but stopped before he touched him. "I don't want to hurt you. Hold onto me." Dayvee hung onto Brando's shoulder. His friend led him out of the cave and down to the creek. Jaycee stayed at Dayvee's side, and Bruno trailed them.

Brando helped him to a seat on a rock near the bank. Brando drew his water bag from his rucksack, filled it, and poured cold water down Dayvee's back.

Dayvee moaned as the water hit the burn. Oh how it stung, but the heat subsided some.

Brando's face twisted in an unusual grim countenance when he stopped washing his back and came around to face Dayvee. His eyes misted. "This has to stop. We have to leave, or you need to challenge him. I think he'd accept yours—his hate won't allow him not to."

Dayvee's voice seemed ragged to his own ears. "If we left, no pack's going to want someone with a white fringe. Elayni won't leave. I'd have to relinquish Jaycee. And I can't see Leeto taking my side if I challenge him. I'm at Nero's mercy and he knows it."

"That's the problem. He has no mercy." Brando's face skewed with deep concern lines. "Maybe Tayro will have something to put on your burns. Do you want to wait here while I go ask him?"

Dayvee didn't know if he could tolerate the agony of moving yet. Jaycee nestled close against the opposite side of the worst of the burn. The wolf kept the slow drizzle from stealing Dayvee's warmth. "I'll wait, but I can't see Tayro doing anything to help me. You're wasting your time."

"If he refuses to help a pack member, he shouldn't be Kwutee's apprentice." Brando's tone darkened. "I'll remind him."

Several minutes later, Elayni pulled Brando by the arm toward Dayvee while Evee and Bruno padded in front of them. "I had to get Brando out of there before he did something rash."

"I didn't think Tayro would help." Dayvee shrugged and sucked in his breath.

"I think Tayro would have, but Nero said he couldn't." Elayni's tone reflected her anger. "He said the bigger the scars, the better to mark you as a coward. Brando asked if Nero forgot you passed the test, and any scar would mark your courage."

Dayvee had to ask. "What did he say?"

Elayni rolled her eyes. "He didn't answer. Then, Brando asked Nero *if* he could pass the test if Brando administered it to him. So I pulled Brando out."

Brando chuckled. "Not before she told Nero it took courage for you to rescue her in the bear cave, and Tayro should treat you."

Elayni hung her head. "He wouldn't listen, and now he may separate us."

"You better think of something nasty to say." Dayvee tried to smile. "Tell them you don't know if I can take pain like a Calupi should or something."

"But that *is* a lie," she said. "I don't think I could have endured his test."

"You'll think of something."

Evee nosed his burn. Dayvee grimaced. Jaycee flew at Evee with his teeth snapping. She retreated. Dayvee had never seen Jaycee show his teeth to Evee before. Evee lowered her head, and licked her mouth.

She didn't mean to hurt me. Dayvee rarely sent twice to Jaycee, now. Must be getting better at it.

She should be more careful. We can't stop Nero, but she doesn't need to help him.

"Evee says she's sorry," Elayni told him.

"I know. It's okay."

"I want to see the damage." Elayni walked around him and gasped. "That hyena. Your back is a torn and burnt mess."

She came back to face him. Tears streamed down her cheeks. "I'm so sorry. This is all my fault. I got you into the mess with the bear, and then I told him. I should have refused like you."

He started to reach out his hand to her but stopped as another stab of pain went through him. "You couldn't and stay on his good side. It's done." Her eyes were muted from tears. "Don't cry."

"I should have just agreed to leave like Brando." Another sob escaped her.

Dayvee shook his head slowly. "Shhh. I wouldn't have let you throw away your future, and I'm not slinking away a failure. I'll mend."

"Burns can get infected." She put a hand on her hip. "Doesn't he realize how dangerous those can be?"

Brando's mouth turned down. "I don't think he cares."

"I almost forgot." Elayni dug in her rucksack. "I have your shirt and coat. Your burns should be wrapped before you put them on, so I brought clean bandages."

Topay loped to them with a flask in her mouth. Brando retrieved it.

Topay says, it's medicine to treat your burns, Jaycee sent.

Did Tayro send her? Dayvee asked.

No, he doesn't know. She took it from his rucksack and brought it. Brando should keep the flask until your burns heal. If Tayro discovers it missing, Topay will tell him she took it.

Brando dribbled some of the liquid onto his burn. The throbbing did subside until Dayvee shifted. Then, a new jolt stole his breath. Brando swaddled his back in the bandages Elayni brought—it took them all to cover the entire length. Each time a bandage hit the burn, the pain ripped through him. Brando helped him into his shirt. He refused the coat. He could barely stand the shirt's weight.

Jaycee stiffened and put a paw on him. *Nero comes.*

Brando capped the flask and slid it into his rucksack.

Nero stalked up. "I thought I told you not to treat his burns."

"Brando had to bandage it, so Dayvee could wear his shirt." Elayni rolled her eyes. "It doesn't seem like all Calupi can take pain."

"He'll learn to deal with it and stop using it as an excuse to do nothing." He pointed to Dayvee. "You have chores to do."

Brando's jaw ticked. "He shouldn't work tonight."

The smirk that crossed Nero's face sent a warning prickle to the back of Dayvee's neck. "Since you keep interfering with a training leader's orders, Brando, Dayvee can gather extra wood, and you need to get back to Pair Cave with your group."

Brando's face turned red, but he didn't say anything more. Dayvee rose and plodded back to the cave.

18

Strange Land

"A powerless man is a nobody." ~ *Varian to Tibalt*

Tib's kagard escort of two hurried to catch up. The one's stationed outside Varian's door opened it to reveal the castle room with its sparse furnishings—a single bed, four plain chairs, and an oil lamp on the wall. Varian's lessons were never dull and the highlight to Tib's blah, blah days.

"Be welcome." Varian's voice bounced off the unsoftened grey stone of the room's floors and walls. He waved a hand at the chairs with a big flourish. Unlike Tib's father, Varian seemed to like flashy gestures.

Tib took his seat between the two guards. After the first few lessons, Varian only let them speak his language. When he corrected them, Varian used their language.

Tolnor, the older burly kagard, peered at Varian and asked haltingly, "How many of the ancient's weapons do your people have?"

Tib had picked up the new language quicker than the kagards. They didn't seem to care as much.

"Between all four kingdoms, each with several hundred weapons, I'd guess maybe two thousand. My people have been making them for a long time." Varian sighed. "We had *some* problems, but we've improved. The ancients had many weapons, but we only make the easiest of them."

The younger, thinner kagard, Drugan, raised his eyebrows. "How do they worf?"

Tib rolled his eyes. *It's work, not worf.* He should be thankful they weren't getting it.

Varian corrected Drugan's pronunciation, then drawled each word out to answer. "We load a pipe with powder and a ball. After lighting the powder, it explodes. The ball is propelled out of the pipe. He gestured by pulling back on a pretend bow. "Like a bow shoots an arrow but much faster." His fingers formed a circle. "It leaves a hole like this in anything you aim at."

Tib leaned forward. He'd like to see that.

Drugan furrowed his brow as his words stumbled out. "How do you make them?"

Varian smiled. "First you need the powder that creates the blast. We collect bat guano from caves, soak it for a day, harvest the crystals, then mix it together with sulfur and charcoal to make the powder. To craft the pipe and balls we melt down the hardest iron ore so it withstands the explosion, and pour it in molds. Sometimes we melt the ancient's things for the iron. If you collect the material, I can help you make one."

It shouldn't be too hard to gather those things. But his father probably wouldn't allow it. Tib didn't want Drugan and Tolnor to know how familiar he was with the ruins, so he raced to say, "There are ruins in the forest outside the city walls."

They never seemed to understand the language if spoken fast. And they probably wouldn't dare to order Tib to slow down.

Varian's eyes lit up. Tib slowed his speech. "Is it true that there are no companions on your continent?"

Varian shifted in his chair. "It's true."

"I'll be leaving soon to stay with a wolf pack and learn about my companion," Tib said.

Varian stared at him as if the idea was crazy. He thought so, too. Maybe Tib should tell his father he didn't want to be king. He could live in Harthome, the capital city around the castle, like everyone else. A merchant or a craftsman must have more fun than a king, and they didn't need a companion.

A scraping sounded as the door opened, and the kagards stationed outside the room opened it to let a servant carry in a tray of sandwiches and drinks. She was pretty with long dark hair that cascaded around an oval face. One of the new ones. What name did his mother call her? Mildred? Mary? Oh yeah, *Maydlan.* Her big brown eyes and smile stayed on Varian and never came to Tib. Was Maydlan just curious or infatuated? She was only a few years older than Tib.

Tolnor and Drugan helped themselves to sandwiches. Varian slid his hand under a sandwich. Was that a tiny piece of paper? Varian's hand circled it.

The kagards didn't seem to notice. Varian caught Tib's scrutiny. "She just wants to learn about my continent." Varian spoke rushed, too quickly for the kagards to translate. "I won't answer, but I don't want her in trouble."

"You need to talk slower," Drugan snapped.

"Why do you need a companion?" Varian paused between each word and annunciated them carefully.

Tib stacked his dishes back on the tray. "To become king, I have to pass tests, and a companion has to choose me."

"Our kings need to be chosen," Tolnor explained. "It's in the Vita."

Varian's napkin seemed bulky as he slid it back on the tray with his dishes. Did he have something hidden in it? Could it be another note?

Whether to disclose Varian's duplicity left Tib torn. He wanted Varian to reveal more about his continent and the ancients. But Varian wouldn't if he didn't trust Tib not to inform his father. Alerting the kagards wouldn't help, but Father believed Varian might be dangerous. How dangerous could notes be? Better to say nothing for now. There were other ways to learn.

As Maydlan left with the tray, Drugan or Tolnor didn't check it. Neither did the kagards at the door. Pericards wouldn't be so lenient.

"I don't understand. What happens if you're not chosen?" Varian asked.

"I'll get first chance in the choosing, but if the companions decide I'm not worthy, they could pick anyone to be king." Tib sped through the next part. "I don't even want to be king."

Varian drummed his fingers on his leg. "As a young prince, I felt burdened by the responsibilities my father thrust upon me. My interests were building my boat and studying the ancients. I didn't care about being king."

Tib blurted out. "I understand completely."

Varian smiled. "I never realized at the time what it meant to be nobody. Growing up as a prince; everyone cared about my concerns and needs."

Tib shifted in his chair. He didn't bother to quicken his speech. So what if Drugan and Tolnor knew he was frustrated? "No one cares about what I want."

"Imagine my shock, after my father sent me away, and I learned about my family and people's fate and the atrocities committed." Varian sighed. "But I no longer had the ability to do anything."

Tib could sympathize. "That would be difficult."

"No one cared any more about my concerns." Varian's lips tightened. "My friends from royal circles abandoned me."

Drugan wrinkled his forehead. "Some friends."

"They were protecting themselves and their families." Varian's shoulders lifted then fell. "I was left without friends, family, or kingdom and fleeing for my life. I learned too late how valuable it is to have the power to do something."

He put his fingers up to his forehead. "Now I'm nobody in a strange land with strange ways, with people who don't trust me, and not a friend to call on." He dropped his hand and gave Tib a piercing glance. "Be careful what you ask for."

Tib's feet dragged once his lesson with Varian ended, and he needed to go to his next. He weighed Varian's words. His reasoning couldn't be right. So what if people cared about Tib's views? And his father didn't have much power. He couldn't take a day off without people griping if their petitions weren't heard. His father sat chained to that throne.

Tib attempted one more time to pray, *Kun, if you're real, prove it. Answer my prayer. Keep me from going to stay with a wolf pack, having a companion, or being king.*

...

The lamps threw soft light on the grey blocks of the castle walls as Tib pressed his body into the concealment of a doorway and waited. The aromas from the kitchen made his stomach rumble—roasted meat, mint, maybe a berry pie—all reminded him how much he wanted dinner. His wouldn't be the only one late tonight.

Tib heard the patter of footsteps against the stone floor. Maydlan approached with her eyes cast down on the floor or the tray she carried. Locks of dark hair nestled around her face, but they didn't conceal the dreamy smile.

He stepped out. Maydlan's brown eyes widened. "Your royal highness."

"Since no one's here, you can drop the royal highness. Just call me Tibalt. My father and Captain Blake believe Varian could be dangerous. Did you realize that?"

She shook her head. "No."

"I know about your notes. You can show it to me or the Pericards."

Her lips formed an O as she sucked in a breath. Maydlan's hand shook as she removed a note from the tray and handed it to him.

"It's nothing." Tears welled up in her eyes. "Please don't tell. I could lose my job, and it's all I have."

Tibalt unfolded the scrap of paper. *I don't know why you seem to care about me, I'm just a servant. They say you're a prince on your continent. To answer your question about why I'm sad, I'm alone, too. My parents are dead. I guess you'd understand. I can tell by your eyes that you're sad, too. I hope this note brings you comfort. And I thank you for the compliment about me being pretty. You're very handsome.*

Maydlan.

It felt as if Tib intruded on an intimate conversation. He didn't really want to hurt her.

She giggled. "I think he really likes me."

What did she see in Varian? But who understood girls? Not Tib. "He's so much older than you."

"My father was older than my mother. You won't tell will you?"

"I don't want you to lose your job, but you can't let Varian know about our conversation. And you need to tell me if there's ever anything to be concerned about in his notes. Otherwise, I'll have to inform the Pericards."

"Don't do that. I'll do what you want."

"I'm sorry about your parents, Maydlan."

"Thank you, Prince Tibalt."

19

Chilly Reception

"An absence of your senses invites trouble." ~ Leeto

The day after Nero burnt Dayvee, he and Elayni again trekked across the grasslands searching for herds. Dayvee did his best to hide the pain. Jaycee and Evee flushed a few birds, and he and Elayni threw their nails. They landed true, and two fell from the sky. He reached to pick his up, slowly.

Elayni shook her head. "You can't fool me. I know you're hurting. I'm really sorry."

"I told you it's not your fault."

"Let's go to camp early."

Dayvee sighed. "It's not even noon, and I'm Calupi. I'll bear it."

She crinkled her nose. "Brando wants to meet at Cracked Rock, so we can spend time together for a change. He said to tell you he misses us."

Hmm…even if his friends planned to coddle him, Brando probably had a hard time with their separation, too. Maybe Rudee's group called Brando tiger.

You should spend time with your pack mates, Jaycee sent.

"Okay." Dayvee nodded once. "I miss him, too."

As they approached, Bruno and Cato loped up to Jaycee and Evee. Brando and Chayla came out of the tree line, arms loaded with branches. Elayni scooted away from Dayvee.

Brando grinned. "You don't have to act. I told Chayla you're not enemies. She's agreed not to tell Nero as long as he doesn't ask her directly."

"Good since Dayvee misses you," Elayni moved back over.

Brando gave Elayni his crooked smile. "Just Dayvee?"

"No. I must be crazy, but I miss you, too."

"I've missed you both." He snorted. "No one screams at a frog quite like you, Elayni."

Their companions finished nosing everyone and raced off together. "I'll gather more wood. Nero wouldn't want you doing it." Dayvee took a step toward the tree line.

"Stop!" Elayni's hand was on her hip. "We're doing the chores today, and you can pretend you did them. You've done more than your share."

"I'm not doing nothing."

"We've got the wood," Brando jiggled his arms. "You and Elayni can cut up everything for the stew."

Dayvee didn't want to argue with his friends. He gave in and went inside.

Brando and Chayla brought more wood in and built the fire. Their companions came back and bounced around each other playing.

"Evee's having fun." Elayni threw her cut vegetables in the pot. "Let's meet again, tomorrow?"

Dayvee added his pile and the meat. "Not for my sake."

Brando pushed his bottom lip up into his exaggerated pout. "We just want to spend time together."

"I don't know." Dayvee ran a hand through his hair. "If me and Elayni are back here early each day, Nero's going to catch on."

Elayni batted her eyes. "Please. One more day?"

Dayvee didn't like it, but he nodded. Hard for him to deny Elayni, much.

...

The next day, Dayvee and Elayni met Brando and Chayla back at Cracked Rock at mid-day. Dayvee and Elayni skewered chunks of meat while Brando lit the fire. Then, Brando and Chayla came over and sat by them.

"We need to leave." Brando's body rocked. "Nero could kill you."

Dayvee stopped his foot tapping and glanced at Elayni. She wouldn't meet his gaze. "You and Brando should go back to the pack and tell your father. I don't think Nero can kick you out of the pack. I'll stay, but I'll be okay. He's not going to hurt me."

"No. I'm not leaving you here." Dayvee hung the skewers off the racks so they dangled above the fire. "After we hunt a herd, we'll have to take the meat back, and I'll ask Codee what to do."

Brando shook his head at Elayni. He acted disappointed in her.

Dayvee shot Brando a hard look. *Leave her alone.*

Brando's face fell. "You may not live long enough to ask Codee."

When Nero arrived that night, he scowled at Elayni. "Why do you and Dayvee have so little to show for your day?"

He must be getting suspicious. "You said to concentrate on looking for herds," Elayni answered.

...

The third day, Dayvee sent to Jaycee, *Will you ask Bruno to tell Brando I'm not going in early today? Nero will ask, and we can't lie.*

Bruno told him, Jaycee sent.

Thanks.

They didn't find any sign of herds, but Evee and Jaycee chased a deer toward them. Dayvee and Elayni's nails struck true. Elayni pleaded with Dayvee not to pull the loaded travois, but he insisted. Injuries didn't stop Calupi, and he'd do his share. His burns opened and blood seeped through his shirt.

He'd heal.

...

The fourth day after the courage test, Dayvee hiked through the grasslands with Elayni and their companions once again to search. The sun shone brightly, and even though his breath still left little steam clouds, the chill seeped in rather than brutalized his body.

The snow was deep, but mostly frozen so not too difficult to traverse. The grass had grown so tall in places they had to crane to see over it. They came to a frozen lake. Dayvee took a branch and carefully pounded the ice. It held. The flat ice made for easy walking, so with no reason to detour around, he led them across.

As the day wore on into afternoon, the sun warmed and melted some snow. With no herd signs found, they turned around to head back to camp. Jaycee and Evee dashed off to investigate another animal scent.

Elayni's cheeks held a rosy tint. While staring, Dayvee tripped over an uneven patch of ground. He righted himself. Elayni pushed back the loose strand of hair that never seemed to stay in her braid. She chewed her bottom lip again—she must be deep in thought.

They reached the lake again, and Dayvee walked confidently out on it with Elayni at his side. They almost reached the far bank when the click of his boots treading on the ice changed to a squish, and the surface felt soft. "Go back, Elayni!"

An ear-splitting crack sounded—like lightning hitting a tree. The ground opened beneath his feet. Cold, icy water. A bolt of pain traveled up his legs, through his body, and over his head. He gasped, swallowed water, and choked. His feet propelled him up and his head broke the surface. Elayni bobbed up beside him, struggling.

The awful stabs of pain ripping through his body changed to a numb, heavy sensation. His rucksack and coat's weight dragged him down. Dayvee struggled free from his rucksack and threw it in the direction of the bank. He helped Elayni get hers off and tossed it. Then, he and Elayni fought to free themselves from their coats, and he flung them. Dayvee tried to lift himself out onto the ice, but the edge broke under the pressure.

A whine alerted Dayvee. Jaycee and Evee paced at the edge of the grass. *Jaycee, don't come out here.*

We'll come around. The wolves raced around the lake.

Dayvee kept breaking ice toward the shoreline until he found some that seemed solid. He hauled himself out of the water and spread out to distribute his weight, then reached back for Elayni. "Come on. I'll help you."

She swam over—a blue tint to her lips. Dayvee grabbed her frigid hands and pulled. The ice cracked, and the cold shocked him anew as the water enveloped him once more.

Dayvee sputtered and swam to the jagged edge again. He broke off several more pieces of ice until he found another stronger patch. Jaycee and Evee stalked the bank. It wasn't far, but Dayvee's body felt like it weighed a ton. Energy seemed impossible to draw. Elayni's teeth chattered and reminded him of their desperate plight. Dayvee couldn't give in. He barely lifted himself out on arms like jelly.

Dayvee crawled backward over his and Elayni's coat and picked them up to use. The bank rose behind him, and he placed his feet on solid ground. Jaycee and Evee greeted him. The wolves' noses and tails brushed against him in their enthusiasm and almost toppled him over.

A hurried knot tied the sleeves of the coats together, and Dayvee flung one end to Elayni. "Grab on."

She clutched it, and Dayvee strained to tow her out. His muscles trembled, and his hands barely obeyed his mental commands. Jaycee and Evee bit the coat with their teeth and backed too.

Elayni rose out of the water, but let go and sank back in. "I'm t-too c-cold. My fingers w-won't hold."

Dayvee lay down and crept back onto the ice. *Kun help us.* Jaycee whined. Dayvee sent, *I have to go. You and Evee keep this end of the coat. When I tell you to, pull.*

Dayvee slid closer. "Give me your hand."

Elayni thrust it toward him, and he clutched it with one hand and held onto the coat with the other. "Now!"

He scooted back, pulling. A crackling sound came from underneath him. Not again. His heart thudded. The fear gave him new strength, and Elayni left the water. The wolves tugged and, between them, he and Elayni reached the bank. Her face was white except for the blue cast to her lips, and Dayvee's legs barely held him. They needed a fire, but for that to happen, he must retrieve his fire kit in his rucksack on the ice.

After a few attempts, Dayvee speared his rucksack with a branch and dragged it carefully to him. *Jaycee, can you and Evee bring me anything that might burn? Twigs, more branches, sticks?*

The wolves left. His body shook, so Dayvee jumped up and down in an attempt to get warm. The exercise didn't work. The tremors in his limbs continued unceasing and Elayni appeared to be unconscious.

Dayvee grabbed her shoulders. "You have to stay with me. I'm going to get a fire going."

Her eyelids fluttered. "I'm tired. Leave me be."

"No, you have to get up." Dayvee struggled to open his wet rucksack with his cold fingers. They wouldn't work. He beat them on his side until pricks of pain shot through them. Jaycee and Evee brought him several branches and twigs. He scooped away some snow to set the kindling down.

His rucksack was treated to resist water, but it didn't take the submerging well. He shook it to get the water out, then searched among his soaked belongings to locate his fire kit with the oil-soaked fungus. Would it light? Dayvee slathered it on the twigs and grabbed his rocks, one in each hand.

His fingers didn't bend the way he told them to. He barely even felt the rocks, let alone gripped them correctly. Several attempts to strike them together failed. His clumsy hands wouldn't work right, and he dropped the stones. No energy. Eyes heavy. So sleepy. Need to rest. He fell and sprawled on his back.

Jaycee nipped him. *Get up or you and Elayni will die.*

Dayvee glanced at Elayni, her lips so blue, almost black. Evee lay next to her.

Jaycee bit him again. *Run.*

Dayvee staggered to his feet and ran in a circle, Jaycee pursued him. If he slowed, the wolf nipped him. He beat his hands against himself again and then stopped. *Jaycee, I need to light the fire.*

Dayvee picked up his fire stones and struck them. A spark flew, and this time, it landed on the twig and lit. He cupped it, blowing softly until more of the tinder lit. He fed it sticks and then a branch and another. He had a fire.

He dragged Elayni closer. He had to get her up and moving. "Come on."

She didn't move. Desperation seized him. He slapped her face—something he never thought he'd do. It didn't work. She only moaned. He couldn't bring himself to do it again. Dayvee threw another stick on the fire. They needed their coats and clothes dry. To spread the items from his rucksack near the fire took so long. Then forever to snag Elayni's rucksack. Why did he move so slowly?

He finally got her rucksack open to spread her things out next to his. He threw another branch on the fire. The shivering continued. His legs collapsed. He lay next to Elayni, Evee, and the fire—unable to make his legs work. *What am I going to do Jaycee? We need help.*

Jaycee nudged him. Dayvee peered through a haze. Maybe he dreamed? *Brando and Chayla are closest. Bruno says they're coming, but they're an hour away.* Jaycee's body pressed against his. *You need to call out. Send a message in your mind to anyone that can hear and ask for help. I'm doing the same. Focus.*

Dayvee sent, *Anyone that can help us, please come.* His brain slow and fuddled—but animals seemed to manifest. Squirrels and raccoons from nearby trees. Coyotes, foxes, rabbits and wolverines jumped and crawled through the grass. They approached to press against him, and some crawled under his clothes to lie against his skin.

Heat sank in and warmed him. He turned his head to Elayni, and a blanket of animals smothered her, too. His clothes steamed from the fire, and he managed to get his boots kicked off. Animals surrounded his feet. As blood flowed into his fingers, toes, arms and legs, sharp pricks engulfed them as if hundreds of bees stung him. His shivering finally ceased, and he could focus. He needed to get up and see to the fire and Elayni. Jaycee moved away and dragged another branch to the fire. Another wolf howled.

Jaycee came back. *Brando and Chayla are almost here.*

Dayvee clambered to a sitting position. No animals lay around him or Elayni. He must have dreamed it. But the grass swayed with movement. Were animals scurrying away as Brando and Renay came closer? Could it have been real? No of course not.

Brando and Chayla ran up to them. "What happened?"

"We fell through the ice on the lake. Can you help Elayni?"

Chayla ran to Elayni's side. "Elayni, can you hear me?"

A moan came—the most wonderful sound. She lived.

"It hurts." Her feeling must be returning.

Chayla turned to Brando. "We need to get them in dry things. Yours should fit Dayvee. Help him out of his wet clothing and put a blanket on him."

"Ours are by the fire." Dayvee pointed to them. "They might be dry."

"Just one side." Brando flipped them. "Wear mine for now."

Brando helped Dayvee, then hung Dayvee's boots and wet clothing over the fire.

Chayla wrapped Elayni in a blanket. Her clothes wouldn't fit Elayni. Chayla wrung Elayni's wet clothes out and put them near Dayvee's.

"Brando, help Dayvee come here," Chayla said. "We'll make a blanket and coat pile, and you and Dayvee crawl under with me and Elayni. Our body heat will help warm Elayni until she stops shivering."

The wolves snuggled close, lending their warmth. Dayvee kept drifting off to sleep, but Elayni's chattering teeth called him back. If anything happened to her…

Finally her teeth stopped their clicking. "I'm okay. I'm warm."

They were the sweetest four words Dayvee could hear. He put his hand up to rub his forehead. "I *am* incompetent. I'm so sorry, Elayni. I should have checked the lake again before we went back out."

"And I could have too. You didn't make me, we went together. But you risked your life to save mine." She turned her gaze to Brando and Chayla. "Thanks for coming."

"Yes. Without the companions and you, we'd be with Kun," Dayvee said.

"You'd do the same for us, and Nero couldn't stop me. But he *will* blame you and won't like that we helped." Brando rolled out from under the blankets. "We know he's wrong, senior or not, so I don't see why we need to inform him."

They all stared at Chayla. "If he doesn't ask, and the companions don't tell, I won't."

Brando went over and felt the clothing. "Fair enough. I wouldn't ask you to lie."

"Are the clothes dry?" Dayvee asked.

"They will be soon. And we're only a little over an hour from Cracked Rock. You should both eat. Food generates heat." Brando threw him his pouch. "Take my rations. They're not soggy."

Dayvee and Elayni chewed several pieces of jerky. The food did seem to warm him some. When enough of their clothing dried, he and Elayni changed. They returned Brando and Chayla's clothes and blankets.

"You two better go. We'll finish drying our things and then leave." Elayni said as she clasped their arms.

Dayvee grabbed their arms, too. "May Kun smile upon you."

As soon as their stuff dried, Elayni insisted they leave. She couldn't move quickly. They'd be late. They made it off the grasslands and to the mountain. They weren't but a few miles from camp when Elayni staggered and fell.

Dayvee rushed to her side.

Her teeth chattered. "I c-can't go on Dayvee."

He took off his gloves and felt her face. It was warm. Too warm. He could build a fire, but what if she needed medicine? Making a travois would take time. She needed help now. He scooped her up in his arms and ran as fast as he could up the rugged steep path. Dropping her wasn't an option, either.

"I'm c-cold."

"Just hang on to my neck," Dayvee pleaded. "You'll be warm, soon. We're almost there. I'm taking you."

"You c-cant," she said. "Nero will know. He'll h-hurt you."

"Shhh. Don't worry. If anything happens to you, *that will hurt me*—so hang on.

Me and Evee alerted everyone, Jaycee sent. *They know you're coming.*

Elayni slipped from consciousness. Dayvee felt the burning heat through her clothes and screamed. "Don't you leave me!"

20

Defiance

"To let a predator know you hurt is to ask them to come in for the kill." ~ Leeto

Dayvee's heart slammed against his ribs. Pair Cave was close by, but they were probably at Cracked Rock taking care of the day's bounty, and they didn't have a healer.

They're at Cracked Rock, Jaycee sent. Dayvee's lungs, arms, and legs all ached, but he dismissed his body's complaints.

He was almost there when Brando sprinted toward him. "Let me take her! Get away before Nero punishes you."

"No." Dayvee's lungs worked too hard to issue more than one word. Cracked Rock came into view. He bellowed, "Tayro!"

Tayro appeared at the cave's mouth. "Bring her in."

Dayvee carried her the last few feet into the cave. A lit fire greeted them. Tayro had a bedroll spread. "Lay her here."

Dayvee drew huge breaths as he searched Tayro's face. "Can you help her?"

"I'm going to try."

Elayni moaned. "D-don't leave me, Dayvee."

"I won't. I give you my word."

"I'm c-cold."

"I know." He pressed his hand to her arm. "Tayro's going to help you."

Evee and Jaycee pushed against Elayni on her other side. The wolves might warm her.

Tayro dug in his rucksack. "Gather some more blankets to cover her."

"Not Dayvee, Renay can assist you," Nero growled.

Dayvee hadn't even noticed Nero on the other side of the fire. Dayvee ignored him and piled his bedroll on top of Elayni. Brando covered her with his bedroll. The other trainees came forward to place their bedrolls on the mound.

"That's enough." Tayro held his hand up.

Nero's voice grated on him. "I'm speaking to you, Dayvee."

"Not now, Nero." Dayvee glanced up from where he bent over Elayni.

Nero moved around the fire and came up behind them. "Now."

Dayvee ground his teeth. "What is so important that it can't wait until I aid Elayni?"

Nero barked, "I had better get an explanation."

"We walked over a frozen lake and broke through the ice. I should have checked it again, but I didn't. So yes, it was *my* fault. Happy now?"

Nero's eyes lowered to slits. "I wouldn't say that." Dayvee'd deal with it later.

Tayro gestured to Dayvee. "Lift Elayni's shoulders and see if she'll open her mouth. She needs to swallow some medicine."

Dayvee gently slid his arms beneath Elayni and raised her. Her eyelids fluttered open. Dayvee made his voice soft and soothing. "Open your mouth."

Tayro lifted up a spoon as it opened. Dayvee pleaded. "Swallow it down." She obediently did. "Good girl." He laid her back carefully.

"I'm tired of being ignored." Anger clipped each word of Nero's. "You're not the only pack member that can help Tayro. Renay, take his place." Renay joined Dayvee at Elayni's side.

Dayvee mentally groaned and turned to face Nero. "What is it you need?"

Nesi stood beside Nero with ruff raised. Jaycee and Evee lifted their heads and low growls rumbled.

Nero crossed his arms. "There's the little matter of your punishment."

Dayvee's exasperation couldn't be hid. "Do you really think you can punish me more than I'm punishing myself?"

"I'm not a gnat to be taken so lightly." Nero's tone was biting. "It's time to face it. I'll excuse Elayni, but everyone else will see Dayvee punished."

"You want to punish me, okay, but not now. I gave Elayni my word I'd stay with her."

Spittle flew from Nero's mouth. "You'll come now."

Jaycee growls grew louder. *Evee and I wish to help our chosen and sink our teeth into Nero, but the law says we can't.*

Dayvee didn't know what Luko, the alpha wolf of the pack, would do to a wolf that broke the law, but he didn't want to find out. *Don't attack, I'll handle him.* Dayvee's jaw tightened. He'd be immovable as a mountain. "No, Nero. I'll stay, and Tayro will continue to treat Elayni. If you try to remove us, I'll hurt you."

Nero's eye twitched. "You're threatening a senior Calupi?"

Dayvee straightened and threw his shoulders back. He winced but that wouldn't stop him. He stared at those cold eyes. "Only if he tries to prevent a pack member from getting treated."

A sick chuckle came from Nero. "Are you challenging me?" Dayvee had never heard Nero laugh, and his neck pricked in warning.

"If that's what it takes to get you to leave us alone until Elayni's okay." Dayvee lifted his chin. "Yes, I'll challenge you."

"No, Dayvee, you're in no shape to fight a challenge, now." Bruno's growl rose. "I'll challenge you, Nero." Brando's tone promised threat.

The sweet taste of Elayni's kiss came unbidden to Dayvee. A reminder of what she meant to him. "It's my fight, Brando."

"I accept *your* challenge, Dayvee." Nero's lips drew back in a big smile to reveal his broken front tooth.

Why did Nero seem thrilled? Now that he accepted, he couldn't claim Dayvee didn't have enough status to challenge a senior Calupi.

"Fine." Dayvee snapped. "I'll meet you in the ring as soon as Elayni's out of danger."

"No." Nero's chin jutted out. "Challenges are decided at Wolf Mountain by the leaders and met within seven days."

"Okay, if you want to wait. But Tayro and I stay or we fight now," Dayvee declared.

Nero licked his lips. "You're not a child anymore but a Calupi who has to exhibit self-control. Strike me outside the challenge ring, and I'll have you bound and taken back to the pack for your sentence."

Dayvee turned to the side, so he could keep watch over Elayni, too. "Whatever, Nero. It would take a lot to bind me, and I'd fight tooth and nails. I suggest you back off."

"To threaten to use your weapons against me breaks pack law." Nero's eyes bulged. "Tayro, stop treating Elayni."

Tayro hesitated. He capped his medicine flask and took a step back. He wasn't going to defy a leader's order.

A warped smile spread across Nero's face. "I control Elayni's treatment, not you. After you receive your punishment, she'll be treated. The longer you stall, the longer she waits."

Dayvee's chest tightened, and he felt as if he couldn't breathe. He knew Nero was evil but this? Why would he deny Elayni treatment?

Evee's growls and Jaycee's rose louder. Nesi's tail dropped. She didn't approve either.

"Elayni needs treated now, and Dayvee should be able to stay at her side." Brando's condescension rang out.

Chayla's voice rose. "Let Elayni be treated, and Dayvee stay." The other trainees' voices melded together. "Let Elayni be treated." But Rudee stood apart and kept his normal silence.

Nero shot them a sneer. "I'll allow Tayro to treat Elayni and Dayvee to be punished at her side if he agrees to some conditions."

Dayvee's mouth went dry. "What?"

"You'll need to practice self-control, admit that you deserve punishment, and allow me to do it. Agreed?"

Dayvee searched each of the other trainees' faces—each dropped their eyes except Brando. Could he blame the others if they didn't want to do more? It surprised him they had spoken up at all. All their lives, they'd been told to follow the leaders' instructions. They didn't want to gain Nero's enmity, like Dayvee, or risk their own pack standing. But Elayni needed treatment. He would have to make the sacrifice. "Agreed."

"I have your word as Calupi?"

"Yes."

"All right, but if you break your word, Tayro will stop treating her. Give me your weapons."

Dayvee undid his weapons pouches and handed them to Nero. It didn't matter what Nero did to him—Elayni's treatment would be worth it.

"First, I'm giving you another white fringe. Then, I'll teach you not to put your pack members at harm." Nero fastened the second white fringe to Dayvee's tooth pouch. *Great.*

"Okay Tayro, treat Elayni."

Tayro undid the flask. "Dayvee, sponge Elayni's face."

"Hot." Elayni moaned.

Dayvee brushed that errant lock from her face. He'd seen her do that so many times. He washed Elayni's face and leaned close. "I'm here with you."

A corner of her mouth tugged up in a little smile. He loved that face. Her long lashes, the pert nose, the high cheeks—now flushed with fever.

"I'll give you five minutes." Nero strode to the fire and drew out a big stick with one end blackened. He started to draw a black line on the stone. "I'm making this big enough you can reach Elayni if she needs you." He finished by joining the lines to leave a large oval. He pointed his stick toward Dayvee. "You should take off your clothes and boots. You'll only need shorts."

Dayvee took a deep breath, removed his coat, and undressed to his shorts. Not this again. His back still hurt.

Nero crowed. "Take off your bandages."

Dayvee hesitated.

"Stop treating Elayni, Tayro."

Tayro was crushing dried roots and leaves in a bowl with a stone. He lifted his hands away.

In a high handed tone, Nero lectured Dayvee. "Your word shouldn't be broken. If you move from the circle, your punishment will be over—and Elayni's treatment."

"Let Tayro help her. You don't have to remind me." Dayvee undid his bandage.

Nero lifted his shoulders. "Go ahead, Tayro."

As Tayro resumed his work, Dayvee recognized the willow tips. A floral scent perfumed the air as Tayro mashed. Was it marsh marigold? Tayro added hot water and strained the tea. No matter how Tayro treated Dayvee, he did know how to help Elayni, and Dayvee didn't. "Thank you, Tayro. I'm grateful for your aid."

"You should thank me." Nero gestured to Geno, then pointed at the water bags. "Fill everyone's and bring them here."

"Choose another. My group's leaving now," Rudee said.

Nero shot Rudee a glare. "You can leave Rudee, but the other trainees should stay and teach Dayvee to protect the pack."

Rudee lowered his head. "Fine." He turned and walked away.

Nero swaggered to the cave's storage area. His voice drifted back. "Dayvee you have three minutes."

Elayni's eyes fluttered. "I heard Nero." Her weak voice could barely be made out. "He's going to punish you?"

"Nothing for you to be concerned about."

Brando's mouth tightened. "Yes, it is."

"Shhh." He didn't want Elayni worrying. Tayro motioned for Dayvee to lift Elayni's head. He did, and Tayro gave her more medicine. Dayvee murmured to her, "Swallow." Afterwards, he held her a few seconds longer just because he wanted to. She was still way too hot. "You just concentrate on getting better. Are you cold?"

"No. I'm sleepy."

"Okay, you rest." He laid her down slowly so as not to jar her.

Brando leaned over and whispered, "Here's our chance. We have to leave before he kills you."

"And who'd take care of Elayni? No Brando. He'll just make me wish I was dead." All the color drained from Brando's face.

I'm worried. Jaycee sent.

You can't interfere, Dayvee focused to send his thought back. *He's not going to kill me.*

Nero stalked toward them. He had some thin strips of leather, a wide leather strap they used to secure loads, and a thinner one with a loop in one end. "Did anyone aid you and Elayni after you fell through the ice?"

Dayvee didn't answer.

"Each trainee will pour water on Dayvee, so he can experience what Elayni did and learn better. The circle's large enough to lie down. Slink, Dayvee. Otherwise, water might splash on Elayni."

The cold stones of the cave's floor pressed against Dayvee's back as he lay down.

Brando's eyes flashed. "He fell through, too."

"I think Brando helped, so he'll go first," Nero's eyes glinted.

Brando locked his jaw. "No. This isn't right, and you just want to make us guilty like you. I won't do it."

"*Tigers* also harm a pack," declared Nero in his pompous tone. "You can either help or share the punishment."

"Don't call him that," Dayvee warned. "Please, Brando. For Elayni's sake—and mine."

Nero's broken tooth leered at Dayvee. "Didn't you act irresponsibly today?"

He couldn't lie. "Yes."

Nero smirked. "And gave your word to accept the punishment?"

Dayvee braced himself. "Yes. Do it, Brando."

Brando poured the water over him. The shock of the ice water hitting him took his breath away and left him gasping. Goosebumps rose.

Downcast faces wouldn't meet Dayvee's gaze as the trainees dumped water on him, and he convulsed. With the fifth bag of water, his body responded differently. His back arched as if hot coals hit him. There were little chunks of ice. The water had to be cold, but his body lied and told him it scalded.

Nero was the last one. He marched over to Dayvee. "If your actions had killed Elayni, the entire pack would be impacted. Evee might never get over it."

"I know. I am sorry."

"You'll be sorrier." Nero's grin split his face as he turned his water bag over on Dayvee.

Dayvee wanted to hit Nero, but he did deserve the punishment. Why hadn't he checked the ice again?

"How do you feel?" Nero paraded around Dayvee.

Dayvee's teeth chattered. "C-cold."

"Good. That's how Elayni felt." Nero smirked.

"All right, Nero, you made your point." Brando's jaw clenched. "You'll kill him."

"No I won't. Dayvee, you can get up to go to Elayni. If you get too cold, you can step out of the circle. Your punishment will be over, but Tayro will stop treating her."

"I'll s-stay." Dayvee went and sponged Elayni's face again.

"Geno refill the water bottles," Nero ordered.

More cold water? Dayvee could take it a little longer to make sure Elayni recovered. Then, he'd leave the circle.

Geno brought the bags back. Nero's voice grated. "Place them near the fire. You'll pour them over Dayvee to warm him and take care of your cold pack member. Renay fill mine. Bring it to me cold and the salt."

The pack used salt for curing meat. What did Nero want with it?

After several minutes, Brando called, "They're warm."

"Wait until I tell you."

Dayvee lost all feeling. So cold. Need to get closer to the fire. Drowsy. Should sleep.

Are you okay? Jaycee asked. The other wolves had surrounded Jaycee, confining him between their bodies. But he still growled.

Yes.

Nero snarled, "Step away from Elayni, and slink." When Dayvee lay back down, Nero ordered, "Brando, you go first."

"But the shock could kill him. When someone's really cold, you warm them gradually."

Nero shook his head. "He could die if you don't. And Tayro *will* stop treating Elayni. So if you care for your friends, you'll do it."

"Do it." Dayvee tensed. The water washed over him. Scalding hot. Burning. A moan escaped his lips. Brando checked the water, it couldn't be too hot.

Nero pointed to Geno. "Go."

Geno's forehead wrinkled as he came hesitantly to Dayvee. It wasn't the first time the trainees had received an order to do something they didn't want to. Geno would do it eventually, and Dayvee didn't need any of the trainees drawing it out longer. "Just get it over with."

The needles slammed into Dayvee as Geno turned his water over on him. Dayvee couldn't help a few groans as the others did the same. After the last trainee's water gushed over him, Dayvee's whole body prickled and tingled.

"Are you ready to plead, yet, Dayvee?" Nero asked.

Dayvee couldn't give him the satisfaction.

Nero gave him his habitual scowl. "I'll give you one more chance to walk away."

Dayvee's searching gaze finally got met from Tayro. He shook his head. Elayni's fever still raged.

Nero circled him like a buzzard. "Clasp your hands above your head."

Dayvee did, and Nero wrapped strips around his wrists, hands, and fingers. He bound them together over and over. Was he that afraid of Dayvee?

"Your pack punished you for Elayni. Now, your leader will punish you for ignoring my orders and threatening me." Nero pulled the other end of the one-inch strap through the loop and slid it over Dayvee's head and around his neck. "I don't trust your self-control. There will be no leaving the circle now until I let you."

Nero gave the strap a tug and it snugged against Dayvee's throat. His hands went to his neck, but he couldn't get his fingers underneath it the way Nero had his hands bound.

Nero growled. "Put your hands above your head."

When Dayvee didn't, Nero pulled on his end and tightened the strap more. Dayvee gasped for breath. Need air. Must breathe. Brando leapt forward, but the other trainees grabbed him and held him back.

A corner of Nero's lip turned up. "You don't want to ignore me. Listen very carefully. Get your hands up." Dayvee obeyed.

Nero stopped yanking, and the strap was loose again. Dayvee drew in deep breaths. Nero doubled the long wide thick leather strap, so it was half its length but twice as thick. He slashed it across Dayvee's chest. The shock and pain hit Dayvee, and he moaned. Another moan filled the room. It was Elayni's.

Dayvee rose to his feet and glared at Nero. "You said I could stay and help her."

"You can."

"How with my hands bound?"

"You don't need hands to comfort her. Tayro can do the rest."

"It's all right, Elayni," Dayvee called.

Nero walked around him and brought the leather strap across his legs. Elayni's eyes fluttered. Dayvee groaned. "I'm here Elayni."

She closed her eyes. Nero slashed his back again. Another quick shock of pain, that turned to a sting, then a steady burn. Dayvee turned around to face him. He'd had it. Enough. He'd hurt Nero.

Yes. Jaycee's thought came.

Dayvee moved forward, and he kicked out at Nero. Fear crossed Nero's face. Dayvee's foot hit him in the stomach. Nero made a harrumph and bent over, but he jerked frantically on the strap, tightening it on Dayvee's neck. Dayvee fell to his knees and gasped for air. Nero tightened it more. Dayvee's chest exploded. He fell forward. The stone abraded his cheek as he hit the ground. Spots swam before his eyes.

Dayvee's awareness slammed back, and he sucked in air. The strap loose against his neck, now. He drew in great ragged breaths. His throat was inflamed and on fire. How long had he been out? Enough time for Nero to bind his feet, too.

"You'll regret that kick." Nero pointed at Chayla. "What was the punishment for refusing to follow the false king's orders?"

A line creased her forehead. "Maybe it was ten lashes."

"You know better Chayla, It was twenty. Dayvee refused to follow my orders at least three times. But I'll only give you forty for disobeying me. And twenty for that kick. I might reduce it more when you beg. All trainees should watch and count aloud. I wouldn't want to lose my place and start over.

"Dayvee, you move again, except for when I tell you to, and your air will be cut off. So you should lie still." A sharp sting to his back. Then another. "That was four, and I didn't hear counting. If I don't hear everyone, I *will* start over."

The trainees' voices melded together in a chant. "Five."

Dayvee rolled into a ball to protect himself, and Nero cut his air off. Dayvee wheezed.

Nero loosened it. "Roll onto your chest, Dayvee." Must breathe. Dayvee quit trying to do anything, but what Nero said.

"Some of us are tired of being led by inept pack leaders who can fight, but aren't real smart."

Kwutee taught them that hate was wrong. It was the deceiver's tool. Dayvee had never hated anyone before. But now hate burned in him for Nero. He didn't deserve punishment for standing up to Nero when he was wrong. The need for revenge filled him. He'd get his chance at the challenge. Nero would hurt, too.

"We're tired of getting passed over. Status goes from the leaders to their children. What about the rest of us? We work hard. We're smarter and more capable."

Nero talked and hit Dayvee, ranted, and beat him again. Nero stopped at ten. "Are you ready to beg, now?"

Dayvee's body had become numb. "I won't beg you."

"I think you will. We'll find out, soon." Nero slowly poured the salt water over him, made him turn, and finished drenching him. The sting and burn was instant on his already inflamed skin. Nero took back up his strap and hit Dayvee again.

It was agony. He sobbed.

"Eleven," the trainees said.

Jaycee's growls had turned to howls and echoed in the cave. For the first time Dayvee was glad Jaycee and him didn't have a full-bond. The wolf couldn't feel his pain.

"The first thing the keeper does when a Calupi is born is slap them," Nero driveled on. "A Calupi trains in the ring to learn to endure pain. We're born in pain, live in pain, and die in pain, so we can't be weak. But I never believed you were Calupi." At twenty, Nero stopped again. "Are you ready to beg?"

Dayvee just shook his head. The scent of salt tickled his nose and stung his flesh as Nero poured more water on him.

The pain consumed Dayvee. It squeezed everything else out. *Can't take it anymore.* Blood from his burn dripped down his back. He knew Nero was right. He'd end up begging him to stop. He saw his father's face and heard his words. *"My son can't be weak."*

Dayvee bit his lip and prayed for the pain to end. His consciousness left his body. Pain free but smooshed between bodies. Hemmed in. A wolf whined.

Topay's muzzle pressed against him, and he heard her voice in his mind. *Jaycee, you cannot attack a human pack member. It's up to them to sort out their own destinies.*

Realization set in. Dayvee shared Jaycee's body. The wolf's stress and sorrow, along with his desire to help, slammed into his consciousness.

Sharing is all I can do, Jaycee sent.

Dayvee watched the other trainees from Jaycee's eyes. Their eyes were averted. They counted after they heard the sickening slap of the strap as it battered his flesh. None watched Nero beat Dayvee but one. Brando's eyes stayed glued and he flinched every time the strap landed. Now, Brando was yelling. He'd wake Elayni. Dayvee's consciousness slammed back into his body

21

Our Hearts Bleed

"No sacrifice you make will ever be too great for your pack." ~ Leeto

Geno, Renay and Chayla held Brando back. He shouldn't punch a pack member outside of the ring. But if they'd just let him go, Brando would hurt Nero. He didn't care if Nero was a pack member and training leader.

I agree, Bruno sent. *Nero's not worthy of respect. Are there any leaders you do respect?*

Why did Bruno keep asking him questions? Maybe the wolf was trying to distract Brando from what Nero was doing to Dayvee. It wasn't working. *I respect Pako and Rodnee. They both lead sub-packs. I respect Leeto's fighting skills—just not the rest. He'd never bind anyone to win.*

The strap hit Dayvee's flesh again. Brando cringed. "Forty."

He could only watch and count as the first ten lashes left Dayvee's skin pink with raised welts. The strap left broad stripes and small cuts at the edge.

Nero spoke over Dayvee's moans. "Do you want me to stop?"

"Yes." Dayvee answered groggily.

"I told you, you'd regret kicking your training leader. You have twenty more, but you should have some cool salt water for relief. Maybe you're ready to beg me to let you go?"

Brando didn't think Dayvee heard him. He didn't seem to be very aware, but, even if he heard Nero, it wouldn't matter. Dayvee'd bite his tongue off first. Stubborn fool. But if it was for Elayni or Brando, Dayvee would beg.

"Nero, I'll beg you to let Dayvee go," Brando yelled. "We need to go back to the pack for the challenge."

Nero turned his cruel beady eyes on Brando. "Too bad you didn't say, sir. Then, I might have been more willing to listen."

"I beg you to let Dayvee go, sir," Brando spit out. "We need to return to the pack, sir."

"We have seven days to meet the challenge, and I'm the senior training leader, so I'll decide when we go."

His anger wrapped tight around Brando like a cloak. "What are you trying to do, kill Dayvee, so you don't have to fight him?"

"I've told you before, your interference only hurts him." Nero smiled. "Since neither of you listened, I'll have to punish him more."

"No," Brando snapped. "If you want to punish someone for that, make it me."

"Do you want to take the last twenty lashes for him?" Nero asked.

He might not stop at twenty once he has you bound, Bruno sent.

I know. I want to say yes, but you'll feel it, too, so I won't if you don't agree.

Do it. Bruno's thought rang clear.

"I'll take them," Brando said.

A small, soft voice spoke out, Chayla's. "I'll split them with Brando. "I'll take ten."

"Split them three ways," Geno said. But they didn't drop their arms and let Brando go.

Renay's voice had a tremor. "Four ways."

Tayro looked up from Elayni. "Five ways."

"My arms are tired." Nero scowled. "Since you begged nicely, Brando, I'll reduce his punishment to forty."

No wonder Nero's arms were fatigued. He'd forced the strap down as hard as he could on Dayvee's body. The thwack had reverberated through the cave and Brando's heart.

Nero leaned over Dayvee, who lay on the ground moaning. "Look at me, Dayvee."

Dayvee opened his eyes.

"Do you still think you could punish yourself worse than I can?"

Dayvee shook his head.

"I want you to remember that, and this." Nero poured the rest of his salt water over Dayvee.

His scream ripped through the cave and crashed into Brando. Dayvee's eyes closed, and his body relaxed and went limp.

Nero let go of the strap around Dayvee's neck. "Brando, you can cut his bonds now. I'll allow him a few minutes before I expect him to start his chores."

Nero strutted like a turkey as he left them. How could he take pride in beating someone bound?

Everyone released Brando, and he ran to Dayvee to take the strap off his neck. He pulled his tooth and cut the bonds to free him. Bruno and Jaycee joined him. The other trainees wouldn't meet Brando's gaze and wandered off, except for Tayro, who still tended Elayni. They should feel guilty for holding Brando back.

Brando carefully washed the salt off Dayvee with his water bag. Nero hadn't noticed he'd used only half on Dayvee. His friend groaned. Brando couldn't choke back his tears. "I'm sorry, but I don't know how to get the salt off without bathing it."

Dayvee's eyes opened. "It's o-okay." His teeth still chattered.

"Maybe we should just leave the salt." Brando didn't want to put more water on him, even if it was warm.

Dayvee shook his head. "No, s-stings and burns."

"Okay." Brando cried as he washed his friend.

A foot rubbed against the stone floor close by. Brando looked up. Chayla had her arms full with Dayvee's clothing, boots, bandages, and a blanket.

"Thank you," Brando said.

"You're welcome. Geno and I are leaving for Pair Cave. Nero said Dayvee has fifteen minutes to start his chores."

"Tell Rudee I'll come later."

She nodded and left. Dayvee stood and staggered forward like someone who had drank too much Razi. "Need t'check on Kays."

Tayro must have understood the broken words. "Her fever broke. She's out of danger."

"Than' you."

"You need to change." Brando grabbed Dayvee's arm but regretted it when he winced. Brando helped Dayvee into dry clothes and covered him with the blanket. Even the blanket's weight made him flinch. Brando couldn't stand it. "Promise me you won't let him hurt you again."

Dayvee blinked a few times. "Not wan' him too."

Brando quieted his voice. "Then walk away. No pack is worth this. If Leeto doesn't agree we did right, and the other packs don't want us, we'll start our own."

"Wha' bou' Kays?"

Brando hoped he was right. "She'll come, too."

Dayvee shook his head. "She be high status here. Y' know what that means to her."

He must be warming. His words were getting clearer. Brando nodded. "Yes, but Nero's hurting me and Elayni. I don't think she'll want to stay. I know I don't."

Dayvee's eyes narrowed. "Thought just me. He hurt you and Kays? How? When?"

"Every time he punishes you." Brando groaned. "Thank Kun, Elayni didn't see that. It might be your body, but it's our hearts. And they're bleeding. I can't watch another person I love try to die."

"I'm not try'n to die."

"Yes, you are. You let him instead of leaving. I won't watch anymore." Brando didn't know if he could abandon Dayvee, but he couldn't take this. Why did Dayvee believe Leeto? The pack wasn't worth any sacrifice.

"You'd leave us?"

"I want you both to go with me." Brando hoped Elayni would agree. "Don't you think Nero knows, now, if he hurts Elayni it will bother you more than anything he could do to you?"

Dayvee set his teeth. "I'd kill 'im."

Since when did Dayvee want to kill someone? Nero had changed him. Brando understood his anger, but he didn't like it. He had to convince him. "You might succeed, but what would happen to you? A ring sentence? We need to leave." Brando helped Dayvee stagger to the fire.

Dayvee tried to put the stew pot on, but he fell and dropped the pot. Some spilled. A scornful humph came from Nero.

Bruno growled as Brando's anger spewed forth like an erupting volcano. "Dayvee can't even stand. I'll do his chores before I go back to Pair Cave."

"This one time I'll allow help, but he'll work too."

Nero must just want to watch Dayvee suffer. He couldn't work after Nero froze him and beat him senseless. The next time Dayvee fell, he passed out. Brando covered him, and Jaycee lay beside him. Grooves deepened around Nero's mouth as he watched.

Brando didn't care if he wasn't pleased. Nero had no hold on him. It was hard for wolves to leave their pack, and he loved Bruno, but they'd find a new place. Would even Leeto expect Dayvee to take Nero's torture? Brando didn't know, but Dayvee was doing it.

#

Dayvee woke. His body was on fire and stiff. Every movement brought him burning pain, but he struggled to get up. He needed to check on Elayni. Jaycee followed Dayvee to her side. She slept peacefully, and her cheeks weren't flushed. Evee lay beside her with her muzzle resting on Elayni's leg.

Jaycee sat and watched as Dayvee performed his exercises near her. With an occasional grimace, he managed to move slowly and awkwardly through the regimen.

A footstep warned Dayvee. Brando and Bruno ducked inside the entrance to the cave. Bruno touched noses with Jaycee. "I can't believe you're doing them this morning," Brando whispered.

Last night was foggy, but Dayvee recalled some. He stopped mid-punch. "I thought about what you said."

"Great. When you and Elayni leave this morning, circle around, and we'll meet up." Brando's brow furrowed. "I'll ask Chayla not to inform them until this evening."

Dayvee took in his friend's serious face. How long had his smile and laughter been absent? The guy who cracked everyone up. Dayvee ran a hand through his hair. Since when did Brando worry about tomorrow? He must be really unhappy. Were they treating him badly, too?

A red tinge swirled around Dayvee's vision. It took effort to keep his voice hushed. "Does Rudee get mad at you for coming here? Are they calling you names?"

"No, Rudee and me have an agreement. If I get to check on my family, I won't pull pranks on him. He just tells me not to get caught, so Nero isn't griping at him. And Geno and Chayla treat me okay, but they aren't family." Brando's blue eyes turned soft. "Ours needs to leave."

"I'm not going, but I understand if you want to." Dayvee didn't know how he'd deal with the loss of one of his best friends, but he made himself say it. "It's okay. You don't have to stay here any longer."

Brando's face fell. "But why? Is it Elayni? I'm sure she'll go with when she learns what happened last night."

Dayvee shook his head. "No, you can't tell her. Promise me."

Brando's eyebrows shot up. "But Dayvee—"

"No, she'll blame herself."

"All right," Brando mumbled. "I won't say anything, but how you going to stop Evee?"

"I can't. All I can do is ask."

Evee said she'd refrain from telling her, Jaycee sent. *But she says what her chosen wants to know, she learns.*

Tell her thanks. Evee had it right about Elayni, but maybe this time it would be different.

"Elayni's not the only reason I'm staying." Dayvee clenched his fists. "Nero agreed to my challenge last night. I will get even. And he *will* hurt."

"Nero's no fool. He knows he's not a match for you." Brando put his hand over his head. "You stand at least a head taller, and you're twice as broad." He dropped his hand.

"That doesn't mean anything. Pako is the smallest, and he can beat everyone except Andee, Leeto, and Codee."

Heart, not size, decides who wins, Jaycee sent.

"Nero's not Pako. When Nero had to prove himself to join the pack, Pako didn't take five minutes to defeat him." Brando's mouth pursed. "You'd easily win, but he's making sure you can't."

"I have seven days. I'll be able to fight by then." Dayvee punched the air again with his left fist, then his right. The punches were weak.

Brando shook his head. Elayni's eyes opened half-way. Dayvee stopped and moved closer. He mouthed to Brando, "Not a word."

Elayni smiled at them. "Hi."

Relief flooded Dayvee. He swallowed past the lump in his throat. "Hi."

"You feeling okay?" Brando asked.

"Yes," she answered. "What aren't you supposed to tell me?"

"Ask Dayvee. I've got to go before Nero wakes." Brando ducked out of the cave.

Elayni turned a raised eyebrow to Dayvee. He'd let her worry about something else. "You should know our secret's out. Nero knows we don't hate each other now."

"I'll have to convince him I've had a change of heart," she whispered.

"I doubt that's possible, but you can try."

"I dreamed he punished you last night." Her nose wrinkled.

"You had a fever and probably had a lot of crazy dreams." Dayvee changed the subject. "Are you able to get up, now? Maybe you should stay at the cave today. I'll search alone."

"I feel fine." She stood. "I'm going with you."

"We'll see what Tayro says," Dayvee said.

Tayro rose from his bedroll, and the others were stirring. Dayvee hurried to feed Jaycee and fix the gruel. When everyone finished eating, he did the dishes. It took Dayvee twice as long as normal. His body kept rebelling. Each arm he lifted, every footstep, sent the shock of pain crashing through his limbs. He suppressed the groans.

"Dayvee, would you hurry up and quit taking all day?" Elayni's voice was frigid. "I'd like to search for herds sometime."

Tayro and Renee glared at her. Why? Dayvee tried to play his part. "Last night you liked me, and now you act as if you hate me? I sure don't understand women."

Nero's face darkened. They'd never convince him.

"I was out of my mind with fever last night." Elayni's tone was biting. "Do you think you should take a person seriously when they're feverish?"

"I guess not. Tayro tell her to stay here. She's probably in no condition to go, and I'll have peace." Dayvee hoped Tayro would. He was far from certain Elayni was fine.

"I already checked her." Tayro grinned at him. "There's no fever. As long as you don't push too hard or go swimming again, she should be fine."

Why had Tayro changed? He'd never spoken to Dayvee so warmly before. Renay treated him nice this morning, too. Did they feel sorry for him because of the beating? He didn't need nor want their pity. And he'd get even with Nero.

Nero must have noticed the changing sympathies, too. He turned his scowl on Tayro for a change. "I don't think even Dayvee'd be so stupid to endanger Elayni again. I don't want to give him lessons, but someone has to teach him not to risk his pack mates."

Dayvee couldn't wait to teach Nero a lesson. Hopefully, Elayni'd think Nero was talking about the courage test.

Nero inflated his chest and rose on his toes. Just another one of his efforts to show he was superior. "This will be our last day here. If no one finds a herd, we'll travel farther into the grasslands before we head back to Wolf Mountain, so concentrate on searching for herds."

As Dayvee and Elayni left the camp with Jaycee and Evee, big fluffy snowflakes swirled through the sky. As they traveled, the snow became deeper and softer. It had drifted in places, so it completely covered the grass. Jaycee and Evee had no trouble, but Dayvee sank in.

He stopped. "I think we better put our snowshoes on."

Elayni took about half the time he did to bend over and lace snowshoes on. Her lips tightened at him. Did she suspect?

Every new move made him draw in a sharp breath to keep from crying out. Maybe she'd think his burn hurt. Once finished, he slowly stood. "Let's check the creek."

Their companions scouted in front with noses held high to pick up scents. Dayvee scanned the creek bank. No fresh tracks. There were a few trees along the creek bare of leaves and covered with snow. Dayvee stopped in front of one. "I'm going to climb this tree, so I can look around." He didn't have any intention of moving too far into the grasslands. Not with Elayni so sick last night, and it snowing. They'd search a little then head back.

Elayni peered up at the tree. "Okay, but be careful. Those branches seem slick."

Dayvee removed his rucksack, snowshoes, and gloves to give him a better grip. He jumped and grabbed the lowest branch."

Cackles that hurt. Had that jarring re-opened his lacerations? That dribble down his back couldn't be sweat. Placing his feet on the trunk, he scrambled up to the branch and maneuvered gently over it. That didn't help, either. He had to ignore the searing through his flesh. Couldn't give in.

Navigating to the next frozen branch, he continued to climb one after another until he made his way to a good vantage point. His fingers were cold and numb from grabbing frozen tree limbs, so he held on to a higher branch with one hand and put the other under his arm warming it. His face tingled while he scanned the grasslands below.

At first the view held nothing more than grass and snow moving in the wind. He cupped his eyes with his hand and located a blur running away from them—a single deer. Nothing else moved in the large grasslands.

He slid down the trunk and put his snowshoes back on, cautiously. "Just one deer fleeing, and it's not close to us."

Elayni's eyebrows lifted. "What do you want to do? Should we go after it?"

"No. It'll take too long to catch up. Besides Nero said to concentrate on searching for herds."

They continued to the next tree line. The trees became scarcer and farther apart. Most grew along the meandering creek's bank, so they followed it. At the next group of trees, Elayni insisted on climbing while he waited with Jaycee and Evee. He didn't like it, but her mouth hardened in that stubborn line. There'd be no talking her out of it.

By mid-morning they still found no herd signs. The snow had stopped falling. A few rays of sun poked out, but the heavy clouds implied the break wouldn't last. He and Elayni each killed a couple quails the wolves scared up but didn't find anything else. The animals must be staying sheltered today. At the next set of trees, it was Dayvee's turn to climb. He'd scale one more tree, then call it a day. He put his rucksack down in front of a catalpa tree.

Jaycee glided up and nudged him. *I smell something I don't recognize up there.*

Dayvee stared at the tree and made out a dark blob mostly obscured by the twigs, beans, and lower branches. Could it be another mountain lion waiting to pounce? Or a bear? No, bears should be hibernating. Some snow fell out of the tree. Branches moved.

"Watch out!" With a few frantic strides, Dayvee jumped in front of Elayni.

22

Wisdom

Wisdom is just learning to trust your instincts so you stay alive. ~ Jaycee

Something launched itself from the tree with a great flurry of wings. "Whoo!" reverberated through the air. Free of the branches, Dayvee could see—dark grey with light grey shades on its underside and a white band of feathers on the upper breast. Round orange circles around the eyes with a tuft of feathers that stood erect on both sides of the head. A great horned owl.

The owl seemed much larger than normal as it flew to the next tree and landed. Those big yellow-orange eyes sparkled with intelligence as it returned Dayvee's gaze—not fearful, but curious.

"That's a companion," Elayni said.

"Yes." Dayvee scanned the area. "If we can find its chosen, maybe we can ask if the owl's glimpsed any herds."

"Good idea. They say owls see and hear for huge distances, but I don't see anyone."

"Me either." Dayvee sighed.

I saw a buffalo herd last night, a voice sounded in Dayvee's mind.

That wasn't Jaycee. Was he going crazy? Or could it be? Dayvee twisted around to Jaycee—the wolf studied the owl. *Jaycee, did you hear that?*

Jaycee cocked his head. *Yes. It's the owl speaking.*

I'm not bonded yet. The owl's thought rippled through Dayvee's consciousness.

Dayvee's jaw dropped open. He stepped back and tripped over Elayni. His arms flew up to clutch the air, and he fell, almost knocking her over. He scrambled to his feet. The sudden movement sent more pain gushing through him. He couldn't let it distract him. Focus.

Elayni's brow furrowed. He shook his head, and she relaxed.

Dayvee peered up at the owl. *I didn't think I could speak to other companions besides my own.* Wait. Hadn't Keeno spoken to him at the choosing? But this wasn't a wolf.

The owl took a few steps on the branch he was on. *You just haven't tried.*

But that's not normal. Dayvee cupped his eyes to see the owl better through the sun's glare and moved closer.

Do you want me to stop talking to you? The owl swiveled its head away from him.

No. Dayvee drew a breath. *Please, I'd like it very much if you told me where you saw the buffalo.*

Elayni shifted. "Are you all right, Dayvee?"

Dayvee nodded once and held his hand up for her to wait. She returned the nod.

The owl ruffled its feathers and swiveled his head back toward Dayvee. *North of here, traveling south. They should be here in another day, maybe two. They're traveling where the snow isn't as deep, moving slowly and foraging.*

Dayvee craned his neck farther back. He had to squeeze his eyes to slits to keep watching the owl, even though the sun was partially covered with clouds. Thank you for your help. *Can anyone speak to any companion?*

No, and those who can aren't always understood or answered. The owl leapt from the tree into the air, spread its wings, and soared away.

The entire thing boggled Dayvee's mind. The owl's answer didn't add any clarity.

It made sense to me, Jaycee sent. *Animals don't always understand each other.*

The sun-gazing filled Dayvee's eyes with water, so he blinked a few times to clear them. *Why not?*

Our ways are too different. When a mouse or bird warns of a threat, it usually isn't to us. But Seemo talks to lots of animals to advise the king on their welfare, and I'll need to, later.

No one's going to believe that owl talked to me.

Jaycee cocked an ear. *Elayni will believe you. Just tell the others I talked to the owl and learned where the herd is. I'll tell the companions the truth, but they won't care.*

Elayni moved a step closer. "What's going on?"

"That owl spoke to me and told me where a buffalo herd is."

Elayni eyes widened. "Wow. How could it do that?"

Dayvee shifted his weight. At least she believed him. "I don't know. Maybe because he was unbonded, but no one else is going to believe me. Can we not mention it to them? Jaycee said I can tell the others he did it."

Dayvee didn't want to admit it, but it scared him. Being different in a pack wasn't good. The distinction of being the alpha's son had earned him nothing but misery.

Elayni's brow furrowed. "We've worked with unbonded animals before, and they didn't talk to us."

"I've never tried."

"Why don't you ask Jaycee about it, now?" The sharp tone warned him Elayni was perturbed. She must want her curiosity satisfied. Even upset, her blue eyes twinkled like one of the cave's stalactites when the light reflected off them. Made it hard to concentrate.

He shook away his clouded thoughts. *Jaycee, do you understand why I could talk to the owl?*

Jaycee cocked his head. *Yes.*

Why?

It is not for me to say. Ask Kwutee. He's the keeper.

"Jaycee says to ask Kwutee. Look Elayni, I don't really need more attention from Nero."

A corner of her lip turned down. "You're right. Just tell them Jaycee did it and ask Kwutee later."

"We better start back," Dayvee said. "If the herd's over a day away, it makes no sense to send for everyone now."

Jaycee nudged him. *I'll tell the companions.* The wolf sat down, pointed his muzzle to the sky, and howled. A few muted howls responded from a distance.

They'd spread the message until Jaycee was close enough to mind speak to them all. Like most wolves, Jaycee didn't like repeating things more than once. When a wolf spoke, it was best to listen.

Mostly, Jaycee communicated with his body. Even a subtle ear twist meant something, and since other wolves paid attention, they didn't need many words. At first, Dayvee felt the partial bond hindered him, but it taught him to keep one eye on Jaycee, and his skill at reading the wolves increased even more. The wolves' hidden language helped him to understand not just Jaycee, but all of them better.

They moved back toward Cracked Rock directly across the grasslands without following the meandering creek. Jaycee sniffed the air, then loped away with Evee. Some scent must have piqued their interest.

As they drew close to Cracked Rock, Dayvee and Elayni left distance between each other to keep up the pretense but found the camp deserted. Jaycee and Evee joined them. Jaycee nudged Dayvee's leg. *Bruno and Cato are close with their chosen. They're going to come here to put their bounty in the cairn.*

When the wolves came into camp, they loped up to Jaycee and Evee. The four of them trotted over to the creek.

A minute later Brando and Chayla strolled into camp. He gripped the feet of a goose with one of his gloved hands and pulled the last feathers, stuffing them in his pouches. "Bruno says you know where a herd will be tomorrow?"

Could Dayvee trust Chayla? She'd helped them when they fell through the ice and didn't tell Nero. Elayni had spent more time with her. He glanced at Elayni, who shook her head. Dayvee felt awful about deceiving Brando, and he was careful how he worded his answer.

"Jaycee was able to speak to an owl that flew over a large buffalo herd last night. They're traveling south, so they should reach us tomorrow or the next day."

Brando whistled. "Jaycee can talk to other animals?"

"Jaycee told me king's companions need to, so they can advise the king on their welfare."

"Great. Hunting buffalo should be fun." Brando threw a punch.

Dayvee recoiled, but too slowly. Brando's fist landed on his shoulder and Dayvee sucked in his breath as pain spiked through him.

"I'm sorry." Brando lifted his gloved hand, palm out. "I didn't think."

"All right, I'm tired of not knowing." Elayni put a hand on her hip. "What happened to you last night, Dayvee?"

The companions came back from the creek and rejoined them. Evee's head lifted at Elayni's tone.

The desire to protect Elayni, and his shame at what Nero did to him, only let Dayvee say, "You had a fever."

"I didn't go blind. How could I miss the red marks on your neck? Or your pain? And everyone's glares? Brando?"

"He made me promise I wouldn't tell you."

Elayni turned to Chayla. "Will you take a walk with me?"

"Yes." They moved off together with Evee and Cato trailing.

"I have to care for our meat." Brando went in the cave, and Dayvee followed him in. "You're both so stubborn." Brando cut up the goose and placed it over a rack to smoke. "She'll get it out of Chayla, so why didn't you tell her?"

"I couldn't." Dayvee sectioned his quails, and threw them on the rack.

In a few minutes, the girls and their companions came back. Chayla's eyes stayed on her feet. Her voice quaked. "Sorry, but she did deserve to know."

"How could you keep that from me?" Elayni's lip quivered, and her eyes misted. "No wonder everyone's glaring at me."

"I'm okay, and you're better now." Dayvee sighed. "Their pity won't last, and neither will their glares."

Chayla shook her head. "It's not pity, but respect. We admired your courage after the first test." Her eyes widened. "But yesterday—was for Elayni. We'd like to think someone would do that for us." Her head dropped, and she barely spoke over a whisper. "But most of us don't think we could have."

Dayvee's mouth dropped open. They respected him? "You volunteered to share my punishment, Chayla. I know you did it for Brando, but still I want to thank you and the others, too."

Chayla raised her head. "I don't know about everyone else, but I wanted to help you. It wasn't anything compared to what you took."

"It was something." Dayvee smiled at her. "And I appreciate you giving Nero the wrong answer to spare me."

Elayni's eyes flashed. "Let me see."

To show her would be to admit that he was helpless when it came to protecting her and himself from Nero. Dayvee shook his head.

"I did that to you. And you won't show me." Tears flowed down her cheeks. "I need to see."

Why did he always crumble at her tears? Dayvee fought his overwhelming desire to do anything to make her stop crying. "You didn't do it to me. Nero did, so you don't need to see."

Elayni took a step forward. "You need your burns treated. If you don't want an infection, your shirt has to come off so I can treat them."

"She's right." Brando crossed his arms. "You need to be treated."

"You can do it." Dayvee beseeched Brando. "She doesn't have to."

"Not this time," Brando mumbled. "Let Elayni."

Did Brando think Elayni'd agree to leave? Is that why he wouldn't help him? But Dayvee couldn't treat the burns adequately himself. If he wanted to fight Nero, they needed to heal. Dayvee pulled his coat off slowly, then his shirt.

He hadn't taken time to look this morning. His embarrassment rose at the puffy red raised splotches on his arms and chest in the shape of the strap. Some were turning black and blue shades. The raised patches were separated by indentations and small cuts. Anywhere there wasn't a welt his skin was pink and inflamed. He guessed his back looked the same.

Elayni undid his bandage. The fresh blood had matted the bandage to his burns. She pulled the wrapping away and reopened them. He flinched. Brando handed her the flask. She applied the cool liquid to his back, and it sank into his inflamed skin.

She wrapped the bandage around him tenderly. A new fire raced through him at the touch of her fingers. When she got to his chest and began to knot it, her hands faltered. He reached for the bandage and tied it himself. She cried great racking sobs.

His hands wrapped around her to hold her gently. She brought her arms under his and clung tightly around his shoulder blades, burying her face against the bandages.

Dayvee bit back the groan. "Stop it. You know that Nero would have found an excuse to do this to me. It wasn't your fault."

"It was," came her muffled reply. "I should have agreed to leave with you and Brando."

"I'm not going anywhere. I'll meet Nero in that challenge, and I'll make him pay for what he put us through." If Brando had asked yesterday morning, Dayvee might have gone, especially if Elayni wanted to. But after last night, no chance. He wanted revenge, and he'd have his opportunity in six days.

Dayvee couldn't help a sharp intake of his breath at the stab of pain when Elayni's arms shifted to clutch even tighter, but pleasure surged in him, too. He patted her back to comfort her, and the fear rose again—she could have died yesterday.

A chagrined look crossed Elayni's face. She dropped her arms and backed up quickly. Maybe she figured she caused him pain, but he'd willingly bear it to stay in her arms. He took a couple of deep breaths to regain control and picked back up his shirt and coat. Elayni helped him struggle back into them, and each time she touched him, his breath caught.

Jaycee brushed against him. *Others are coming.*

"Chayla and I are going back to Pair Cave," Brando said.

"I have to start chores before Nero gets here." Dayvee tried not to wince as he walked into the tree line with Jaycee following. He needed to put space between him and Elayni and he didn't need another of Nero's lessons tonight. Prickles of unease over his deception about the owl kept Dayvee on edge. He made sure he was too busy to answer questions, and hopefully, keep Nero happy.

The snow had changed to a cold rain and made it difficult to find dry wood. His condition kept him moving at a turtle's speed. Jaycee carried a branch in his teeth to him. Dayvee grabbed it. *Thanks, Jaycee.*

He finally gathered enough and carried the wood to the cave. With a strike of his stones, he lit the tinder, and soon the fire lapped at the wood. After washing the root vegetables, he diced them, and added meat chunks and seasonings for another stew.

When Elayni explained to the other trainees how Jaycee spoke to the owl, they praised his cleverness. He *was* clever to come up with a plan the others would believe.

When Nero came in, Elayni relayed the news. Nero's face didn't hold his normal scowl. Maybe he was pleased. Would he want more details about Jaycee talking to the owl?

Nesi trailed Nero to walk closer to the fire where Dayvee stirred the stew. Jaycee's hair rose, and a low growl rumbled. *Cackles, here he comes.*

23

Hunting Buffalo

To live, you must eat. To eat, you must hunt. Now or never. ~Wolf Companion saying.

Dayvee steeled himself. Nesi lowered her head as Jaycee's growl grew louder.

Nero ignored Jaycee's reaction. His steps drummed louder against the cave's stone floor as they drew closer. "Tell me about the terrain where you met the owl."

"There are a few trees along the bank of a small creek," Dayvee answered. "Nothing else but grass and snow."

Nero stopped, only an arm's length away. "Are there any hills or valleys close?"

"No, the ground's flat."

A line wrinkled Nero's forehead. "What about the creek—is it deep? Are the banks steep?"

"The bank's knee high, and the creek didn't seem to hold much. It's frozen now, but you could easily jump it."

"So what does Jaycee say about the herd's location?"

Dayvee shifted, uncomfortably. "They're north of where we were, but the owl thinks they'll be at the creek in a day or two if they continue on. That's all Jaycee knows."

Would Nero ask Nesi if his story was true? He didn't directly lie, so she might not disclose it, anyway. No one acted like they doubted Dayvee's story.

As soon as they hunted the buffalo, they'd have to take the meat home, and they'd hold the challenge. Dayvee couldn't wait.

After they finished eating, he put up the stew, cleaned the dishes, and stacked them for everyone to collect. He stowed his and Jaycee's bowls and prepared his rucksack for their morning departure.

Nero came to get his dishes. "Dayvee, these aren't clean. Wash them, again."

Dayvee couldn't find anything on them, but he didn't argue. No one mocked him, and his chores weren't sabotaged. No soggy messes lay in the fire, and Nero's complaints were the only ones. After cleaning the dishes again, he laid out his bedroll by the door away from everyone else. Jaycee lay next to him. Topay and Nesi's tails hung low, and their ears drooped.

Jaycee, Nesi, and Topay seem depressed. Will you ask them if they're all right, and if there's anything I can do to help?

Jaycee gave them a sideways glance. *They say thanks, but there's nothing you can do.*

Sometime during the night, Dayvee awakened. He shivered. Cold seeped into his body. Jaycee had left. He moved closer to the fire and away from the entrance but left plenty of room between him and the sleeping trainees. After he settled, Jaycee, Nesi and Topay padded back in the cave and returned to their Calupi. Maybe they went out to howl. He flipped over and fell back to sleep.

#

Nero's voice broke the quiet as Dayvee stoked the fire to prepare breakfast. "Let's go Calupi. We'll eat our rations cold on the trail, and Rudee's group will meet us there."

Not even light yet. Nero must be in a hurry. A thrill ran through Dayvee. He could hardly contain his excitement about hunting buffalo. A test of their abilities—beasts so massive they'd need all their wits to bring them down.

"Dayvee, stow everything else in the cache."

He quickly piled everything in the recessed area in one wall of the cave and slid the slab shut as the others grabbed their rucksacks and left the cave.

Dayvee had stuffed his belt pouch with jerky the previous night for Jaycee and him. He needed only to secure it to his belt and put his rucksack on, and he'd be ready to go.

Where was his rucksack? Not where he left it. He searched the cave. It wasn't there. Did Nero or someone else pull another trick to make him appear inept? He didn't have time to look longer, and Nero would yell at him if he slowed everyone down.

Dayvee could do without his rucksack except for food. He removed his gloves and stuffed jerky from the cache into his pockets. That should be enough to feed him and Jaycee for the day. At least his weapons hung at his side, and he had his coat and gloves. He pushed the slab closed again, and threw water over the fire to extinguish it. He and Jaycee rushed out to join the group.

Clouds rolled in to obscure the sun. Stiff winds carried a sweet, sharp zing to Dayvee's nostrils. The moisture-laden air pressed against his skin.

Snow on the way, Jaycee sent.

Dayvee shook his head. That was their weather—changing every other minute from sun to rain to snow. They didn't follow the creek but cut across the grasslands and detoured around the ruins.

Before they made it to the tree line, Rudee's group joined them. Grunts, bellows, and bleats filled the air, along with the heavy thud of hooves. Jaycee's head rose and his lope held a bounce.

The other trainees must share Dayvee and Jaycee's enthusiasm. Every one of their faces was marked with a smile as the hundreds, if not thousands, of brown, hump-backed, shaggy buffalo appeared and stretched into the far distance. Codee had said buffalo herds could span over a distance of five to six miles.

Before the Vita, Kwutee told of a time when the buffalo were very few and considered novelties. During Dayvee's lifetime, the buffalo had never been scarce, and the grasslands teemed with great herds of them. Nero led them to a position downwind, far enough away from the shaggy beasts not to alert them, and stopped.

Dayvee joined the other trainees for their instructions in the half-circle they formed around Nero and Rudee. Nero faced them, head up, and chest puffed. "Sometimes we use the terrain or deep snow to hunt buffalo. It isn't ideal here, so circle the herd like wolves and find an easy target. Look for the young, injured, or old. They'll be the easiest to separate and kill."

Nero pointed toward the buffalo. "We'll try for three. An adult female weighs one thousand pounds, a bull twice that. That's plenty of meat to carry home, along with what's already in the cairn. We'll split into three groups of three. Buffalo aren't easy to kill, and one nail strike won't do it. Rudee, choose someone from your group to go with Elayni and Dayvee."

Rudee waved to Brando. "You can join them."

Nero didn't contradict him, but his nose wrinkled. "Stay outside the herd to choose a target. Wait for my signal to throw your nails, then yell. We want them to stampede, so they don't protect each other." He licked his lips. "Remember their horns can be deadly, as well as their weight. So be careful. Good hunting."

Brando, Dayvee, Elayni, and their companions moved away from the group. Brando glanced at Dayvee. "Where's your rucksack?"

"I couldn't find it. Nero or somebody else probably thought it'd be funny to hide it and claim I was inept when I lost it."

Elayni cheeks fired. "They shouldn't take someone's rucksack."

"They'll deny it if I complain. At least my weapons weren't in it. I stuffed some jerky in my pockets."

"I'll share with you," Elayni and Brando said in unison.

Dayvee smiled. "Thanks."

They crept closer to the herd and circled around. The long grass of the grasslands hid the Calupi and their companions. Dayvee kept his eyes peeled to find a target. There. An old bull and a yearling calf on the outside of the herd. Dayvee pointed toward the calf and raised his eyebrows to signal his preference for the yearling. The tender meat of a calf tasted much better than a tough old bull's.

Good choice, Jaycee sent.

His friends nodded their agreement. A yearling might still be a challenge. Dayvee and Jaycee crouched low in the grass by his friends and waited. They couldn't see Nero or the other trainees. The signal would pass from Nero to Nesi. Dayvee watched Jaycee for a sign.

Now, Jaycee sent.

They all leapt at the calf. Elayni led, and her nails flew first. They hit the calf in the rear left stifle. Brando's landed a second later and buried in the front left hock. The calf bawled and stumbled before falling to the ground. Dayvee and his friends yelled as their companions growled.

The herd took off, their hooves beating the ground like rolls of thunder crashing. The calf's mother still heard its cry of pain. The buffalo cow turned toward them and charged the interlopers to defend her baby. Brando and Elayni had already thrown their nails at the calf. It was up to Dayvee to protect them. *Kun help me.*

Time slowed. He strained and used every muscle to throw his nails. Adrenaline provided him extra strength. His nails hit true and buried in the cow's neck. How much damage did they do? The mother didn't even slow. Over a thousand pounds headed straight toward them, with increased momentum. And she wasn't the only one. Other buffalo followed her like a river after a dam burst.

Dayvee and his friends scrambled away from the onslaught as the companions rushed in. If they made enough noise, they might be able to turn them. Dayvee screamed like his friends and waved his hands. The clamor of hundreds of buffalo feet shook the ground and drowned out their shouts. The trainees' only hope lay in getting distance between them and the buffalo to escape. Dayvee ran faster, peering over his shoulder to see. The snarling wolves slowed the mother down. The buffalo behind her swerved and turned away from the wolves.

The companions snapped at the mother's legs. She kicked out, and they dodged. Her feet barely missed them. She moved slower, now, but still gained on him and his friends. She'd squash them. Dayvee needed to run faster. He looked back again over his shoulder and into her bulged eyes. Her head shook, and the beard and mane whipped around her face. Hot steam billowed from her nostrils and touched Dayvee's neck. The musky scent of wet buffalo fur surrounded him. She lowered her head. Her horns might be short, but they looked sharp.

Her loud bellow filled his ears. *We're going to die.* A huge mountain of shaggy hair cast a shadow over him. Her legs trembled, and her knees crumpled. She toppled. Dayvee dove away from her in tandem with Brando and Elayni.

The huge thud filled the air. Mud-churned snow sprayed their backs. Dayvee's breath rushed out. They were alive. He scrambled to put a safety zone between him and the cow, then stopped and turned. Was she seriously injured? Could she be dead? His nails must have penetrated deep enough in her tough skin to do damage.

The rest of the buffalo disappeared in the distance, and the rumble receded. The cow, the calf, their companions and them were all that remained. Perspiration dripped from Dayvee's brow, so he wiped it. "Whew, we came really close to seeing Kun."

Elayni had bent, and she slid a hand in her boot as she struggled to catch her breath. "No kidding. Good throw."

Dayvee's lungs stopped burning. "Did she hurt you?"

"It's nothing. Her foot only clipped mine." She took her hand out of her boot and straightened. "At most a bruise, but I sure thought we'd die."

"You weren't the only one." Brando's hand slid away from his side. "I saw all the most memorable moments of my life flash by in a second."

Elayni rolled her eyes. "The memorable moments of your life couldn't have taken an entire second."

"I've had several, like the time I put the frog in Dayvee's towel." Brando grinned. "I'll never forget your scream as you tried to escape the terrible toad."

Elayni's hand moved to her hips. "That's what you call memorable?"

Their companions turned their attention to the calf. It had managed to get back up on wobbly legs. Bruno attacked its rear right leg, and it went back down. Jaycee's teeth ripped the calf's throat, and it lay still. Dayvee slowly approached the mother, ready to flee if he needed to. The cow's eyes appeared glazed. She made one last jerk, her eyes rolled back, and her tongue rolled out of her mouth. She was dead.

The grasslands grew quiet. A huge swath of flattened grass and churned up mud in the snow left a scar to show the path the buffalo took. No other Calupi were in sight. Each group spread out to select their buffalo. They might be a long way from the others.

His friends and the companions joined Dayvee at the dead cow's side. He said the hunter's prayer.

Elayni moved to the calf. "I'll work on the calf since Dayvee and I aren't supposed to be friends."

Dayvee and Brando went to the cow. Dayvee made a cut in the hide on the cow's underside and down her legs. Brando reached in and took out the intestines and organs. To free the meat from the hide, they sliced the ligaments and muscles with their knives, and then in one piece, Dayvee slid the hide over the cow. They both worked to cut the meat from the bone into smaller, manageable sections. Then, they collected branches from the trees by the creek and built a rack to hang the meat.

The buffalo cow and calf were too heavy for the three of them to carry until they dried the meat. Afterward, it would be bulkier but lighter—weighing only one sixth of what it did before. When they discarded the bones, the three might be able to pull the load distributed between them.

Brando stopped cutting. "Nero will probably be mad we killed two, but if you hadn't thrown your nails, we'd be trampled, and we shouldn't waste the meat."

"I know." Dayvee sliced the meat into thin strips to hang. "He'll have another reason to be angry with me."

Brando exhaled heavily. "I'll claim I killed the cow."

"What if he asks Nesi? I don't want you punished. I'll face the consequences."

Brando raised his eyebrows. "You can't take any more consequences."

Brando was right, but Dayvee didn't want to admit it. "Surely, even Nero can understand I had no choice but to defend us."

"We'll soon know. Isn't that Nero headed here? Maybe someone else wasn't as lucky, and we'll still have the number he wanted."

Dayvee looked up to see a figure with a companion in the distance.

Jaycee's ruff rose. *Nero and Nesi come.*

24

Up in Smoke

"Dawn always follows the blackest night." ~ Kwutee

Dayvee stood from cutting the meat to face Nero. What would he say and do now? Nero and Nesi stalked closer. He was angry. Dayvee took a deep breath, and prepared himself for another confrontation.

Brando rose and turned toward Nero. "Did every group get a buffalo?"

Nero stopped a few paces from them. "Yes, one apiece. Why did your group kill two? Didn't you listen to my instructions?"

Dayvee motioned to the cow. "The mother charged us. I had to try and stop her." Surely Nero could understand. He had to kill her.

Nero narrowed his eyes. "So your group chose the calf, but *you* killed the mother. Are you sure you weren't showing off, again?"

Jaycee growled, and Dayvee squared his shoulders. "I'm certain her death was an accident, but necessary."

Chills rushed through him at Nero's evil smirk. "If that's true, then figure out how to *accidentally* get the cow's meat home alone with one-third of the calf."

Dayvee's mouth gaped. He shut it. "What?"

Nero leered at him. "I won't ask others to carry more when they're already burdened because you can't follow directions. And there's no reason to waste the meat."

Dayvee's shoulders fell. "How do you expect me to carry it all?"

"Maybe you should have thought of that sooner." Nero's chin jutted out. "I'm sure you'll figure it out since you know more than the training leader. Did you even think about the quotas when you decided to hunt more?"

"Self-defense isn't deciding to hunt more." Red hues moved up Brando's neck. "The buffalo clan would understand and allow us one less next year."

Dayvee stopped swallowing his anger. "What did you want me to do, Nero, let it kill us?"

Nero ignored his question. "Brando and Elayni, load your share of the calf on a travois and join the rest of us. Dayvee, smoke your meat and bring it back to Wolf Mountain by yourself."

Dayvee's head spun. He didn't know what to do. Couldn't absorb it. Nero really expected him to carry that much home alone?

Nero glanced at Jaycee. "I don't think the prince's companion needs to stay with you since I can't trust you to train him. He can go with us, and I'll finish his training."

Dayvee's stomach churned. After everything he'd gone through, Nero would kick him out of training for killing a buffalo, and he was going to take Jaycee without his father or the pack's approval? He didn't want to separate from Jaycee.

Jaycee took a few steps toward Nero. A ridge of hair along his back stood on end to join his ruff. *No Calupi can order a companion from his chosen.*

Relief flowed through Dayvee. Whatever else happened, Nero couldn't take Jaycee.

Evee and Bruno moved stiff legged with ears pinned back to stand beside Jaycee. Nesi, Nero's companion left his side to join the other wolves. Growls erupted from the wolves and their muzzles pointed at Nero.

The color drained from Nero's face, and he retreated a step from the wolves.

Are the companions going to attack Nero? Dayvee asked Jaycee.

Nesi halted. Her head was cocked.

Jaycee still bristled, but he didn't advance more. *No. He's a pack member, but Nesi let him know he needs to follow the Vita, or he might be judged unworthy of her. We decide, not him.*

Nero shifted his feet. "I thought Jaycee would want to go. I'm certain the older companions will agree an experienced Calupi is better than an inept youth, but he'll stay for now."

Jaycee circled to Dayvee's side. Bruno followed Brando as he stomped closer to Nero. Inches separated them.

Brando's fists clenched. "Surely you don't intend to send Dayvee and Jaycee home alone with all that meat. How will he stop a predator attack, if he can even move the travois?"

"It's all right." Dayvee didn't want Brando kicked out next, so he tried to project confidence. "I'm not the first Calupi to have to drag meat home alone."

"It's not a deer. There's too much there for any one person to haul." Brando's eyes narrowed at Nero. "I'm willing to help. You should let me stay."

"I already gave you your orders." Nero licked his lips. "You need to obey them if you wish to remain Calupi." He shifted his gaze to Dayvee. "If you value your friend, you'll make sure he listens, and quickly. Snow's coming." Nero strode away.

Dayvee didn't give into his despair. He'd love to have Brando with him, but he couldn't endanger him. "Brando, please go."

Brando set his jaw. "No, I won't abandon you. You need me, and I'm not leaving. I'll take the punishment."

Not if Dayvee could prevent it. "Elayni, can you gather wood to build a travois to carry the calf's meat? Brando and I need to talk." She nodded and walked away with Evee.

Dayvee put a smile on his face. "I'll be fine. Trust me."

"I think Nero's planning something." Brando's face scrunched. "I'm worried he wanted you alone for a reason."

"I'm concerned, too, about Elayni if neither of us are there. Nero is crazy. You heard him. He wants anyone with high status to pay. If I'm gone, who's next?"

Brando drew a sharp breath. "Tayro would be, and then Elayni."

"Exactly. I don't think he'll bother Tayro. He already owns him, but I don't think he's convinced about Elayni. She'll be his next target, and she won't leave. I'll be okay. But if anything happens to her...."

Brando's forehead wrinkled, and he frowned.

"I'm sure Nero will keep the groups together to take the meat to Wolf Mountain. I need you to go with, and if he decides to torture you or her, get out if you have to carry her. Can I count on you?"

Brando clasped his forearm. "Always."

Dayvee returned the clasp. Elayni rejoined them, and Dayvee helped them fasten the calf's hide to the poles, with their share of its meat on top. She touched Dayvee's shoulder. "Keep your fire large, and do your best to keep predators away. Don't travel alone. When we get home, we'll explain and send help. I know the pack will see it differently than Nero."

Dayvee slumped as despair threatened to overwhelm him. *Be strong.* He straightened. "How can you be certain?"

"I know you're in the right. You had to kill the buffalo. This will be an affront to the entire pack, and Nero will be judged harshly."

It would probably take two days for them to make Wolf Mountain carrying loads, and two back. In four days he should have help, but he hated to wait. He could build a cairn and stash the meat. In winter, the meat would keep if animals couldn't get it. Then, Jaycee and he could go home and come back with help. But Nero ordered him to bring the meat and was trying to kick Dayvee out for not following his orders.

Dayvee wanted to tell Elayni he'd move the meat as far as he could each day, even if he had to make several trips. But her focus was on Evee. One glance at Brando told Dayvee he spoke to Bruno.

After a few seconds, Elayni took her rucksack off and dug around in it. "Evee says the companions have a plan to help you."

Yes we do, Jaycee sent.

Elayni took out her blanket and a water bag. "Brando and I can share our things since we'll be together."

Brando plucked his fire kit and a hide from his rucksack.

"I don't want to short you." Dayvee shuffled his feet, embarrassed to be so needy.

Brando pulled the flask with the burn medicine from his pocket. "Don't be too prideful to take help you need. You'd share with us."

"Listen to Brando." Elayni's arms shoved her things toward him. "When we get back to camp, we'll find your rucksack and have extra."

"Okay, thanks. I'll take the water bag, the fire kit, and the burn medicine, but I won't need the rest. I have the buffalo hide if I get cold. Besides, I have plenty to carry." He took their supplies and clasped arms with them. "May Kun smile on you."

"And on you." Elayni's lip trembled. She and Brando dragged their travois away. Evee and Bruno trotted out in front of them.

Jaycee nudged him. *Cut some of the buffalo hide into short and long strips.* As Dayvee followed Jaycee's instructions, two wolves appeared in the distance.

Cato and Graydee are coming, Jaycee sent. *To lose the meat a pack needs doesn't protect it, so all the trainees' companions will help me guard.*

Relief surged through Dayvee as they greeted the new arrivals. *Jaycee, ask them if they could eat.*

They said only a little since they shared in their chosen's kills earlier.

Dayvee piled meat on the ground for each. His meat piles weren't even dented. He fixed his own dinner. The buffalo tasted too much like cinders of despair. Same as his dreams. Nothing remained. Nero wouldn't let him finish training. He wouldn't be part of the pack. Wouldn't be able to life-mate with Elayni. He choked a few bites down past the lump in his throat.

Keeping busy might hold his despair in check. But why fight it? What was the point? Unable to focus or really care, he doggedly continued. He rotated the meat on the racks around the fire so it cured, then staked out the hide. He rubbed the buffalo's brains on it to waterproof and treat it.

When he finished, Jaycee brushed against him. *You'll need to make two travois. One will need to be very large.*

Dayvee searched the creek bank and found several branches and a dead tree. He dragged it all to his camp.

With four of the longest, thickest branches he made poles for the two travois. Then, he braided prairie grasses with the skinnier branches to form a mat and wove them over and under the poles. He fed the fire more branches as the meat smoked.

Did the trainees miss their companions? Did they know where they were?

The companions didn't have to share where they went with anyone. Nero couldn't stop them from helping Dayvee. In a few hours, two new companions came, and Cato and Graydee left. The companions continued to come and go through the night. Each pair stayed a few hours.

Gratitude overwhelmed Dayvee. Jaycee's safety was his biggest concern, but the wolf was determined to protect the meat and Dayvee.

The grass in front lay smashed from the buffalo's passage, but it wasn't an ideal place to camp. Predators could sneak up on either side or from behind them to get close. Every sound sent his hands flying to his weapons pouches. If anything happened to Jaycee because of Nero, Dayvee's anger wouldn't be contained.

Just thinking about it set his teeth grinding. Dayvee glanced at the wolf's grey head and it hit him—his bond with Jaycee was as strong as the bonds of love that tied him to Brando and Elayni. To separate from the wolf might be extremely difficult.

The fire and his anger at Nero kept Dayvee warm. The buffalo hide would make a good bedroll, but he needed to stay alert in case of trouble. He sat with his back to the fire to keep his night vision keen and searched for movement in the waist high grass behind their campsite. Jaycee and the other wolves trotted circuits around the camp, then returned to sprawl by Dayvee. As he worked to finish the travois and smoke the meat, a constant prayer passed his lips. *Kun, help me.*

Time passed slowly. No stars were visible. The overcast sky matched his mood.

Would he be able to continue training Jaycee? Would they let him stay? He clasped his hands over his face and looked out between splayed fingers. A sob threatened to escape. He choked it back. His mind churned the day's events over and over in an endless, repetitive cycle. What could he have done differently? Preventing the cow from harming his friends and their companions wasn't something he'd change.

He mulled over the last two weeks and recalled every time Nero became angry. Perhaps if he made better decisions, he'd have avoided this. He doubted that Elayni guessed right about the pack's reaction. Nero was senior.

A few hours from sunrise, he heard it—a rustling sound in the grass. It came from several different directions. Jaycee jumped to his feet, and Dayvee gained his as the rustling grew louder. Bruno, Topay and Jaycee moved stiff-legged toward the sound. Soft growls rumbled in the wolves' throats. Dayvee pulled his tooth and nails from his pouches.

A series of short, fast, high-pitched whoops from several points filled the air. Could it be? Oh no.

25

The Scent of Trouble

Attack each day like it's your last. ~ Wolf Companion saying.

The wolves stood with Dayvee, facing the blackness. He strained to see. With the amount of grass moving, several must be approaching.

Jaycee, ask Bruno and Topay to let them come to us. There're too many to chase off.

Shorter ears than wolves emerged above the grass, then the black muzzles, the wide face. The black spots on the brown bodies weren't completely obscured by foliage. Dayvee shuddered. Hyenas. *Kun, help us.*

Another one of the animals Kwutee said hadn't always flourished here. The ancients kept a few caged along with many other types of animals. The wars freed them all. Some, like hyenas and buffalo, adapted and thrived while others died out or migrated south.

The fire's heat licked at Dayvee's back as the hyenas approached from different angles. At least thirty. His stomach contorted in a spasm. The hyenas held their heads and hindquarters high, and their tails were straight or curved over their back. They planned to attack. His heart sped up. The sudden impulse to run came over him.

Should we flee, Jaycee?

No, they're hyenas. Even if we gave them the meat, they'd chase us. We have to teach them better.

Dayvee took a deep breath and steeled himself.

Jaycee bumped him. *The one in front—she's their leader. I'll convince her she's on a fool's mission. Try to keep the others from aiding her.*

Dayvee had to admire Jaycee's courage and his belief that he could make their leader think a few wolves and one human were too much for them to handle.

Jaycee snarled and charged. With his teeth snapping, he slammed into the hyena leader. She rolled but regained her feet. Her ears folded back as she bared her teeth. The two animals circled. She made a loud, rattling, low-pitched growl. More hyenas—at least ten—formed a ring around Jaycee and her.

Dayvee grabbed his nails. The weapon slid into his slick palm. He tightened his grip, brought his arm back, snapped his wrist to fling his hand forward, and released. His nails flew and bit deep into the middle of a hyena's front leg. "Yes."

The injured hyena howled a cackle and shifted its weight off that leg. Blood poured from around the nails. Dayvee took a branch from the fire and moved toward it.

The other hyenas stepped slowly back from his burning stick. A hole in the uneven ground caught Dayvee's foot. He tilted sideways and fought for his balance. The hyenas drew in closer, ready to pounce if he fell. The weight of his tooth in his hand reassured him. Dayvee gained his balance. He flung his tooth out overhand, and the blade sunk into the wounded hyena's throat. Only the hilt protruded. The hyena dropped to the ground. He thrust his branch at another hyena too close. It whipped back a step.

Three more paces brought him to the dead hyena. Dayvee pulled his weapons from its body. The odor assaulted him, and he choked. It filled his eyes with water—like lye soap as it cooked or burned bugs. The smell of trouble. Hyena scent.

A thud sounded. Jaycee had crashed into their leader again. Their teeth clunked together as they met amidst a flurry of growls. Dayvee looked over his shoulder at Bruno and Topay. The other twenty or so hyenas moved in and attempted to circle around the wolves to get to the meat racks. Dayvee caught a fast movement from the corner of his eye. A hyena rushed Jaycee's back. Dayvee flipped out his arm to throw his tooth. It sank into the side of the hyena's head.

Blood painted the hyena's face. Its tongue lolled out, and it went down. Other hyenas closed to tear the flesh from the two Dayvee killed. The distraction let Dayvee advance a few more steps toward Jaycee, thrusting his torch ahead of him. He needed to keep the other hyenas at bay and off Jaycee.

The wolf still struggled, locked in battle with their leader. There were so many. Jaycee's teeth latched onto their leader's neck, but they couldn't seem to penetrate the tough hyena skin. Jaycee let go and bit her face below her ear. The face ripped, and the skin hung open.

Two hyenas ran at Jaycee. One from each side. Dayvee sucked in his breath. He snapped his wrist, and his nails buried into the hyena's neck on Jaycee's left. It fell over. The other hyena clamped its teeth on Jaycee's front, right leg. Jaycee turned his head to confront it. The hyena leader moved to re-engage with the wolf.

Dayvee hurried to retrieve his weapons. Hyena bites could crush bones. He glanced toward Topay and Bruno. Several hyenas ringed them—closing in. There'd be no help from them. *We're doomed.*

The night air filled with new snarls and growls. The stiff wind parted the grass to reveal forms racing through it. Dayvee could just barely make out the shapes in the dark. Nesi led all the rest of the trainees' wolf companions toward them.

The hyenas' woops turned to low pitched grunts. They broke off and stopped their attack, lowering their hindquarters to flee. Their short tails with the little tassels faded from sight. The rattles of their low-pitched staccato grunts receded in the distance.

Dayvee's held breath rushed out as relief flooded through him. They'd live. He filled his lungs with new air, so crisp and sweet. The six other wolves from the sub-pack joined Jaycee. The hyenas must not realize how they outnumbered them—hopefully, they didn't figure it out.

Dayvee ran to Jaycee's side. The prince's companion held up a foot and limped. Dayvee examined the leg with his still burning branch. Nothing appeared broken, and the bite marks didn't tear much flesh or extend very deeply. Dayvee retrieved his weapons from the carcasses. Would the hyenas come back?

Jaycee, was anyone else hurt?

Not seriously. Topay's ear's torn. Bruno has a few slashes.

Dayvee picked out the other wolves in the dark. "Thank you for coming to our aid."

If they responded, it was too dark for him to tell. With his torch he examined Topay and Bruno's bites. None looked serious. He washed the bites of all three wolves.

Jaycee, tell Bruno and Topay to let Tayro know they were bit by hyenas. He may want to put medicine on them to keep infection out. You could go to Tayro and have him treat you, too.

No, mine doesn't require treatment. I'll stay here with you.

Graydee, Cato, and Jaycee stayed with Dayvee. The night's darkness swallowed the other wolves as they moved away.

Thanks be to Kun, they'd escaped serious harm, but Jaycee limped. Dayvee didn't know how he'd carry the meat, and if Jaycee couldn't walk home, they'd have to stay and wait for help. But if the others left, and the hyenas came back, Dayvee couldn't fight them all alone. There was so much to worry about. The anxiety threatened to overwhelm him as he sat by the fire again.

The snow flurries stopped, and the sun rose, partially shining through the mist and grey clouds. His thoughts circled as he searched for a ray of hope to brighten and lift the despair that enfolded him. Jaycee joined him. He didn't seem to favor his injury now.

He rested his head on Dayvee's leg. *You aren't alone. Don't worry. I am here.*

Dayvee stood and turned the meat again. Less than an inch of snow accumulated, so the fire stayed lit and the meat cured. Something crinkled. Grass stalks bowed. Something raced through it. He swallowed hard. What now?

26

Wolf Power

"When a wolf pack hunts together, they don't work as a group but as one." ~ Codee

Dayvee recognized the ears above the grass—wolves.

Pack mates, Jaycee sent.

A heavy breath escaped Dayvee. All nine wolf companions from the training sub-pack surrounded Dayvee to greet him. His loneliness and desperation lightened. For the first time since Brando and Elayni left, his stomach stopped churning, and the knot between his shoulder blades eased.

Jaycee brushed against him. *Load the small travois with meat.* Dayvee heaped meat on top until Jaycee placed his paw on it. *That's enough. Put the rest of the meat on the other travois, and tie both loads down.*

When Dayvee finished, he eyed the larger load. The meat was mounded almost as high as his waist, the length and width of the travois. How could they ever move it? He covered the larger pile with the hide and tied both loads down with the strips.

Dayvee looked at the travois, at the leather strips in his hand, then at the wolves. Comprehension finally sunk in. They must plan to drag the large load along the ground behind them.

Jaycee, isn't this too much for you?

Not when we all pull it together. The hardest will be the start. If you want to help, you can push as we pull to get the load to move.

Dayvee smoothed his cowlick. *Should you do this with your injury?*

I'm fine. It doesn't even hurt now.

As Jaycee directed him, Dayvee slipped the leather strips around each wolf's chest and their middle. He attached the long lines to each band carefully so as not to tangle them.

His fingers chilled, he hurried to form the slip knots to tie the lines to the travois. *I've never heard of this before.*

Jaycee pulled a little on his harness as if to test it. *We don't usually do it or share that we can since it limits our fighting abilities, but it was necessary today. If anything threatens us, you'll need to release the lines quickly.*

Dayvee scanned his temporary camp to make sure his fire was out, and he'd left nothing behind. *Will we rejoin the others then?*

No. Jaycee's hair rose. *We go to Wolf Mountain as Nero ordered. The companions have told their Calupi they're doing something important, and they'll rejoin them this evening.*

Dayvee sent, *They'll be missed.*

They are many, and you are one. We'll keep pace with the trainees to be in range if they run into trouble. Pack members will be here to help you as soon as they can make it.

Dayvee scratched his head. *How does the pack know I need help?*

Nesi. After she and Nero left here yesterday, she ran back to where she could reach Luko and Keeno and asked them to send help. Calupi are on their way.

You've thought of everything.

Jaycee leaned against Dayvee. *I told you not to worry, and you weren't alone. Your difficulties are mine.*

I don't know what I'd've done without you. Dayvee faced all the companions now attached to the travois. Remembering the owl, he tried to address them all in his mind. *Thank you all for everything you did to aid me last night and today. I'm very grateful.*

The wolves' flicked their ears. He narrowed his focus. *Jaycee, will you tell me if you need a rest, or if your injury bothers you again?*

Yes. Jaycee cocked his head. *You should know your father is coming.*

Dayvee sucked in his breath. *Do you know if he's angry at me?*

Jaycee glanced over his shoulder at Nesi. *Luko said Leeto needs to have fun, but she doesn't know if you're the one who raised his hackles. We better go, or we won't keep pace with the others, and it will snow soon.*

The confirmation of Leeto's anger sent Dayvee's heart galloping. And Luko thought he'd challenge someone—Leeto's fun. He took a deep breath and pushed his worry aside to concentrate on the task at hand. The sky had changed from ash gray to a dark charcoal. He didn't have Jaycee's nose, but it smelled like snow to him, crisp and damp.

He grabbed the load to push. The wolves leapt together to pull against their harnesses. Their feet scrabbled in the snow. Dayvee leaned in to shove harder. His muscles tightened as he strained with all his strength. Heat ran through his biceps from the pressure, but the travois inched forward and then picked up speed. Dayvee let go. The wolves flew over the tundra. Dayvee grabbed the poles to the other travois and rushed to join them.

Around lunchtime, Kun opened the clouds. Large flakes of snow rained from the sky like white flower petals. The pristine flakes danced through the air, but on the ground the white powder soon piled up. The accumulation made it harder for Dayvee to pull the travois since the load sank through the powder instead of gliding over the top.

He trudged along and tried to avoid the deepest drifts. To make it easier to drag the travois after him, he stomped down a path. Maybe it would stop falling soon. It was getting much harder to see. This could end up as one of those few snowstorms that required Calupi to hole up and wait for it to pass.

When they come to a creek, Jaycee stopped. *The other wolves are in mind range of their trainees. They and Nero stopped to rest and eat. Release the lines so we can.*

If Nero would let Dayvee, he'd like to be with Brando and Elayni. But the man was impossible. Dayvee untied the wolves and grabbed some meat to heap in front of each wolf. They gulped down their food as quickly as a squirrel could grab a nut. Dayvee still had no appetite, but chewed a few pieces anyway and went to the creek.

He swept aside the lighter snow under the trees by the bank and found the thin ice. A heavy rock broke it. The wolves came to the creek and lapped up water. He cupped his hands to get a drink.

It's time, Jaycee sent.

Dayvee reconnected the wolves' lines, gave their load another push, picked up his travois poles, and followed.

The amount of falling snow had lessened, but it changed to sleeting rain. Ice hitting the snow made a crackle sound like little pebbles falling down a mountain. The footing grew slick, and the water-ice mix sent chills through him as it soaked his clothing. The icy sheen gave the trees and ground a sparkle like the stalactites in the caves.

Dayvee couldn't help but admire the crystals. If only it weren't so treacherous. The crust it formed on top of the snow crunched under his feet. It crinkled underneath the wolves' lighter paws and screeched under the travois. Dayvee struggled. He skidded several times but managed somehow to keep from falling. They made good progress in spite of it.

The snow and freezing rain stopped as they moved higher, but the temperature also dropped. Even with the exercise the cold sank in. He clamped his teeth together to keep them from chattering. Visions of sitting around a warm fire tormented him. He couldn't feel his toes anymore, but stubbornness wouldn't let him admit it. It was mid-afternoon when Jaycee stopped at a wooded area. Dayvee hurried to his side.

Jaycee tilted his head. *Nero and the others are at Cracked Rock, now, and your father's not far. They pushed hard. Release the other companions, so they can return to their Calupi while you and I wait for your father.*

Dayvee disconnected the lines, slipped the harnesses over their heads, and thanked each for their help. *Should I feed them?*

Jaycee took several bounds as if happy to be free. He shook the snow and ice from his coat. *No, they wish to return to their Calupi and will eat with them.* The other wolves loped off. *You can tell those coming that we helped you, but they don't need the details.*

Dayvee gathered wood and started a fire. He rubbed his hands over it and soaked up the warmth. As the blood rushed into his toes, they tingled and then hurt. His legs grew too hot, so he took a step back. Threading large chunks of buffalo through a branch, he hung it over the fire to cook. He prepared enough meat to feed his father and the Calupi with him.

Dayvee's nerves were stretched to breaking. He paced around the fire between tasks. What would Leeto do? Dayvee had two white fringes, and he'd been kicked out of training. Leeto might renounce Dayvee, even challenge him. The pack's welfare would be his first concern, and Nero was senior.

Jaycee came up to him. *Take apart the harnesses you made for the companions and put the strips back on the travois. Then, you should make two more travois and distribute the meat between them as you will have human help now.*

Dayvee searched through the yellow pines, red cedar, redbud, and a few white oak trees in the copse to find wood to make the travois and set to work. When the meat finished cooking, he and Jaycee ate, but Dayvee barely touched his. Not long afterward, Jaycee nudged him. *Your father and five other pack members are here.*

Facing Leeto after he learned of Dayvee's failings would be the hardest thing he'd ever done to date, but it couldn't be prevented. Dayvee stood and took a deep breath. His heart hammered against his ribs.

27

Leeto's Wrath

"An alpha cannot show any weakness to those who circle below."
~ Leeto

Dayvee lifted his head and straightened his shoulders. A new stab of pain hit him, but he ignored it. He wanted Leeto to see a Calupi, not a scared, weak child.

Six wolves ran with tails wagging fluidly into his makeshift camp. They surrounded and pushed against him to smell and nuzzle him.

A step back secured Dayvee's balance. "It's good to see you, too." He almost smiled but stopped when Leeto entered the camp with his men.

The wolves parted as Leeto strode through them. Dayvee's stomach clenched, and he searched Leeto's face for the anger Jaycee had warned of. Leeto's face revealed nothing, but Luko's legs were stiff. His father stopped a foot away, and his arm rushed toward Dayvee.

Dayvee flinched, but Leeto clasped his forearm. "I'm glad you're all right."

Water pooled in Dayvee's eyes. He opened his eyes wider in an attempt to stop his tears of relief from spilling. "Thanks."

Codee enfolded his arms around Dayvee in a big hug. "We were worried about you."

A small moan escaped Dayvee's lips.

Codee dropped his arms, and his eyes softened. "Are you okay?"

"I'm fine."

Codee raised one eyebrow. "Huh."

The other men took Dayvee's forearm. He returned the clasp eagerly. "Thank you for coming."

After he greeted them all, Dayvee turned back to his father. "Are you hungry? I have food ready." Would Leeto notice how quickly Dayvee fulfilled the Calupi rule to offer hospitality when meeting?

An approving nod provided his answer. "We could eat."

Dayvee's nerves calmed a little. After they fed their companions, the men gathered around the fire to enjoy the meal. Leeto and Codee sat on each side of Dayvee.

The furrows in Leeto's face made Dayvee's foot tap the ground again. He pulled his leg under him to stop it.

Codee winked at him. "Look at all the meat. That's good hunting, Dayvee."

Nods, grunts of agreement, and smiles came from the other Calupi. The praise warmed Dayvee—a nice change.

His father finally turned to him. "Our companions have been talking to Jaycee since we've been close enough, and they relayed most of what went on. I want you to stand, take off your shirt, and show us."

Heat flushed Dayvee's face. He rose, faced his father, and removed his coat. Like a little kid, he undid his shirt lacing and drew it off for his father's inspection.

The Calupi's eyes widened and lips tightened. Some of the marks on his chest and arms had faded, but he still sported a multitude of raised red welts, bruises in shades of yellow to black, and crimson cut-lines from the strap. It looked like someone used his body as a strange wall mural.

Leeto's voice was gruff. "Undo the bandaging."

Dayvee unwrapped it. He had to pull where it stuck to his back from the fresh blood. He started, but it came free.

His father's face was frozen. "Turn around."

The men behind him gasped. Codee snarled. "That hyena."

Dayvee glanced over his shoulder. He couldn't read the steel mask, but Leeto's jaw clenched, and Luko's hair bristled.

Leeto rose, examined Dayvee's back, handed him his shirt, then sat again. "Why did you let him do it?"

Dayvee turned around and hung his head. How to answer? He needed time to think. Since his shirt and bandages were removed, he better treat his back. He grabbed the flask from his pocket and lifted it to his shoulder to pour the burn medicine down his back.

Codee stood. "Give me that." He splashed some liquid on the burn. It stung, but Dayvee was used to it. Codee took his bandage and wrapped it around him.

A sharp intake of breath escaped Dayvee when he pulled his shoulder back to slide his arm in his shirt. He struggled into his coat and raised his head. "Nero said if I refused his courage test, I'd have to leave the pack and Jaycee. He claimed you'd be an unfit alpha if you raised a coward. Brando offered to go with me, but I couldn't let him throw his future away."

His father raised an eyebrow but didn't say anything.

"Maybe, I should have challenged him then, but even after I did, nothing changed. I wasn't going to let him force me from the pack. So I made the sacrifice. I took his test and passed it."

Leeto crossed his arms, but he remained silent.

What? Didn't Leeto agree? Dayvee had to know. "What could I have done differently?"

Leeto's eyes flashed. Anger radiated each word he punched into the air. "Nero never had the power to force you from the pack or hurt me without a challenge. And we both know he couldn't win. I'm the only one who can exile a pack member, and I wouldn't without everyone's agreement." Leeto uncrossed his arms. "What could you have done differently? So many things. I don't even know where to begin. What makes a leader?"

"The respect of the others, their abilities, their experience."

Leeto shook his head. "Respect and ability yes. Not experience. I took the leadership of the pack at eighteen, so what's the other one?"

Dayvee scratched his head. "Their status?"

"Yes. So what do you think I'd have done before I submitted to Nero?" Leeto spit out Nero's name.

What would Leeto have done? Dayvee let out a heavy breath. "You'd probably challenge his right to lead the sub-pack and taken control yourself—but as a trainee—I didn't have the knowledge to train the others."

"I didn't have Miko's knowledge when I assumed the pack's leadership. I consulted with him and others and drew on their experiences, but a leader doesn't have to hold it to access it. Who decides a sub-pack leader?"

The memory rose of Leeto's congratulation to Rodnee on being selected. "The Calupi they lead."

"Yes, even if I assign a sub-pack leader, Calupi have the right to change it. Would the other trainees have supported you? I don't know, but I'd have tried. You were assigned the first room, weren't you?"

"But Nero said it was Jaycee's status, not mine, and since I only trained Jaycee, I had none."

"And you let that pass like so many other things. What did Jaycee tell you about your status?"

"That it was only as low as I let Nero convince me it was."

"Correct. The highest status pup wouldn't select someone unworthy of their status, no matter what amount of time you shared together."

I chose the best, Jaycee sent.

"So to answer your question, you could have informed us what he said before you left, sent a companion with a message, came back to tell us, challenged him, or taken the leadership of the sub-pack. No one expected you to submit to torture at a training leader's whim, senior or not." Leeto ground his teeth, then shouted, "He only had the power to hurt you because you gave it to him!"

Dayvee's mouth dropped open. How stupid was he? He couldn't look at his father or anyone else. His head sunk, he turned and fled. He couldn't let them see him cry.

Inside the stand of trees, he buried his face against the trunk of a White Oak and punched the tree with his fist. Tiny fissures of blood appeared along the ridge of his knuckles. A nose pressed against his pant leg. He turned his head. Through a mist of tears he quickly wiped away, he saw Jaycee. *How could I have let him?*

Nero convinced you he was alpha and could do anything he wanted.

Codee found him and put a hand on his shoulder. "Your father still has more questions, Dayvee. You need to come back."

He looked at his uncle and choked out. "I can't face him."

"Yes, you can. You faced worse. Leeto isn't mad at you, maybe disappointed, but his wrath is with Nero. Since he's not here, his anger spilled out a little."

"I let him down."

"You just made a mistake. Something tells me Nero couldn't have passed his own test."

"That's what Brando told him." Dayvee wiped his face with his sleeve and tried to compose himself.

"Come on."

Dayvee followed Codee to their seats near his father. Codee turned his gaze back on Dayvee. "So when was it that you challenged Nero?"

"Four days ago." Dayvee's foot tapped. "Don't you think I should have?"

Codee's forehead furrowed. "Of course. You needed to, but you're in no shape to fight. He's right about one thing—the challenge needs to be met within seven days."

Leeto's face was frozen again. "That's when you threatened to use your weapons on him?"

Dayvee's foot tapped furiously. "Yes, but Elayni needed treatment and I gave her my word. I handed them over when Nero agreed I could stay, and Tayro could treat Elayni if I'd submit to his punishment."

Codee looked at Leeto then turned to Dayvee. "I would have submitted under those circumstances. But even the threat of using a weapon against another pack member is serious."

"I know, but I wasn't thinking clearly." Dayvee's head sunk to his chest. "I just wanted to make sure Elayni was treated."

"You didn't use them, and he was wrong, too." Codee's mouth tightened. "We don't torture Calupi or refuse a pack member treatment. There're three days left for you to heal enough to fight. Unhurt, he's no match for you."

Dayvee shrugged. "I'll survive."

A glint sparked in Codee's eye. "You'll do more than that—like win and teach him to give up bullying." He grinned at Dayvee. "I'd love to give him that lesson, but he'd never agree to a stand in."

"Oh, don't worry." Dayvee clenched his fists. "I plan on letting him experience what he put me and my friends through."

"I need to know what you thought during yesterday's hunt." Leeto's stern tone commanded his attention. "Would you have been able to get away without throwing your nails?"

Dayvee shifted. They had to understand. "I didn't think so. The cow's breath touched my neck when she collapsed, and I'm not sorry. When she died, we escaped."

A corner of Leeto's mouth turned up, a smile almost broke through his mask. "It must have been a good throw. It usually takes more than one nail to down a buffalo."

Was Leeto proud? Dayvee held his breath.

Leeto nodded once. "You were right to kill the buffalo. And we're here to help. Can you travel further?"

Dayvee let his breath out. Leeto had agreed and would back Dayvee. *Thank you, Kun, for answering my prayers.*

"Yes." Dayvee threw snow on the fire, packed the food and his few things on his travois, and grabbed the handles. "I'm ready."

Leeto came over and placed his hand on one pole. "You won't have to carry a load. There are enough of us to handle it now."

Dayvee didn't relinquish his hold. "But I want to do my share."

"Okay, we'll take turns. I'll take the first." Dayvee let go of the travois. "You can join me and finish explaining."

Luko nudged Jaycee as they walked beside his father. Luko's pride in Jaycee was plain. Dayvee took note of the Calupi with his father. They were the ones Leeto trusted the most. Coincidence? He didn't think so.

"I did make mistakes," Dayvee admitted. "But I don't believe running from the bear's cave was wrong. We escaped harm. And others made mistakes, but Nero punished only me."

His uncle strode directly behind them and pulled another travois. "Every trainee makes mistakes. Sometimes they're the best teacher. If you escaped from a bear unharmed, you did the right thing. I'd have backed for the exit."

Dayvee looked over his shoulder at Codee. "He gave me two white fringes, can Nero give them out?"

"Any sub-pack leader can give a Calupi a white fringe if they admit they intentionally chose an action knowing full well that it would risk pack mates. Like Nero when he left his guard post." Codee's face furrowed. "Did you know ahead your actions would risk a pack mate before deciding on that course?"

"No, I forgot about backtracking to check if anything trailed me before going to camp, and I thought the ice was safe, but I should have checked it again before letting Elayni walk on it."

"Yours were mistakes, and I'm sure you learned better." Codee frowned. "He shouldn't have given them to you. Take them off and hand them to me."

Dayvee smiled. Those were something he'd be glad to be rid of. He untied the fringes and gave them to Codee. "I knew you'd give me good advice. I was going to ask you what to do when we got back, but Nero kicked me out first."

Leeto grimaced, but it quickly disappeared.

They were nearing where Dayvee killed the elk. He scoured the area. None grazed today.

Dayvee's heavy rock of worry he carried lightened with the weight shared. He and Jaycee weren't alone anymore. His fog of despair lifted. He extended his stride and struggled to keep up. "Why are we racing back?"

"Nero's remarks and actions shout a challenge for alpha," Leeto answered. "But, he'd need to win a challenge against me. He can't, so I need to learn if others are involved."

Leeto treated Dayvee's question as if it came from an adult. A first.

Dayvee rubbed his forehead. "I hope there aren't others. But Nero *did* say low-status Calupi were tired of being passed over."

"If there are others, they'll soon learn what a mistake they made." Leeto's crisp retort revealed his fury.

Was Dayvee dreaming? His father would side with him against a senior Calupi?

Codee cleared his throat. "You should tell him the rest."

His father gave a wry look to Codee. "Nesi informed us that Nero and another trainee plotted to kill you. He needed you alone and without help."

Jaycee pressed against him. *But I wouldn't leave.*

Dayvee sucked in his breath. Nero *really* wanted to kill him...someone else did too? Brando warned him, but he never believed it. A visible shudder from cold chills coursed through his body.

Nero hadn't succeeded. So would Leeto and the pack consider it breaking pack law? Probably not. "I don't know what to do. How can I keep training Jaycee if he wants to kill me?"

Red splotches spread up Leeto's neck. "You'll meet him in the challenge ring. Afterwards, you won't have to worry about working with him again."

Did Leeto think if Dayvee won that Nero'd leave him alone? Maybe Leeto planned to send Nero or Dayvee away. He'd seen pack members separated before, sent on long trade trips, or to other packs when they lost a challenge and couldn't accept it.

His attempt to hold his voice steady failed. It quaked. "Who else wants to kill me, and how did they plan to do it?"

"I don't have all the details," Leeto answered. "Nero's blocking Nesi, so she can't tell us much, but when I find out everything, I'll let you know."

Dayvee slid across a slick patch. "How do you block?"

Leeto maneuvered the travois around a fallen tree. "The keepers know how but don't share it unless it's needed. They think it hinders us, and so do I. Kwutee taught Nero so he could block out his first companion's thoughts when the rabies stole his mind."

"Most of us wouldn't want to do it," Codee explained. "As long as the block is in place, our companions can't speak to us, but we'd still feel their emotions. Their alarm might make our heart pound, but we couldn't ask the cause until we took the block away. Wasted time could kill us and them."

The game trail they traveled twisted to make sharp turns down a rugged slope. Sure didn't seem like the game always picked the easiest path to tread as Codee had claimed. Dayvee stumbled repeatedly. His feet kept finding an abundance of slippery rocks beneath the small snow cover to slide on. The lack of sleep, his pain, the steep descent, and the cold temperature made their trek almost unbearable.

Dayvee gritted his teeth and forced his feet forward. Jaycee's normal glide had lost its spring. *Are you okay, Jaycee?*

Yes, but those hyenas better not steal our rest tonight. I won't be as pleasant.

As the sun sank deep on the horizon, his father stopped to camp where the creek rose from the ground near a thick grove of trees. A few brown leaves still clung to branches. The telltale twin line of a spear-shaped leaf caught Dayvee's interest. Butternut trees stood among the familiar yellow pines, hickory, oaks, and cedars.

The skies partially cleared to offer them a brilliant red sunset with a great fire-ball in the center that descended until they could no longer see it. Dayvee's tired brain still registered awe at Kun's ability to paint such brilliant colors across His canvas.

Dayvee ran his fingers across his eyelids to pull the grit out—they wanted to close. His vision blurred and thoughts circled. Out of energy, and unable to garner more, Dayvee's feet dragged. In the growing darkness, he decided a search for butternuts would be futile although he loved them in Milay's nut crisps. Maybe in the morning he could find some. Instead, he helped gather enough wood for the fire.

Dayvee stumbled on the rocky ground again and dropped his load. The branches scattered. He rushed to pick them up and stack them on the pile. His body might not be working very well, but he wouldn't admit it to Leeto. "I can take a turn on guard duty."

"We'll handle guard duty tonight." Leeto motioned with his thumb. "Get some sleep."

Dayvee found some dry leaves under a rock overhang to cushion the ground. Between the folded buffalo hide, he soon warmed. Jaycee curled up beside him. Dayvee let his eyes close and forgot his troubles.

28

Mixed Messages

"An urgent message is almost always a harbinger of bad news. We let good wait." ~ Chayla

Codee rubbed his finger to his lip. "I'll take second watch."

Leeto acknowledged the signal by widening his eyes slightly. Codee couldn't speak to Leeto in front of the others. The alpha and his second needed to show a united front. Leeto would call Codee before first watch ended.

Dayvee thrashed in his sleep and woke Codee with screams. Nero must haunt Dayvee's dreams, and his nephew's tortured body invaded Codee's own. He closed his eyes again, but before sleep reclaimed him, a hand brushed his arm. Leeto stood over him. He rose. Wilee sprang up, too, and they followed Leeto and Luko away from the sleeping Calupi to the other side of the fire's flickering flames.

Codee asked softly, "What will you do about Nero?"

"Dayvee challenged him. We'll see if he can hold his head up and be strong. I'll wait for my fun."

Whether Nero won his challenge against Dayvee or not, he'd still face Leeto's wrath. But why make Dayvee go first in his current shape? Codee flung the stick into the flames.

"I won't stop it." Leeto crossed his arms. "The pack wouldn't like it. He issued a challenge, and Nero accepted. He has to meet it."

A noise came from the tree line. Wilee and Luko's heads went up. Leeto and Codee drew their nails in tandem. The hoot of an owl broke the silence.

Wilee's muzzle swiveled as he sniffed the air. *I smell no threats. Just the owl and a few small animals.*

Leeto's shoulders relaxed as he secured his weapon. "Dayvee knew what Nero did was wrong. So why let him? Was he that afraid of him?"

Codee slid his nails back in his pouch. "Dayvee didn't fear Nero, but maybe he should have." Couldn't his brother see? "Nero couldn't hold Dayvee's feet in that circle, you did."

Leeto's eyes narrowed. "What are you talking about?"

"Dayvee would do just about anything to gain your love. Didn't you teach him that to be Calupi requires sacrifice? Then, you told him he was wrong and shredded his confidence."

Leeto drew a deep breath. "Dayvee doesn't think I love him?"

"No, and if you do, you should tell him."

"If he thinks he needs to strive to gain my love, I won't change it."

"You make it too easy for our pack members to hate their leaders." Codee sighed. "Sometimes, I have to remind myself I love you to keep from resenting what you do to us. Will you make Dayvee hate us, too?"

"Sometimes, I hate myself." Leeto frowned. "But how many are alive now from father's pack?"

"Four."

"That isn't very many. We lose a lot less now, and if they hate us, so be it. That goes for Dayvee, too. I can live with the hate easier than I can live with more deaths or the pack destroyed."

"Most everyone loved our father."

"Yes, but did it help him? If we'd been more skilled, we could have saved him from that bear. I won't be that weak again, and that's why I pushed myself, you, and Dayvee." Leeto clenched his jaw. "No more coddling. That ends, now."

Codee gaped as the shock hit him. "Pushed me? I thought Miko must have been angry at you. Were you the one responsible for how everyone acted after our father died?"

Leeto didn't confirm or deny it. "How did you respond?"

"I challenged." A low growl rumbled from Wilee as the heat poured into Codee. "No." His voice shook with the effort to contain his rage. "Did you tell Nero to make Dayvee's training harder when you know he hates you, and your son would make a great target?"

Luko's hackles rose as Leeto drew himself up. "I don't have to answer to you unless you become alpha—are you challenging me?"

"No, but I'm working awful hard to remind myself again that I love you."

Leeto's brow furrowed. "Remind yourself too, that you're my second, and whatever you suspect I did, it won't get back to Dayvee."

"Right now I'd be happy to forget I'm your second, but I won't."

Leeto gave him a sharp glance. "I'm *proud* of the role I played in making us unbeatable. And I will tell you this much, Nero *never* had permission to torture Dayvee or call my leadership into question." Leeto bit the words out. "He'll pay for both. And Dayvee should have come to me."

Leeto's actions drove Dayvee away from both him and Codee. "Dayvee is a fine Calupi who made a few mistakes. You've made judgment errors, and so have I."

Leeto harrumphed. "You think you'd have been a better father, but I don't believe it."

"Maybe, but we won't know, and I'll keep silent about it."

"I'm sorry. I shouldn't have brought their deaths up, but I'm doing the right thing. He needs to be stronger than us."

"Because of what Kwutee said?"

"No, I'd drive *my* son to succeed, no matter what his future holds whether you like it or not."

Codee ran a hand through his hair. "What if he gives up trying?"

"Then, Nero will beat him, and he'll learn what a terrible choice he made."

Codee stalked to the other side of the fire with Wilee. His job was to support Leeto whether he agreed with him or not. And Leeto usually got it right. He knew how to motivate Calupi, and they did live longer, now. But did he have to crush Dayvee and expect Codee to support it? Nothing could be more difficult since he loved them both.

Dayvee woke to a hand shaking his shoulder. Leeto bent over him with a grave face. "Time to get up."

His mind was foggy. Where was he? It all came rushing back, and why Leeto looked upset. His leadership could be in peril. Only a few scattered stars lit the black sky. Dayvee grabbed some meat to give to Jaycee and ate his breakfast in darkness. As soon as the grey of early dawn appeared on the sky's periphery, they were on their way.

Dayvee and Jaycee plowed down the steep mountainous terrain trailing Leeto and Luko. Shades of red, purple, blue, and pink set the sky ablaze. Finally, the golden-yellow sun rose to illuminate their day. Dayvee's breath puffed out in steam clouds. The chill seeped through his boots and gloves to nip at his toes and fingers. The sun shone bright and the exercise warmed him.

Leeto stopped. "Luko says a messenger from the pack is coming, and he'll lead us to meet him." The alpha wolf turned to the East, and they followed.

Why had they turned east? Wolf Mountain lay south, and why a messenger rather than sending the message through the companions? Did they need to deliver something? Maybe the message was confidential. After several minutes of brisk walking, a Calupi emerged from the trees running toward them.

Chancee. His companion loped beside him. "Greetings, Leeto. I have an urgent message for you from Jonesee."

Brando's father. A chill ran through Dayvee. Something must be wrong.

Gloom etched Chancee's face. "There's been an outbreak of rabies among the wild packs. Jonesee needs Calupi to come quickly to help contain it."

Rabies. The faces turned white around Dayvee. If the rabies outbreak spread, their own companions might be affected.

Only one answer to foaming sickness, Jaycee's ears flattened.

Dayvee's stomach flipped. The diseased wolves would need to be tracked down and killed before they carried it further. A grisly job.

His face devoid of color, Leeto's mouth set in a grim line. "Where is he?"

Chancee shifted his weight and studied his feet. "He's in Shadow Canyon keeping an eye on some rabid wolves."

"That's closer to us than Wolf Mountain. We'll need to go." Leeto waved a hand toward Dayvee. "Dayvee has a challenge to meet day after tomorrow, and if he fails to show, Nero will win by default."

"He can go with me," Chancee said. "I came in person so I could help. We'll carry some of the meat and build a cairn to stash the rest until we can come back for it."

Leeto put his hand on Dayvee's shoulder, "I hope you understand, but if it's bad, it will take us all. Shadow Canyon's a day's trek. Your challenge has to start before sunset, day after tomorrow. Wait as long as you can. I'll do my best to get back in time, but if I don't, I know you can defeat Nero."

"I understand. I'll be okay." Dayvee wanted Leeto and Codee with him, but he would never ask them to ignore rabid wolves.

When Nero's companion had rabies, they had to shut him away to die alone. The disease took his mind long before death, and his howls couldn't be shut out. Dayvee shuddered. They'd do whatever they could to prevent another outbreak.

Leeto grabbed a piece of their rare parchment paper out of his rucksack and wrote a message on it. He rolled the parchment, wrapped a twine around it, and knotted it. "I'm sending this with you to Kwutee. Make sure he gets it." He met Dayvee's eyes. "Kwutee will make sure my instructions are followed, and your challenge is taken seriously no matter what Nero claims."

Chancee reached for the note. "You better hurry. He'll be fine."

Leeto released the paper, and Dayvee clasped his father's forearm. "May Kun go with you."

"And with you." Leeto returned the arm clasp, then he and those with him hurried away at a lope.

When the group disappeared, Chancee pointed to the east. "There's a small cave just a little farther. We'll each pull a travois and then come back for the others. Our companions can guard the meat here."

I'll keep it safe, Jaycee sent.

Dayvee grabbed the travois he and Leeto had carried. After a five-minute walk, the cave entrance appeared. Not big, just a small jagged hole in a cliff face.

"Go ahead and take yours in." Chancee pointed to the hole. "I'm going to grab some of these rocks to build a cairn."

Dayvee put down his poles. "I better make a torch first."

"Are you going exploring? It's a small cave. We've used it to store in before. Just take the meat inside and go until you meet the far wall to leave room for me and the other travois. It's not more than ten steps. Then come out."

"Are you sure there're no bears?"

"Yes. I just came from here."

The terror Dayvee experienced when he was young and lost in the nowhere tunnels at home haunted him, but he wasn't a child anymore. He could take ten steps in a dark cave. Sweat from his hands made the poles slick when he lifted them and strode forward. A small pile of rocks lay scattered in front of the opening.

The jagged hole looked like a mouth with teeth. A prickle went up Dayvee's spine. Would it swallow him? He pushed down his fear and ducked through the small entrance.

The light didn't penetrate far, just enough to discern a high ceiling. He straightened to stand erect and pulled the travois through the tight hole. His gaze met a pitch-black void. Dayvee gulped and forced himself to tromp forward blindly. After his count reached ten steps, he put down the travois and extended his arms out, but his fingers groped only air—no wall.

A slight creaking, then a rumble sounded. It grew louder. One thud, then another. A huge crash thundered and reverberated all around him. Falling rock. A cave in!

29

Dark Times

"When things look their bleakest, pray. You won't face the hardship alone." ~ Kwutee

Dayvee fell to the floor and covered his head. Anyone who lived in caves like they did dreaded the sound of falling rock.

Dust spewed, filling the air, and he choked. He turned his head to look behind him. Nothing. He waited for the dust to clear. No light met his eyes. The deep black void overtook him, and his heart slammed inside his chest.

Jagged rocks scraped against his skin as he crawled back. A pile of rubble met him where the doorway had been.

"Chancee!" No response. Dayvee gulped for air like a fish out of water. "Chancee!

"I hear you." A muffled voice came from beyond the rocks.

"Can you dig me out?" Dayvee screamed.

"You don't have to shout. I can hear you fine." Chancee replied in a calm voice.

Maybe Chancee wasn't upset. He wasn't the one trapped.

"Okay." Dayvee lowered his voice to an almost normal decibel.

"It would take forever to move this many rocks by myself. I'll have to go to the pack for help."

"Can you hurry?" Dayvee couldn't keep the desperation from his voice.

"Yes. My companion asked Jaycee to stay here with you."

Goosebumps rose on Dayvee's skin. "The meat will draw predators. Jaycee can't guard it on his own."

"I don't expect him to. We'll have to let the predators have it if you want aid in a hurry. Jaycee can stay hidden. Don't try to get out until we return so we can drive off the predators."

How long would that take? Dayvee's body pulsed as if toads leaped around inside. "Okay."

"I'm leaving, now." Chancee's voice came through the rocks.

Trapped and alone in the dark, Dayvee's desperation rose. His mind spun like a whirlwind. Was there still a little light? A finger brought right in front of his eye couldn't be seen. He gasped for breath. His lungs hurt.

I'm here. Jaycee's quiet whisper in Dayvee's mind helped him fight his fear down.

He grasped at reason. If he quit taking such huge breaths, he might stop choking on the dust. He steadied his breathing and focused on Jaycee. *How far are we away from the pack?*

Maybe three hours. Too far for me to mind reach, but Chancee won't have to go the entire way before he can reach them.

I know. Thanks, Jaycee.

Dayvee had to get free. No matter what he told Chancee. His skin crawled at his entrapment. He couldn't wait. How deep were the rocks? He needed light. His pocket held Brando's fire kit, but rock didn't burn.

The buffalo's hide would. The travois rested somewhere in front of him. But without light, he might get lost. Did he want the black void to swallow him? On shaky legs, Dayvee placed one foot carefully in front of the other, counting steps until he bumped the travois and found the shaggy hide. With one hand grasping his knife hilt, he carefully cut thin strips to twist and braid around each other. The fashioned torch wasn't stiff enough for him to hold, but it should cast light.

He opened Brando's fire kit and groped. His fingers recognized the greasy, sticky glob of the oil-soaked fungus, and then clutched at the fire stones—their smooth and pitted areas—a few sharp edges. One stone slipped from Dayvee's grasp and fell to the floor.

Dayvee's heart missed a beat. He patted the floor around him, and his hand brushed the knobby bark of the travois pole. How stupid could he be? The poles were formed from branches, and he could use *them* to make better torches. He continued groping and felt rocks everywhere. Without light, how would he tell which one? Those in reach, he snatched wildly and formed a pile near him. He'd try them all. As he grabbed another, his fingers recognized the harsh grooves.

He struck it. A spark flew. Even the tiny light made his eyes blink. He placed the fire stones carefully aside and fashioned a better torch, cutting one end from the travois pole. When he finished, he used the stones again. A small flame erupted. He had light. Tears welled up in his eyes. He blew on the torch until the end burned cheerfully.

The flame might last long enough to get out. Even by torchlight, the rock pile at the entrance appeared thick. His heart sank as he pulled the travois over to the entrance. Next, he fashioned a rope from lines he'd used to attach the companions to the travois. After securing one end to a boulder at the entrance, he tied the other around his wrist. If the torch went out, he'd find his way back.

He held his torch higher, took a deep breath to calm his rattled nerves, and pressed forward. The room was huge. Brown lines and cracks checkered the stones that formed its walls and ceiling. The light bounced off openings with tunnels beyond. This wasn't a small cave.

Could Chancee have forgotten? Calupi memories were too good to forget a cave they supposedly used all the time. Chancee had deceived him.

I suspected Chancee was deceitful more than once, but I wasn't certain, or I'd have warned you, Jaycee sent.

Cackles. So what else had Chancee lied about? Was he working with Nero? Maybe Chancee wasn't coming back. Maybe Dayvee would be trapped forever. His chest tightened as he gasped for air again. Stop it.

He had to calm down and think. How could he get out of this? Could there be another exit? Dayvee checked the four openings for a breeze by holding his torch in front of each. The flame didn't flicker. The feather hanging from his pouch didn't move. He inspected the corridors for the smallest light in the darkness. Nothing. They could be like the nowhere tunnels back home. Was there anything else in the room he could use? It held nothing but rock and the travois.

I don't think Chancee is coming back. Dayvee sent to Jaycee. *I'm going to try and find a way out.*

I'll see if I can find an entrance out here.

You shouldn't go too near the meat. I'll search inside.

Should I go for help?

Please. But just go to where you can reach Elayni or Brando's companion and ask them to come. Be wary of other Calupi. If Nero's willing to kill me, he might harm the messenger.

Dayvee went back to the entrance and dumped the travois, letting the load slide to the floor. Using every bit of wood and most of his hide, he made nine short torches. Normally, they soaked torches in oil and let them freeze or dry overnight so they'd last for an hour, but Dayvee had no oil. His torches might burn twenty to thirty minutes before they lapped at his fingers.

To be safe, he should turn around before he burned through his fourth torch and mark his route. Now, which of the four tunnels seemed the most promising? The flame on the one he held wouldn't last much longer. He filled his pockets with meat and grabbed his water bag. The slight slosh reminded him how little was in it. If only he'd filled it before he was trapped. He found a few rocks that left a black mark when pressed against stone.

In its final throes, his torch flickered. The fire's last remnant lit Dayvee's second torch. He examined each tunnel by going down a few feet to smell it. If an entrance lay anywhere near, he should be able to see some graying in the blackness or smell the crisp scent of fresh air. Only the damp smell of soil greeted him.

If Calupi had explored this cave, they should have marked it. He found none. A brush of the walls with his hand determined one might be a little chillier than the others. Fresh air would be colder this time of year. He ventured farther and came to a branching. Would his flame flicker? No. He trudged on and marked the rock. The cave reminded him of home. The tunnel would switch between twisted corridors to be squeezed through to large expansive chambers.

A few times the passage ended, so he retraced his steps to a branching and changed his wall marks. As Dayvee explored, his light bounced off stalactites and stalagmites reaching from floor to ceiling. He passed formations that showed Kun's awesome ability to carve works of art from rock. The torch didn't illuminate much, and he didn't have time to examine them closely, but Kun's work was impressive.

Two torches died. Should he use all his light on one tunnel? He couldn't turn back before he found a way out. Was the air not so damp, maybe fresher? The branchings were many. After three torches died, he took a sip of his water. Hadn't he come too far? Didn't the air smell less of soil here? Just a little farther and he'd go back.

His dim light barely exposed the missing floor. Dayvee flailed his arms to stop himself short. His foot sent a rock tumbling over the hole's side and he swayed on the edge, fighting for his balance. The remote clatter of the stone landing told him to fall meant his death.

#

When Codee and the others located Jonesee, the Calupi informed them no rabies threat existed—it must have been a ruse by Chancee. "He must be blocking his companion from his mind, too," Codee told Leeto. In a hurry to contain an outbreak of rabies, they'd missed the signs.

But why send them to Jonesee? All that trouble to keep them from Wolf Mountain for Dayvee's challenge. That might be terrible for Dayvee, but what could Chancee hope to gain? He must know Leeto and Codee would confront them on their return.

Jonesee joined them on their race back to Wolf Mountain. They stopped to fill their water bags at a creek. Cackles broke the quiet—announcing hyenas—nearby. A chill ran up Codee's spine. The wolves answered with growls as they came into view. More hyenas in their territory? Had the clan council approved the hyena's move north?

Wilee's ears pinned back. *Focus on the fight.*

Right. The hyena pack had to be seventy strong. Seventy against seven men and seven wolves.

Codee's stomach twisted as he followed Leeto's instructions. "Fall back to the cliff! Keep your tooth in hand and don't use nails. They'll cut us off from retrieving them."

They formed the fight ring and backed together, Calupi and wolf. They didn't have long to wait before the hyenas slammed into their circle. They stopped moving as predator met predator. A growl rose in Codee's throat as his knife found a hyena's throat. The beast dropped. Teeth clunked together as Wilee locked in a struggle with another.

Codee reached over and stabbed his knife into the back of the hyena's neck fighting with Wilee. His tooth sunk deep. He pulled it out fast to meet the next springing at him. The hyena's teeth gripped his shoulder as Codee buried his knife in its ribcage. Pain radiated up his arm. Codee's knife found its heart. The bite pressure released, and Codee flung the dead hyena off him. Blood soaked his shirt.

That hurt, Wilee sent.

The hyenas circled.

Leeto's voice rose over the cackles. "Keep pressing. We need that cliff."

#

An acrid tang covered the sweet scent of pine and fresh snow. Brando's nose wrinkled as he trudged down the trail, pulling the weight of the loaded travois. He picked out the print of an animal, partially filled with snow—five small nail marks above a round toe print and a conical pad. It confirmed his suspicion. The scent that still lingered belonged to a skunk—like the one at the front of their line—Nero. Brando placed his feet carefully since the familiar trail had turned slick.

Elayni walked at his side. "Isn't it my turn again?"

"No, I can finish up." Brando slid and caught himself. "We're not more than an hour from Wolf Mountain." Would Leeto and Dayvee be there?

I'm in mind-reach of Wolf Mountain, Bruno sent. *Neither Leeto nor Dayvee have come home or can be contacted. When we left them, Luko wasn't that far away, and they were keeping pace with us.*

"I'm worried about Dayvee." Elayni's bottom lip was in her mouth.

A group of five Calupi strode toward them. It was Rodnee's sub-pack. Rodnee had helped Brando more than once, like Miko, and if pity motivated Rodnee at least he hadn't made it obvious.

Nero held his hand up to signal a stop. "Pack members are here to greet and aid us in carrying our loads."

Elayni would be safe now. Nero couldn't hurt her with other pack members there.

As Nero greeted Rodnee and the other Calupi, Brando whispered to her, "I'm going back to find Dayvee. They may be in trouble."

Her nose wrinkled. "I'll go with you."

"That will end the pretense."

She put a hand on her hip. "I don't care."

Brando raised his voice. "Elayni and I are returning to see if Dayvee needs more help. Would any of you be willing to carry this travois to the pack?"

Nero snorted. "I don't think you'll be needed."

Brando squared his shoulders. "We're going."

"I'll carry it for you," Rodnee said. "Leeto won't mind more aid." Rodnee outranked Nero by far.

"I really appreciate it." Brando gave him a smile.

"You two are only trainees," Petee said. "I'll go with you."

"Thanks," Elayni replied. Brando gave him a nod. Petee was a good tracker, and surely Nero wouldn't argue with Rodnee's backing and an adult Calupi offering to go.

"All right, Elayni and Brando." Nero shrugged. "Go help your inept friend."

"You'll find out in the ring he's not inept." Brando snapped.

Nero's mouth turned down. "I don't think so."

"I'll catch up." Rodnee waved Nero on.

Rodnee and Petee came over to them as Nero left with the others. Rodnee chuckled. "So Dayvee challenged Nero. Is the pup trying to fill his father's prints and give us another year of challenges?"

"Nero really deserved it." Elayni's tone was indignant.

"Yes, he did." Brando lifted his chin. "I challenged Nero, first, but he wouldn't take mine."

Rodnee laughed. "I see you can still growl."

"Not just growl."

"I know. Walk with me, Brando." Rodnee led him a little several feet away and spoke in a hushed tone. "I'm considering a few changes." He glanced back at Petee. "When you finish training, I could use you in my sub-pack."

Hmmm. Petee might not like taking Rodnee's orders after losing the sub-pack leadership. It was really important for a sub-pack to be cohesive. They spent too much time together to be at each other's throats. "You know what they call me."

"Yes, and I know they're wrong. I've seen how you treat those who treat you right. I'll treat you right and make sure the others do, too."

"If Leeto lets us decide, my first choice would be with Dayvee and Elayni, but you'd be my second."

"Leeto rarely puts new Calupi together. He divides them between experienced Calupi, usually with family. I suspect he'll assign Dayvee to help Codee and Elayni to Franko. I'll let him know, if he divides you, I want you." Rodnee grasped Brando's arm.

"Thanks." Brando returned the clasp, and followed Rodnee back to Elayni and Petee. He didn't want to separate from Dayvee and Elayni, but if he didn't have a choice, he'd rather be with Rodnee than any other beta.

Rodnee grabbed the travois poles. "I'll miss seeing that challenge. We'd have left for rotation this morning, but I wanted to talk to Leeto." He glanced at Petee. "You'll have to catch up. Let Leeto know hyenas have been spotted in our territory."

Elayni gasped. "What if hyenas found Dayvee?"

Brando tried to reassure her. "He'll be fine. They probably don't want indigestion." She gave him a weak smile.

"May Kun go with you." Rodnee pulled the travois away.

"And with you." Brando, Elayni, and Petee replied.

Since they carried no loads, Petee led them at a trot. They had packed the snow down the first time, and it made the trail easier although it was still slick in areas. A few hours passed taking its toll on their energy levels.

Petee slid and sprawled on the ground. Elayni and Brando stopped, offering him a hand up.

He held his leg. "I tore something. Can any of your companions reach the pack?"

No, Bruno sent.

Brando and Elayni both shook their heads, no. Petee grimaced. "Okay, Brando, go find some branches I can use for crutches, Elayni, help me bandage my leg."

Brando moved off in the woods with Bruno and located one good one. A scream split the air—Elayni's. Evee's growls erupted.

Elayni's in trouble, Bruno sent.

Branches slapped Brando's face as his heart and feet raced to get back.

30

Decisions

"After you've made a decision, don't look back, but embrace it and accept the outcome." ~ Leeto

Codee put his back close to Leeto's to keep the hyenas off his brother and walked backwards. Leeto forced their ring against the line of hyenas cutting them off from the cliff base. The hyenas gave way, and they reached it. Codee sighed. The stone would prevent attack from one side.

Leeto raised his eyebrows at the blood on Codee's arm, "Does any Calupi or companion have life threatening injuries?" No one answered. His voice turned sharp. "Here they come. Use your nails, now. If they fall at our feet, we can retrieve them."

The hyenas targeted the end of their line, Jonesee. Several flew at him. Jonesee's tooth found one's throat. Another grabbed his leg and started pulling him away. Codee threw his nails, and others landed, too, dropping the hyena. Codee rushed to help Jonesee and retrieve his nails.

The hyenas targeted the other end of their line, pulling Grego down. Codee pulled his nails and switched directions. One at a time, the hyenas were trying to pick them off. They had the numbers. Jonesee's leg sprayed blood.

"I'll take this end, Codee, you get that one." Leeto gestured with his hand. "Those in the middle help Jonesee." Codee took up his place on the outside. Three Calupi ringed Jonesee while another helped him attend to his wound.

"Leeto, I think I remember a small fissure in this cliff, past Codee," Jonesee hollered.

"Take us, Codee," Leeto calmly ordered.

Codee side-stepped to keep the rock at his back as he moved down. The hyenas charged again. He stopped. With his nails in one hand, tooth in the other, he wove them in a dance to deliver death to his foes. His nails found one's throat. Another pressed him. He slashed its chest with his tooth, but another wrapped its muzzle around his leg. Codee's tooth stabbed the hyena's eye. It released him, and he kicked it.

Nails scrabbled on the rock above. A hyena plunged down the cliff toward Codee's back. He jumped to the side, bracing his tooth upward against the rock and slashing another hyena's cheek with his free hand. The plummeting hyena landed on his tooth and Codee twisted it up farther to rip its gut open. Entrails and blood washed over his hand. He pushed the hyena off his knife into those advancing. They tore into their dead pack member.

Codee used the distraction to move again and found the small fissure. A narrow line broke the cliff face, but it didn't go through. Should provide some safety. He stepped aside and waved the others into the opening. Calupi and companions disappeared inside the crevice.

Leeto came last and gave Codee a head tilt toward the crack. Codee and Wilee backed in. Codee's shoulders brushed both walls. Another hyena rushed toward the fissure. Luko met the charge. The wolf and the hyena's bodies slammed together, teeth flashed. Luko's sunk into the hyena's face, ripping it open. The hyena retreated. Luko bounded in. Leeto joined them.

Not much space for seven wolves and seven Calupi. They stood squished against each other with little room to move and just enough width for one Calupi in front. They'd have to take turns fighting in that confined spot, but the hyenas could attack only one at a time.

Codee's eyes traveled up to see the sky through the narrow opening. The hyenas might be able to make it through and could conceivably drop onto them.

Leeto glanced over his shoulder at them. "Take everything out of your rucksacks but water, food, bandages, and medicine and pass the rest to me. We'll block the entrance and make a barrier they have to cross. It might slow them down. Then see to each other's injuries. Treat whoever's closest."

Every single one—except Leeto—held at least one injury. Codee passed his things to Leeto. "Did the clan council approve the hyena clans' request?"

"No," Leeto answered. "Nero must be behind this, so he and those helping him just harmed the Vita."

Sharp intakes of breath came from behind Codee. JoKayndo taught Herrick—Wolf Mountain's first alpha the Vita—to safeguard Kun's creation and live in balance with it. To break pack law made them a traitor of their pack, but to hurt the Vita betrayed every clan and all the blood that had been spilled in defense of it. Didn't Nero worry about repercussions?

Wilee nudged him. *Nero isn't concerned about answering for it since he believes you'll be dead.*

The reality slammed into Codee. They couldn't stay in there forever—their water'd run out. The hyenas could wait—still probably fifty to sixty out there. Eventually, they'd have to leave and fight to gain the creek again.

We can't send for help. Wilee's thought crashed in. *There's no one in range.*

A few wouldn't help, Codee sent. *We'd need several.* But how many were loyal to Nero?

Leeto's mouth had set in a grim line. "We'll stay until the water runs out, but not until we're unable to fight." Leeto gave them the signal. A fist under his nose. 'Until their last breath.'

Codee joined his howl with Wilee's and everyone else's. Leeto had their agreement. Doubtful they'd win this one, but they'd give the hyenas a fight to remember and take as many with them as they could.

But what about Dayvee? Nero'd never meet him in a fair challenge. He'd kill him. Codee and Leeto underestimated Nero.

"How many times did I tell Dayvee he shouldn't worry so much?" Leeto sighed. "I should have worried more." Leeto twisted to look at Codee. "You were right. I should have told Dayvee. If we get out of this one, I'm going to have to change that."

Codee raised his brow. Which thing was Leeto talking about?

#

When Brando emerged from the trees, Petee stood silhouetted behind Elayni with a knife to her throat. Her arms curved behind her back. She must be bound. What was Petee doing? Brando reached for his weapons.

"Don't think it, Brando. I don't want to break the law and kill her but, I will." Petee tightened his grip, and Elayni gasped.

Brando lifted his hands up palm out. "Don't hurt her." His heart crashed to his toes. Dayvee'd never forgive him if anything happened to Elayni. He'd never forgive himself.

Bruno and Evee approached Rodnee stiff legged. *I wish I could sink my teeth in him,* Bruno sent.

"If you or your companions threaten me or Polo, I'll slit her throat." Petee's voice was low and threatening—like he meant it.

Cold fingers of ice spread from the pit of Brando's stomach. *Please, don't do anything, Bruno.*

"Take your weapons pouches off unopened and throw them on the ground over here." Petee gestured near his feet.

Brando hurried to comply. A lump squeezed his throat. He got his pouches off and threw them. Maybe Petee'd turn Elayni loose? He didn't.

"Turn around. Put your hands behind you and slowly walk back to me."

Brando did. Ideas kept crashing into his mind. He considered each and rejected them as too risky. Brando glanced over his shoulder. Petee's arm was linked through Elayni's. Even though his tooth wasn't at her neck now—but in his hand—Petee could quickly bring his blade up again.

"Eyes forward," Petee ordered.

He grabbed Brando's arms. The stiff scraggly texture scraped against Brando's flesh as the bindings wrapped around his wrists.

Brando's heart careened. "What do you intend to do to us?"

#

Dayvee's wind-milling helped him get his balance on the chasm's edge. He gulped and backed up. The hole filled the width of the tunnel, and its length made it impossible to cross without longer ropes or a bridge.

Tears stung his eyes. Disappointment threatened to crush him. He wanted to sink to the ground and give up. Instead, he trotted back so he'd waste less light. Two torches later, he came to his rock pile.

He sank down by the provisions, and his despair welled up. With no obvious exits and the amount of tunnels here, it might take weeks, months, even years to explore them all. Dayvee dreaded his torch going out, but did he want to burn through them all? He had only three left. The rope went around his wrist again. The light flickered, and died. The darkness closed in to suffocate him.

His heart raced. *Breathe.* One deep breath. In then out. His heart slowed. Now, think. He'd been here a long time. His internal clock claimed it was night. No one had come—not Chancee, Brando, Elayni, or Jaycee.

He was worried about the wolf and his friends. He couldn't believe they'd turn their backs on his plight. Something must have prevented them from coming. They might need help. But he couldn't aid them when he couldn't get free. And his challenge needed met. His mind circled. No answers presented themselves. Exhausted, he lay back. Must rest for a few minutes.

The little hide remaining went around his shoulders. He put a hand under his head and closed his eyes. Nero must be home spreading his lies. He'd have painted his picture of Dayvee as an inept trainee. And Nero had help.

His foot tapped a rhythm against the cave's floor, and his eyes snapped open. He needed to remove the rocks from the entrance. There was an opening here. He had no torches or time to find another if he was to be free in time to meet his challenge.

By Dayvee's reckoning, it was the morning of the eighth day since he challenged Nero. He'd spent three nights in the cave, all that time lifting rocks. His challenge was yesterday. He missed it. He failed. The despair weighted him down and sapped his strength—like he had treaded water all this time.

The mound blocking the door was smaller, but still too thick. No light came through. He allowed himself one more sip from his water bag. The slosh told him that only a few remained. Long before he freed himself, his water would run out.

No. No! He would *not* die trapped. He wanted out. Recklessly, he pulled another rock from the bottom. Rocks cascaded over him, bruising his body anew. He unburied himself, rose, and lit his last torch. Just a small spill. He might kill himself before that worked. Since he had his last torch lit, he should investigate another tunnel.

He squeezed through a narrow one. The ceiling lowered, and he crawled, then wormed on his belly until he could go no further. Another dead end. He backed out. All he needed to do was get stuck. His body trembled until the cave opened up. When he came back to his rock pile, he extinguished his torch. It had almost reached his fingers.

His only hope left was someone coming. How likely was that? Maybe Chancee would return since Dayvee missed his challenge. If Chancee wanted to kill him, wouldn't he have just used his nails? Dayvee hated feeling so helpless. Needles of unease pricked him.

Rabbit in the hole. Leeto should have been back. Why hadn't he come and found Dayvee? The rabies outbreak must be bad. What if Leeto contracted it? And who was in charge now? Would Nero have convinced them to kick Dayvee out? Probably. If he ever got out, Dayvee could find himself without a pack, home, or companion.

How he craved companionship. Never had he been alone for this long. Even when Nero isolated him, he had Jaycee. Raised in a pack with others always around—that was one of the hardest parts. His head went in his hands. Anguish came spilling out in sobs. No one would hear. Dayvee was abandoned.

He wiped his tears with his sleeve. Kwutee said they were never alone. Kun would send help and guidance to those who asked. Where was his help? His guidance? Why was he so isolated?

An unmistakable soft flutter came to his ears. And several chirps. Then squeaks. Then a cacophony of chirps. It almost sounded like crickets. What was it?

His last torch couldn't burn much longer, but he had to know. He struck the rocks. The torch lit. Several small flying creatures with ugly faces and pointy teeth swooped through the large room. Bats. Startled by the light, they fled.

Bats would know the way out.

Dayvee ran to follow, slipping the rope off his wrist. *Don't leave me. I need to find a way out.*

Had the bats slowed? Were they waiting for him? He hurried, following the flying cave- dwellers farther in. His low torch gave off a dim light, and it fell on one of his marks. This was the same tunnel he'd explored. The chasm was ahead. Dayvee couldn't fly over it like the bats. His heart clenched.

His torch flame went out. The darkness closed in. Fear rose, and his rapid breathing filled the silence. Could he make it back without light? No. Tears flowed. Why had he left? At least there he had the faint prospect of someone coming. Now, no one would find him. Dayvee had no light, no water, and no hope.

Dayvee crawled on his hands and knees forward. He couldn't give up. One hand fell through the floor. A shiver ran up his spine. He pulled it back and felt the edge of the abyss. He retreated and sank to the cave floor. Everything he'd tried had failed.

If he went on, he'd fall in the abyss. If he turned around, he wouldn't find his way back to the entrance. He couldn't fight anymore. Just one small person trapped in this vast cave. He'd die alone in the dark he hated. Abandoned by everyone and everything. Even Kun. His tears flowed. How Dayvee longed to hear a voice. *Kun, before I die, could you please let me hear a voice and give me some light?*

How about mine?

Was Dayvee imagining things now?

Don't you want to talk to me? The thought crashed into his head. *Who are you?*

A bright light shined in front of him. Dayvee blinked rapidly as his eyes tried to adjust. He'd longed for light, cried out for light, but it was so intense he had to look away. His hand went up to shield his eyes and he glanced again. A giant white wolf stood there bathed in light.

JoKayndo! Townspeople said the first Kayndo was a man. The Kwin claimed JoKayndo was a horse. Calupi stories related JoKayndo as a wolf. Dayvee had no doubt. The wolf had to be JoKayndo.

Wolves are pack animals. Why must you do everything on your own? JoKayndo's head tilted. *It broke Kun's heart to see your pain. Why didn't you ask sooner?*

I prayed for help. My prayers went unanswered.

Each of your prayers was answered. Look at the help you were sent. Family to turn to, friends gave you council. Animals aided you. Didn't Kun help you endure the pain? But why didn't you ask for the pain to end? You didn't believe in Kun's power.

How many times had Brando advised Dayvee to leave? How many times had Elayni recommended he tell his father? Dayvee had escaped the pain. Dayvee's prayers had been answered. Could Kun be blamed if he refused to listen? Or didn't ask? Dayvee hadn't really believed they'd be answered. They were just desperate pleas.

All this time, you've been here, and only now you prayed for help. Kun has plans for you, just as he had plans for me. You're important to Him. He wants to help you, but you need to stop being a lone wolf.

Wait, he was important to Kun? All his life he'd been told an individual wasn't important. The pack was.

Each individual is important to Kun. You need to call Him first— believe in HIS power—trust HIS path for you, and take the aid sent. Even now, you yearn for help but you don't believe I'll help you.

Belief is difficult when I'm trapped in this cave. Nero has everyone turned against me. And my companion, family, and friends could be in peril.

Then ask for help believing. Hasn't Kwutee always taught all things are possible with Kun? How many rocks must you move, how lost do you have to be before you realize you can't do it on your own?

I can't do it on my own!

Do you want Kun's help?

Yes, Dayvee cried.

You must believe in Kun's power.

Please, help me believe.

The wolf turned around and took a few steps. He looked back over his shoulder.

Did JoKayndo want Dayvee to follow?

Dayvee sprang to his feet and ran after the light. JoKayndo led him back to the rock pile at the entrance. The wolf moved into the rock pile and disappeared. The light left, and the blackness returned.

No. Please. Don't leave me in the dark again. Seconds elapsed. Dayvee was abandoned.

"I believe Kun has the power to help me. Please, Kun help me." His shout filled the room.

A crack sounded. The unmistakable sound of a rock fall. Dayvee covered his head, but the rocks blew from the cave as if a giant hand picked them up and threw them. The hole was open, and light streamed in.

Dayvee walked out of the cave, blinking in the bright morning sun. Rocks from the pile lay scattered in front of the cave's mouth for some distance. Some were even stuck in tree trunks. It looked like a tornado had picked them up and tossed them.

Dayvee fell to his knees. *Thank you, Kun, for my escape and for JoKayndo's aid. Please, protect Jaycee, my family, my friends, and the pack.* As he prayed, the light moved toward him and embraced him.

Warmth and peace filled him. *Believe, Dayvee, and you don't have to fear being trapped alone in the dark. The Light will always be with you.*

What should he do now? A soft whisper sounded in his head. Dayvee focused. *Jaycee?*

Yes.

To hear Jaycee's thought brought mist to Dayvee's eyes. *Where are you?*

Coming back. Brando and Elayni weren't at the cave. I tracked them. Petee has them tied up.

Dayvee sucked in his breath. Petee must be working with Nero, too. *Has he hurt them?*

No. Just threatened them. Then, I went to find Leeto in shadow canyon. They weren't there, and I lost the scent. It took a lot of searching, but I finally reached Luko. They are fighting hyenas and outnumbered. He told me to return and tell his story well so I'm almost back.

Dayvee's heart plummeted. Luko didn't think they'd survive. But Leeto and Codee wouldn't be easy to kill. Was that part of Nero's plans, too? *How far away are they?*

Brando and Elayni a few hours. Leeto's further. We can do something, right now to help them.

What?

Remember when you needed to get warm, and we called for the animals to aid you?

Turmoil churned in Dayvee. *That was real?*

Yes. We both should do the same now. Call out for the animals to aid Leeto and your friends. Send a mind picture of what they look like.

Would that help any or be a waste of time? Hadn't JoKayndo told Dayvee to believe? Being different scared him, but he needed to face it. He focused. *I'm asking any animals that can to aid my friends and family, and the hyenas to leave Leeto's group alone.*

Good, Jaycee sent.

Do you know what's going on at the cave?

No they're not in my mind reach, but I'd guess Nero's hoping you don't show for your challenge today.

Dayvee's jaw dropped open. *Wait, that's today?*

Yes. You have until sunset.

Dayvee had only spent two nights in the cave. *I still have time.* Hate for Nero burned through his veins. He clenched his fists.

If that's the choice you make, Jaycee sent.

Leeto expected him to put the pack first. And Dayvee wanted revenge. Nero needed to pay. Maybe his friends and family would be okay.

I haven't heard the death howl.

That didn't mean much. Dayvee sighed. A companion had to be near enough to hear it to pass it on.

31

Evil's Lair

"Hate is like poison ivy. It might start with a little sprig but it spreads to choke everything else out." ~Kwutee

Rough bark scraped against Brando's back. Scratching above alerted him to a squirrel clinging to the trunk. The little gray rodent with its big fluffy tail froze, looked at him, then shimmied up the tree as easy as wolves tread across the ground.

Brando glanced at the sky. The sun's western position announced evening. His entrapment caused his skin to crawl as if worms slithered underneath it. The chafing from the ropes acted as a hard reminder—he'd sat in the same spot too long.

His shoulder brushed against Elayni tied next to him. The small shift sent tiny pin pricks traveling up Brando's feet and legs. Petee stood by the fire. His belt brimmed with all their weapon pouches.

"You have our weapons. Why do you need to keep us tied?" Brando asked.

"Your life depends on not doing anything stupid, so I'm helping you." Petee threw some wood on the fire. "When Dayvee misses his challenge, I'll free you tomorrow, and we'll go home."

Did Dayvee even know they were in danger? And if he did, what would he choose to do? Leeto had told Dayvee for years the pack came first. Now, Dayvee was so intent on revenge, he might leave his friends to fend for themselves.

If Petee tries to kill you, Evee and I will attack him and face the judgment for killing a human pack member, Bruno sent.

What's the penalty?

It would break our trust and cohesion with Calupi pack members, so it's not pleasant.

Bruno seemed reluctant to tell him, but Brando wouldn't be put off. *A ring?*

Yes.

Brando feared he knew which of the two. *Are there any exceptions?*

If he was an outsider or wanted to harm everyone in our pack, we could attack.

He's not, so please don't. Brando had to get free. For the hundredth time he strained against the ropes pinning him and Elayni. They gave. Huh? He hadn't expected it to work. Elayni's eyes widened. Hope surged and gave him new strength as he pulled against the bindings around his wrists.

The leather broke. Yes. But what would Petee do if he caught them? Every rustle sent Brando's heart lurching as he helped Elayni free her wrist bindings. Next, he slowly wriggled his body around. Needles pulsed through his legs. Would they hold him?

He needed to act before Petee's attention bore down on him again. He grabbed the rope that had bound them and ran toward Petee with a prayer on his lips. *Please, Kun help me get to him before he draws his weapon.*

The older Calupi looked up, his eyes widened, and he jumped at Brando, knocking him from his feet. Brando sprawled on the ground, and Petee fell over on him. Brando couldn't lose the most important wrestling match of his life. His desperation gave him the strength to fling Petee to the side and climb on top. Petee's arms pummeled him. Brando got one pinned to the ground, then the other.

Petee twisted and heaved to throw Brando off. It took all he had to keep him pinned. The rope lay on the ground beside them where he dropped it. Brando got his knees over Petee's arms, then grabbed for the rope. He slid it around Petee's neck like Nero had done to Dayvee. "Lie still, now."

Petee thrashed and kicked, so Brando pulled the rope tight. Polo growled. Bruno and Evee moved toward him with teeth showing. Polo backed away.

Petee's body sagged under the rope. Brando loosened the rope a little. Petee gulped to draw breath.

"I'll choke you more if you don't stop resisting," Brando threatened. Petee stopped and lay still. "Elayni, can you grab the weapons?" She removed the pouches from Petee's belt. "I'm going to get off and let you sit up. Put your hands behind your back." He used the other end of the rope to bind Petee's hands together and took it off his neck. "Now, we're going back to that tree." Brando led him there and wrapped the rope around the tree.

"I've got the rucksacks," Elayni called.

He took Petee's from her and threw it up in the tree. Then, Brando loosened his bonds. "It shouldn't take you long to free yourself, but remember we have your weapons."

"You're not even going to leave me a weapon?" Petee's eyes flashed.

Brando drew himself up. "I could kill you. After you retrieve your rucksack, you shouldn't have any problem making it with Polo. Your weapons will be at Wolf Mountain." He pulled his tooth, grabbed Petee's hair, and laid the blade against Petee's throat.

Polo growled. Brando ignored him, trusting Bruno to make sure Polo didn't forget the law.

As Petee's eyes grew wider, Brando snarled. "You did this to Elayni, so you made my list to be taught better." Brando pulled his knife away. "Give us a huge head start, because if I catch you on our back trail, I *will* kill you." Brando turned his back and slammed his tooth into its pouch.

#

Dayvee's feet fought the slush on the trail, softened by the day's warmth. The thin gnarly pine trunks lay scattered around him, and the pines didn't tower, so the boughs let plenty of sunshine in. He and Jaycee moved at a fast lope, but his chest squeezed as he labored for each breath.

Jaycee brushed against him. *I just spoke to Evee—Brando and Elayni are free and making their way toward us.*

Relief sank in. Dayvee stopped and drew in a huge breath to fill his lungs with air. *How?*

A squirrel chewed the ropes, so Brando broke free and took Petee captive.

Dayvee angled over to the creek and quenched his thirst. Then, he continued toward his friends, but at a trot. Roughly an hour later, Evee and Bruno came into view with Brando and Elayni following. Bruno and Evee loped up to Jaycee. Dayvee's heart skipped as his friends raced toward him.

When they met in the middle, Elayni and Brando's arms encircled Dayvee. Pain stabbed him, but he didn't care.

Dayvee took a step back and examined his friends. Brando's grin spread across his face, and Elayni's smile showed her dimples.

After greeting Jaycee, Evee and Bruno pressed against Dayvee. He touched each on the head.

Brando's mouth took a serious line. "Bruno told me that hyena, Chancee, trapped you in a cave."

Dayvee clenched his fists. "He's working with Nero and Petee."

"My list is getting long." Brando's brow wrinkled.

"What will you do now?" Elayni's face tilted up at him.

Dayvee cupped his hand over his eyes to check the sun. If he hurried, he might be able to make it. If the hyenas left Leeto, he'd head for the pack, and he'd expect Dayvee. "I'm going to meet Nero for that challenge."

Elayni's eyes filled with tears. "Don't give Nero another opportunity to kill you. We'll leave the pack."

Her tears pulled at him to make them stop. "You'd regret it later."

She shook her head. "Never."

"Listen to Elayni," Brando said. "Nero will have a plan if you show up. I told you, I won't watch you die."

Would he understand? "We're Calupi. Hyenas are in both our territory and our pack. I can't forget my vow to protect the pack."

"They aren't your pack. They stood by while Leeto or Nero said and did things to hurt you. You just want to get even with Nero."

"What's wrong with making Nero suffer like us?" Dayvee demanded.

Brando's piercing blue eyes met his. "Because you've changed. And it won't hurt him, but you. Your need for revenge is turning you into another him."

Dayvee lowered his voice but couldn't keep the rage from it. "I'm nothing like him. And what about your list?" Dayvee pointed his finger at Brando. "You want to get even with those that hurt us."

"It's not about getting even, but to teach people to reconsider before they hurt our family, again. I don't hate anyone—dislike, yes, but I don't want to see them dead."

He teaches respect, Jaycee sent.

Elayni put her hand on Brando's arm. "You won't change his mind."

"I'm not slinking away," Dayvee snapped. "I won't turn tail again."

Brando shook his head. His gaze met Dayvee's, "I can't follow you this time. I'm leaving."

"You have to do what you think's right for you, and I have to do what I know's right for me."

Red flooded Brando's cheeks. "What are you trying to call me—a tiger?"

"I've never once said that."

"Will you go with me, Elayni, before he gets you killed, too?" Brando asked.

What would she say? She turned cheeks that glistened with tears to Dayvee. "I agree with Brando, but I can't let you die alone."

Brando pivoted and strode away with Bruno following.

I'll miss Bruno, Jaycee sent.

Dayvee watched them go. A lump rose in his throat. Was the pack worth losing Brando? He turned away from Elayni's wet face. "If you're coming, we have to go."

Dayvee broke into a run. They had to make it in time. He mulled over what Brando said. Yes, Dayvee had changed, but for the better. He was tougher now, and Nero would pay. Leeto'd be proud of his son.

#

Which way should we go, Bruno? Brando asked the wolf that padded at his side.

Bruno cocked his head. *The best place to find a new pack would be the clan meeting.*

Of course, the clan meeting would be held this year. Once he and Bruno made the trip, they could wait. As soon as spring arrived, the clans would gather. And every Calupi pack in their area would have representatives there.

That's a great idea. Brando turned northeast. He and Dayvee had always wanted to go to a clan meeting. If only Dayvee wasn't so stubborn, they could.

Why did this always happen to Brando? He had failed. Not only was his family miserable, but Dayvee was willingly throwing himself off a cliff. And Elayni might follow. The only two people who cared about him.

Thanks to Leeto and Milay, Dayvee never pitied Brando for not having parents around. Dayvee admired him and called him brilliant and confident—but Dayvee's belief made him confident.

Brando's foot landed on a large jagged rock and slipped. Pain stabbed his ankle as it twisted and sent him falling.

Ouch, Bruno sent. *How bad?*

The throbbing gave him the answer. *Sprained at least.*

Brando didn't try to rise but wrapped his head in his hands. Tears came to his eyes as he rocked. He wasn't confident, now.

Was this any different than his parents abandoning him? Why was he leaving Dayvee and Elayni? Brando's guilt called him a tiger—not Dayvee. What if he could prevent their deaths, and he wasn't there? He couldn't bear to watch them die, and he couldn't leave.

#

Jaycee and Evee ranged ahead of Dayvee and Elayni. *When we get close enough, I'll contact the pack to learn more,* Jaycee sent.

Dayvee glanced over his shoulder. Elayni struggled to keep up. She'd been tied to a tree all day. She tripped again. He slowed to a walk and let her catch up.

"I know that look," she said. "You're frustrated at me, aren't you?"

"Sorry. I have to go, but you don't."

"Do you remember when I broke my leg?"

"Yes."

"Brando wanted to get Kwutee, but I begged you not to leave. Do you remember what you said?"

"I said never."

She grabbed his arm, and moved to face him. "I knew you wouldn't leave me. If I'd have left with you, Nero wouldn't have hurt you. None of this would be happening." Elayni threw her arms around him. She rose on her feet to brush her lips against his.

Her kiss was like a near lightning strike. The ground rocked beneath Dayvee, and it set his blood sizzling. As if she were a rope he needed to keep him on the mountain, he pulled her closer. Flames roared through his body. His lips pressed down to devour hers. They responded and fanned the fire. The sweet taste of rose hips. His breath turned ragged. A howl surged inside. And reason stopped for a second.

Thought returned. Why was she doing this? To keep him from going to the pack? His emotions sank as if he dropped off the mountain's peak to plummet down its snow-covered face. She shouldn't manipulate him like that. The fire wasn't completely quenched, but it was banked.

He stepped back and broke the kiss. "It won't work."

Her chin quivered. "That could be your last kiss."

Please, not more tears. He steeled himself. Focus on Nero. He broke into a trot and put space between him and Elayni. The gap between them widened, and she fell further behind. Dayvee craned his neck to check the sun. Could he make it by sunset?

A thud sounded. He glanced back at Elayni lying on the ground. To make it in time and for her own safety, he should go without her. He took a step.

"Have you changed so much you'd leave me now?" she called.

How could he even think it? Dayvee went to her and offered his hand. "Sorry. Let me help you."

"I'll be able to go again. Just let me catch my breath."

"All right, but it will be slower. If we don't make it, they'll just have to give me an extension."

Jaycee nudged him. *I'm in mind range now. Nero's leading the pack in Leeto's absence. He's asking for your exile.*

Nero? He's not even beta.

Chancee must have changed Leeto's instructions. The alphas and betas are gone. Kwutee and Milay left to help someone with an illness.

Maybe feigned? Understanding flooded Dayvee. Brando was right. Nero planned well. Who was there to dispute him? Leeto had suspected Nero wanted to be alpha. He'd managed it. And Nero wouldn't relinquish it easily.

The pine sentinels finally came into Dayvee's view. He was running out of light. There were only a few rays left from the setting sun.

Elayni's forehead held worry lines. "We better pray. Kwutee says all things are possible with Kun."

He should pray first like JoKayndo said. But Kwutee taught them that Kun wanted them to forgive their enemies. Dayvee's hate for Nero and the rage he felt was too powerful. He couldn't forgive.

Shame filled him. He must be a terrible Calupi. His guilt cut him off from Kun. How could he pray when he didn't deserve Kun's help? He looked to the side, unable to meet Elayni's eyes.

Another trap must wait, but he had to go. Dayvee turned back to Elayni. "You better not be seen with me. Nero won't hesitate to come after you."

"I'm done hiding our friendship." Her pert nose wrinkled and her mouth set in that stubborn line. "To get to your back, he'll have to come through me."

Dayvee didn't like putting her in danger, but there'd be no talking her out of it. Calupi came spilling out, and all the pack's companions surrounded them. Dayvee bent down and greeted the wolves—old friends, that they were. Bunjee ran up.

Dayvee straightened and clasped Bunjee's arm. "Hello, brother." Nero stalked toward them. Dayvee tilted his head toward the rest of the pack. "Get back with them," he warned Bunjee.

Bunjee retreated as Dayvee turned toward his enemy. He met the darkness in the cave. Now he had to meet the darkness in Nero. Jaycee and Nesi both stiffened.

"What are you doing here?" Nero hollered. "You've been voted from the pack."

He didn't say an exile. Apparently, Nero could only get them to kick Dayvee out. Not welcome, but if caught trespassing, not marked for death. But why did they do it already?

Dayvee straightened, pulled his shoulders back, and lifted his chin. "A little premature, wasn't it? I challenged you, Nero. Even after you had me trapped in a cave, I'm here and in time."

"Everyone here knows about your incompetence." Nero smirked. "They're not about to believe you."

The Calupi stood rigid with downcast faces to greet Dayvee. So, that much was true.

"You don't have to believe me. Ask the companions to judge the truth. Leeto's fighting hyenas, and he never left Nero in charge."

Elayni's parents came forward. "Elayni, come away. Dayvee's jeopardizing your future."

"No." Elayni shook her head. "I won't leave him."

The grooves on Miko's face deepened. "Nero explained how upset you were at failing your training, but wild accusations won't help. If that was true, the companions would warn us."

"Nero's been blocking his companion," Dayvee said. "The others aiding him must be, too." Nero snorted. Dayvee glared at him. "I have the right to be judged for truthfulness."

"Not anymore." Nero licked his lips. "You're no longer a pack member. Leave or suffer the consequences."

Jaycee's growl pierced the air. *You should growl, too.*

"I'm not leaving." Dayvee threw his chest out. "It's time you meet my challenge if *you're* not a coward."

"I'm the acting alpha," Nero crowed. "You're defying me and trespassing. Maybe you should receive the Ring of Pain."

Elayni put a hand on her hip. "Nero's doing wrong, and that proves it. A ring sentence is reserved for those who commit terrible acts like rape or murder. And everyone has to agree."

Several in the pack shuffled their feet. Nero must be losing their support. Dayvee smiled at Elayni.

Nero must have realized it, too. "Not the Ring of Pain, but I'll make your feet match your back so you learn not to go places you're not wanted. Bind him."

Most of the Calupi faces held puzzled expressions, but some moved toward them.

Dayvee's quick count revealed the odds, twelve against two. "Take my back, Elayni." They'd have to come through him to get to her.

32

The Challenge

Brando's stomach clenched. Would he be too late? The tall pine trees appeared. The pack stood outside the cave around Dayvee and Elayni, who retreated back to back from the others. None of them looked up at Brando's approach.

"You'll pay for your lies," Nero yelled.

Several Calupi moved forward in an attempt to ring his friends and cut off their escape. Brando broke into an awkward run. His ankle wrapped and supported with sticks, it barely held his weight as he and Bruno hobbled through an opening in the ring.

His friends' faces lit at his arrival, but worry quickly lined them again. Brando turned a steely gaze on Nero. "Anyone who knows Dayvee can tell you, he doesn't lie." Brando lifted his chin. "But you have no such scruples. You lie as easy as you breathe."

A few Calupi stopped and moved away. Ten still approached.

Brando gestured to Elayni. "I'll take the back, get in the center. They'll have to come through us to get to you."

"No, I fight with you."

"All right, then." Brando grinned. "We'll make them rue the day."

"I know you love to fight," Dayvee said softly. "But you do realize we're facing ten to three odds, don't you?"

Brando chuckled. "Don't make me feel sorry for them."

The circle of Nero's supporters still had gaps. Chayla, Geno, and their companions ran through and joined them. "Dayvee wouldn't run off like Nero claimed," Chayla asserted. They put their backs up against them and joined their ring. Brando took a step out to make room.

Renay and Tayro raced through another space, followed by their companions. "I don't believe Dayvee lied," Tayro said.

It surprised Brando. Tayro had never been one of Dayvee's supporters, but he wasn't about to question it, now.

A couple more pack members stopped which left eight closing toward their seven. Better—but some of those held weapons. They weren't just threatening them with fists. Would they force them to break one of the pack's most strict rules—to never use a weapon on a pack member? Their foes seemed determined to force the issue. Maybe Nero's cohorts.

A whispered plea came from Dayvee. "I know I don't deserve it, but, Kun, please help us."

Are you willing to split and be in Dayvee's pack? Bruno asked.

Of course.

Their companions jumped in front of them. Companion's teeth snapped in the air. Brando's mouth gaped open, and he shut it. The wolves made it clear, not just growling, they'd attack. They were going to break pack law.

Aren't you risking a ring, Bruno?

"Those with me, and our companions, have split to form our own pack," Dayvee declared. "We don't wish to be members of Wolf Mountain with Nero in charge."

No, Jaycee asked Dayvee to announce that, so we don't. Our attackers are now outsiders and threatening our entire pack. Jaycee is alpha wolf for Dayvee's pack, so we are upholding pack law, not breaking it.

Jaycee's one gutsy pup. I hope Luko agrees. It's risky.

We know. Dayvee wasn't happy about it, but Jaycee did it, anyway. Dayvee's not happy much.

Brando couldn't contain his mirth and his laughter spilled out. *No, he's not. If we survive, maybe we can change that.* All the trainees looked at him like he was crazy. They should try laughing. Brando straightened his face. We're still outnumbered.

Feeling sorry for them? Bruno cocked his ear in a wolf laugh.

Nesi moved from Nero's side, bounded up to the ring of wolves, and flipped around to growl and show her teeth to Nero.

What's Nesi doing?

She just joined Dayvee's pack, too, Bruno sent. *She told Nero that his actions are making him unworthy of her.*

Dayvee's wide-eyed gaze fixated on Nesi.

That swayed most of the others not to side with Nero. Bruno's thought rang in Brando's head. *Most Calupi are neutral, but all agree Dayvee should have his challenge; and if he wins, take over as alpha for Leeto's pack in his absence.*

Nero scowled. "You're late, the sun's last rays are down."

Brando glanced to the west. It was true. The last rays were gone, now.

"Your challenge to me is forfeit," Nero said. "Since some want me to allow you a challenge, I'll permit you to fight another I select." Nero's lip turned up in his creepy little smile. "If you win, I'll step down, and you can challenge me again. But if you lose, you'll leave our territory forever, and I'll punish you and your friends for defying me." Nero's chest puffed. "Those are the conditions. Do you accept?"

Would Dayvee's hate for Nero allow him to consider carefully? He didn't have to agree to Nero's terms.

Sweat beaded Dayvee's brow. "Can I pick someone to fight in my place, too?"

Nero glanced at Brando, then back at Dayvee. "I doubt many will fight for you, but you can have one stand-in. Same as me."

"I'll accept those conditions with one exception." Dayvee's shoulders rose. "You don't punish my supporters."

"You're in no position to make demands, but to show how fair I can be"—Nero's smile spread to span his face and display his broken tooth—"I'll let you take their punishment, too."

Heat rose to Brando's face. "Don't agree to that—let him try to punish me."

"No, Dayvee," Elayni whispered.

Dayvee nodded his assent. He said softly, "It doesn't matter. If I lose, he'll kill me anyway."

"I choose Andee to fight on behalf of the pack," Nero boasted.

"I knew he'd pick Andee." Brando shook his head. "Leeto and Codee are the only two who have won against him." He spoke quietly to Dayvee. "I have a better chance than you in your condition. I can be your stand-in."

"What about your ankle? I only get one stand in, and I don't think either of us can win against Andee." Dayvee's shoulders fell. "I'll just stay away from him as long as possible. Pray Leeto and Codee make it back, or the other help Jaycee and I sent for arrives."

Brando lifted an eyebrow at Dayvee. What other help?

Dayvee turned to Nero. "The one who will stand in for me is coming. Can we wait?"

"No, you've already had seven days." Nero grinned. "You'll have to fight until they make it. The challenge will start in five minutes in the ceremony ring."

Brando drew in a sharp breath. Five minutes didn't leave much time.

Nero's eyes roamed the crowd. "Everyone is welcome to attend. Youth, too." His gaze settled on Andee. "I hope Andee gives Dayvee a painful lesson about trespassing in Wolf Mountain territory." He stalked away.

Everyone, but those around Dayvee, left. "I want you to know, no matter what happens, I'm thankful for your support, and I'm proud to claim you as pack members."

Each of them in turn clasped Dayvee's arm. The companions pressed against him. Brando went last. Dayvee grabbed his arm. "I can't tell you how happy I was to see you. But if things turn bad, I don't want you to watch. You and Elayni should leave until it's over."

Brando tried to smile. "You can't let that happen, and I'm not leaving again." His fingers tightened around Dayvee's arm. "Now listen, you know every one of Leeto and Codee's moves, and they beat Andee. Trust me and the training. You can win this." He released him and Dayvee moved toward the cave entrance shaking his head. Brando trailed him with the other trainees. He sharpened his tone. "Yes, you can if you don't hold back."

"I always try hard."

Brando snorted. "Really?"

"All right, not against you, but Andee's not you." Dayvee ducked to enter the cave.

Brando almost ran into Dayvee, who had paused to inhale deeply. Brando should have expected it. Wolf Mountain had always meant so much to Dayvee. He was home, if only for a short time. Brando drew a deep breath, too, and his heart lurched. They'd been gone only a few weeks, but it seemed much longer. The familiar terra scent with wood smoke, herbs, and leather brought a new, warm sensation of belonging. It rocked Brando to his core.

Hadn't he always felt Wolf Mountain belonged to the pack—not him?

Bruno sent, *What's your heart say, now?*

It screamed Brando had come home, too.

Sweat poured from Dayvee's face as he strode through the corridor. Brando moved up beside him. "I win wagers by knowing someone's strengths. I realized a long time ago, you don't use half your abilities, but you still win against every trainee but me."

No one appeared. The pack must be at the ceremony room, already. Dayvee scratched his head. "Are you trying to tell me that I want to lose?"

"No, but you worry too much about hurting people, and against the really good fighters, you let your doubts beat you. You won five fights in a row when you believed you could."

"I only fought two, the rest rolled over."

"You only have one this time. And it's no different. You say you want revenge on Nero—put Nero's face on Andee. Just believe it, and you'd win even against Leeto."

\#

Dayvee entered the huge room followed by his friends. Sand brushed his feet as he forced himself to plod forward. Calupi already sat crowded on the ledges that pocked the wall above, and Andee waited in the ring. The lamplight glistened off the stalactites as Brando, Elayni, and the others moved up the steps to join the pack. No-one but those who fought and the leaders were allowed near the ring once a challenger stepped foot in it. Dayvee removed his coat, rucksack, and weapons and placed them down.

He blinked a few times to clear the sweat trickling in to sting his eyes and wiped his sleeve across his forehead. His heart sank as he stepped past the stones that marked the ring and took up his position opposite Andee. The giant Calupi turned a face to him that crinkled with disdain. Andee's biceps strained against his shirt, and his arms were as big as Dayvee's legs. Any belief he had in his own abilities fled.

Nero's voice mocked him. "The challenge test will be a fight until you beg for mercy, leave the ring, or a hand is placed around your neck."

Dayvee trudged to the ring's center to meet Andee, whose stride revealed his confidence. Andee howled.

You should howl, too, Jaycee sent.

Nothing to howl about—this fight isn't the one I wanted, Dayvee sent back.

"Begin the challenge," Nero called.

Andee lunged, and Dayvee jumped back. For a large man, Andee was quick. Dayvee retreated, and Andee advanced. The ring's perimeter neared. One step out meant a forfeit. He ran to get around Andee but not fast enough. Andee lunged and grabbed Dayvee, digging vice-like fingers into his arm. Frantic, Dayvee struggled to pull free. Andee's fist slammed into his stomach, distorting it as it sank in.

Dayvee's air rushed out as the ache doubled him in two. Andee grabbed his head and pushed. The room tilted as Dayvee's legs flew from beneath him. A thud filled the air as his body slammed into the ground. Lights flickered before his eyes.

Andee leaned over him. His meaty hand drew close to Dayvee's neck. Was it over? No. His shirt choked him as Andee's fingers grasped it tight under Dayvee's chin and lifted him up. His feet swung for purchase in the air. Tossed, like a pebble, his body collided into the ground. The shock jolted through him. Dayvee rolled and regained his feet. Must stay away from him.

Andee blocked his path, an impenetrable wall. What would Leeto do? Not run.

Yes, Jaycee sent. *Fight.*

Dayvee balled his fist and drove it into his Andee's stomach. His knuckles stung, and the burn traveled up through his hand to his elbow. Andee's rock-hard stomach didn't move.

His heavy fist bashed into Dayvee's eye. Pain rocketed through his skull. His legs swayed beneath him. He staggered back. His vision blurred. Andee pressed forward. Dayvee swung but only grazed Andee's cheek, who backpedalled. Andee recovered and closed the gap.

His fists rained down on Dayvee again and again. Dayvee's face, chest, and stomach took the onslaught. His old injuries opened and bled again, along with the new. Wet, sticky blood filled his mouth and soaked his shirt. His return volleys didn't seem to faze Andee any more than a mosquito would. One finally got a reaction—it landed on Andee's nose—and he recoiled with a grunt. Then, he struck back.

Andee's fist slammed into Dayvee like a hammer. Dayvee careened backward, crashing to the floor. Lying in a pool of his own blood, he moaned and squinted through swollen eyelids. Surely his death approached. To die at Andee's hands would be easier than to die at Nero's. Either way, one thing was for sure—his body couldn't take much more agony.

Fight until your last breath, Jaycee sent.

33

The Pack

An absence of pack, is an absence of love. Death is preferable. ~ *Jaycee.*

As Dayvee struggled to rise, the blood ran into his throat and choked him. He coughed. The stalactites above swayed as the room spun like a tempest.

I'm here, a new voice whispered in Dayvee's mind.

Who?

It's me, Shakree. I came to fight when you and Jaycee called.

"Nero." Dayvee made it to his knees.

"Are you ready to beg?"

Dayvee got his shaky feet under him and spit the blood from his mouth. "No, I won't beg. My stand-in is here."

There was a stir in the cave. Two Calupi guards came in the room with a man and a bear companion. Bunjee ran to them. "Santo and Shakree."

Santo hugged Bunjee, then raised his head and voice. "Greetings, Calupi. We have come to fight a challenge."

"You'll fight for Dayvee?" Bunjee asked.

"No." Santo laughed. "Shakree wishes to. He's not too happy after waking from hibernation for this." Shakree rose on his two rear legs and roared—a giant grizzly bear.

Nero's eyes narrowed. "You can't have a bear stand-in, Dayvee."

"The agreement wasn't to choose a human." Dayvee clutched his ribs. They hurt even more when he talked. "The agreement was that I could have one stand-in. Shakree is one."

Andee backed and held his hand up, palms out. "I'm not fighting the bear. I'll leave the ring and forfeit first, or you can fight him, Nero."

Nero glared at Dayvee. "If you'll continue on and agree not to take Shakree's help, I'll fight you myself in the rope challenge."

To win the rope challenge, he'd have to drag Nero out of the ring or get him down and put a hand on his neck. A chance at Nero—all Dayvee wanted. Nero wasn't Andee. Dayvee could beat Nero. Elayni and Brando were shaking their heads no.

Sometimes it's better to fight another day, Jaycee sent.

Dayvee's blood boiled. *I don't want to wait*, he sent to Jaycee. "I'll fight you, Nero."

Nero came into the ring and took off his weapons. So what if he was fresh? Dayvee's anger gave him new energy. He needed to hit Nero and make him pay.

Before Andee left the ring, he caught the ropes, Franko tossed. He threw one to Dayvee and then to Nero. Dayvee wrapped an end around each of his ankles. The short rope stretched between his feet. It would allow him to move but only with small steps. Andee tied the longer line to the bindings between Dayvee's feet and Nero's. Then, he left the ring.

Nero looked at Dayvee and chuckled. "You still don't know when to quit. A toddler could beat you now."

Dayvee shuffled to close the gap between them. Nero reached down and caught the rope between them and pulled. Dayvee's feet flew up, and his arms spun as he fell. Nero leapt on him, but Dayvee caught Nero and rolled on top. Shards of pain hit Dayvee's eyes as Nero tossed sand in them. Tears streamed forth. The haze only allowed him a glimpse as Nero slid out and wrapped the rope around his neck.

"You should remember this." Nero pulled the rope tight.

Dayvee thrashed and struggled to work his hands up under the rope. He gasped for breath. Black spots swam in his vision.

"We'll get this over quickly," Nero snarled as he crouched over Dayvee. "There's a branch in the fire ready for your feet."

Kun help me. All the moves Dayvee had been taught, all his training, clicked in his brain, and he knew what to do. He lifted his legs and wrapped them around Nero. Dayvee pushed with all the force he could muster from his tired legs. Nero released the rope as his body slammed to the ground. Dayvee jumped on top, straddling him.

Yes, go for his throat, Jaycee sent.

He could put a hand on Nero's throat, but first, Nero had to pay. The weak punch Dayvee threw barely brushed Nero's nose.

He heard a shout. Through the blur, he watched Leeto and Codee come into the room with Jonesee and the others. Kwutee and Milay followed.

Nero used the distraction to heave at Dayvee with his arms. He slid off. Nero jumped to his feet. Dayvee wobbled as he regained his. JoKayndo's words came to mind. He was part of a pack and should let others help him.

Yes, Jaycee sent.

Dayvee's gaze darted to Codee, his uncle tilted his head toward Leeto. Dayvee nodded, then turned his attention back. "I'll have my stand-in now, Nero."

Bruno says Brando wants to fight Nero, Jaycee sent.

Tell him if he didn't have a hurt ankle, I'd let him.

"You can't go back on your word," Nero said. "You already agreed you wouldn't use the bear."

"I'm not talking about Shakree." Nero must not know they were here. Dayvee smiled. "I take my father."

Nero's eyes shot up and widened. He glanced at Andee. The giant shook his head. He wouldn't fight Leeto.

"I'll forfeit." Nero's eyes darted. "I don't want to fight more."

"Then, you shouldn't have made yourself alpha." Leeto's voice rang out. "Alphas can't refuse to meet challenges. But if you won't finish this one, I'll ask the pack's agreement to form a ring of pain since you tried to murder pack members." Leeto's face was hard. "Which is it?"

Nero's shoulders fell. "I'll finish the challenge."

Leeto strode into the ring, followed by Codee. Dayvee untied his ankles while his father scrutinized him. Leeto took the rope from him and tied it around his own ankles. Codee fastened the end of the long rope to it. Dayvee lurched out of the ring and over to where the bear, his human companion, and Bunjee stood. "Thank you, Shakree and Santo, for coming."

"No problem. Shakree wants to sleep so we'll leave, but he says if you need him again, just call." Bunjee hugged Santo again, and they left.

Rayvo came over to Bunjee. "Are you coming?"

Good, Bunjee was making friends. Dayvee waved his hand. "Go, on." They ran off as Dayvee climbed a few steps to where Brando, Elayni and the other trainees sat together in a niche.

Their companions and Jaycee all sprawled together behind the trainees on the wide ledge. All of them scooted down, making room. Brando patted the spot he just left, closest to where Dayvee stood. "Sit here. As ugly as your face is now, you're going to make me look really good."

Dayvee chuckled but stopped when it hurt. "I'm glad you appreciate my efforts. It's not easy to make you look good."

"Your face *is* a mess," Renay said.

Brando and Elayni both turned frowns on Renay. Elayni snapped, "He doesn't look that bad."

Dayvee liked the return to normal. Elayni could tease them, and for the most part she gave up trying to stop them from ribbing each other. But no one else could.

"It's all right," Dayvee said. "I guess I do look bad, but Nero might look worse in a few minutes."

"Anyone want to wager?" Brando asked.

"Not against Leeto." Dayvee turned his attention back to the ring as Codee stepped out of it.

One corner of Leeto's mouth turned up. "Time for my fun, now."

Nero's eyes darted around wildly. With small steps he raced toward the ring's perimeter. The rope tightened, and he stopped. Leeto anchored it. Nero grabbed the rope and pulled, taking Leeto's feet from under him. Nero struggled to drag him. Leeto rolled, thrust his hands between his ankles, and caught the rope. He leaned back and yanked. Nero fell to the ground.

The audience of Calupi cheered. Dayvee joined in.

Leeto stood, rope in his hands. He shuffled forward and hauled Nero closer. When Leeto reached him, he dragged Nero to his feet, then punched him under his chin. Nero reeled back and landed on the floor.

"Woohoo! Hit him, Leeto," someone in the pack called.

Leeto smiled. Then, he cast an ice cold glare back on Nero. "Leadership is gained through respect, not deceit. You've earned only our contempt."

Leeto leaned over Nero, his hand grasping his shirt. Nero threw sand in his eyes. Leeto's hands flew to them. Nero leapt up, clutched the rope, and in a part-hobble, part-run, towed Leeto off his legs behind him. Would Nero be able to drag Leeto from the ring and win?

Leeto's red eyes streamed water as he rolled into a crouch. He snatched the line with his fist, wrapped a coil around his forearm, and jerked. Nero staggered and fell.

Several Calupi leaned forward. One shouted, "Yes. Show him, Leeto."

Leeto stood and drew in the rope, hand over hand. When Nero reached him, Leeto brought him to his feet. Nero tried to toss more sand, but Leeto grabbed his wrist and pushed the hand back. "Open your fist and drop the sand."

Nero hesitated. A pop, then crunch followed. He cried out and dropped the sand. Leeto let go of his hand and plunged a fist deep into Nero's stomach. Nero grunted as he bent, clutching his middle. He gasped for air but lifted his face up in time for Leeto's next punch to strike his nose. Nero's face flew back, then forward. Blood sprayed from his nostrils.

Leeto's teeth are sharp, Jaycee sent.

Dayvee sent his thought back. *Very.* Was Jaycee disappointed in Dayvee's performance?

I don't think I could win against Luko or Wilee, Jaycee sent.

Huh? Jaycee must have guessed what Dayvee had been thinking.

Nero flung his fist at Leeto, who sidestepped to let the punch land in the air. He slugged Nero. Codee and the Calupi that had been with them moved up the steps. Codee usually stayed near the ring during a challenge. Dayvee's gaze darted between Codee and the ring where Leeto pounded fist after fist through to Nero's face and torso.

Codee came to Petee and said something. He sprang up to push Codee and tried to dart around him. Codee grabbed him. With both arms, he lifted him off his feet while the others grabbed his weapons. Codee sat him back down, and they bound him. Codee must be apprehending the traitorous Calupi.

Codee confronted Chancee next. Chancee threw a punch, but Codee ducked under it and grabbed him. Rudee handed his weapons over to Codee and turned for them to bind him. Then, they came to where Dayvee sat with his friends and the other trainees.

Codee moved past Dayvee to Tayro. "Get up slowly, Tayro. Don't try to use your weapons."

Dayvee's head spun. Tayro must have been the trainee that wanted to kill Dayvee, but why did he stand with them and support him?

Codee grabbed him roughly and tied his hands. They led the four down to stand outside the ring. Leeto glanced over and gave Codee a chin lift.

Nero's nose bled now, one eye had swelled shut. With his unharmed hand, he held his ribs. He was outmatched, and Leeto made him suffer. But that's what Dayvee wanted, wasn't it? Nero to hurt like he had. Nero tortured him, trapped him in a cave, and had Andee give him a beating. Dayvee's rage welled up and consumed him again.

Leeto's fist slammed into Nero's stomach. Nero landed on the ground, retching and sobbing.

Dayvee glanced over at Elayni and Brando. Elayni's face appeared green, Brando's pale. Nero's beating wasn't making them happy, even after Nero hurt them, too.

Both Nero's eyes were now puffed and swollen. Was Leeto making sure Nero's injuries matched Dayvee's own? Nero crawled, attempting to get away.

Dayvee hated Nero. He deserved it. But was Brando right? Was Dayvee turning into Nero? If Dayvee had made different choices, couldn't it all have been avoided? Wasn't he responsible, too? But Nero put him through agony. Hate was the deceiver's tool. He had to let it go. *Kun, help me let go of the hate.*

Nesi helped you, but she suffers through the bond, Jaycee sent.

He found Nesi surrounded by the other wolves. Her head hung low with ears down. A whine escaped her. Nesi hadn't done anything wrong, yet she suffered. And Nero would be ostracized now, like Dayvee had been. After the hyenas attacked Leeto, Dayvee was sure Nero'd be exiled. No home. No future for him or Nesi. Compassion welled up in Dayvee.

Nero staggered to his feet. Leeto caught Nero, and then drove his fist up under Nero's chin again. Nero careened to the floor. He cried and scratched at the dirt, unable to move.

Leeto's eyes locked with Dayvee's.

Hadn't Nero had enough? Nesi certainly didn't deserve more. Dayvee mouthed, "Mercy." Leeto nodded once at Dayvee. Did his father understand?

He put a hand on Nero's neck. "You're fortunate JoKayndo taught us to show mercy. Otherwise, you'd suffer much longer for what you did to me, my son, and to this pack."

"Yea," the pack erupted. Whistles and foot stomping filled the room.

"Leeto has won the rope challenge in Dayvee's stead." Kwutee had to shout to be heard.

Codee and the Calupi who'd been with his father led the bound men into the ring. They went to Nero and tied his hands. There were five bound Calupi—Chancee, Petee, Tayro, Rudee, and Nero.

Leeto looked up at the crowd. "Nero and these other Calupi have betrayed our pack. I've asked the companions to judge each person's truthfulness. Dayvee and the other trainees should come down, so they can be judged, too."

34

The Judgement

"You're actions will be perceived as a credit or disgrace and reflect on your pack because they'll judge us by you." ~ Leeto

Dayvee took a hard swallow. Codee and a few others led the bound Calupi into the ring, but he didn't bring them to the center. They must intend the trainees to go first. Kwutee took his place beside Leeto.

Dayvee's legs shook, and the sand caught at his feet as he staggered through it to the middle of the ring to face Leeto and Kwutee. The other trainees and their companions surrounded him and Jaycee. Dayvee held his ribs. He was meeting Leeto as an alpha, and he better act like it for the sake of those that supported him. With a struggle he straightened and lifted his chin. The other trainees raised their heads, too.

One corner of Leeto's lip curled up. "I'll begin with you, Dayvee. You split to form your own pack?"

Dayvee's mouth dried, and his tongue felt like a wad of jerky. "Yes."

"Then, you have a choice. One alpha doesn't usually judge another, but all this occurred while you were our pack member. You can submit to our judgment or the Calupi councils. But if they determine you and your pack wrong, they could mark you as lobos. So which is it?"

Dayvee sucked in his breath. A Calupi wouldn't be allowed near one pack after an exile. To be marked with the L for Lobo meant a Calupi would be barred for certain from every pack and all their territories. Brando still looked belligerent, but the rest of the trainee's eyes widened.

Dayvee wouldn't risk their futures. "I'll submit to your judgment." He lowered his head. Everyone but Brando did the same. Dayvee stuck his elbow in Brando's side, and he lowered his head.

"Remember the rules for the judgment," Kwutee cautioned them. "You don't speak until we ask you, and one at a time, so the companions don't have to verify everyone's truthfulness at once."

Leeto's voice was stern. "Dayvee, relate what happened between you and Nero. Start at the beginning."

Jaycee nudged him. *They just need to know what happened with Nero. Don't reveal the aid from the animals until you talk to Kwutee.*

Dayvee focused on all those Calupi faces. They'd already believed him wrong once. The words wouldn't come out. Then, he found Bunjee leaning forward—eyes big and round. Dayvee's words flowed as he shared with Bunjee what happened until he was trapped in the cave. Several gasps and murmurs sounded during parts of his story.

Dayvee's gaze returned to Leeto. "JoKayndo helped me escape. I knew I might forfeit the challenge, but Brando and Elayni's safety was my first concern. They broke free and met me. Then, I returned to the pack to warn them about Nero and fight."

Leeto's mouth kept its serious line. "Take off your shirt and bandages, and turn around."

Dayvee's swollen fingers kept losing their clumsy grip on the lacing that kept his shirt shut. Brando and Elayni reached over to help him.

Dayvee accepted their aid. Leeto might believe him weak, but he didn't care.

Pack members should give and take aid from each other, Jaycee sent.

Dayvee slowly pivoted around to allow the pack to see his burn still bleeding, his cuts, and his old and new bruising. Mumbling filled the room. His face flushed.

Leeto flipped a hand. "You can put it back on." His focus went to the trainees. "You may speak one at a time to add anything you think we should know before we judge Dayvee's actions and yours."

"Dayvee saved my life. Yet Nero punished him for it." Elayni's hands went to her hips. "We should have stopped Nero."

Renay shuffled her feet. "I helped Tayro and Nero sabotage Dayvee's chores. Later, I realized Dayvee's a better Calupi than Nero, senior or not." Her face lifted to Dayvee. "I'm sorry for adding to your misery."

Geno's thick brows crinkled together. "Nero called Dayvee inept, but he did most everything better than us. I held Brando back so he wouldn't be hurt, but I should have helped him stop Nero."

More murmurs swept through the room. "Dayvee didn't do anything wrong." Chayla's quiet voice spoke with conviction. "We did, and so did you when you decided blame without having the companions' judge."

"I should have never left Dayvee to come back here alone." Brando's eyes locked on Dayvee. "I'll never abandon you again." Then, he turned back to Leeto. "Bruno and I are part of Dayvee's pack. If you throw him out, we go, too, whether the council marks us as lobos or not."

Elayni's voice rang out. "Evee and I, too."

"Us, too," Geno, Chayla and Renay said together. The words echoed in the large room.

A lump rose in Dayvee's throat, and the corners of his eyes stung. His heart overflowed with gratitude for their loyalty and defense of him. He hadn't wanted anyone to throw their futures away. But if they needed to, they'd embrace new ones.

"Wolf Mountain is ranked first, so you might want to let us finish the judgment before rushing off." Leeto gestured to Kwutee. "Can you ask the companions if Dayvee and the other trainees told the truth?"

Kwutee's wrinkled face turned to the pack. "The companions didn't sense any deceit from them."

"Will you ask the companions if they judge Dayvee still worthy?" Leeto asked.

What would they decide? Dayvee held his breath.

Kwutee's tone was solemn. "The companions say Dayvee is worthy to be Calupi and should continue to train Jaycee."

Yes. Dayvee exhaled heavily. He was still Calupi.

Jaycee's head lifted high. *I chose right.*

"So be it." Leeto touched Luko's head. "He stays Calupi. Now we decide whether Wolf Mountain pack wants Dayvee. All pack members may vote, except those being judged. Those who believe Dayvee shouldn't be in Wolf Mountain pack, say, nay."

The room was silent.

"All who believe Dayvee should be in our pack, say, yea."

The room shook from shouts and stomping feet. "Yea!"

Leeto turned back to Dayvee. "We invite your pack to rejoin Wolf Mountain, but the other trainees' still face judgment. And Luko will decide if your companions acted wrong. Are you willing?"

Jaycee, you ready to give up being alpha?

Yes. All the companions agree.

The other trainees nodded to him. Brando chuckled. "I wouldn't want to deprive them of pranks."

Dayvee lowered his head to Leeto. "We wish to rejoin Wolf Mountain Pack."

"Welcome home," Leeto said.

Jaycee went over to Luko. Luko snarled, and Jaycee lowered himself to his belly. Then, Luko extended his muzzle, and Jaycee licked it.

Is it okay? Dayvee asked.

Luko nuzzled Jaycee's ear. *Yes, my father said there's only one alpha wolf in this pack. But he didn't use his teeth, so he's not too mad at me.*

Each of the other companions went to Luko and submitted. He greeted each the same.

Leeto pulled out four red fringes. "Dayvee never risked a pack member deliberately, so he shouldn't have received any white fringes. He did choose actions that protected a pack member and endangered himself four times—in the bear cave, going on the ice for Elayni, when he insisted on her treatment, and coming back here to help the pack. I think he's earned four red fringes. Does the pack agree?"

"Yes," they shouted. Applause filled the room and Leeto handed Dayvee the fringes. Joy filled Dayvee as he tied them to his tooth pouch.

Leeto gestured at the other trainees. "Now, I'll judge the rest of you." He shook his head. "Every one of you should have stood together against Nero, senior or not. Yes, burning sticks and water can be used as weapons. No, you can't hit another Calupi outside the ring if you bind them first and use a strap instead of your fist. Nero broke the law, discarded the Vita, and acted against Kwutee's teachings."

Each face held a glum expression. Elayni bit her lower lip. Dayvee's foot tapped. How harsh would Leeto be?

"I feel each of the trainees who took part in Nero's punishment earned a white fringe, but since you volunteered to take lashes and you stood against Nero with him, it cancels out the white." Leeto gestured to Renay. "You will help Kwutee with teaching the children the Vita and the law. You'll rejoin the others when I'm sure you know it. The rest of you will continue training. It seems you've figured out how to growl together, but you need to work on when to use it." Leeto's gaze pierced Brando. "And who to use it on."

Only a warning, Jaycee sent.

A heavy weight lifted off Dayvee. He didn't want them in trouble when his own poor choices caused so much of it.

"Elayni and Brando, you tried to aid your pack mate. You might have succeeded if you had asked your companion to send a message. An attempt that doesn't get the job done is a failure, and I don't reward them. Brando, you endangered yourself, letting Petee bind you to protect Elayni, so you earned a red fringe."

The clapping was loud and long as Leeto handed a beaming Brando a red fringe. Dayvee smiled, too. Finally, the pack showed his friend some appreciation. Maybe they'd finally give Brando the respect he deserved.

Leeto pointed at Tayro. "Now to judge the other Calupi and their involvement." One of the men put a hand on Tayro's back and pushed. He staggered up to stand in front of Leeto.

Kwutee turned to him. "Tayro, as my apprentice, you learned the law. Tell me when a Calupi can take another human life."

Tayro's lip quivered. "There are three times. The first is in a war. The second is when we defend the wolves. The third is if the pack hands out a death sentence."

Kwutee's eyes seemed to glitter as they pierced Tayro. "If you kill a person for your own reasons without a threat to the Vita, what is that called?"

Tayro's Adams apple bobbed up and down. "Murder."

Kwutee shook his staff. "Dayvee never threatened the Vita, so why did you aid Nero with his murder plot?"

Tears flowed down Tayro's cheeks. "He only told me he wanted to make Dayvee sick. He said I had to help him defend the pack, so we didn't suffer when Dayvee got the prince's companion killed."

Jaycee's hackles rose. *He's claiming I'm not capable and needed a hyena's aid.*

"I picked a few winter berries and dug up a daffodil...."

Dayvee gritted his teeth. They'd all been taught to avoid winter berries because of the cramps and diarrhea they caused, and daffodil bulbs were extremely poisonous.

"...I only used a little and mashed them together. I diluted them with liquid." His eyes beseeched Dayvee, "I swear I didn't want to kill you."

Dayvee's jaw tightened. Tayro had to know someone too sick to defend himself might not survive.

Tayro dropped his gaze. "I soaked the jerky and wrapped it. Nero said he'd put it in Dayvee's rucksack, and when Dayvee became ill, have Brando and Elayni take him home."

After Topay told us what Tayro did, we took your rucksack, Jaycee sent. *I didn't know if the poison leaked, so we buried it all.*

Thanks.

The entire pack seemed to glower at Tayro. His voice cracked. "Nero claimed Dayvee ran off before he had the chance to use it."

Lines creased across Leeto's forehead. "Didn't you know what Dayvee ate could be shared with his companion?"

"Yes, but Nero said Dayvee fed Jaycee from a separate pouch."

"That's not true." Dayvee couldn't stop even after everyone turned to stare. He wasn't supposed to talk, but Tayro should know. "I only packed one jerky pouch to share."

"Nero told several lies." Leeto crossed his arms. "If Dayvee and Jaycee had eaten that meat—the poison, the storm, or predators would have killed them."

"After Dayvee's second punishment, I knew Nero was wrong." Tayro hung his head. "I should have told Dayvee, but I thought if he became sick and returned to the pack, he'd escape Nero."

Leeto uncrossed his arms. "Dayvee, you were the one most harmed. Do you want to challenge him?"

He was in no shape to fight, but in seven days, Dayvee could do it. He had bested Tayro in every training bout. But Tayro's tears cooled his anger, then tugged at his heart. He knew what Tayro felt, just having gone through it.

"No, I don't believe he intended to kill me. Kwutee teaches that Kun wants us to forgive. I'll forgive him."

Tayro's eyes widened and a heavy breath escaped.

Leeto glanced at Kwutee. "How do the companions judge him? Is Tayro still worthy?"

"The companions say he spoke the truth," Kwutee answered. "But he gave into Nero and did wrong although Topay urged him not to."

The blood drained from Tayro's face to leave it pasty white. His shoulders slumped as his chin fell forward. Would he faint?

Kwutee stomped his staff. "If Tayro learns to control his jealousy, he may prove worthy of Topay, so they'll let him remain Calupi for now."

Tayro's chin lifted. He straightened.

Leeto surveyed the room. "Now, we vote on whether he remains in our pack. If we reject Tayro, I doubt another will accept him."

Kwutee's fingers tapped his staff. "I'd prefer we gave Tayro the chance to earn our trust back, but I won't let him assist me again until he does."

Topay's head and tail were down. She had brought Dayvee the burn medicine and alerted Jaycee about the poison. Companions weren't happy without a pack.

Leeto shifted. "All those who can vote and wish to have Tayro remain Wolf Mountain, say, yea."

Unenthusiastic yeas rippled through the room.

"All those who wish for Tayro to leave, say, nay."

Dayvee heard fewer than ten nays.

"Any who voted nay, can you explain why?" asked Leeto.

Franko spoke out, "Calupi don't poison pack members. If he had a problem with Dayvee, he should have challenged him. Who will he poison next?"

"It's true his knowledge could be used to harm again." Leeto shook his head. "Tayro, how can we trust you?"

"Can't you ask my companion to inform you if I do anything wrong?"

Lines wrinkled Leeto's forehead. "How can you feel a partnership with Topay if she's doing that?"

"I deserve it. I'm willing."

"All right. We'll ask her to inform us, but only if you plan to harm a pack member." Leeto raised an eyebrow toward Kwutee.

"Topay agreed," Kwutee said.

Leeto turned back to Tayro. "You should know you'll probably have the lowest status in the pack. Calupi have long memories, so it might never change. Do you still want to stay?"

"Y-Yes," Tayro choked out past his tears.

Leeto twisted toward the keeper. "Is Topay willing to stay with him at a lower status?"

"She says, yes," Kwutee answered.

"Calupi will need to work with him. Will anyone in the training group?" Leeto's face turned to them.

There was a long, awkward silence. Tayro's lips moved, and Dayvee made out his prayer. *"Please, Kun, give me another chance."*

It's okay with me, Jaycee sent.

"I'll work with him," Dayvee announced.

Tayro startled. Murmurs filled the room.

"If Dayvee wants to, I will," Brando spoke up.

Elayni, Geno, and Chayla joined in, "Me, too."

"Explain why, Dayvee?" Leeto asked.

"He treated Elayni, and stood with us. I believe Nero misled him."

"So does anyone say nay now?" Silence answered Leeto. "So be it, he remains Wolf Mountain pack. You may release his bonds." When they freed him, Leeto handed Tayro a white fringe and a red. "For endangering a pack member with poison, you've earned a white, and for aiding Elayni, you earned one red."

Pity surged in Dayvee. Until Tayro earned another red, most Calupi would treat him as omega.

"Tayro, you'll help teach the younger children the Vita with Renay until I allow you to rejoin the trainees." Leeto's mouth pursed. "Rudee, come forward. I'm really disappointed in you."

His companion's tail dragged the ground as they stood in front of Leeto. Rudee lowered his head. "I never participated in his punishments. Nero has more status, so I couldn't change anything in his group, and I didn't know his murder plans."

"You should have been the first to stand against him and to counsel the trainees on what to do. Instead, you encouraged him."

If the older Calupi had given Dayvee advice, would he have followed it? Probably.

He's a buzzard, Jaycee sent. *Just watching and waiting for the kill but doing nothing himself to cause or prevent it.*

Rudee shuffled his feet. "I never knew how far he'd go. I thought it was just talk."

Dayvee took in his thinning hair and long neck. Rudee did resemble a buzzard. Remorse pricked Dayvee for his unkind thoughts.

Do you think wolves are always kind? Jaycee sent. *Every pack has an omega, but think how much better they're treated than buzzards and hyenas.*

Dayvee recalled Wilee tearing into a buzzard that wouldn't wait for the leavings. But Dayvee wasn't a wolf and was supposed to follow Kwutee's teachings.

Leeto eyes pierced Rudee. "You tried to play both sides. Maybe you thought your status would rise if Nero became alpha. Now, your status will fall, and you'll join Tayro and Renay with Kwutee."

Leeto's attention shifted. "Bring Petee and Chancee forward." Franko and Pako escorted the two to him. Jaycee's, Bruno's, and Evee's growls pierced the air. Petee and Chancee's companions slinked behind them as they approached Leeto. "Who else was involved in your plans?"

Silence greeted his question. "How does the pack vote?"

"Exile! Exile!" The words resounded.

"Is there anyone against the exile?" Leeto asked. Silence reigned. "The pack sentences you to exile. Kwutee, make the mark."

Kwutee must have expected it. He signaled, and Santo brought a bowl into the ring to him. Pako and Franko untied Petee and Chancee's hands.

"Give them to me." They each held out their left hand. Kwutee took out the needle, dipped it in the die and tattooed a white X over their pack marks. Dayvee felt sorry for Petee and Chancee, but not too much. They left him in the dark and threatened his friends. If they left Wolf Mountain willingly, an open circle would be drawn around their pack mark. But they would bear the shame of the white X. It was much worse than a white fringe. Would anyone offer them a pack home, now?

"You should leave our territory at once," Leeto said. "To come back under exile would mean your death." Their acting guards, Pako and Franko, escorted them to the exit.

Leeto's eyes narrowed. "Bring Nero forward."

Dayvee heard the rumble of growls echo through the cave. Was every companion giving voice to their displeasure with Nero?

Codee and Andee carried Nero and laid him in front of Leeto. Nero moaned, half in and out of consciousness. "Pour some water on him." Leeto ordered. "He needs to be awake for this."

Codee grinned and dumped water on Nero, who spluttered and his eyes widened in shock.

Leeto touched Luko's head. The companions all quieted. Leeto's contempt was written on his face as he peered down at Nero. "You're being judged for harming the Vita and breaking the law. Who else was involved in your plot?" After a minute of silence, Leeto clenched his jaw. "Do you have anything to say for yourself?"

"I did it for the low status members," Nero said. "If they aren't big enough to win a challenge, they get palssed over. We're not stupid, and we deserve status, too."

"Pako's the smallest Calupi, yet he's beta. Size doesn't hold anyone back. Your hearts do." Leeto's anger turned his words brisk. "I think you're a pawn of the deceiver, but the companions will judge since I follow the Vita."

All the companions were led by his own Nesi to circle Nero. Their lips curled revealing their teeth.

Kwutee hit his staff on the ground. "The companions say Nero is no longer Calupi. His actions hurt the Vita and broke the law. He's not sorry, so he's unworthy of a companion."

Nero glared at Dayvee. Did he still blame Dayvee for everything?

"They say he has too much hate in his heart and should die. If you exile him, he'll return and try to do harm, again."

Leeto's face was frozen. "The companions don't kill people unless they're defending us, the Vita, or we're at war. If we sentence Nero to death, we'll need to carry out his punishment. How say the pack?"

They shouted their answers out with venom. "Death! Death to Nero!"

Leeto nodded. "Does anyone believe Nero shouldn't receive death?"

Silence.

"We sentence you, Nero, to the Ring of Death. To be carried out immediately."

35

The Ring of Death

Dayvee gulped. Nero was to die. Reluctantly, he trudged over to form the circle while Jaycee and the other companions left to wait outside of the ring.

The cave lamps picked up the sparkle of the stalactites far above. The ceremony room was stunning with its rock chimneys, alcoves, crystal formations, and striations. Too beautiful to die in. A somber silence filled the room, broken only by the shuffle of feet and the drip of water from the cave.

Dayvee took a place between Brando and Elayni in the ring of Calupi around the condemned. His stomach roiled. He couldn't stand Nero, but he didn't want to end his life or anyone else's. Nero would never again touch his companion or a friend. He'd never find a life mate, have children, walk again through the woods, or have a breeze play on his face.

Sweat broke out on Dayvee's forehead. No one had received a death sentence in their pack since long before his birth, but he'd heard the stories. He understood what was expected. To take a man's life.

Leeto's voice was grim. "Unsheathe your weapons. It's time for us to serve justice and for Nero to explain his actions to Kun."

Kwutee and Leeto joined the ring. Nero moaned. He tried to stand but fell. His fingers scrabbled at the ground.

Dayvee stared at the moaning man. His hands shook and stomach churned. Nero humiliated him, hurt him, and tried to kill him, but he only felt sorry for him.

A keening whine filled the air, Nesi's. She would feel Nero's pain until his last breath. *Please Kun. Don't let her suffer more. I'll take her pain.* None came.

Leeto gave the signal. "Now."

All the Calupi in the ring released their nails on Nero. All save one. Dayvee couldn't. He slid his nails back in his pouch and hoped no one noticed. He glanced up. Leeto's gaze was trained on him and a frown crossed his face.

Dayvee dropped his head, shamed. He'd been weak. Could Nero have survived the ring of death? No one ever had. Dayvee looked. Nails had found Nero's jugular. His eyes were rolled back in his head. Tears stung Dayvee. Leeto would remove the nails and never disclose which found their mark. Dayvee's hadn't, but he still felt responsible.

Nesi's muzzle pointed up, her mouth opened, and she released a death howl. Her eyes closed to slits and her legs buckled. She collapsed on her side as if grievously injured—a spirit injury.

Her soft voice whispered in Dayvee's mind. *It's over. I protected the animal master, I defended the Vita, but now I have no one. I failed to turn Nero from hate. Now he's dead, so I choose to guard his body.*

Dayvee's mouth fell open. A companion that chose to guard their Calupi's grave refused food or water and mourned until they died. It didn't take long. A wolf that grieved alone was weak and easy prey for a predator. The companions howled as they began to mourn her.

Dayvee hobbled to the ring's center—the haze of his tears obscured the people around him. He couldn't let Nesi die. Jaycee came up beside him. His howl reverberated through the cave.

No, Dayvee shouted in his mind. The wolves immediately quieted.

The memories came rushing in. Nesi was one of the smallest companion pups, but what she lacked in size she made up for in courage. She led when the companions came to Dayvee's aid as they battled hyenas and paced vigilantly around the meat when it was her turn to guard. Her body strained hard against the harness to pull the travois.

Dayvee reached Nesi, kneeled, and cradled her head. Her thoughts pummeled him. *Kayndo, I informed the leaders, I aided you, and I defended you showing teeth to my chosen. Now I wish to guard his body. Haven't I earned it?*

Dayvee's mind reeled. What did she just call him? He pushed it aside. *You've earned my gratitude and loyalty, but how can I repay you if you die?*

Jaycee pressed against Dayvee. *I'm so sad. I'll miss her.*

Help me stop her.

It's too late. Her spirit is already with Kun.

The Vita wasn't the same for wolves as humans. Each species existed as Kun created them. The wolves had their teachings, and the Calupi had theirs.

Kwutee approached and leaned over Dayvee. "You must let her go."

"We have Calupi in training, why can't she have another?" Dayvee asked.

Kwutee's frown was deep. "I'm not sure anyone would accept her since she was Nero's companion."

Dayvee gave him a short nod. "I'll take her."

"You have Jaycee."

"Not for long. He'll go to the prince. I'll train him, but I'll bond with her, too. Don't I owe her that much?"

"We need to talk."

"Yes, we do. She called me Kayndo."

Kwutee glanced around them. "Not here."

Dayvee looked to see his father and others milling about. He didn't think anyone but Kwutee heard.

"We need to go to my den, now." Kwutee signaled to Leeto.

Calupi carried Nero's body from the cave. It would be taken a long way before they left it. Nero wasn't considered Calupi anymore and wouldn't be buried like one. As a pawn of the deceiver, his body would feed carrion.

If only Dayvee had handled things better. Nesi lifted her head a little and turned it to watch. *I'll go with and protect him.*

Please wait, let me talk to Kwutee so we can help you. Dayvee removed his hands from her.

She cocked an ear. *You're the animal master.*

I'm not your master, I'm Calupi. I can't order you, and if I could, I wouldn't. I'm asking you to wait. I want to do something for you.

You can do something for me. You can honor my wishes, but I'll wait. Her head slumped back to the floor.

Jaycee, Luko, and Keeno accompanied Dayvee and Kwutee to his den. "We'll make this short. Your father may need us."

As Dayvee entered, Kwutee turned to face him. "The companions, Leeto, Codee, and I are the only ones who know you could become Kayndo. But nothing is certain."

So why hadn't anyone told Dayvee? He tried to absorb it. That must be why the wolves showed him respect at his choosing, and why the animals kept aiding him. "What do you mean by could?"

"We might need an animal master if the prince is found unworthy. You've been selected, but no one knows for certain. You're training Jaycee, so if you become Kayndo, you'll have the best. Then, what will you do with Nesi?"

To think he could become Kayndo seemed about as plausible as believing he could reach up and pluck a star from the sky, but Kwutee waited for an answer. "If that happened, couldn't I keep her as a companion, too? Doesn't an animal master have many?"

"He can talk to all animals but usually holds one companion. The second animal master might have had two. I'm not sure. We'll ask the companions." Kwutee glanced at Keeno.

Dayvee heard Keeno in his mind. *He actually had three. At first, when people died serving the Vita, he'd offer to bond with their companion. He learned too late it wasn't fair to them. All his companions suffered since his thoughts, attention, and care were so divided.*

"It wouldn't be fair to Jaycee if you fully-bond." Kwutee's face twisted.

Dayvee shook his head. "Jaycee may never become my companion, but if I bond with Nesi, I'll have a companion regardless, and I can repay her. She turned against her chosen for me."

Luko stepped toward him, and the wolf's thought whispered in Dayvee's head. *Have you asked Nesi what she wants?*

Nesi was still in the ceremony ring, but Dayvee called to her in his mind. *Nesi, would you like to be my companion?*

You honor me, but your burdens will be heavy. I want to be with Nero.

What if someone else wanted you for their companion? Dayvee asked.

I don't want another. I couldn't be loyal to Nero in life—I chose to defend the Vita—but I wish to be in death.

I owe you so much more, but I'll support you, even in your desire to die.

Keeno, Luko, and Jaycee rose and moved toward the entrance. Kwutee gestured to them. "We have to go back. Return after the meeting. I'll explain more and treat your injuries."

When they reached the ceremony hall, Luko helped Nesi up. Luko spoke to her, and Dayvee heard it in his own mind. *For your service to the Vita, we honor your wishes. We don't believe Nero deserves it, but we'll take you to him and leave you.*

None would stay to help. If she didn't die fighting, Nesi would refuse food and water. A quick death by predators would be easier. Companions surrounded and supported her. She reeled slowly toward the entrance.

Do you wish me to carry you? Dayvee asked. *It will be far.*

I'll make it. Be worthy, defend the Vita, and make my sacrifice count, she sent weakly.

I'll remember you always. Dayvee sent back. *I'll tell your story and sing your song.*

That will be good. Bye, Kayndo.

Bye, Nesi. Dayvee turned away. He couldn't stand to watch. He found a deserted alcove to hide his tears.

Kwutee's voice rose to inform the pack. "Nesi's chosen to guard her companion's body. Nero's not worthy, but she is, so we will honor her wishes."

Brando and Elayni found Dayvee. He stood in the alcove, doing his best to choke back his grief. His friends entwined their arms around him and the three shut out everything and comforted one another.

Leeto's voice resounded. "Returning trainees may sleep in the communal den or in their family dens while we mourn Nesi. Then report to your assigned area."

Dayvee gained comfort from Brando and Elayni a short while longer, then dropped his arms and stepped back. The companions returned, minus Nesi. Jaycee approached.

Are you okay? Dayvee asked.

I'm sad. I'll mourn Nesi and sing her song tonight.

Most everyone left the ceremony room, including Kwutee and Leeto. Dayvee turned to his friends. "Kwutee wants me to go to his den for treatment. I'll find you later." He forced his sorrow down into his stomach. Later, he'd mourn. Now, he needed to learn what Kwutee could tell him about animal masters.

As Dayvee and Jaycee walked the short distance through the cave's corridor to Kwutee's den, he mulled things over. So hard to wrap his mind around everything. Why did everything seem so hazy? Why couldn't he concentrate? And why was he dizzy?

"Come in, Dayvee and Jaycee." Kwutee called when they arrived.

Dayvee pulled aside the hide and wobbled in. A fire crackled in the hearth. Kwutee's den seemed warm and familiar. Keeno and Jaycee touched noses, and they sprawled together on the rug.

"Have a seat." Kwutee smiled at him and motioned to the bench. "Would you like something to eat or drink?"

"I'm not hungry." Dayvee sat on the bench.

Dayvee heard Nesi weakly in his head. *Farewell, frien....* Then nothing.

Nesi's gone, Jaycee sent.

The death howl reverberated through the cave as the mournful notes were carried by all the wolves. Jaycee and Keeno joined their lament to the chorus. After a long moment, the clamor subsided.

Dayvee couldn't keep a tear from running down his cheek.

Kwutee's face twisted. Dayvee bore the fault for Nesi's death. He should have gone to Leeto before they left. If only he could go back. The room spun, and his heart pounded again. He had to pull himself together.

Dayvee took a deep breath and remembered why he had come. "Kwutee, can you explain more about being an animal master?"

Before Kwutee could answer, a sharp slap sounded. "Come in, Leeto," the keeper called.

Dayvee sank back. Would his father confront him now?

36

Kayndo

"Do not underestimate the power of Kun. With Kun, all things are possible." ~ Kwutee

As Leeto and Luko came in to the keeper's den, his eyes slid over Dayvee. Maybe Leeto wouldn't criticize Dayvee for not using his nails on Nero.

Kwutee gestured to Leeto. "Have a seat. Would you like something to eat or drink?"

"No thanks." Leeto continued to stand. "Most of the threat is eliminated, but I'm not convinced that was everyone. I think it would take more than three."

Kwutee's forehead wrinkled as he rubbed his chin. "We may never know, but I don't believe we'll have any more trouble after Nero's sentence."

"He could have avoided the death penalty by letting go of the hate." Leeto shrugged. "He gave us no choice."

Kwutee inclined his head toward Dayvee. "Dayvee knows now he may become the next animal master."

Leeto's gaze locked on Dayvee. "Then maybe you can understand. The Kayndo may have to kill. How will you do that?"

Dayvee drew a breath. "I probably could if someone was trying to hurt us, but Nero just lay there moaning."

Leeto's lip curled down. "Didn't you understand he'd be back to threaten us, again?"

"Yes."

One of Luko's ears flopped and revealed Leeto's disappointment. "Nero would have killed me and you. If everyone was like you, Nero'd still be a threat."

Dayvee studied his feet. Leeto sighed. "We can't afford a weak Kayndo. You have to be stronger."

What could he say? He wasn't a good choice for Kayndo at all.

Leeto and Kwutee's faces both held concern lines. Dayvee had let them down. They should choose another to be Kayndo. He wouldn't be good at it, and no one had asked him.

Leeto turned toward Kwutee. "I think it's time to inform the pack."

Kwutee asked Dayvee. "How do you feel?"

Not that long ago, Dayvee couldn't wait to have his view heard, but now he didn't trust his choices. "I don't like deception, but we don't know yet. It would be like claiming I was Calupi before I was chosen."

"You'd be respected." Leeto took a step closer.

"It wouldn't be respect I earned." Dayvee's foot tapped. "And I don't like being treated differently."

"I think that's wise, but maybe Leeto should inform a few of those we trust." Kwutee shifted his weight.

Dayvee lowered his gaze to the colorful Kwin rug on the den's floor. He spoke softly. "Nero and Nesi are dead because I didn't make good decisions. Do whatever you think is best."

"You're not responsible for the paths they chose," Leeto said.

Dayvee lowered his chin back onto his chest. "B-but Nero was a good Calupi before…"

The sound of Kwutee's staff thudding against stone came closer, then stopped. Dayvee lifted his eyes to see the keeper standing in front of him. "If you hadn't been there, he'd have found another target. The fault was his."

A hyena always finds someone to turn on, Jaycee sent.

Leeto put a hand on his shoulder. "Don't worry about your next training leader. Codee will teach you."

"Thank you." Dayvee clasped his forearm. "I am grateful for your help."

Leeto nodded, then strode out with Luko following.

Kwutee's voice rang with authority. "Take off your shirt and pants."

Dayvee stripped to his shorts and perched on the low bench. Made from a stone slab, and supported by others, its chill seeped into him, and goose bumps rose on his skin. The fire's warmth on his side didn't do much to dispel them.

Kwutee gathered things from his shelves, clean bandaging and a water bag. He washed Dayvee's face. Then, he took some dried and crushed leaves and wrapped them in a soft piece of hide. After tying the small bundle and dipping it in water, he handed it to Dayvee.

"Hold this to your face to help with the swelling." Kwutee moved to his back, chest, and legs, washing and treating his various scrapes, cuts, and bruises. "I didn't know you'd receive the Kayndo's gifts, already. But Keeno says several animals have assisted you."

The poultice on his face and the cold liquid Kwutee used to wash and treat his injuries sent shivers up Dayvee's spine. "Yes. Will they all aid me, now?"

"I don't know." Kwutee leveled an embarrassed half-smile at him. "No living person can tell you about a Kayndo's ability."

Dayvee sucked in his breath as Kwutee pulled bandaging tight around his ribs. "So how will I learn?"

Kwutee wrapped the rest of Dayvee's burn. "The companions can help you the most because of their memories."

We pass our memories on mind to mind. Jaycee's head rose off the rug. *Wolf companions aren't forgotten.*

"Jaycee can draw on the memories of the second Kayndo's wolf companion and share them with you."

"It isn't going to help me if the situation isn't the same." Pain stabbed Dayvee's head. He rubbed his right temple. "If I make mistakes, others might die, and I'll be responsible."

The keeper shook his head. "I'll tell Leeto and Codee light duties only until these heal."

Dayvee cringed inwardly. Leeto would think him weak. "You don't need to do that. I'll be fine."

"I'll make certain." Kwutee spoke in his keeper voice again—the one Calupi didn't argue with.

Dayvee struggled back into his clothes, grateful for their warmth. Kwutee reached out and squeezed his shoulder. "You can only do your best. And everyone makes mistakes." Kwutee smiled. "Even Leeto, but he tries hard to get it right."

"And he has Codee, you, and Milay to help him."

Kwutee's mouth reverted to a serious line. "You need to surround yourself with good people, too. But even if you make every decision right, people and animals could die."

Dayvee shook his head. "It sounds like a terrible job."

"Your job is to defend the Vita regardless." Kwutee's voice turned somber. "If we need a Kayndo, war's usually the outcome, and the companions still shudder at those memories."

Dayvee trembled at the thought. "Can't someone like Leeto be the next animal master? He can have the gift of speaking to animals."

Kwutee's fingers tapped his staff. "You can't give away the gift."

"Why not? I'm sure he'd do a better job. Look at all my mistakes." Dayvee gritted his teeth. "I'm too weak. Just ask him. I can't make decisions about war." They couldn't force him. Someone else could have the job.

"You can't change the selection. The only choice you have is to refuse to do anything and let us lose the Vita." Kwutee straightened, and his eyes softened. "Hopefully, you'll prevent war. But remember, most of us would rather die than live without the Vita."

"How can any one person carry that load?" Dayvee's stomach churned again. He jumped up and paced the room.

Kwutee's voice took a soothing tone. "We didn't tell you sooner to protect you from the burden, but you won't be alone. You'll have Kun, all the people, and animals that will answer the Kayndo's call to defend the Vita."

"I'm willing to risk my life, just not others." He sent to Jaycee, *Can't the companions choose another?*

You don't understand, Jaycee replied. *We didn't select you, Kun did. Luko and Keeno were shown your face as the next Kayndo. We cannot change Kun's decision.*

"I can offer you only one other thing." The wrinkled face smiled. "My assistance."

"Thanks, Kwutee," Dayvee said.

Keeno and Jaycee sprang to their feet. *The companions mourn Nesi, now,* Jaycee sent. They both trotted from the den.

Kwutee motioned to the entrance. "You should rest but come back anytime."

Dayvee left the den but stopped in the corridor and sank down at the conical rock formation in front of it. He cried out to Kun. *I'm not worthy, I can't do this. Please don't ask me to bear this responsibility.*

In his mind he heard a voice. He wasn't sure if it was Kun's, JoKayndo's, or Jaycee's, but the answer was clear and didn't brook argument. *You must!*

The walls swayed again. How could he not be overwhelmed?

Don't worry, I'll be with you! the voice said.

Dayvee pummeled his fists into the floor. He staggered to his feet and fled the cave in a clumsy run. His feet pounded on the hard ground and jolted his knees. The frigid air sent a shock through him as he skidded on a patchy spot of ice. His weary feet plunged into the cold snow. He stumbled over a branch on the creek path and righted himself. His body refused to continue. Bent over, he drew huge breaths of air.

Dayvee visualized Nero's face when he lay moaning in the ring of death, Nesi's eyes when he held her head, Nero's limp body when they carried him out. *Kun, do I really need to be responsible for more deaths?* He retched and lost what little was in his stomach. A semblance of calm returned. He didn't have his coat, and his body shook from cold, so he hiked back. The companions had gathered outside the cave. Someone had carried wood past the pines and started a large fire. Flames leapt toward the sky.

Jaycee met him. *Remember, when you said you didn't think that humans had a star grouping? I found one. Look up and follow my muzzle to it.*

Dayvee scrutinized the sky until he picked it out. *It looks like a man with an arm extended.*

It's a Calupi, ready to embrace those who defend the Vita or throw a weapon to stop anyone harming it. I told you Kun's rewards are great. He's showing us his love for Calupi.

Jaycee's tail almost touched the ground, making the wolf's grief evident, but he still made an effort to lift Dayvee's spirits. Got to love that wolf. *Thanks, Jaycee.*

Brando and Elayni came and each grabbed an arm to pull Dayvee closer. Geno, Chayla, and Renay joined them. The warmth soaked in. The wolves and Calupi filled the night with Nesi's song, and he joined his voice with theirs.

The rest of that day and the next, the companions drank little and had no appetite. Their heads and tails stayed close to the ground. Calupi comforted them and grieved with them. Any pack member's loss was painful. They weren't many and worked close together. Several had called Nero friend, and they grieved him, too, but not openly.

The second morning after Nesi's death, the nights of little and troubled sleep caught up to Dayvee, and he woke late to a ravenous hunger.

After Jaycee bolted down his food, he held his head up. The wolf's grief seemed alleviated some. The deaths were Dayvee's responsibility, but he was determined not to make the same mistakes again. The aroma of cooking gruel wafted through the air and made his stomach rumble.

He found the leftover gruel, but it was cold. The fire held only a few hot coals, so he added some more wood and stoked it back to life to heat his breakfast.

A coal from the fire flew out to land on Jaycee's paw. Dayvee let out a holler, and jumped back as pain pulsed through his foot. His boot wasn't burnt. Why did that hurt him? He poured cold water over Jaycee's injury, and his own pain subsided to a sting. Then, he went to find Kwutee. Jaycee limped behind him.

At Kwutee's den, the keeper called out. "Come in, Dayvee and Jaycee." As soon as they were inside, Kwutee examined Jaycee's foot. "It's not bad."

Kwutee retrieved a flask from a shelf. He poured the liquid on Jaycee's foot, and Dayvee's sting disappeared.

Dayvee smiled. "Thank you. I felt Jaycee's pain. He seems to be reading my mind, and I'm speaking to him without focusing, so are we fully bonded?"

The keeper raised his eyebrows. "I'll ask Keeno."

Jaycee established the full bond after you were trapped in the cave. Keeno answered directly in Dayvee's mind. *He didn't want to lose contact again since Nero was trying to kill you, but he should have asked.*

I'm sorry I didn't ask. Jaycee's head sank low.

Dayvee glanced at Jaycee. *I'd have told you to do it.*

"Once you establish a full bond, it can't be turned off," Kwutee said. "Only, if he fully-bonds with another, can he relinquish yours, and when he dies, it will disappear."

"I know it will be difficult, but I can take better care of Jaycee when I know what he feels."

Dayvee left the keeper's den. Why didn't he notice sooner his and Jaycee's bond had changed? He had felt Jaycee's sadness at Nesi's death and his hunger. The emotions he had been having trouble with lately must be Jaycee's.

The wolf didn't try to keep his emotions in check. When he was happy, he was overjoyed. If angry, he was fierce. And when he was sad, Jaycee moped. How did Leeto control his emotions when he felt Luko's, too? How could Dayvee stay in command of his, now? Any type of detachment from Jaycee was impossible since they shared thoughts. Now, he understood why so many Calupi said we when they answered questions. *Jaycee, did you feel my pain in the ring with Andee?*

Yes.

I'm sorry.

Don't be. Pain is part of living, and I'm not ready to see Kun yet.

...

After Dayvee and Jaycee ate breakfast, they went to his family den. Leeto looked up from cleaning his knife as they walked in. During the time set aside for mourning, he didn't seem as busy as usual. Luko nosed Jaycee in greeting.

"Where're Bunjee and Milay?" Dayvee asked.

"At the pool."

Dayvee tapped his foot. "I wanted to ask you something. How do you know if you're making the right decision?"

His father met his gaze. "I don't. No one does."

"Then how do you make decisions which could lead to someone dying or war?"

Leeto slid his knife back in his pouch. "I ask those I trust for advice, and if it affects the entire pack, I try to give everyone a say. Sometimes there isn't time."

"I know." Dayvee thought of how quickly he decided not to tell his father about Nero.

Leeto rubbed a mixture of oils onto the outside of his pouch that helped with waterproofing. "It's difficult when a decision could result in someone's death." He shook his head slowly. "I've never had to make the decision to go to war. I don't envy you the Kayndo's job."

Dayvee paced. His boots slammed against the floor. *I don't envy me either, but I don't have a choice.* He stopped. "If you had to, how would you do it?"

Leeto stroked his chin, and spoke slowly. "I'd listen to my companion's advice. I'd surround myself with good people to consult, and I'd pray to Kun for guidance. Then, I'd do what my head and heart tell me I need to do to defend the Vita."

"Thank you."

"You're welcome. I'm glad you came. I wanted to talk to you."

"Yes?" What would Leeto criticize now?

Jaycee sent him reassurance and love through their bond. *I'm happy with you.*

Amazement filled Dayvee. Jaycee thought Dayvee worthy of his love. And he knew Brando and Elayni loved him. Did it really matter what his father thought? He didn't really need his father's approval, did he? No, but he wanted it.

Leeto hung his knife pouch back on his belt. "We were certain our fight with the hyenas would be until the last breath, but they broke it off. Luko says I owe you thanks for our escape."

"It was Jaycee's idea."

"Thank you, Jaycee." Jaycee pressed his nose against Leeto. He touched the wolf's head. "After we learned of Nero's treachery, a few things became clear. If I lost my place as alpha, it would not be the end of the world."

What? Did he really say that?

Leeto let out a heavy breath. "I realized to lose you would be worse."

Could this mean...Leeto cared more about Dayvee than leading the pack? Joy bubbled up inside.

"I know I've been hard on you." Leeto ran a hand through his hair. "I'm just trying to help you be the best Calupi you can. Just like my knife, I want you sharp. A dull knife isn't much good to anyone and won't be valued."

Could he really believe his criticism made Dayvee a better Calupi? "What if I don't want to be alpha?"

Leeto put a hand on his shoulder and squeezed. "You'll be a Calupi, so you need to be sharp, but I'll love you whether you become an alpha, a Kayndo, or neither." He wrapped both his arms around Dayvee and hugged him. Then, Leeto stepped back and dropped his arms.

Tears welled up in Dayvee's eyes. He'd always longed to have Leeto tell him he loved him. His father's eyes brimmed, too. Could this be a dream? Never had he seen Leeto show any weakness.

You're awake, Jaycee sent.

\#

Dayvee hurried to the ceremony room with Elayni and Brando. His father and Kwutee had asked everyone to gather there this evening. Dayvee joined the pack as they sang and told Nesi's story. Many shared pieces of her life. Dayvee told how Nesi led the companions to help him when they fought hyenas. The pieces were like patches on a quilt—together they assembled a beautiful whole.

"The time for mourning is over." Leeto said when they finished. "Tonight we celebrate and feast in Nesi's name without sadness. We'll carry on with the same zest and courage she displayed. She chose to serve the Vita. We'll honor her by doing the same, and we'll learn from her story. Our companions won't be forced to choose between us and the Vita because we and the Vita will be as one."

\#\#\#

-Epilogue-

Tib hefted the rucksack. It had come by messenger as a gift for him from the Calupi at White River pack. Just two more days to convince his father not to send him. Tomorrow he'd meet with Father to discuss what he'd learned from Varian and the next day he'd be gone.

He pulled out the water bag, bedroll, fire kit, and examined them. The bedroll was just two hides sewed together. He ran his hands over them. Rough like the rucksack. They'd itch for sure. The only other things were a bowl, and spoon. His stomach clenched. This wasn't going to be fun.

The note attached said to take no more than what would fit in the rucksack. To bring warm clothing, a coat, boots, and any weapons he used. How would all that fit? And once he got it all inside wouldn't it be heavy?

And what about his other belongings? He opened the box that held his treasures. Things he'd purloined from the ancient ruins. A spoon, a comb, and the knife. He had to take them. But he better not let the Calupi see them. They believed the ancient things contaminated the soul. He wrapped them in a cloth and put them inside.

He sorted through his clothing. Not that warm. This was useless. He'd go see Blake. He'd be the one to ask what weapons to take from the armory. Maybe Tib should purchase warmer clothing before he left. He went into the hall and plodded down to his father's meeting room, carrying the rucksack with him.

Pericards stood stationed at the door. "Is Blake inside with my father?" Tib asked.

"Yes."

"Anyone else in there?"

The pericard shook his head. "Not at the moment."

Blake's voice resonated in the hall. "Maybe I should send a few guards with him. The messenger said they'd do their best to keep him safe but they can't guarantee it. Calupi live dangerous lives."

Father's reply came easily to Tib's ears. "He's had plenty of defense lessons. It's time to let him leave the nest."

Tib gulped. So if the wolves didn't kill him, something else would. He knew this was a mistake. He turned around and fled. Somehow he had to get out of going.

His father had given him the afternoon off to pack his belongings and prepare. He'd spent enough time doing that. Now he'd do something he wanted to do.

Tib took the familiar path through the woods outside Harthome. Not as overgrown in winter. The trees opened up and piles of crushed stones and bricks with jagged metal pieces protruding came into view. They looked dark and twisted against the backdrop of snow and trees, and it sent a shudder through him. He took a deep breath. Varian said the ancient's things didn't harm you. And Tib agreed. Their things amazed him. He just needed to be careful not to get cut or have one of the piles shift.

Some of the ruins in the clan's territories were reported to be much larger and cover miles. Footprints in the snow drew Tib's attention. He scanned the area. No one appeared to be around, but some of the rubble had the snow disturbed. Hmmm. Someone else had been there. Tib wasn't surprised. It wasn't the first time he'd seen evidence that the ban didn't frighten everyone away.

He picked up a branch and poked around. The ancient's stuff could easily slice open a hand. He pulled out something with writing. It crumbled at his touch.

A shiny bauble caught his eye. Some type of necklace. He examined it and put it in the rucksack. Then dug again through the rubble.

A shiny handle. A dagger. Not like his knife. He'd leave it. Not much use when it was all rusted. Too much work to clean.

Tib kept prodding. The shadows lengthened. He had better return to the castle. Dinner would be soon and his father expected him. If he didn't arrive, the kagards would search for him. A broken piece of some stone covered in writing drew his attention. He threw it in the rucksack, too. Maybe Varian could tell him what it said, if he could speak to him alone.

A stick snapped. Could it be a kagard? Tib's heart leapt to his throat as he darted around the pile to the other side. If Father learned he was in the ruins, he'd be furious. Tib raced to another and maneuvered around it. Halting steps sounded closer.

As furtive as they approached it couldn't be a kagard. It was probably someone who shared his interest in the ancients. Tib didn't have any intention of letting them learn he was here. If they got caught, they might reveal to the kagards Tib had broken the law, too. Better to stay hidden.

He peeked out, from a small hole and got glimpses. Petite. Long hair. Maybe a woman? The movements were more graceful than a man's. Her back was to him as she explored the pile he'd just left. She picked up something and pocketed it. Tib couldn't stay longer. He needed to get rid of her.

Maybe he could scare her by making some noise. He reached out, grabbed a rock and threw it over to the side.

"Who's there?" The voice sounded familiar and definitely feminine.

He waited until she rummaged in the rubble again before throwing another. A clatter sounded as it hit the pile. She ran. Phew. She paused and turned to look back. It was Maydlan. Then, she hurried away.

Tib gave her a few moments and then followed. On the trail, he found a folded piece of paper. She must have dropped it. Did he want to read another intimate note to Varian from her? He stuck it the rucksack unopened.

#

Glossary

Andee – Wolf Mountain Pack Calupi
Animal Master – Kayndo
Blake – Captain of pericards (the king's guards) in kingdom of Taluma
Brando – one of Dayvee's best friends, Calupi of Wolf Mountain Pack
Bruno – Brando's wolf companion
Bunjee – Dayvee's adopted younger brother
Cato – Chayla's wolf companion
Chancee – Calupi of Wolf Mountain Pack (friend of Nero's)
Chayla – Calupi trainee of Wolf Mountain Pack
Clay – Milay's former companion
Clunee – Clan writer
Codee – Dayvee's uncle
Codee's mate – Jolay
Dayvee – son of Leeto, the alpha leader of wolf clan
Drako – Wolf Mountain Pack - Calupi messenger
Elayni – one of Dayvee's best friends, Wolf Mountain Calupi trainee
Evee – Elayni's wolf companion
Franko – Elayni's father - Wolf Mountain Pack Calupi in the trading sub-pack
Geno – Calupi trainee of Wolf Mountain Pack
Graydee – Geno's wolf companion
Grego – Wolf Mountain Pack Calupi
Harthome – capital city of the kingdom of Taluma - Western continent
Herrick – first alpha of Wolf Mountain pack
Hugo – Scarred Calupi, Running Creek Pack
Jaycee – Dayvee's wolf companion
JoKayndo – first animal master (Kayndo)
Jonesee – Brando's father, Wolf Mountain Pack Calupi
Juno – Drako's wolf companion
Kayndo – animal master
Keeli – Brando's mother, former Wolf Mountain Pack Calupi

Keeno – Kwutee's wolf companion
Kagard – kingdom of Taluma's soldiers
Kwutee – keeper of the Vita, Calupi healer of Wolf Mountain Pack
Kun – (God) creator of universe, master and maker of all things
Law of the Pack – Protect the pack and defend the Vita
Layton – current king of Taluma, Western continent
Leeto – Dayvee's father, alpha leader of Wolf Mountain Pack Calupi
Luko – alpha wolf of Wolf Mountain Pack, Leeto's companion
Marcello – (nicknamed the false king) former king of Taluma, Western continent
Miko – Wolf Mountain Pack senior Calupi, lamp lighter, former alpha leader
Milay – Dayvee's mother, Wolf Mountain Pack Calupi
Nails – Calupi weapon (chakram with several blades)
Nesi – Nero's wolf companion
Nero – Wolf Mountain Pack Calupi and senior leader for trainees sub-pack
Nolan – king of the Kingdom Lucendo on the Eastern continent of Terra
Owen – mayor of Portia, city in the kingdom of Taluma
Pako – Wolf Mountain Pack Calupi
Pericard – detachment of kagards that protect the king (his fists)
Petee – Calupi of Wolf Mountain Pack (friend of Nero's)
Polo – Petee's companion
Portia – Port city
Rayvo – boy of Wolf Mountain Pack
Razi – alcoholic beverage
Reed – Botanee Clan member
Renay – Calupi of Wolf Mountain Pack in Dayvee's training sub-pack
Rodnee – Beta sub-pack leader in Wolf Mountain Pack
Rudee – leader of training sub-pack from Wolf Mountain Pack
Santo – Ursan clan member
Shakree – Santo's bear companion willing to fight on Dayvee's behalf
Seemo – King Layton's eagle companion
Shonee – Calupi from Wolf Mountain Pack

Skylay – Milay's companion
Stuee – Shonee's companion
Taluma – Western Continent Kingdom – (King Layton rules it)
Tayro – Calupi in Dayvee's training sub-pack (Kwutee's apprentice)
Terra – The planet
Tibalt (prince of Taluma) – King Layton's son
Tinay – Wolf Mountain Pack Calupi (Elayni's mother)
Tobee – crippled adult from Wolf Mountain Pack
Tooth – Calupi weapon (knife)
Topay – Tayro's wolf companion
Varian – Visitor to the Western Continent from the Eastern
Vita – (Way of Life) a set of rules and religious beliefs taught to Terrans by JoKayndo.
Wilee – Codee's wolf companion

-Acknowledgments-

They say it takes a community to raise a child. It certainly takes a community to put out a book. It wouldn't have been possible without the aid of my incredible team so I want to acknowledge and thank them.

First there's the One who gave me the inspiration and words. My Lord and Savior.

Second is my awesome family and amazing friends who always had words of encouragement. Their belief in me has been unfailing.

Third is my critique group, Fantasy for Christ members Scott Abel, Katie Clark, Azalea Dabill, Karen Deblieck, Sarah Grimm, Loraine Kemp, Kathrese McKee, Tami ONeal, Jennifer Rogers, Aaron Schlegel, Sarah Witenhafer and Precarious Yates. Even in the first terrible drafts, they bore with me and offered advice, contacts and encouragement.

Fourth are my beta readers: Jennifer Rogers, Precarious Yates, Sarah Grimm, Tami ONeal and Suzanne Galla. And I can't forget my editor and proofreader, Nadine Brandes and Stephanie Van Wyk. I shudder to think what this book would look like without their help.

Then there's my cover artist Yvonne Less with Diverse Pixel, cover model Matt Luckey, photographer Katherine Cobert with Cobert Photography, web-site designer Joe Vanderjagt, web-site ruins artist Josh Anspach, and for e-publishing answers, Terri Main and CIA. All of them gave of their time and energy to help me.

Last but not least, I want to thank all of you that read this book and everyone that's promoting it. Your support is really appreciated.

Made in the USA
Middletown, DE
26 December 2014